THE SAND MEN
CHRISTOPHER FOWLER

SOLARIS

First published 2015 by Solaris
an imprint of Rebellion Publishing Ltd,
Riverside House, Osney Mead,
Oxford, OX2 0ES, UK

www.solarisbooks.com

ISBN (UK): 978 1 78108 373 4
ISBN (US): 978 1 78108 374 1

10 9 8 7 6 5 4 3 2 1

A CIP catalogue record for this book is available
from the British Library.

Designed & typeset by Rebellion Publishing

Printed and bound by CPI Group (UK) Ltd, Croydon, CR0 4YY

PART ONE

*The ultimate gated community is a human being
with a closed mind.*

– JG Ballard

Chapter One
The Beach

A SKY SO blue it looked like the atmosphere had evaporated into space.

Mandhatri Sahonta stared into the infinity, then lowered his blue NYC baseball cap over his eyes, adjusting his hardhat on top of it. He was unimpressed by the sky. It was always this blue here, always this bright.

Mandhatri dressed as if he was expecting the weather to suddenly turn cold. When he saw the crimson-faced, fat-bellied holidaymakers waddling past in their Vilebrequin shorts and Diesel tanktops like oversized toddlers, he thought of them as ghosts. He was an engineer. His world did not touch theirs. Tightly wrapped in a vest, shirt, scarf and workboots, he passed their oiled bodies roasting in the sun and assumed they were living proof of what happened when you ate pork.

At noon, with the temperature hitting 38⁰C, even the mad English had abandoned their beach chairs, heading back to air-conditioned buffet lunches beside sun-fractured swimming pools.

Mandhatri stopped the Jeep on scrubland at the edge of the lot. Grabbing his steel toolbox, he set off across the sand. The landscape was bare and unforgiving, a table-flat geometry of grey and yellow patches bordered by piles of breezeblocks. In the distance he could hear the rumbling of the gravel trucks that never stopped, swerving past each other on the peninsula like tin toys on a track.

The date palms had been transported fully grown and impatiently planted into the unfinished esplanade, where many of them promptly died. As he walked, he thought about his father and wondered if he was still alive.

Mandhatri and his daughter Sakari had abandoned their village in the South Kanara coastal district of Karnataka and moved to Delhi, because their father's house had burned down in mysterious circumstances. Not for the first time, the old man had made enemies from unpaid debts. After arguing with him Mandhatri had moved north, where he'd heard they were recruiting. He spoke perfect English and had found employment in Dubai on a two-year contract. He transferred money and called home every month, and when he spoke to his wife she avoided any mention of the father who had brought them low.

Mandhatri tightened his checked scarf and consulted his handheld tracking system. The GPS device overlaid an installation grid on the landscape, enabling him to pinpoint work locations. The problem was somewhere around here, but even the foreman hadn't been sure of the exact spot.

To his left, the high wall of a hotel screened guests from the ugliness of the site. The tourists had been lured by pictures of unspoilt beaches. They did not want to look up from their sunbeds and see tractors and diggers.

He set down the toolbox and checked inside, but found nothing that could help him. Kits were leased from the company and repaid with loans. Specialist equipment was extra, so his mates clubbed together and time-shared items. During busy hours, the foremen charged extra rental fees on certain wrenches and drill attachments. Lately, some of the crew members had started refusing to pay the bribes. Instead, they altered their shifts around times when the tools were available. There was talk of starting a union but nothing ever happened.

Mandhatri reached the broken end of the esplanade, walked beyond stacks of white plastic beach loungers and found himself standing on a plain where hot breezes scrawled their signatures across ridges of loose sand.

He knew at once that something was wrong.

Fine diamond granules lifted from the peaks of the dunes and swept around his bare ankles. He studied the sand carefully, trying to make sense of what he saw. The patterns were wrong.

He knew that the barchan dunes were carved by winds that struck the sand from a consistent direction. They should only appear as wavy crescents until they reached the sea-table. After that, the beach was flattened out by water. But just ahead, the curving lines broke and ran in a wide concentric circle.

If there was one thing Mandhatri had come to understand since he arrived here, it was the movement of the sand.

He walked out into the circle's centre and set down his toolbox. Kneeling, he removed a small spade and an oscilloscope to pick up any sounds beneath the faint rustling of migrant silica. Digging into the scorching granules, he inserted the device's metal probe and waited for the reading to settle.

The beach was radiating fearsome heat. He placed his palms down and lay as close as he could to the surface, listening intently.

Now he could actually hear it—a bad sign. He had no equipment to deal with this. Feeling for his mobile, he speed-dialled his foreman. The line was engaged.

My body weight, he thought suddenly, trying to rise. The faint hiss grew louder, turning into a roar, then a blast.

He realised what it was and forced himself to move, but the sand suddenly burst upwards and air began to condense around him. His face and hands were hit and immediately started turning numb. The crystallisation spread across his bare arms, down through his torso and into his thighs like the brumal deadness of dental Novocaine. It thickened the blood in his veins until he was no longer able to move. A thin, stinging craquelure of iridescent frost formed over his skin, sheening the backs of his hands with tiny diamonds. *My fault,* he thought dimly. *I knew the signs to watch for and ignored them. My clothes...*

But the material had already stuck to his skin and hardened so that he could not tell flesh from fabric. The fissures beneath him grew. He knew that if he suffered serious injury, his wife would not be sent her monthly money. If he died, she would be destitute.

He remembered what had happened to his daughter, and wanted to cry with the unfairness of it all. Even now he tried to hold Sakari's face in his mind, but her features grew dark and were lost, until all that remained were the lights in her brown eyes.

At 11:47am on the burning beach of Dream World, at the edge of the shimmering Arabian sea, Mandhatri Sahonta froze to death, the wavering rolls of heat dancing around his ice-ferned body.

Chapter Two
The Arrival

'My God.'

The aircraft door opened. The rectangle of light was a blazing revelation, hard, hot and even. Mobile phones flashed on. As Lea disentangled her hand luggage ready for disembarkation, a fine sweat broke out on her forehead. She had changed into a floral summer dress but the light fabric already felt as constricting as bandages.

She looked across at Roy, fanning her hand at him and blowing upwards at a loose curl. He smiled back: *Warned you.*

The noon shadow beneath the Emirates A380 was so sharply delineated that it could have been painted onto the ground. The outside air was fan-oven fierce. She stopped at the bottom of the steps. At first she saw nothing but baking flat concrete. As her eyes adjusted, the rippling heat-mist revealed a collection of distant silvered towers whose heights were impossible to gauge. She might have been looking at Xanadu or the Emerald City of Oz.

'Like a science fiction movie,' said Cara, shielding her eyes. 'Like special effects or something.'

'The business district,' said Roy, pleased that his daughter had been provoked into a response. These days any reaction was welcome. 'You'll see it better on the way to the house. We can drive right through the city centre.'

Still craning her head back to stare at the glistening mirage, Cara stepped into the refrigerated terminal. The vaulted steel sepulchre instantly banished memories of Heathrow's chaotic, claustrophobic crowds. Lea looked about, amazed. Everything was so bright and pristine that it appeared unused.

They were fast-tracked through the electronic customs system and met at the baggage carousel by a tall Arab. Disappointingly, he wore a modest Armani business suit, a freshly-pressed white shirt and a thin black tie. He was so slender that his jacket hung loose at his waist. He gravely introduced himself as Tahir Mansour, the compound's general manager. He nodded to each of them in turn. '*Salaam aleikum*. I hope your flight was not arduous.' He had very white, sharp teeth.

Lea raised an eyebrow at Roy, who smiled back. Mr Mansour shook hands with Lea first, perhaps to dispel the idea that more devout Muslims preferred not to shake hands with a woman. 'Please, leave everything here. I will have your bags brought to the villa at once. We can go on ahead. I understand this is your first time in Dubai, Mrs Brook.'

'I was hoping to visit before Roy accepted the position,' Lea replied. 'A wife should have a say in these things. Everything happened so fast.'

'Your husband tells me you are a magazine writer.' There was no disapproval in Mr Mansour's voice. 'I hope you will be able to continue here. Of course, this is not London. We do not have so many media outlets. But the state encourages the creative arts. We wish for writers to visit, unlike India or China, where you must acquire additional letters of authority before being issued with a visa.'

Roy shot her a look. *Don't say anything smart.* Lea had read him online articles about censorship.

'Thank you, Mr Mansour,' she said. 'I'm sure I'm going to like it here.'

The formal courtesies over, Mr Mansour turned away and spoke with Roy.

Outside, the heat was furnace-like, fiery and desiccating. It seemed to Lea that she could actually see the sunlight falling. The air itself was a solid thing. They walked through carefully arranged areas of shade, led by a smiling, silent Indian chauffeur.

An avenue of transplanted palms looked Riviera-fake, the spiked emerald foliage immaculately clipped, as glossy as PVC. Mr

Mansour strode ahead with her husband, Lea and Cara trailing behind in unconscious simulation of the Arabic family order. She was dying for a cigarette. There was a packet of Davidoffs in her bag. She wondered if she had time to surreptitiously smoke one before they reached the car.

Her daughter blinked at the all-encompassing heat.

'You okay?'

'Surprised,' said Cara. 'You think it gets cold at night?'

'Apparently it drops by twenty degrees. Still warmer than an average summer's day in London. You going to cope with that?'

'Does it make any difference if I can't?'

'Not for two years, young lady.'

The darkness of the garage danced green spots before their eyes. They reached the first of two immense black Mercedes saloons. 'Why have we got two?' Cara whispered, peering over her shades.

'I thought it would be more comfortable for you, after your flight,' said Mr Mansour, clearly blessed with powerful hearing. He ushered Roy into the first car and indicated that Lea and Cara should enter the second. 'I hope you don't mind, Mrs Brook. I need to take your husband out to the site. Your driver will take you directly to your new home.'

Disappointed by the arrangement, Lea seated herself in the back of the freezing Mercedes. It seemed as if Mr Mansour had deliberately separated them. She had not expected Roy to be put straight to work. The chauffeur offered bottles of iced water.

'It would have been nice if we could have entered the house together,' she said to no-one in particular. 'His contract doesn't start until the first.'

'That's only the day after tomorrow.' Cara checked the view as they drove off. 'Very flat, Dubai,' she said in her Noel Coward voice. She could be perversely old-fashioned when she chose. It usually meant she was happy. Lea sometimes had to remind herself that Cara was clever; playing dumb was part of her public persona, like the dour, unsmiling Facebook shots she posted.

'It looks like a building site,' said Lea.

'That thing wasn't there on Google Earth.' Cara pointed to the half-finished steel exoskeleton of a tower looming from the soft pink mist. The traffic was heavy and slow. It appeared that nobody drove a car more than three years old. A brand-new Lexus and a Lamborghini Aventador rolled at a stately pace on either side of them, their powerful engines wasted.

The Mercedes saloon coasted along a broad avenue of construction zones, then switched lanes onto a curving flyover. An immense chasm of steel and glass opened up before them.

'I think we just went into the future.' Cara stretched her neck back but could not see to the tops of the buildings. A uniform row of cranes appeared along the horizon like the raised drumsticks of a distant marching band. There was a glitter of water between the bases of the tower blocks. The streets were deserted. 'Where is everyone?'

'I guess they're all inside,' Lea replied. 'It's too hot to be out in the open.'

'It kind of looks like Los Angeles. I mean, what Los Angeles looks like in movies.'

'No honey, this is bigger and newer. There's supposed to be an older area near the creek. Look over there.' They passed a wide man-made river that meandered between the glassine offices. 'Maybe we can hire a boat, take a trip around the place to get our bearings.'

'Cool train.' Cara pointed to a curving armadillo-hood of polished steel, one of the stations on the monorail line leading out to the Palm Jumeirah, the great man-made palm tree island that jutted from the coastline. Its concrete fronds were supposedly visible from space.

'The Palm Atlantis monorail,' said Lea, reading from her guide-book. 'You'll be able to get about until you pass your driving test.'

They reached a T-junction, where the first Mercedes took the filter and turned off, to be eclipsed by soaring steel cliffs. They were alone now. Lea was bothered by the ease with which Roy had been spirited away. She reached for her phone.

'Don't embarrass Dad on his first day,' said Cara without looking over. 'We've only just left him. We can manage.'

She wanted to protest, but reluctantly returned the phone to her pocket. She could feel the edge of the cigarette packet.

They passed beneath a gigantic electronic poster featuring a beautiful girl tossing glossy brown hair, smiling as if she had just discovered a secret reason for living. The slogan read: *Live a bespoke lifestyle—Dubai Pearl.* The billboard's pixels shone brighter than any cinema screen.

So that's what we're getting, a bespoke lifestyle, Lea thought. *Men come out here with their families, fulfil their contracts, bank their cheques and head home. It's all mapped out for us. It'll be good to have a system for once.*

The journey took almost an hour. They emerged from the cliffs of grey steel and silvered glass. The chauffeur did not speak, but tapped on the windscreen with a manicured fingernail.

'Look, Cara.' Lea pointed.

The compound was surrounded with date palms and high walls of yellow English brick. Its houses were invisible from the main highway. A slip-road brought them to the perimeter.

At the main entrance, a metal barrier rolled back. Its folksy wrought-iron design was unable to disguise its real purpose. *Dream Ranches.* The name was stencilled in gold pokerwork on a slab of laminated teak, and underneath, *A Division of DWG Estates.*

The company had constructed the compound to house the families of Dream World's engineers, architects and technicians. The resort's designers were known as *imagineers,* a Disney term that felt infantilising, considering the pressures they faced; Dream World had been scheduled to open in February but was already four months late.

The chauffeur stopped at the gate house and nodded to a pair of young guards in crisp khaki uniforms. The boys ran pole mirrors beneath the Mercedes. The gatekeepers wore spotless white *kanduras* and *guthras.*

'They've got string ties,' said Cara.

'It's called a *kerkusha.* You can soak it in scent.'

'How do you know?'

'I read, my dear.' One guard promptly dropped to his knees and checked behind the tyres. 'I think they're looking for explosives.' The country was on a medium-level security alert, but so was everywhere these days. If you followed the Foreign Office advice on travel you'd never go outside again, especially not in London.

The chauffeur finished chatting to the gatekeepers, and the saloon rolled inside. After fields of ochre sand and gravel, the sudden mouth-watering burst of greenery came as a shock. Behind the acacia trees stood identical beige ranch-style homes. They were arranged in pairs, low and wide, with shallow red-tiled roofs and spotless garage bays.

The roads were uniform and identically matched, from the colour of their fences to their regiments of kerbside eco-bins. The houses were constructed close enough to each other to suggest that a subtle point was being made; they were for executive employees, but employees nonetheless.

'Welcome, please,' said the unsmiling driver, pulling to a stop. 'This is your new home.'

'I CAN'T BELIEVE you packed teabags. We're not on holiday. You've finally turned into Nan.' Cara was impatient to explore. She roved fractiously from room to room, anxious to see over the dense green hedges that surrounded the property. The street outside was deserted and silent.

'As you will one day turn into me, darling,' countered Lea. 'Or if you're lucky, the me I might have been.'

'Don't start.'

'We should have a cup of tea first.' She opened each of the cupboards in turn and found them packed with groceries. She had forgotten that she'd filled out an online form requesting kitchen provisions. Most of the produce was from Waitrose.

'Can I go outside?'

'We'll have to go out later and get some fridge stuff. There's supposed to be an amazing mall nearby. We've got a shared swimming pool, and there's a lake and a golf course.'

'Then let's *go*!'

'Let's wait for the luggage to turn up first. You'll need to unpack today if you're going to start school straight away.' She had enrolled Cara in a British School run by ex-pats who had stayed on after the country had been handed back. The classes were small, and the Albion High School prospectus suggested she would get a better education than she would have done by remaining at her cash-strapped state school in Chiswick.

Lea walked through the house, making mental notes about how the furniture would need to be rearranged. The property came with chairs, tables, beds and sofas, finished in safe tones that matched the cream and beige walls. There were three flat-screen televisions. The beds were made. There were even towels in the bathrooms. The rooms smelled of lavender air-freshener.

Opening the French windows in the lounge, she stepped out onto the area which had been described in their orientation brochure as 'the entertaining deck'. Tipping her face to the sun she closed her eyes, feeling the encompassing calm of light and heat. It was raining in London and 14°—she had already taken pleasure in checking the conditions on her phone.

'Turn your data roaming off until you get a local provider,' Cara called. 'Do you want me to do it for you?'

'I'm not completely useless,' Lea called back. 'I've already done it.' She quickly checked her mobile settings and disabled the internet access.

The deck had comfortable rattan sofas and pretty peach-shaded lamps. Beyond it was a small square garden filled with unfamiliar plants. She could smell the flowers, pungent and cloying.

It was wonderfully quiet. No circling helicopters, no sirens, no continuous thrum of traffic. *I won't be able to get away with the odd cigarette out here,* she thought, *the air is too still.* Roy thought she had given up, but she felt sure Cara knew. She knew too much about everything.

'The luggage could be ages,' Cara called, trying again. 'Come *on*, there are cars in the garage. They're ours, aren't they? The keys must be around here somewhere.'

She was going to argue, but decided Cara was right. There was no point in simply wandering around the empty house. Whoever was delivering the luggage presumably had keys. 'Okay,' she said, 'let's go and see what's out there.'

There was, indeed, a double garage containing two cars. The little blue Renault was emphatically intended as a woman's shopping vehicle, complete with a decent boot for grocery bags. When she turned the ignition, she found the gas tank full. Roy's new BMW X5 had been parked in the shadows like a glistening black diamond, manly and expensive. Not that she was complaining; the company's attention to detail was everything Roy had promised. All their immediate needs had been catered for. This, she decided, was no mere courtesy. It allowed her husband to start work immediately. Various permits and laminated ID cards had been provided in orientation packs that made her feel as if she too was now working for the company.

She paused before getting into the car and looked across the street. A curtain shifted, and for a moment a man's face watched her from the darkness of his living room.

'Are you okay to drive?' asked Cara.

'I've driven in other countries. Incredible as it may sound, I did have a life before you.'

'Just checking.' Cara had confidence beyond her years. Her mousey hair was London-tough, her chin a little too pointed, eyes blue and thoughtful, with a cool indifference that hid her emotions. She had become good at hiding herself, so that when a genuine emotion surfaced it was like the sun coming out.

The guards opened the gate and released them into the afternoon traffic. The soft-spoken female voice of the sat-nav was a nice touch. It guided them along a series of identical dual carriageways in the direction of the mall. Driving was stately and at a fixed pace, as in America. You hardly needed to be awake.

Lea caught sight of herself in the mirror. The same high cheekbones and brown eyes, almost dark enough to be mistaken for Arabic, but she was tall and lacked the fluidity of movement she associated with Middle Eastern women. Instead she saw the restlessness of an awkward Englishwoman who was always slightly too aware of her surroundings.

'You can go anywhere you like, so long as you keep your shoulders covered and don't wear a short skirt,' she said, looking out for the turn-off sign. 'Maybe I should help you choose a new summer wardrobe.'

'Forget it, not going to happen,' said Cara.

'We'll figure it out when we go shopping. It's super-safe. Apparently there are some towns where women aren't allowed on the beach and even men can't wear shorts. It's more relaxed here. It only rains about three times a year. We can go to the desert. You can try dune surfing. And there's falconry, and—'

'You don't have to sell it to me, Mum. Left here.' Cara pressed a pale finger on the tinted windscreen.

'I'm excited, aren't you?'

'Interested,' Cara conceded.

They parked on a virtually deserted floor, wrote down the location of their car, B769 Orange, and headed into the Arabia Mall.

The scale of the building induced agoraphobia; five pastel floors with a vast golden glass atrium, fluted fountains and a forest of tropical plants, hundreds of stores selling high-end luxury goods, mostly aimed at women. 'Check out the shoes and handbags,' said Lea. 'It's how the local ladies show their wealth.'

'No different to home, then,' said Cara, pushing her mother towards an Apple store. 'Can I get the iPad now?'

Lea had promised Cara she could have one if she made the move without a fuss. She hated using bribery but had been worn down by her complaints. Only a few women were wearing *abayas*, the traditional black gowns used to cover day-wear. Many wore *hijab* head-scarves but there were very few *burqas*, the hoods that sometimes still came with metallic coloured face coverings. Most were dressed in the kind of designer wear you saw all over the Mediterranean.

'How come the women cover up and the men don't?' Cara asked.

'The Prophet Muhammad issued guidelines for female modesty,' Lea explained. 'You're not allowed to outline or distinguish the shape of the body, so skin-tight jeans are out. He once warned that in later generations, there would be people who are dressed yet naked.'

'What, he saw the future?'

Lea looked about. 'Seems pretty accurate to me.'

'The women must get hot.'

'The clothes are very light. Feel that.' She showed Cara a gauzy, pretty *hijab*. 'And it's only for going out. At home they jazz it up for their husbands.'

They found what appeared to be the largest supermarket on the planet, and were paralysed with indecision when faced with seventy types of breakfast cereal. Cara stood before a display featuring thirty different brands of honey. 'Why would anyone need so much choice?' she asked, genuinely bemused.

'I guess eating is a serious family business. Not drinking alcohol probably makes you enjoy food more. Remember when the three of us used to sit down at the meal table together?'

'No.'

'I'm just saying. A real dining table. Conversation. The odd night in front of the TV.'

'Is that what you want?'

'What, for us to be a real family? Well, yes, it would be nice.'

The process of shopping was slow and laborious—everyone seemed to be moving at a third of the speed she was used to. Lea pushed the giant red plastic trolley between rows of shocked fish arranged on ice like jewelled purses, past jars of exotic pickles as mysterious as foetuses in a medical museum, through a corridor of arranged meats that glowed acid pink under sterile counter lights.

'Next time, we need to make a list,' she said. She watched Cara reading the back of a can, the way her lank brown hair fell forward over her eyes, shielding the world from her thoughts. She had sprung up in the last year, but still dressed in her dark London uniform of grey hooded Adidas top and jeans. There would have to be some variation in her wardrobe now. The local girls were more traditionally feminine.

Still unsure about the contents of the can, Cara replaced it on the shelf. She never asked for help; the age of independence was upon her. She had left behind very few friends of her own age, and needed a good peer group.

Lea steered the trolley away, feeling a little sad. Nothing made her more aware of the passing time than looking at her child. But here it might be possible to roll time back just a short way, and recapture something lost.

Unable to decide on foodstuffs, they bought too much. They spent ages in the computer store, and finally left the mall two and a half hours later.

'We won't do that every day,' Lea said, searching for the turn-off to Dream Ranches. 'I wouldn't get anything else done.'

There was no response. Cara was busy taking the iPad out of its box. She had a flair for technology, and was the house guru for everything electronic.

Their luggage had arrived, along with a welcome letter from the company, details concerning the shipment of their belongings and a great bouquet of lurid flowers. Cara claimed a bedroom and set up her laptop. She located English-language TV channels.

Lea made a salad. She tried leaving the back door open but the alternating blasts of hot and freezing air brought on a headache, so she closed it and sat in the lounge to watch the sun setting behind the silent garden.

The sound of sprinklers starting up in unison made her jump. They sounded like the rain that had pattered onto the leaves of the plane trees as Lea waited on the front doorstep of their Chiswick home, convinced that she was leaving something valuable behind.

Throughout that final morning she had circled the cold empty rooms, trying to pinpoint the nature of the loss. Two Bishops removal vans had splashed into Belmont Terrace and filled up, one with furniture going into storage, the other with the personal belongings they were taking with them.

Cara had questions she couldn't answer; would the PlayStation work? Would they need to put transformers on all the electrical items? Was there anything she wouldn't be allowed to take into the country? Was it true the internet was censored? Would she still be able to use Facebook?

'You're a big girl now, check it out online,' she'd said. 'You'll have to ask your father about the rest.'

'Will we have a fast Wi-Fi connection? I don't know which cables to take.'

'Take them all, I don't want to have to buy them again. If they get packed in the wrong van you won't be able to get your hands on them for two years.'

'Two years is a long time. We could all be fighting each other for food by then.'

'Thanks for the cheerful thought.'

'Not my fault. The world's running out of water thanks to your generation.'

'Yep, that's right, blame it all on us. Why don't you make a list of all the things we screwed up for you, I'll try and deal with each item in turn. Meanwhile can you see if I've packed my ginger cat mug? And while you're at it, write on this.' Lea had picked up a cardboard box and handed her a marker pen. 'Your old board games. I found them in the attic.'

'What do you want me to write?'

'Their destination. England or the Middle East.'

Cara pulled a grossed-out face. 'I don't even want them. I'm never going to play Cluedo again.'

'You may not want them, but I do.' She pinched Cara's cheek. 'Somewhere inside there you're still my baby. I'm talking my opera CDs, so make sure you've got everything.'

'I keep telling you, you don't have to take them. I loaded everything onto your phone.' They moved off the stairs so that the removal men could get past.

'But what if I have to update the phone or lose it?' said Lea.

'I thought we were finally getting away from all that wailing. You'll be able to play it on a dock.'

'Nice try but they're coming with me. Mark the boxes.' Stripped, the house was depressing. Its bare windows looked onto a corpse-grey London street where drizzle sifted from an tarnished sky. Opposite, a traffic warden slowly and patiently wiped excrement off his shoe. *A fresh start*, she'd thought. *Say goodbye to the dim light, the endless cloudy skies, the tired faces. Cara locked in her room avoiding anything that could embarrass her. This will bring us closer together. The last couple of years haven't exactly been...*

A crash from downstairs had made her start. The removal men had dropped something big. She ran out to the landing and looked down to find Cara standing in a nimbus of shattered glass.

'Your Aunt Jen's water pitcher. That was a wedding gift.'

'I was just trying to help.' Cara in defensive mode. 'It slipped out of my hands.'

'Leave it to the professionals, Cara. Just concentrate on your own things.'

'I'm not a child. It was disgusting anyway.' Cara had stormed off beyond her line of sight, furious at being admonished in front of the removal men.

Now they were in a land where rainfall would become a distant memory. She wondered if her daughter had any inkling of how much she was loved. With each passing day she saw less of herself in Cara, and longed for a way to reconnect. The thought stayed with her as the sun sank below the treeline and the golden garden fell into shadow.

Chapter Three
The International Dream

ROY DIDN'T GET home until 9:45pm. 'Wait until you see the resort,' he said excitedly, pulling off his jacket and kissing her. 'It's incredible. The stats are surreal. I mean, I knew the architects were going for something really futuristic but this is—you need a hand with that?'

'It's salmon salad, I can manage,' said Lea. 'Hang your jacket up.'

He aimed himself at the refrigerator and found a beer. 'I'm sorry Tahir took me off like that. I wasn't expecting it.'

'What was so urgent?'

'A workman had an accident.'

'Was it serious?'

'The guy died. There was nothing to be done.'

'What happened?'

'They're installing pressurised refrigeration pipes under the sand to cool the beach down for tourists, and he was sent to repair one of them, but it exploded. Talk about bad luck.'

'That's awful,' said Lea.

'The company will take care of all the bills and pay his family compensation.'

'That's not the point.'

'It's a massive project, Lea, a lot of people involved, accidents happen. It's the biggest train set I'll ever get to play with. I never had an opportunity like this before.'

She rested a hand on her hip, leading him to look at the rearranged lounge. 'Do you want to check out the house first and tell me you approve?'

'I already saw it last time I came out.'

'You didn't tell me.'

'Sorry, I figured I could leave it to you. I'm just jazzed. The resort already generates more power than the entire country used in the seventies. The Persiana's main atrium is so big that they're having to install a computerised airjet program to stop it from creating its own internal weather system.'

'Its own weather system? How does that work?' She dipped slices of courgette into lemon juice.

'The hot air separates out, then cools and condensation builds up. They're constructing glass-walled executive suites with bathrooms that are below the water line so you can watch the fish while you're taking a shower, but the glass gets heated from the freshwater side and they're having problems with the rubber seals.'

Whenever Roy described technical problems, he had the enthusiasm of a child. He been brought in to find solutions to architectural faults in the main hotel of Dream World, the multi-billion dirham resort nearing completion on the country's reclaimed coastline. Experts from around the globe had been hired at great expense. There was never a question of not taking the job. By the time the offer of employment came through, Roy had been out of work for over eight months.

'You think there are going to be enough rich people to fill the place?' Lea asked.

'You're kidding, right? The board of directors don't have much taste but they know the market.'

'Aren't they the ones you were supposed to meet at the Mandarin Oriental? The ones coming over from Guangzhou? I thought they didn't show.'

'Well, they didn't. I met their people. All they're concerned about is getting the place back on schedule for its revised opening date on September 9th. Where are we eating?'

'The table's laid outside. I'm not sure if there are mosquitos so I bought some citronella candles anyway.' She shook her head. 'Maybe you can get in with the board and persuade them to make you a director.'

Roy followed her about, as excited as a dog. 'Apparently they're famous for rewarding hard workers. I've got to sign a shedload of non-disclosure forms. And there's a limit on who we can discuss the project with. We're not allowed to bring in freelance consultants whenever there's a problem. There are a couple of guys at NASA who know about heat-resistant materials, but we can't access the specialist advice we need because of the conflict with their own confidentiality agreements. I'll have to work with as many lawyers as engineers, but you know I can do that.'

'Tell me more over dinner,' said Lea, taking a salad bowl to the patio. 'Cara, come and eat.'

'Is it salad?' Cara called.

'Yes, with cold salmon. The green stuff won't kill you, it's not kryptonite.' In London, Cara mostly lived on tomato soup, cheese and toast.

'I'll have it later,' she yelled. 'I'm trying to get the Wi-Fi set up.'

'It'll take you ten minutes to eat, honey. The internet will probably still be there when you finish. It's our first dinner.'

'Let me do this and I'll set you up with a dock so that you can play your wailing opera women.'

'Always with the bargains. Okay, just this once.'

'So—the central tower of the Persiana is over 430 metres,' Roy continued, seating himself and grabbing a fork, 'which means it'll be the tallest hotel on earth. There are three hotels, the Persiana, the Atlantica and the Arabiana. Dream World sticks way out into the sea and weighs over a million tons, plus it has to withstand everything from earthquakes and gulf storms to tidal waves, so they've got to get it right. Everything has to be ready in three months. Fifty years ago this place was a backwater used by pearl divers, camel traders and Bedouin. Everything changed when they struck oil, of course, but that'll all be used up in a couple of years, so they're future-proofing the country.'

'By building resorts no-one else will be able to afford to visit?'

'Come on, show some enthusiasm. The Russians and Chinese own the franchise but guess who gets most of the money? Two thirds of the investment returns to the UAE. This is the flagship resort that'll prove the model can work. Then they can build others all around the world.'

She pushed a bowl of rice at him. 'I know it's a really exciting opportunity for you, but don't you think it's kind of grotesque? I mean, all you need is another credit crunch and it'll become the world's most expensive slum.'

'Darling, if we took that attitude, nothing would ever get built. I'm still a New Yorker at heart, I can still walk down 34th Street and marvel at the buildings. Manhattan took the lead a century ago. Okay, its skyscrapers aren't as big as those in the East but they have more cohesion, more character.'

'They also serve a practical purpose.'

'So will Dream World. We're all working harder and playing harder, Lea. And this is going be the best playground on the planet.'

Lea had always loved her husband's optimism. It seemed to be a quality bred into New Yorkers from birth. He'd just started working downtown in an architectural practice soon after the Twin Towers collapsed and, typically, had seen the 9/11 tragedy as a structural engineering problem. After that, the failure of his own company and the killing damp of London winters had encouraged him to seek opportunities overseas. Arab, American, Muslim, Christian, Hindu, what did such differences really matter? Everyone needed to construct; it was an instinct as natural as building families and friendships.

'What?' said Roy, not chewing. 'You're looking at me funny.'

'I can look at my husband,' she said. 'You make me remember why I married you. Like a big kid with those eyes. Finish what you were saying.'

He pushed his blond fringe back from his forehead. It was just starting to grey at the sides. 'You know I appreciate your support, Lea. This is my only chance to get into the big time. I had to come here, the shit we went through.'

'Shh, Cara might hear you.'

Roy clapped his hands, dismissing the subject. 'Anyway, it's our life for the next two years, but the good news is that you won't have to do any food preparation from tomorrow.' Roy waved a fork across the meal. 'They're sending over an Indonesian maid. She won't live in, she'll just come and help you out during the day. You can become a lady of leisure.'

'I'm not sure I want to do that, Roy.' Lea laid down her cutlery. 'There's not going to be much work. Do we really have to have her?'

'She's part of the package. All the senior executives have them. She's fully paid for, so we might as well use her. Besides, I thought you wanted to concentrate on your magazine writing.'

'I'll have to find some freelance contacts first. The house is hardly going to be any trouble to look after. I was used to fixing broken pipes and clearing mud out of the hallway in Belmont Terrace every time it rained. I think I can manage a place like this and hold down a job at the same time.'

'All I'm saying is that you won't have to work if you don't want to. Didn't you do enough of that in London?'

'But I want to work, Roy. I don't think it's going to be enough just being a housewife.'

'That's what I mean. You'll have someone to do the boring chores. Anyway, I already agreed to take her on.' Roy shrugged. 'But if she doesn't work out we'll let her go, okay?'

Lea picked up a fork and toyed with her food. She imagined it would be easy to become trapped within the compound, only seeing other wives and venturing out with her family at weekends. In London she had worked at a women's magazine called *Eva* for five years. It never achieved a huge circulation but had prided itself on a certain level of literary merit. She had suggested sending pieces from Dubai, but her boss had implied that she needed to be based in London to maintain her edge. There wasn't going to be much chance of finding similar work here.

I won't argue with him, she thought. *We did enough of that in London. This is a fresh start for all of us.*

Chapter Four
The Resort

ON SATURDAY MORNING, Roy drove Lea and Cara out to Dream World.

They parked on a white stone peninsula that jutted into the cobalt gulf waters, at the entrance to the private marina. In the distance, hundreds of brown figures toiled with *keffiyehs* tied around their heads, protecting them from the relentless sun. An infinite ant-march moved across the isthmus as crews shifted locations. Behind them a line of red trucks, as neat and orderly as toys on a track, rumbled over the tamped-earth highways.

Three glittering obelisks rose from the scrubland, connected by arabesques of white concrete that swept in streamlined fractals through the sand. Arabic designers shared the geomancer's dislike of hard lines and sharp angles. The immense hotels owed more in design to the calligrapher's plume than the technician's grid. Two were finished and the third, the Persiana, was almost complete. They rose in the early morning haze like jewelled artefacts from a lost civilisation.

James Davenport, Dream World's public relations officer, gave them a tour of the development. He was as awkward as an ostrich, and had peppery hair and white freckled arms, as if his body could not settle to one colour. Lea wondered how he managed to keep his skin from getting burnt, considering he was on site all day and wore short-sleeved shirts. Already the temperature was in the high thirties and he didn't even look warm.

Lea wiped droplets of sweat from her eyes and tried to concentrate. Her cream linen suit felt damp and crumpled.

27

Everyone else appeared to have stepped out of a dry-cleaning advertisement. She wondered how much starch the local businessmen used in their white cotton *thobes* to get their creases so sharp. At least Cara had dressed for comfort in three-quarter length baggies and a yellow cotton top.

'You'll hear people saying that Dream World is the future,' Davenport told them, his broad Glaswegian accent sounding out of place in such an exotic setting. 'And they're right. It's a truly international project, financed by the Russians, engineered by Americans, designed by Europeans, built by Indians, raised on Arab land. If you ever want to find a way towards world peace, I'd suggest getting a dozen different faiths and ideologies together and making them construct something like this.' He laughed, exposing a frightening array of strong yellow teeth.

'How do you build out into the sea?' Cara asked.

'See over there?' Davenport pointed to the furthest outcrop of white stone in the water. 'The base of the resort is made from cement blocks that stand just seven metres above sea level, but they're designed to hold up against freak waves. They get abnormal tides in the Arabian Gulf once every century, so we had to test all kinds of scale models and be ready for any kind of extreme weather.'

He led the way to an etched steel site map built into a stone stand, a visual orientation point for any visitor entering the resort.

'We had to demolish all the old hotels that were put up during the oil boom, then level the shoreline and start from scratch. Many of the older hotels were trapped in the shadows of the new skyscrapers surrounding them, so it wasn't difficult to buy up the land. People come here for sunshine and luxury, and that's what they'll get. There are over a hundred and sixty separate fountains in the resort and they all work at different pressures. There's a canal flowing through the Persiana, and the world's largest resistance pool. Then there are the "atmosphere environments", in semi-submerged domes around the three hotels. For Snow World we've artificially created snowflakes without spurs on their surfaces, so that they don't appear fluffy. Our model is more crystalline and flat, which meant it packs down harder and is perfect for skiing in our biodome. Sea World has a huge aquarium, but has yet to be fully stocked. We had a problem with rare breeds of fish cannibalising one another.'

Even Cara looked awed, if only by the publicist's enthusiasm.

'We work around the clock, 24/7, 365 days a year,' said Davenport. 'We've got Indonesians, Vietnamese, Sudanese, Somalians, Filipinos, Egyptians, Koreans, just about every part of the world represented on the construction payroll. We live, sleep and breathe the resort. When it's finished, the top suites are going to cost around $35,000 a night. There are celebrity chefs opening signature restaurants in the marina, and we're hoping to host world-class competitive events in the sports complex. The whole thing will be ecologically independent within two years and computerised by a unique digital management program.' He noticed that Lea and Cara were starting to suffer in the heat. 'Sorry, but when you see what we're trying to achieve here, it kind of gets to you. Let's go inside.'

Davenport led the way to the hotel's chilled staff canteen. The huge shed-like steel structure was divided into sections so that the architects, technicians and engineers did not have to eat with the labourers. A vast buffet of salads, chicken, fish, eggs, beef, curries and *shawarmas* had barely been touched by the few other staff members in the restaurant.

'What happens to the food they don't eat?' Cara whispered. 'Does it get offered to the workmen?'

Davenport joined them at the table. 'We're very pleased to have your father here with us,' he told Cara. 'He's going to help us solve some of the problems we still have in the main atrium.'

'What kind of problems?' Cara asked.

'Things we couldn't take into account in the modelling process. CAD allowed us to deal with windshear and sand particles, corrosion from sun and salt air, but you have to imagine this place with thousands of people in it. In July and August the temperature is often above forty-five degrees. Getting the guests around without frying them is a trick in itself, especially as the seasonal movement of the sun constantly changes the shaded areas, so we're installing motion-sensor shades and water sprays along the walkways. We're using over twelve billion litres of water on the site.'

'In the sea air the exposed parts of the jets have a tendency to clog and corrode,' Roy added, 'so the valves have to be made of rubber, but rubber contains oil that dries out in the heat. Many solutions cause problems of their own.'

'It's true,' Davenport agreed. 'Every day presents a different challenge. There's no natural tide movement around the reclaimed land, which means that the seawater becomes stagnant. We've fixed that, but it's a learning curve. What we're attempting is unprecedented. It's kind of like terraforming a new planet. You saw *Star Trek*, Cara, right?'

Cara had overfilled her mouth with chicken, and didn't respond. She looked past Davenport to the horizon. The PR officer was clearly thrilled to be part of such a project, and was seized by the excitement of rising to the challenge. But *they* were doing the manual labour, those hordes of stripped brown figures out there in the sun. They were carrying out the really punishing work with drills and jackhammers, like slaves building pyramids.

Davenport finished describing the technicalities of geothermal cooling structures, then sensed that he should change the subject. 'Have you met many of the other residents yet?' he asked Lea.

'We haven't seen a soul, except at the school.'

'Ah—you're enrolled at Albion, aren't you? How was your induction day?'

'Okay,' said Cara. The Albion was attended by nearly four hundred English-speaking pupils from all over the world. The place was as quiet and orderly as a private hospital. Some of the other kids had led interesting lives in different countries, unlike Cara's classmates back in Chiswick, who had only ever gone to

Provence and the Algarve with their parents, or had stayed shut in their bedrooms on spliffs and Playstations.

'We work late during the week,' Davenport warned. 'Hopefully Milo will come to the residents' party. He's on the welcoming committee. He lives just across the road from you. He's a real character, the last of the original architects.'

'I think I've seen him at the window,' said Lea, recalling the glowering old man who watched her unapologetically when she went to the carport on their first day.

'Milo doesn't like the heat so you won't see him outside much.' Davenport dabbed at his mouth with a linen napkin, then pushed back his chair. 'I must get on. I know it must seem strange to you, Mrs Brook. But most of our regular staff do this for a living.'

'What do you mean?'

'They go from one construction project to the next in different countries on two-to-five year contracts. I came here from Cambodia, and before that, Korea. But I gather you've always been in London. This is an odd place at first, not quite Arabic, not quite Western.'

'So how would you describe it?' Lea asked.

'International. The way all cities will be one day.'

'But it's not, is it?' said Cara. 'The Arabs are at home, the Europeans are in offices and the Indians are out there in the sun. How can it be truly international if they don't socialise with each other?'

Lea looked at her daughter in surprise. It was unlike her to ask a virtual stranger such a question.

'Oh, that'll come in time, I'm sure,' said Davenport good-naturedly. 'It's a balancing act, and has to be recalibrated all the time. Rome wasn't built in a day. I'm sure you'll get to like the life here. We're a testing ground for the future. And who doesn't want to be part of the future, eh?' He glanced over at Roy. 'You must excuse me, I've got the senior directors' team coming in for an update.'

'Well, he seems happy in his work,' said Lea, watching Davenport stride out of the canteen.

'Why shouldn't he be?' asked Roy defensively. 'It's one of the most advanced construction projects in the world.'

'You think it's sustainable? I mean, something like this relies on continuous growth. Look what happened after 9/11. Tourists stopped visiting Muslim territories overnight. Most of those places were perfectly safe. The locals abandoned their traditional skills to cater to tourism and ended up suffering. Whole towns were obliterated. It could happen again if the global downturn deepens.'

'The credit crunch doesn't affect the super-rich half as much as it affects us,' said Roy. 'There are over seven billion people on the planet, Lea. Do you think some of those will be wealthy enough to pay $35,000 a night for a suite at the Persiana? Of course we have to make the most of it. The next generation may not have so much money.'

'Talk to your daughter about it,' said Lea. 'She's always complaining that we spent her future.'

'We could still be back in Belmont Terrace trying to make next month's mortgage payment, with me stuck out of work.'

'Are you guys going to have another row in public?' Cara asked, 'Because if you are I'll go outside and wait.'

'We weren't arguing, it's called a conversation.' Lea laid a hand on Cara's arm. 'And you gave Mr Davenport a pretty hard time.'

'Get off me, I'm not a child.' Cara shook away her hand and rose.

'Hey!' Roy watched as his daughter headed outside to sit and sulk against the shaded patio wall. 'You have to let her form her own opinions, Lea.'

'Me?' Lea repeated in surprise. 'If she doesn't make friends here she'll just become an outsider again, you know that. She's at an awkward age.'

'She's smart enough to have an open mind.'

'I hope so.' They watched Cara as she sat texting, one leg folded under the other in the kind of awkward position teenagers seemed to find comfortable. 'Actually she says she's already hooked up with a couple of girls from the school. Remember how long it usually takes her to make friends?'

'Good, I'm glad about that. I want you to be happy while you're here too.'

'I know you do,' Lea assured him. 'Don't worry about me, I'll be fine. I'm looking forward to it. It's a very different world to the one I'm used to, that's all.'

They finished their coffee in comfortable silence as Filipino waiters collected the plates.

Chapter Five
The Housewives of The Future

THE INDONESIAN MAID'S name was Lastri. She was nineteen, slender, silent and serious, with an unnervingly still gaze, and her size belied her strength. Each morning she changed into a pink and white nylon outfit supplied by the compound's store, and quietly set about her duties. She seemed fluent in English, but went blank whenever Lea moved away from the day's agenda to ask about her family.

Lea soon realised that her second language was confined to a narrow path of subjects mainly involving the kitchen and cleaning materials. She tried to shorten Lastri's hours just so that the house would sometimes be empty, but failed to make her understand. With the beds made, the floors polished to a lethal gleam and the kitchen scoured to operating-theatre sterility there was nothing else to do.

She met Maruf, the gardener, and Kamal, the cleaner who took care of the shared swimming pool, and the men who tended the tennis courts, the lake, the fountains and the hedgerows. At 8:00am each day the pristine compound was filled with the drone of trimmers and leaf-blowers, after which silence returned and nothing stirred.

The neighbourhood looked like a magazine brochure, its plants and emerald lawns meticulously weeded and watered. But it felt oddly artificial. Perhaps it was the sheer brightness of the colours, as though a TV image had been turned up too high, or the knowledge that beneath the thin layer of topsoil there was nothing but sand and rock. The immaculate swathes of grass were faintly absurd, laid across the natural landscape like a nylon carpet, dressing for doll houses.

Each day grew incrementally hotter. Soon, Lea realised, there would be nothing to do except sit in air-conditioned shadows, hiding from the summer temperatures. On days when a breeze stirred, the horizon was dotted with red and yellow hang-gliders, sawing down through the zephyrs toward the shore.

The sparkling swimming pools left behind a tracery of neon waves when she shut her eyes, like the remnants of a dream. Beyond these azure rectangles were security fences and ID cards that needed to be shown, groundsmen standing bored at the edge of the lake, guards with their mirrors on poles to check for bombs, maids clearing untouched breakfasts from patio tables. The changes in security status were posted without explanation on the compound's corner-store message board, and were just as mysteriously retracted.

In the house, everything was calm and ordered.

Cara had set up a dock for her iPod, and now that Lea was alone she played her recording of Maria Callas in *Lucia di Lammermoor.* Sopranos had the power to still her restless energy and bring shape to her thoughts. Roy had no response to music at all, beyond a few terrible old rock albums that reminded him of his teenaged years, and Cara fled the room whenever an aria started.

Lea looked out of the window, sipping tea from her ginger cat mug, and saw a woman standing on the front path. She was clearly waiting to be noticed and greeted, rather than walking up and ringing the doorbell. She was squat and rotund, Anglo-Indian, in a cornflower blue smock over beige slacks, a helmet of mouse-coloured hair that might have been a *sheitel* and too much shiny coral lipstick. Turning down the music, Lea opened the front door and stepped out.

'Can I help you?'

'Hello there,' the woman called in theatrical surprise, 'I was just seeing if anyone had moved in and well, there you are.' She held out a hand. 'I'm Rosemary Busabi, it sounds like busy bee doesn't it, and I suppose that's what I am.' She gave a little squeak of a laugh. At first Lea thought Mrs Busabi had overdone the foundation on her cheeks, but there was a smell of baking about her, and she realised her neighbour was covered in flour. Mrs Busabi pointed behind her. 'I'm diagonally opposite. I teach at the primary. Are you here with little ones?'

There was clearly no way of avoiding a coffee morning, so Lea invited her in. Mrs Busabi peered and prodded and checked everything she saw, blatantly pricing and comparing the furnishings. She had a middle-England accent tempered with something that hinted at a more exotic past, probably time passed in India. 'I said to Harji, that's my husband, someone's moving into Tom and Sally Chalmers' old place but he said surely not so soon, he hadn't heard anything about it.'

Lea knew nothing about the history of the property. It appeared to be no more than two or three years old. 'So there was someone here before?' she asked. She was about to start making tea, but Lastri insisted on taking over, so she led Mrs Busabi to the lounge.

'Didn't your husband tell you? Tom was the original compound manager. He was here right from the start. I was good friends with his wife for a time. He had this place for about six years. I know what you're thinking; the villa looks brand new, but it's not. It's the climate, you see. Things don't age, they just get a bit dusty. Even the sandstorms don't do much damage because we clean everything after they've passed, so it's all spic and span again. You just have to keep a broom handy and remember to refrigerate your perishables. Because terrible things can happen if you don't refrigerate your perishables.'

'So, when did the Chalmers leave?' Lea awkwardly sat back as Lastri served coffee and pastries.

'Tom died about two months ago. The silliest accident. For some unearthly reason he decided to trim the grass in front of the house—that little patch you've got before the edge of the pavement? At *night*. And he went through a power cable. It turned him quite black and fried off all his hair.'

'That's awful.'

'Oh, he didn't die here, but in the old Creek Hospital. He was overweight, of course, and had high blood pressure. He was always doing silly things.' Mrs Busabi took a sip of her tea and didn't appear to find the taste entirely to her liking. 'His wife went home to—Sheffield, I think it was. They'd lost their only child, so she didn't have happy memories of being here.'

'Why, what happened—' Lea started to ask, but Mrs Busabi ploughed on.

'We were very good friends for a time. I do miss her. We used to play cards together. Do you play bridge?'

'I'm afraid not.'

'Mr Mansour took over but he hasn't got the same *warmth*. He lives in town, a Muslim of course, so he can't really be expected to understand our little problems.'

'I met him the day we arrived. He seemed nice.'

'Oh, everyone's very nice,' said Mrs Busabi, absently touching her hair. 'But I liked India more. The people in Delhi were so friendly, and you couldn't get better servants. Of course, you had to keep them in line or they would take advantage, inviting their relatives in to sweep your yard, that sort of thing. Where have you come from?'

'Oh, just London,' said Lea with an air of apology.

'So this is your first tour of duty? You don't usually trail spouse?'

'I'm sorry?'

'Oh, that's what it's called. Wives who follow their husbands around.'

Lea felt the need to explain. 'This is going to be my only tour of duty. Roy's contract is for two years, and our daughter is fifteen. She'll be sixteen in September. I'd like to get her into a good college in England. She doesn't know what she wants to do yet, but she's very good with technology. I don't understand half the things she does.'

'Does she have to do anything? Couldn't she just do what you do?'

Lea decided she probably wasn't going to be Mrs Busabi's new best friend.

'We don't have little ones, unfortunately,' her neighbour continued. 'I have my children at the school, of course, so it's like one big lovely family.' She paused, and it seemed to Lea she had suddenly lost her train of thought. 'Your husband, what have they put him on?'

'His background is in architectural engineering,' Lea explained. 'These days something like a concrete pillar isn't just a support anymore, it's a conduit for electronics and sensors and all sorts of other stuff. He makes studies of the structural problems.'

'My husband Harji is the public water projects manager,' said Mrs Busabi. 'It's very demanding work. There's a fire-and-water fountain at the centre of the Persiana park where all the jets are meant to rotate and light up to music every fifteen minutes, and it doesn't work properly. It's all he ever talks about.' There was a hint of desperation in her voice.

'What about you?' Lea asked. 'What do you do?'

Mrs Busabi looked puzzled. 'What do you mean?'

'In your spare time.'

'My dear, I never have a moment to call my own, there are so many clubs and charities and societies. Cookery classes and reading groups and makeover evenings, all sorts of lovely things. A lot of them are run by our younger ladies, so I don't tend to go to those.' Lea studied her neighbour. Mrs Busabi couldn't have been more than forty. 'I'm sure the Americans will try to enlist you.' She sounded disapproving.

'The Americans?'

'Your next door neighbours. Very *friendly*. They've been away visiting her family in Ohio. You won't have to seek them out, they're bound to come and find you.'

'My husband is American. From New York.'

'Oh, but that doesn't really count, does it? New York is so much more...' The thought trailed off.

'These clubs.' Lea tried to come up with a way of framing her question so that it wouldn't offend. 'Are they just for the wives?'

'Mostly. The men are all at work. But there are the dances and dinners at the golf club, the husbands usually attend those if they're not too busy. We have shopping expeditions, and the children have their computer club, and outings to the desert. I take the little ones on nature rambles with Dr Vance, he's the compound's GP, such a lovely man. You're not planning to work yourself, are you?'

'I'm hoping to,' Lea said, almost feeling guilty. 'I wrote for a magazine in London. I'm looking for freelance assignments. Articles and so on.'

'How marvellous,' said Mrs Busabi unenthusiastically. 'You must submit something to our local residents' newspaper. We're always looking for new recipes and home decorating ideas. Well, I must be getting along. It's baking day. We'll have to enrol you in our cookery classes.' She shone a happy smile in Lea's direction. 'I absolutely insist you become a member of the Dream Ranches Pastry Club. And we should get your daughter started as soon as possible. Future housewives!'

Chapter Six
The Nasty Old Man

'I DON'T SUPPOSE they're all like her,' Lea told Roy as they sat together for a dinner of sea bass in fennel. 'God, they can't be.'

'Sounds like she was just being friendly,' said Roy. 'She's probably used to a certain kind of person living here. Where's Cara?'

'She called to say she'd be late. Some of the girls in her class are planning to go swimming at sunset on one of the public beaches near the Palm Jebel-Ali.'

'Really? Is that a good idea?'

'What harm can it do? Her social calendar seems to have suddenly filled up. I had this fantasy that the three of us might get to eat meals together.'

'Look on the plus side. We have the place to ourselves.'

'Good point. Give me a kiss.'

He leaned over and raised his hand to her face. 'Hey,' she said, looking at the shiny redness on his left arm, 'you've burned yourself.'

He examined the mark. 'We have to get our hands dirty here. No more sitting behind desks sending emails. I'm out in the field now.'

She savoured the taste of his kiss.

'So your day,' he said, reminding her. 'Mrs Busabi.'

'I can't remember her first name, and we've got beyond the point where I can comfortably ask her to remind me.'

Roy laughed. His teeth looked white against his new tan. 'You are so English sometimes.'

'She's going to try and recruit me and Cara for the Pastry Club, whatever that is. Actually I feel a bit sorry for her. She's obviously lonely, stuck at home while Mr Busabi does something demanding with rotating fountains.'

'Go on, make fun now,' said Roy, 'but wait until Dream World is open. You'll be proudly pointing out that your husband was the one who discovered why the marble walkways were splitting.'

'Why are they splitting?'

'Wrong usage. They're too fine. The Chinese have been buying specialised high-finish marble for the heavy-traffic areas, and it's not suitable. The water-sprays make everything slippery, and because it's hard water we're getting calcification in the natural texture of the marble, which causes it to split. There's a lot of trial-and-error.'

'Do you think you'll make the opening date? It's only three months away.'

'It's not impossible, but there'll have to be cuts.' Roy carefully deboned his fish. 'People don't realise how much work it takes to keep hotels looking good. Most resorts have teams of marble polishers that work through the night.'

'I suppose it really is like Oz,' said Lea. 'The guests don't want to see what's going on behind the curtains. Maybe you can't transform a country into something entirely different overnight. It's like the Victorian English in India, passing out in their crinolines and planting rosebushes everywhere, only to watch them die.'

'Well, the region can't go back to being a desert populated by nomadic tribes and fishermen. The UAE member-states have ancient alliances; everyone's watching, anxious to learn from our mistakes. Nobody wants to end up with a string of ugly Vegas-style resorts.'

'But isn't that exactly what Dream World is going to be? The British press says they're ignoring safety precautions and won't allow the workforce to unionise.'

'The British press.' Roy made a sour face. 'They tell their readers that celebrity footballers are buying luxury holiday homes on the Palm Jumeirah, then run stories about the sewage pipes backing up. Build and destroy. You were a writer, Lea, you know how that works.'

She bristled at his use of the past tense, but it was impossible to be angry with Roy for long. His enthusiasm was so boyish and energetic that it could spread like brush-fire. 'What will happen if you miss the date?'

'I guess they'd have to renew my contract, for a start.'

'You mean we'd be here for more than two years.' The thought hung between them. 'Oh, I didn't tell you—the previous tenant here died in a freak accident. He went through a power line and electrocuted himself.'

Roy did not look up from his partially deboned fish. 'Really? I didn't hear about that.'

'Something happened to his daughter and he went a bit odd. He was gardening at night. Mrs Busabi didn't tell me the full story.'

'You certainly got a lot of information out of her, considering you didn't like her.'

'You don't think it's kind of weird?'

'What, that someone failed the Darwin test?'

Lea watched as Roy carried on eating.

THE NEXT MORNING, a minor accident brought Lea into contact with Milo. She returned from the mall and was parking the blue Renault when she heard a bump. A red electric scooter had appeared behind her at the kerb. She was sure it hadn't been there when she left. The old man came out of his house with such speed that she felt sure he must have been watching her.

'I'm so sorry,' she said, bending down to check the scooter for damage. 'It's just a tiny mark. I can get it out and you won't be able to see a thing.'

'Woman driver, eh?' said the old man, waving a tanned hand at the Renault. 'Menaces to society, the lot of you.' He had the kind of German accent she had only ever heard in old British comedy shows. 'Don't worry, I'm joking', he said quickly, seeing embarrassment in her face.

'You must be Milo.' Lea remembered Davenport's description

of the retired German engineer who lived across the road. 'Mr Davenport told me about you.'

'Well, you can assume that anything James told you was a lie. He's a company weasel. He has no opinions of his own. So cheerful, so enthusiastic. He can brighten any room just by leaving it.'

Lea stifled a shocked laugh. 'Listen, would you like to come in for some tea?'

'Why not? That's what we do around here, we drink buckets and buckets of tea until it's time to start hammering the alcohol, which is any time past midday. At my age tea makes me piss like a horse every ten minutes but what the hell, I'll accept a good strong Arabic coffee if you have it.'

Milo Melnik was small, stocky and sun-creased, with fine white hair and sharp blue eyes that seemed to be searching for signs of rebellion. In his baggy red cardigan and trousers pulled halfway up his chest, he reminded her of Mickey Rooney. Instantly drawn to him, she introduced herself and took him inside.

Lastri obediently appeared with cups and cinnamon date cake. 'It's shop-bought, I'm afraid,' Lea apologised. 'Our furniture only just turned up and I've been busy unpacking.'

'At least you got Arabic food,' he said. 'Nobody does that here. They spend most of their time setting up little kingdoms and copying the recipes they used to have at home. Have you ever eaten something called Battenburg cake? I'm sure we never had it in Germany. Disgusting. The Americans and Australians are always hosting god-awful barbeques and the English are forever complaining that you can't get a decent cup of tea.'

'I won't be doing that,' said Lea. 'I'm interested in Middle Eastern culture. I'd like to get involved, not hide away. Back in London I was a writer.'

'I thought I recognised a kindred spirit. Please don't turn into a little housewife like the rest of them. And don't let them tell you they've got nothing better to do. There's plenty to do. People arrive with good intentions but instead of being useful they spend their days creeping around the malls like ghosts, staring at all the stuff they don't need. But what do I know, I'm an old man, there's nothing in the malls for me.'

He seated himself in the kitchen's only comfortable chair. 'I was going to visit you yesterday but I saw old Busy-Body Busabi heading over here and thought I'd better stay out of the way. That woman makes my balls ache. Wait until you try her sponge cake, it's like eating a cushion. How are you settling in?'

'Everyone seems very nice.'

'Bullshit, you thought you were making an entry into an earthly paradise, but you're slowly finding out that you've landed in a snakepit.'

Lea laughed. 'Well, let's just say I'm not really interested in shopping and taking cookery courses.'

'Hooray for that. It means we can be friends at least. It may not endear you to the other Stepford Wives, though.'

'How do you fill your time, Milo?'

'Haven't you heard?' He leaned forward and held his palm against his lips in a theatrical whisper. 'I'm the nasty old man who frightens the children. I'm the fly in the ointment around here, a German Jew working in an Arab country. They look at me and ask themselves, how did that happen? I tell them it's simple, I have no roots, I've outlived the rest of my family, I go wherever I damn well please and I say the things nobody is supposed to say. We're all meant to toe the company line, even the retired ones.'

'Well, I guess they're paying for us all to be here.'

'They!' he exclaimed. 'They! It used to be we, us. I was a founding member of the original project team. I started as a marine engineer, working on the concept of building on reclaimed seabeds. Several of us shared parallel ideas. But ideas aren't enough. They have to be financed, monetised, packaged, so a new board of directors was formed. Needless to say, I didn't make *that* team. They pay the UAE, they pay us all, and look what they get in return! Have you seen much of your husband since he started work?'

Lea's smile fractionally faded. 'He's putting in long hours.'

'You won't see him at all from now on, and when you do he'll be so exhausted he'll just want to sleep.' He sighed wearily. 'We knew it would be hard, but it didn't turn out as I'd imagined. Things never do.'

'You sound disappointed.'

'I would hate to become known as the grandfather of a project that's a future watchword for all that's wrong with the world. I'm not full-time anymore, they just come to me whenever they have a problem nobody else can fix. I guess you heard about some of those?'

'Only what I read in the papers. The stories seem to have stopped now.'

'That's down to Davenport's latest PR onslaught.'

'I heard about the workman who froze to death.'

'It's the price we pay for leaping into the future.'

'So everyone keeps telling me,' said Lea. 'The business district reminds me of the Emerald City. I keep expecting the Tin Man and the Cowardly Lion to come dancing out of the bushes.'

'That's because it's a fantasy. We're trapped between Eastern and Western ideals. The Arabs don't have to work. They have an Indian workforce triple the size of their own population. Do you know how many couples here meet for the first time just before their wedding? Is it surprising that when they come out of the mosques and see Western women in tiny bikinis, it offends them? They want tourists but they can't pick who comes, except by raising prices.'

'Britain is the same,' said Lea, 'only more secretive. Our government is stuffed with Old Etonians who don't give a damn about the underprivileged.'

'Good God, a woman with an opinion.' Milo laughed. 'You'll have to be careful about that.'

'I'm hoping to get a job here.'

'I wish you the best of luck. Most of our magazines just print glossy guff about sporting events and fashion shows. There's less moral outrage than in the other UAE countries, of course—you should try living in parts of Saudi Arabia, it's still the Stone Age there—and here sometimes, just below the surface.'

'What do you mean?'

Milo waved his hand airily. 'Oh, raids take place and people go to prison. You never quite find out what's going on. Everyone knows about the secret police. They had a perfectly workable system before the West arrived. Now they have a sort of polite totalitarian state. Hey, I don't want to frighten you. I'm meant to be part of the welcoming committee.'

'It's a pleasure to find someone I can talk to,' said Lea.

'Let's change the subject. How's your daughter coping with the move? I assume that's the pretty girl I see charging about on her bike.'

'Cara seems to be taking to it well. Of course the weather's still a novelty. She's joined the computer club and is going to the beach. The kids at her London school were a pretty wild crowd, and she's easily led. I didn't want her getting into drink and drugs.'

'There's not too much chance of that happening,' said Milo. 'They don't publicly whip offenders here like they do in Saudi, but arrests are made over tiny quantities of soft drugs and even over-the-counter medicines. In theory you can get a mandatory sentence for being in possession of flu medication. One guy was held after poppy seeds were found on his clothes. It turned out they had fallen off a bread roll he'd eaten at the airport.'

Lea's eyes widened. 'Is that for real?'

'It was in the papers, it must be true.'

She couldn't tell if he was joking. 'Do you think Dream World will work?'

'I don't see why not. So long as people are rich and stupid enough to want novelties like underwater casinos and refrigerated shops selling fur coats. The Americans won't come here and the Europeans are too broke, so it's the turn of the Russians, the South Americans and the Chinese.'

'That's what Roy says. But what happens after that?'

'My dear, there'll be plenty of things to worry about before we reach that point,' said Milo, sipping his coffee with a smile. 'The road to democracy is filled with nasty surprises.'

'I heard our predecessor got a nasty surprise right outside this house.'

Milo raised an eyebrow. 'You mean Tom? Old Busabi *has* been busy. I was here the night he died.'

'How did he manage to cut through a power cable?'

'Nobody knows that he did. He'd certainly been using a fairly lethal electric saw to take out dead tree roots—the garden wasn't like it is now. But he was found dead in the street. It was an odd thing—'

'Why?'

'Darling, it was *dark*. What the hell did he think he was playing at?'

'What happened to his daughter?' Lea instantly regretted asking the question.

Milo turned aside and made a fuss of checking his watch. 'Look at the time, I must be getting on. It's nearly noon—the safe hour.'

'What do you mean?'

He pointed up to the ceiling. 'The sun is directly overhead. There are no shadows at noon. Middle Eastern cultures believe that death hides in the shadows. You're fine for now.' He rose and made his way to the front door, turning to her. 'Oh, don't look so serious. Silly old men love to tease pretty women. But do one thing for me. Keep an eye on your daughter.'

His change of tone surprised her. 'Why?'

Milo shrugged. 'There's an unhealthy lassitude that descends on rich people at the equator. The heat breeds strange notions.'

'What do you mean?'

'She has your looks. This is a place where the most primitive beliefs can suddenly resurface.' He cut himself off. 'Don't worry, I'll be here to keep an eye on you.'

And with that he was gone.

Chapter Seven
The Next Doors

A YELLOW SCHOOL bus dropped Cara back at the entrance of Dream Ranches every day at five. On the afternoons that Lea took her car to the mall, she drove by the school and collected her daughter. The low white building that housed the classrooms sat in a perfect oblong of brilliant green lawn, surrounded by acres of beige rock and dust.

Cara stood waiting beneath a flat-topped acacia tree, whispering conspiratorially into her phone. Her pale skin had darkened to a permanent soft brown tan, her hair lightening to dirty blond, and regular immersion in seawater had thickened it. Ever since she had been small, she'd rubbed the knuckle of her thumb against her chin when she was stressed. Out here she had suddenly dropped the habit. Her new physicality had become readily apparent, and—shock of shocks—she had started using the school gym most mornings. Perhaps this was what she had needed all along.

'You have to get a haircut,' Lea said, pushing open the car door. 'You're starting to look like a surfer-chick.'

Cara got in. 'I'm not going to catch a wave around here. The sea's like glass.'

'There's surf at the Hilton Beach.'

'It's mechanical, it's not the same. Can we take Norah with us?' She pointed to a girl hanging back by the bushes. 'She just needs to get to the Arabia Mall.'

'Hi,' said Lea, checking her rear-view mirror, 'I'm Cara's mother, Lea.'

Norah shot back a salute, two middle fingers from her eyebrow ring, but remained silent. She wore a black woollen cap and heavy black jeans, despite the heat, and went back to checking her emails.

'Norah lives next door to us,' said Cara. 'She's been away with her folks in America.'

'I'm looking forward to meeting your family, Norah,' said Lea.

'Yeah.' Norah continued texting, and didn't look up again until they reached the underground car park at the mall. The girls climbed out.

'Well,' said Lea, 'it was nice meeting you.' But Norah had already gone, loping toward the elevator bank with Cara in her wake. 'Bye, then,' she said to herself. *So Norah's the cool new pal she can't tear herself away from*, she thought. *I guess they find more to talk about when I'm not there.*

The next morning at 11:00am on the dot, Lea opened her front door to a tall, burnished blonde in her mid-forties, too studiedly thin, with a turned-up nose and a smile that revealed a palisade of artificially whitened teeth.

'I hear you met my oldest daughter yesterday,' she said, stepping inside without waiting to be invited, 'We're the Next Doors. I'm Colette Larvin. I thought I should drop by and apologise for her. Not that I suppose she said anything.'

'She was probably shy,' Lea suggested, as Lastri once more scurried off to begin the mid-morning ritual of setting out coffee and cake.

Colette recognized the remark as politeness and waved it aside. 'You couldn't shut her up when she was small. Then she hit her teen years and turned into a deaf-mute. Occasionally I manage to starve her into conversation. Stopping her privileges works too. Sometimes I hide her laptop charger.'

'Mine's the same.'

'Seems like they're already great friends. What are you doing here?'

'Oh, I'm—what do they call it?—trailing…'

'Trailing spouse. Me too. Ben is one of the DWG planners. He specialises in electronics, how to fit them into buildings. I think he's going to be working with your husband. Something about marble—ring any bells?'

'Believe me, I've heard all about it.'

Colette flopped down onto the couch. 'We're so sorry we missed your arrival. I'd have been here with the welcome wagon. We were visiting my family in Columbus. But don't worry, you'll hear us now we're back. Rachel's a little deaf and tends to shout. Don't mention it, though, because she's convinced nobody notices.'

'Rachel's your other daughter?'

'No, That's Abbi. Rachel is my mother-in-law. She insisted on coming out with us to look after the children, but she hates the sun.'

'So the company paid for all five of you to come here?'

Colette laughed. 'They must value Ben's ability to get the job done. He's putting in crazy hours, shedding weight, going grey, stressed to the max, although weirdly he's looking kind of hot these days. If this keeps up I'll be pestering him for sex.'

'It seems like they have a pretty big responsibility.'

'Tell me about it. Dream World starts losing around seven million dollars each day it goes past the opening deadline.'

Lastri's strong coffee and Arabic cakes appeared, set out in their usual place. Lea checked her watch and noticed that she was setting it out at exactly the same time every morning. Clearly the neighbours knew how the system worked and arrived accordingly, subconsciously controlled by their maids and gardeners.

'I'm glad Cara and Norah have hooked up,' said Colette. 'Norah runs her computer club most weeknights. We don't see her much—Abbi's the homebody— but at least I can be sure she's not getting into trouble now.'

'Why, did she have a habit of getting into trouble?'

'You're kidding. We had her on Ritalin for years. We were both out at work and it got too tricky raising children without pharmaceutical help.'

Lea wasn't sure about putting children on medication. It reminded her of Victorians dosing their babies with laudanum. She changed the subject. 'So you've been here for a while?'

Colette helped herself to a miniscule sliver of cake. 'Two years, nine months and counting. Ben's on an open-ended contract.'

'So you'll stay after the opening.'

'If everything goes well and the consortium decides to go ahead with the DWG project in Athens we may stay with them, depending on the girls' schooling. I told Ben I won't do Africa, no matter how much they promise to sort out their power supply. Things have been a little strained here since the bombs.'

'There were bombs?'

'Didn't they tell you? Only a couple exploded, they were just low-level pipe-bombs, but no warning was given. Protest groups have to give warning call signs. One of the site foremen found them by the reservoir.'

'Who do you think put them there?'

'The cops arrested some Indian workers on the site. It's convenient for everyone. They're always upset about working conditions.' She set down her cup and glanced back at Lastri, lowering her voice. 'How are you getting along with your maid?'

'I'm not used to this kind of thing,' Lea admitted. 'It feels weird having her around all the time. I don't need any help running the place. It's not like anything gets dirty.'

'You say that now, but you'll come to depend on her,' said Colette. 'You should be careful what you say when they're in the room. I heard that some of them report back to the police. There's a rule around here; what happens in the compound stays in the compound.'

'Why? What's likely to happen?'

'A few months back, there was supposedly an attempt by Muslim extremists to radicalise the area, and security was tightened. I mean, we all heard about it but nobody saw anything first-hand. And the maids—suddenly half of them disappeared and were replaced. These new girls just turned up on Monday morning and nobody said a word. It's like we weren't supposed to have noticed. You hear some pretty odd things and never get to find out if they're true.'

'Milo was regaling me with his fund of horror stories yesterday.'

Colette sat back sharply. 'Oh, we all talk too much, and a lot of it's just gossip. Actually it's kind of zen here, a blank slate you can write what you like on. Listen, did you get yourself a drinking licence?'

'No, do I need one?'

'Ex-pats need an alcohol licence to drink, even at home. The police don't check, but you should get one just in case. Sometimes we do booze-runs to Sharjah and the cops wait to issue us with tickets on the way back.'

'You mean they know what's going on?'

'Sure, it's all just a big game to remind us that we're only guests. Speaking of booze, I came over to tell you we're throwing a welcome bash for you on Saturday. I hope the date's okay? We're using your arrival as an excuse for a party. If Ben can get off work he'll fire up the barbecue. He likes to do it himself. A man is at his happiest when he's poking a fire with a stick. Rachel and I will do the invitations, and the maids can handle the catering. You have to agree you'll be there. It'll be too hot if we leave it until next month.'

'That's great,' said Lea, 'We'd love to come.'

'I'm sure we're going to be good friends.' Colette rose to leave. 'People will want to tell you things. Don't believe everything you hear. I have to get back. It's cookery class this afternoon. I always look forward to it. Has anyone enrolled you in the Pastry Club?'

Chapter Eight
The Swim

CARA AND NORAH carried the blue plastic icebox between them. A tangerine slice of sun glowed muddily as it reached the lip of the sea.

'Pollution,' said Norah, pointing at the horizon. Although she was in a khaki vest and baggies, she still wore her woollen hat. 'The rays are reaching us through thirty metre bands of shit from the tankers in the navigation channel. The water's okay, though. Most of the beaches are fake but this one's real.'

Norah had travelled a lot with her family, and nothing impressed her. 'They're building new beaches all along the coast,' she told Cara. 'A year ago everyone was broke. Now everyone's spending like fucking maniacs.'

'You come down here every evening?' Cara asked.

'Most nights, around sunset. A bunch of us from school, and some boys from the compound who go to the French college. They're glad to get out of their school because of the cultural fucking imperative.'

'What's that?'

'It's financed by the French government, so they're only allowed to speak French in class. Sometimes we have barbecues. The cops drive down to the shoreline and sit in their jeeps watching us, but they don't do anything.'

'What are they looking for? Drugs?'

Norah gave a mirthless laugh. 'You're in the wrong place if you're looking to smoke dope. It happens, just not around here.' She squinted back at the sun. Her face fell into a natural pout and her pencil-straight hair looked as if it had been dyed black, but this confrontational pose was mitigated by signs of wealth; a Breitling watch, a series of jewelled rings on a chain at her throat. Sudden movements brought out a cat-eyed wariness in her.

'No dope?' Cara repeated. 'You know that for sure?'

'The clubs in town, they got these pole dancers who put on private shows. Their bosses keep the girls half-starved and pay for their tits to be enlarged. The Chinese are crazy for big tits. That's where all the drugs are, in the bars. You can get anything if you have enough money and the right connections. It's sick.' Cara was unsure whether Norah meant good-sick or bad-sick; she had heard no slang at school or in the compound, probably because there were so many nationalities using the common language of basic English.

Norah high-fived a couple of other kids joining them. 'The cops are watching for booze,' she explained. 'The whole mixed-minors thing freaks them—come on.' They padded over the hot sand and joined the rest of the group, who were stacking driftwood above the tideline. Half a dozen boys and girls from the school sat in a semi-circle, generic hip-hop playing on a music dock. Cara was surprised by their sombre mood.

'Anyone got a brew?' Norah asked. Someone popped the lid of a cooler and threw them one apiece.

'We're not allowed beer on the beach,' said Lauren, a blandly pretty American blonde with a heart-shaped face and lip implants. Cara had seen her before, seated behind her parents in their silver Mercedes, queuing to get into the estate. 'Dean keeps a second icebox buried in the sand.'

Dean caught the name-check and leaned forward, hand raised to Cara in greeting. He wore his curly brown hair in a ponytail knotted with coloured bands and beads. His wide smile invited complicity and revealed perfect bleached teeth.

'But the cops could be a pain if they wanted to, couldn't they?' Cara asked.

'They're not serious,' said Norah, 'they just come around so that we'll tell our parents we've seen them.'

'Do you ever go into the desert?'

'Sometimes,' said Lauren. 'My brother takes us, but he won't roll his jeep or anything cool like that. He's such a fun-suck. He sticks to the main highways. If you go off-road you have to let your tyres half-down to get traction in the sand, and he says it damages them if you do it too often.'

'He doesn't come to the beach?' asked Cara.

'No,' said Norah. 'Her bro hangs around the mall cruising for underage *poo-say*. They should get him chipped.'

'We got plenty of other stuff to do,' said Dean. 'There's a ski-slope at the Mall. The cinemas show English language movies but we don't get the really gross horror movies. The censorship is fucked up. I've got some sites you can stream from. You're London, right? We haven't been back for two years. What's it like now?'

'Same as ever,' said Cara, 'cold and wet. There's some good bands though.'

'Bring some music down next time,' said Norah. 'If we like it, it goes on the playlist.'

'Do you ever go out to the resort?' asked Cara.

'Dream World? No, the security guy there watches for us. There have been some really fucking weird accidents. One guy got a scaffolding pole through the top of his skull. Another one got killed when a stack of pallets slid over on him. The heat loosened the metal ties.'

'Tell him about the ice-man,' said Lauren.

Dean drew them in with his smile. 'Okay, there's this beach out at the end of the resort where they're building this exclusive restaurant? You can only reach it across the sand, but it gets too hot to walk on, so they installed pipes under the ground to cool it down. They didn't want people to complain about burning their feet, so they filled the pipes with some kind of coolant like liquid nitrogen. There was a leak, so they sent one of the Indian workers down to fix it and he had to lay on the ground to uncover it, but it turned out his buddies hadn't shut the pressure off properly. The pipe exploded and froze him to death on the sand, right in the middle of the day. His lungs turned to ice. When they came to take his body away, it was still frozen solid. Amazing, huh?'

'What happened?' asked Cara.

'What do you mean what happened? They shipped the corpse back to India and charged his wife for the freight.' Dean checked his watch, some kind of neon Japanese model. 'I have to go home soon. Let's swim.'

The group waded out into the warm water together. Cara wasn't used to swimming with boys, and felt self-conscious about her body. Most of them took athletic practice and worked out. Nobody seemed to be paying any attention, though, and after a while she grew more comfortable. She was a strong swimmer, and led the way into deeper, cooler water. Speedboats droned past, and a red acrobatic plane was performing stunt-rolls, corkscrewing down through the bare blue sky, a lone participant in a dogfight.

Looking down between her feet she could see all the way to the bottom, where small black fish darted over the rippled sand.

'Sometimes they swim over you,' said Dean, floating alongside her. He tipped his head back and allowed his body to rise, the water gently lapping his broad chest. 'I like it out here. You don't have to think about anything, just hang in space, like you're floating in the clouds. Sometimes the mist blurs the horizon line and you can't tell which way up you are, if you're in the sky or the sea. You might be looking down at the earth from the distant future. Like you're in another life.'

Cara watched as his tanned form floated slowly past her. He was so close that she could smell the coconut oil on his sun-warmed skin. The lotion sheened his body in a golden carapace. Droplets shone on his chest like diamonds. He drifted and shone like some polished component of a luxury yacht, then sank beneath the surface of the glassine ocean, still gleaming, swimming slowly around her, encircling her. She could tell he was smiling, even underwater. He watched her for a long moment, then turned with a flick of his leg, sinking deeper, a lapidary merman returning home.

Back on the shore, behind the open space of the beach, two policemen sat silent and motionless in their blue and white jeep watching the teenagers, the setting sun reflected in their mirror shades.

Chapter Nine
The Underpass

THE LAST OF the boxes had arrived from Chiswick and their contents had been set around the house, but most of the pieces looked out of place, as if an effort had been made to reassemble their home from a poorly remembered dream.

Disappointed, Lea drove back from Spinneys supermarket with several days' supply of groceries. There could be no distractions next week; she was determined to find freelance work. She had bought a sombre high-necked suit in grey silk, and two light jackets that covered her skin. The outfits felt cooler than her London summer clothes. Catching sight of herself in the car mirror, with her dark hair tied back and large sunglasses, it seemed that she offered up the perfect image of Arabic modesty.

It was, unsurprisingly, another beautiful day.

The road to the compound curved from Highway A6 in an architectural arabesque, passing between several dusty single-storey buildings, the remains of an old village that had been cleared for the route. The last few stores were still open for business—stacks of beach chairs and blue plastic laundry baskets framed their doorways—but no customers could reach them through the tangle of on-ramps and roadworks.

Clearly, some locals were missing out on the property bonanza. Lea was so busy studying the shabby row of stores that she missed her turn-off. Suddenly nothing looked familiar. The Renault's sat-nav sounded confused, telling her to turn left where there was no left turn, so she looked out for signs.

'Turn around at the first available opportunity,' said the sat-nav. She could see the compound wavering in the distance, a low mushroom-coloured wall studded with date palms, but could not find a way to get to it.

The traffic faded away, funnelling from the sculpted steel towers of the financial district toward the coastal districts. Taking the first slip road that presented itself she watched as the manicured verges broke up, to be replaced by rubble-strewn sandlots and stony ground littered with abandoned appliances.

At first she thought she had reached the city dump, but ahead was another compound. This one had no security walls or statuesque palms. The eight rows of utilitarian blocks were arranged like army barracks. Most were fitted with narrow, rudimentary windows. A pair of sentry boxes guarded the only way in, and she was forced to brake.

One of the uniformed guards came out to her car. 'You are in an unauthorized area,' he said, peering in to see if she was travelling with anyone.

Lowering her window was like opening an oven door, and she did so reluctantly. 'I took the wrong exit from the highway,' she explained. 'What is this place?'

He ignored her question. 'Where are you trying to get to, Ma'am?'

'The Dream Ranches Estate. I could see it from the road, I just couldn't—'

'You need to turn around here, go back and take the third road on the right.'

'Turn around at the first available opportunity,' said the sat-nav, as if in corroboration.

'Thank you, but what—'

The guard had already turned smartly on his polished heel and was heading back for the white wooden box.

Lea did as she was instructed. When she glanced in her rear view mirror, she saw the sentries in their shadowed huts, as immobile as nutcracker soldiers, boles of beige dust blustering around them.

As she followed the road beside the barracks she realised how close they were to her compound, and was surprised that she hadn't noticed them before. But through the acacia bushes at the end of her street she realised she could now glimpse them, even if she could only see the tips of the roofs.

On an impulse, she drove past her front door in the direction of the perimeter wall. The houses soon petered out. The central reservation's sprinklers were spread further apart and the grass withered to scrub. The estate housed over a thousand residences, but most were gathered around the golf club at its centre.

On the outskirts the lawns turned to empty lots. The sun shone dully, baking the dead earth into rock. A few wild dogs scratched at the dirt. The Renault coasted quietly along the back roads, mapping the topography of the compound. Drifts of wind-carved sand shimmered between a handful of maroon and yellow desert hyacinths. Most of the stems had been strangled by tough parasitic plants. Little else grew in the salt-heavy soil.

The first three streets proved to be dead ends. The furthest point of the fourth dipped beneath a wide, noisy highway. It appeared to be an unmanned exit from the compound. The sat-nav failed to recognise it, and told her to continue straight on.

She slowly drove toward the embankment, trying to see into the deep shadows of the underpass, but her eyes had trouble adjusting. Something had caught her attention, a faint wavering movement in the darkness.

By the time she realised her mistake, it was too late.

Braking sharply, she narrowly avoided a young man. Gathered in the gloom of the underpass were at least thirty people, who grew agitated as soon as they saw her car steadily approaching. She attempted to make a U-turn, but realised that the road was too narrow. If she left the tarmac, there was a danger that her tyres would slip in the loose sand.

Suddenly the crowd surged forward. There was a dull thud behind her. Someone had thrown a chunk of sunbaked earth at the car. It bounced and broke on the trunk, to be followed by a second and a third, this last one skittering across the roof.

Panicking, she ground the gears and frog-hopped the Renault, trying to reverse it. A hubbub of complaint rose around her. Forced onto the waste ground at the side of the road, she slammed the accelerator and fantailed gravel, pulling away as the crowd retreated back into the penumbral harbour of the tunnel.

She found another exit and drove for a while, passing beneath a vast poster that read: *Visit the largest shopping mall in the world*. She was heading in the direction of the Dubai Mall.

Later, standing in the icy blue light of the outsized aquarium, where sharks drifted behind magnifying crystal, shrinking observers to the size of children, she practiced breathing exercises and lowered her pulse. The mall's bright anonymity removed any sense of time and place, calming her more effectively than any pharmaceutical prescription.

She took tea beneath a dizzying man-made waterfall through which a dozen sculpted steel divers burst in inverse cruciform. Many of the stores she had left behind were replicated by the same English brands here. There was even a Patisserie Valerie. It was odd to think that a tiny cake shop that had first opened in a bohemian part of Soho could now be found in an Arabic country, its louche clientele replaced with severe Muslim wives.

Outside, she smoked a cigarette and stared up at the dazzling gilded towers of the Burj Khalifa, a series of transcendent repetitions that formed a hallucinatory futuristic Babel. There was a soaring grandiloquence to those slender spires that mitigated suspicions of vulgarity and doubts about economic sense, as if it was man's purpose to grasp at the heavens whatever the human cost. The crowds of shoppers seated at its base appeared to share a communality that was missing at Dream Ranches, or perhaps it was just the illusory effect of so many people gathered together in one place. No alcohol, no litter, no spontaneity; it was almost appealing, like being gently medicated.

Every few minutes the crowds thickened, gathering to watch the dancing fountain show, a matrix of circuitry that switched thousands of water jets back and forth in a preprogramed display of technical wizardry, and always earned a burst of noisy appreciation. Its audience might have been applauding a television set, she thought, or a computer.

It comforted her to stroll through the anonymous, orderly throng. She feared she might soon come to dread the thought of returning to the anarchy of London. London was like the underpass, unpredictable and threatening. Here life was as predictable as the robotic fountains. It could deliver the thing she most wanted right now, the return of her daughter and husband. She decided not to report what she had seen. Chaos was best left in the shadows.

Chapter Ten
The Welcoming Party

LEA HAD BEEN expecting to see plastic chairs and a barbecue appear in the Larvins' back garden around lunchtime, but at 8:00am a team of Indian workers began to erect a large red and white marquee, which they filled with bunting-trimmed trestle tables and a silver-painted bandstand.

'Have you seen this?' she called from the bedroom.

Roy poked his head around the door, goateed in shaving cream. 'They always put marquees up for parties,' he explained. 'It's too hot otherwise.'

'But it looks like they're going to have live music and everything. I hope it's not just for us.'

'Why not? The company's paying for it.'

'It's just so extravagant. I don't like all this fuss.'

'Enjoy it while you can, honey, we're all only here for two years.'

'Not according to Colette,' said Lea, following him back to the bathroom. 'Her husband is contracted indefinitely.'

'Did I tell you I met Ben?' Roy wiped foam from his chin. 'I've never seen a more worried-looking man in my life. He has satchels under his eyes.'

'That's what Colette says. She thinks the project will overrun and they'll have to stay on.'

'That won't happen. The board of directors has everything in hand.'

'So why is Ben so stressed?"

'He's a director now too, he has more responsibility. They're—'

'Darling, are you really going to wear those?' Lea stifled a laugh. Roy had donned a pair of shorts with purple stripes that made his legs look like candles.

'I picked these up at the mall on the way home last night. I thought they were kind of hip.'

'Hang on.' She went to Cara's room and knocked. 'Cara, would you come out here for a minute?'

Cara emerged looking dishevelled and tired. 'What's up?'

'Your father needs to know what you think of his shorts.'

Cara studied them for a moment. 'Utterly gross.'

'Thank you my sweet, you may return to cyberspace.' Lea grinned back at Roy. 'If you kept the receipt you could take them back.'

'No, it's small acts of defiance like this that keep me sane. What time are we going over?'

'Colette said noon but I think that's a little early.'

'I guess we'll hear when the other neighbours start to turn up. Then add twenty minutes before we leave. My old man gave me two pieces of life advice; he said *Never arrive early for a party* and *Never turn right on a plane.*'

'It's that where you get your ambition from? At least it means I still have time to write my speech.'

'You're not—'

'No, honey, it was a joke. Remember those?'

Roy was right. By 12:30pm the garden was crowded. 'I can't believe I'm actually nervous,' Lea said, smoothing out her floral shirt in the mirror. She caught Roy looking at her. 'What? It's just that you work with all their husbands. I want to make a good impression. Oh God, look at them, all so perfect. I'm the only one in jeans. Aren't there any working women at the resort at all?'

'Apart from Irina I haven't seen any others.'

'Who's Irina?'

'She handles the architects' correspondence and appointments, but she's based off-site. Apparently there are some women in accounts and on the PR side. Come on, I'll introduce you to the guys I've met so far.'

As they reached the front door of the Larvins' house they spotted a banner across the garden entrance that read: *Welcome Brook Family!*

'Oh my God. Do you think she gets these specially made every time someone moves into the neighbourhood?' Lea asked from the side of her mouth.

Roy leaned in. 'Give 'em a smile, honey. And remember, you're the prettiest woman here.'

Moments later they were surrounded and everyone was talking at once. The Larvins' home had the same layout as Lea's, but their furniture was more extravagant. Norah targeted Cara and pulled her aside. Her sister Abbi was a doll-like eleven year-old, curled and painted in an uncomfortably adult style, dressed in bows and flounces as if she was auditioning for a children's beauty pageant.

Colette hauled Lea through the families to the marquee, piling on introductions. Roy had been stolen away by Ben, probably so that they could discuss drainage.

A band consisting of four middle-aged European men in red-striped blazers and straw hats struck up, playing soft jazz. The quartet's lead singer was the compound's medic, Dr Vance, twinkly, avuncular, perfectly suited to the bandstand. From the corner of her eye, Lea saw James Davenport with a heavy red-haired woman, presumably his wife. Children scampered around the rear of the garden, chasing a young fox terrier. Maids served sickly purple punch from a silver tureen the size of a paddling pool.

Although she heard a great many accents as she passed through the guests, Lea couldn't help feeling that she was at a party somewhere in the Thames valley, Teddington or Twickenham perhaps. The guests sheltered from the sun's unforgiving gaze at the shadowed edges of the tent, darting through the unprotected areas as if avoiding rain, as they would have done at home.

Introductions were made. They met an absurdly handsome tennis pro and his wife who looked like characters from an old soap opera, a Swedish couple who were in charge of the stables, several American engineers, a mural painter from

Estonia, a Spanish interior designer and her artist partner, one of the few women working at Dream World. Lea tried to remember who they all were, but found herself forgetting them moments after each pair had moved on, as if their names had been written in sand.

Mr Mansour visited early on in the proceedings and stayed for the minimum time he thought propriety allowed. Everyone was connected to the resort's construction in some way. The air felt dead and sullen, as if a storm was approaching, but the sky revealed nothing more than a high, pale sliver of moon. Lea had not seen a cloud since their arrival in the country.

Fat blue lobsters were split, brushed with butter and set upon a gas-fired barbecue grill. Immense red steaks were turned until they resembled sunburnt flesh. Vast lurid salads were drizzled in yellow oil. Roy had gone off somewhere. Lea felt someone tapping her shoulder and turned around, spilling white wine.

'Oh God, I'm so sorry!' She looked at the spreading stain on the shirt before her.

'My fault entirely. I made you jump. I remember the first time I attended one of these little shindigs. I felt exactly the same way. This is the whitest crowd I've ever seen, and we lived in Ohio.' The speaker raised a pair of gigantic sunglasses to the brim of her hat and squinted at her with tiny blue eyes that she had accentuated with thick false lashes. She was tall and underweight, frail-looking, like a flower-child who had become unmoored from her era. She wore brightly-striped slacks and a pair of gaudy silver trainers. 'I'm Rachel, Ben Larvin's mother. I only go to the pool before dawn and after dusk, but I've seen you heading down there.'

'Hi, I'm Lea. Colette told me you don't like the sun.'

'I break out in blisters unless I factor up to 50. Really, it's quite the worst place on earth I could have come to, but Ben and Colette needed help with the children and I couldn't refuse them.'

Lea saw now how pale Rachel was. She looked to be in her early seventies, but had good posture and a model's figure. Her white hair was tied back with a cluster of tiny blue flowers. Her arms rattled with heavy silver bangles.

'It's an awful lot of fuss, isn't it?' said Rachel. 'I'm sure it's the last thing you wanted.' She dabbed vaguely at her blouse with a tissue, unbothered by the stain. 'You'll be relieved to know it's not just for you. At the start of every summer there are always parties to welcome the fresh influx of talent. Do you need a guide?'

'I'm sorry?'

'To know who you should be speaking to. You have to figure out who's important and who to avoid.' Lea must have looked surprised, because Rachel added, 'Darling, I'm a New Yorker, we take our parties very seriously.'

'Oh, so is my husband.'

'Thank God. This place needs a healthy injection of East Coast cynicism. I heard you playing *Addio del passato* from *La Traviata* yesterday. God, I miss the Met. I used to go to the New York Opera every season as a child. There's nothing here like that, not yet anyway.'

'Hasn't Zaha Hadid designed an opera house?'

'Yes, but it'll never get finished. There's not much call here for the arts. There's a lot of talk about becoming a "cultural capital", but this is a city that runs on press releases. Meanwhile, the local husbands pin-protect their wives' TV channels. I imagine they're only allowed to watch stuff about makeup, cooking and children. And don't get me started on the new climate-controlled Mall of the World, it looks like Walt Disney threw up on the plans. Sometimes I feel like I'm living in that *Twilight Zone* episode, "It's A Good Life". But you're too young to remember.'

'No, I saw that show. My husband has the DVD. He's a big science fiction fan.'

'I understand you're a writer. You were working for a magazine in London, is that right?'

'The usual story. Once I wanted to be a famous reporter, but I ended up getting married and writing women's features. It wasn't quite what I'd had in mind.'

'Is that why you came here?'

'What do you mean?'

'Well, you're not just following your husband, are you?' There was a forensic edge to Rachel's question. 'Some wives stay behind and rely on monthly visits. Others are looking for something more.'

Lea decided to be honest, only because she felt sure Rachel would find her out if she lied. 'I want us to be close again. London is tough on families. It was tough on us.' She sipped her drink, embarrassed.

'Well, this is the place if you want to be a wife.'

'How did you hear about me so quickly?'

'News travels fast around here. We've nothing else to do but sit and talk.'

'So, who should I be talking to?'

'You've already missed Tahir Mansour. I guess you met him at the airport. Our compound manager is dry as a stick, but a decent man. I think he regards us as an alien species. Humour never touches him. I don't think he knows how to smile. He has a huge family tucked away somewhere, but no-one's ever seen them. He was promoted after Tom Chalmers died.'

She craned her long neck forward and checked out the crowd. 'I expect you've been given the resort tour by James Davenport, although you may not have met his wife Madeline. Shaped like a beachball, over there. She's very *sweet*.' Rachel clipped the adjective and made it sound poisonous. 'If you absolutely have to get into conversation with her, don't try anything complicated and stay away from religion. And of course, Mrs Busabi will have called on you by now. Has she started leaving photocopied recipes in your mailbox yet?'

Lea laughed. 'No, not yet.'

'Don't worry, she will. I once asked her why she didn't just email them to me, and you know what she said? "I don't approve of women using computers."'

'You're joking.'

'If only I was. You know what they say; all men love working in the Middle East and all women hate it. Your other neighbour should be here with her son, but I haven't seen—ah yes, there she is.' Rachel wagged a discreet finger over Lea's left shoulder. 'That's Betty Graham and her boy Dean. They live next door to you on the other side. She's adorable, very ditzy. English. Dean's been a bit of a handful since his father went to work in the DWG sister resort in Abu Dhabi—he's there most of the year. I think their marriage is in trouble.'

'Ah, there you are,' said Milo, kissing them both. 'Lea, how lovely to see you again. Welcome to Sodom-Sur-Mer.' His cadenced German accent made the title more comical.

'We shouldn't stand together,' Rachel laughed, 'the little rebel clan, they'll think we're corrupting poor Lea here.'

'You're right, we should seat her with the other wives. You'd like to get tips on how to roll your dough, wouldn't you?'

'I don't think that's very me,' said Lea. 'Why did you call it Sodom-Sur-Mer?'

'My dear, haven't you read your company induction brochure? It's a piece of PR bullshit.' Milo was wavering slightly, already a little drunk. Lea looked about, making sure they were not being overheard. 'The bordellos make a fortune while women are imprisoned for a kiss in public. The men do as they like, of course.'

'Oh Milo, don't start that again,' said Rachel.

'Everyone's having affairs in the compound.' He waved his arm at the guests. 'Theoretically, having an affair is an automatic prison sentence. At least we're not under Sharia law, where they stone adulterers to death.'

'Really? They're having affairs?'

'You'd better believe it,' said Rachel. 'See that couple of there?' She aimed a painted nail in the direction of a bony, brilliantined man as Italian as a Tiepolo, and an attractive dark-eyed woman barely half his size. Her augmented breasts seemed absurdly disproportionate on her tiny ribcage. Both were checking their

Blackberrys for emails. 'They're the Ribisis. Bruno is in infotech, a glorified handyman for the resort's computer system. Elena Ribisi has an appointment with Ramiro, our tennis coach, every other afternoon, and she's getting more than just help with her back-hand.' She drew an invisible cord across the room to a well-built man in too-tight white shorts. 'Ramiro's a walking cliché, poor soul. See the woman next to him? The one who looks like Penelope Cruz? That's his wife, Palmira.'

'I was just introduced to them.'

'They've been married just nine months and she's apparently getting it on with your pool man. You wouldn't think it to look at him, would you? Furtive sex, it's just something to do around here. It only works because everyone's lives are so regimented. God knows what would happen if the timetable got thrown off.'

'Their parents were probably doing the same thing in commonwealth Africa in the 1960s,' said Milo rather too loudly. 'Everybody's getting an illicit fuck around here except me.'

'I think we'd better take Milo inside,' said Rachel.

Lea saw Cara balefully watching them, and knew she was becoming annoyed,

Yeah, I'm doing it again, Cara, embarrassing you, she thought. *Always talking to the wrong people, always standing out. We wanted a clean break from the past and here I am doing it again. Well, I can't spend my life worrying about your teenage sensitivities.*

EVERYONE BROKE OFF conversation and turned in the direction of the sea, looking up into the sky. The stars were eclipsed by immense gold and violet blossoms. Elliptical rings of fire expanded like shell-bursts, the glittering sprays lighting the distant black mirror of the ocean in a percussion of sonic booms that bounced back from the glass cliffs of the financial district. Between the buildings, the sea was spackled with orange and green shards, so that for a moment it seemed that great shoals of phosphorescent fish had risen to the surface.

Milo had fallen into a phlegmy slumber on the Larvins' couch. Outside, Rachel nudged Lea. 'I used to love firework displays,' she whispered. 'Now I look at my watch and turn up the TV just before they start.'

'You sound as if you disapprove.'

'Of fun? Never. It's just so damned predictable. Laugh here, gasp there, we're the biggest, the glitziest, the most expensive. Part of me wants it to fail, just to bring back a little spontaneity.'

'Sounds like you're just an old hippy at heart.'

'You don't know how true that is. As a teenager I went looking for America and couldn't find it anywhere, just like Peter Fonda and Dennis Hopper in *Easy Rider*. Then I came home and started a family.'

Lea laughed. 'I suppose it does all seem kind of immature, but innocent in a way.'

Rachel peered over the top of her glasses. 'Oh, don't you believe it. There are very specific limits placed on our freedom here. Once in a while I have to get away from it all. Don't ever tell Colette, but sometimes when the kids are on playdates and I have the day to myself, I borrow the runabout and take off to the desert. I don't go all the way in, just to the edge where the pylons end, to look at the bare unspoiled space. All that sky. I clean the sand off the tyres when I get back and nobody knows. Little acts of rebellion, they're what get us through.'

'Have you been to the far side of the estate?' asked Lea. 'There's an underpass full of people there. They dented my car.'

'Oh darling, you must have taken a wrong turn. It's not safe down there. They were going to build more homes for the executives but the villas never got built. That's the badlands.'

There was a crash from the lounge. Lea followed Rachel through the French windows and found that Milo had awoken and dropped his walking stick on the coffee table.

'Hey sleepyhead,' said Rachel, 'let me get you a strong black coffee. Lea, sit with him a minute, would you?'

'I'm fine, damn it, I don't need a nurse,' said Milo. 'That

woman's always fussing.' He curled the arms of his glasses behind his ears and looked around. 'Where is everybody?'

Lea nodded in the direction of the garden. 'They're out there watching the fireworks. You managed to sleep through it.'

Milo smacked his lips. 'I'm as dry as a nun's fanny. I could use a brandy.'

'Milo, who are the people in the underpass?' she asked.

'Why, did they give you any trouble?'

'I nearly drove into them. They threw a few stones at the car.'

'And they frightened you.'

'No—I was just surprised.'

'That's the trouble with the good life here. It comes at a cost.'

'I don't follow you.'

'Please, stay away from the underpass. The workers live in the dorms on the other side of the compound wall, and they're not too happy about their conditions. They go to the underpass between shifts. It still connects the two areas; the company never got around to sealing it up.'

Rachel had returned with coffees. 'It's unsafe for Europeans to go onto the workers' territory. They hang out down there because it's cooler than in the dorms.'

'They threw rocks at Lea's car,' Milo told her.

'I think I startled them,' said Lea. 'I was travelling quite fast.'

'They're upset because they're not allowed to form unions,' said Rachel. 'They left a couple of pipe bombs at the resort.'

'Ach, *pipe bombs*—little farts of fire, fireworks, not bombs,' said Milo. 'If they wanted to blow something up they would have done. A few small gestures of protest and everyone acts like it's World War Three.'

Lea was still enjoying the conversation when Roy came to find her. 'There you are,' he said, kissing the top of her head. 'You're missing all the fun. Come back outside.' He turned and left. She didn't like the way he automatically assumed she would follow, but preferred not to risk a disagreement, and rose. Rachel raised her eyebrows at Lea and gave her a look.

We've been told off.

Lea stepped outside with her coffee and dutifully watched the end of the display.

'Darling, this is Leo Hardy,' said Roy, presenting her to a huge brick-skinned man with hard eyes and a downturned mouth. Hardy's green Polo shirt was pulled too tightly over his barrel chest. He wore razor-edged khaki shorts and socks pulled up too high, like an overzealous scoutmaster.

'Pleased to meet you, ma'am,' he said, leaning forward to squeeze her hand in a meaty fist. There were coarse black spider-hairs on his fingers, even on the backs of his thumbs. He had a strong Dutch South African accent.

'Mr Hardy's the unit commander at the workers' barracks,' Roy explained.

'You're in the big yellow buildings?' Lea asked. 'Unit commander—that sounds military.'

'It's security terminology,' Hardy explained. 'I have my work cut out over there, and they respect a title.'

'Really? Why do they need security?'

'We keep the units ethnically divided to prevent territorial problems, ma'am. The Indian sector is the largest. They're my responsibility.'

'I think I bumped into a few of them,' said Lea, 'down in the underpass at the end of the road.'

'You never mentioned this to me,' said Roy, affronted.

'It didn't seem that important.'

'You shouldn't have been down there,' said Hardy.

'So everyone keeps telling me. I think I frightened them more.'

'We're trying to get the police to impose limits on the size of public gatherings. They want to reduce the length of their shifts, but it's not going to happen.'

'Don't they have a case?'

'They're paid ten times the amount they could earn back home in their villages. It's their choice, *ja*?'

'But the stories in the press—'

'The press want us to fail, Mrs Brook. Any problems we have here are created by foreigners. Most of my workers keep their heads down and get on with their jobs. It's only a small minority who make their grievances known.'

'What are their grievances? Is it about working conditions?'

'They're well looked-after, in the same way that you and your husband are here. If you take my advice, you'll keep away from troublemakers. I'll see you on Monday, Roy.' Hardy gave a small, brisk nod of the head to each of them and left.

'YOU COULD HAVE given me some support tonight,' Roy said finally, as they were undressing for bed.

'I was interested in what Milo and Rachel had to say, that's all,' said Lea.

'And what the hell were you doing near the barracks?'

'I was curious. Is that a crime? Would you rather I was like Mrs Busabi and Mrs Davenport, having endless conversations about cupcakes?'

'They're nice, ordinary people, Lea. They're not trying to stir up trouble. They're not the ones hanging around with the crazies.'

Lea was amazed. 'Rachel and Milo are not crazy, they just don't gush on about the resort like the rest of them. I wasn't trying to upset anyone. At least in London our conversations were actually *about* something. We could go to parties and hold opposing views without being frowned upon. The women around here are throwbacks. It's as if feminism never happened. And I think the men all secretly like it that way.'

'That's bullshit, Lea, and you know it.' He lowered his voice. 'This is as tough on me as it is on you. I had nowhere left in London. It was killing us.'

'I just don't want this to be like it was before,' said Lea softly.

'Is that was this is about?' He came over to take her shoulders, but she shrugged him away. 'I swore to you, didn't I? I swore it would never, ever happen again.'

The circumstances of his infidelity still nagged at her. She had discovered the affair in the most mundane manner. She'd needed to replace a brake light and had been looking for the number of their local garage on Roy's phone when she'd found some undeleted messages. 'Would you have told me if I hadn't found out?' she asked.

'You know how difficult things had been between us, what I was going through.'

'You weren't the only one suffering, Roy. I supported us while you were out of work. I had to deal with the day-today practicalities of getting by while you were sitting around at home, talking to her online.'

'I told you, I knew it was wrong. I was about to end it.'

'That's what all men say when they get found out.'

'Listen, you have to work with me here. There's a lot at stake, for all of us. Can't you just be like the others for a while?'

Lea felt chastened. She knew the transfer had been hard on Roy, and the last thing she wanted to do was upset him. 'I'm sorry,' she said softly. 'I didn't think I was causing a problem. I've never been around people like this. It rankles me, the whole good life thing. I'm not used to it yet.'

'You were the one who thought that the school here would be better for Cara.'

'Yes, because you know how easily influenced she is. And we couldn't always be around her to supervise.'

Roy would not be mollified. 'You could have, but you decided to work. Don't kid yourself, Lea. You wrote because you didn't want to be called a housewife. You were never very good at it.'

Lea was stunned into silence. She hadn't wanted to be lumped in with the immaculate beige women of Chiswick, their valeted 4X4s and unnaturally clean houses, their endless chatter about holidays and gardeners over salads in Twickenham and Richmond. She'd planned to create some distance from them and some respect for herself, but then Roy had lost his job and Cara had got into difficulties at school.

She thought she might read for a while, but Roy snapped out the lights moments after pulling back the sheets. Now she lay awake, listening to the darkened villa, trying to temper her anger, concentrating on the week ahead.

Roy had always acted hurt whenever she worked late. He considered himself a modern urban male, but his confidence had been damaged by losing his job and watching her become the breadwinner.

She could see the trap that lay before her; to get back the things she wanted most, she would have to become someone she hated.

Chapter Eleven
The Lifestyle

LEA KNOCKED ON Cara's bedroom door and waited for an answer. They had lately come to an arrangement; she would not barge in unannounced, and in exchange Cara would turn up for meals on time.

'Hang on a minute.' She waited while Cara came to the door, opening it a crack. The blinds in her room were drawn shut. 'What do you want?'

'I'm going into the Old Town this afternoon. Want to come?'

She smoothed down uncombed hair. 'It's Sunday.'

'Yeah, which means that everything's open. We could get you a haircut. Come with me, I could use the company. I'm going to try and find some freelance work.'

'How are you going to do that?'

'I've got a couple of leads. Something called *Gulf Coast* magazine. Milo put me onto them. And Dream World is putting together a quarterly magazine about the resort.'

'I'm supposed to go over to Norah's this afternoon. We're building a website.'

'What time?'

'Four.'

'No good, I won't be back by then. I have to update my CV and sort out examples of work before I go.'

Cara looked sceptical. 'You really going to find a job?'

'Don't make it sound like I'm going to track down the Ark of the Covenant. I can freelance from here. You can help set me up with an office in the spare room. I can't seem to get my contacts onto my phone.'

'I saw you had some synchronisation issues.'

'When? Have you been in my stuff?'

'I'm just trying to get everything to work together. I'll set up your office.'

'Okay. Just do me a favour and don't make a big deal about it with your father.'

'You're going to tell him you're looking for work, aren't you?'

'There's no point in us talking about something that hasn't happened yet. I don't want another argument.'

Roy was on site, supervising the relaying of the first of the damaged marble walkways, so Lea headed to the Old Town alone. The area around the creek came as a complete contrast to the high-rise modernity of the coastal hotels. Here, she saw just how separated the imported Europeans were from the Arab world. The older men still wore black *dishdashas* and white *kiffiyeh* scarves, and the women had robe-like dresses that covered the whole body. In clothing store windows, the word 'modest' appeared as a desirable description, yet discordant bolts of fabric clashed against each other in retina-searing limes and golds. Lea noticed that many of the young *Muslimah*s were now dressed in western jeans and shirts.

Arranged around the mouth of the creek was a terrace of dilapidated two-storey buildings, flat-roofed and covered in plastic signs and satellite dishes. Lethal-looking necklaces of electrical wiring festooned the peeling facades of shops selling fruit and vegetables from plastic baskets.

She parked, checked her notebook and found the office. The rickety, dark staircase to the first floor office did not look promising.

Andre Pignot was an elegant fifty year-old French-Algerian, a former archaeologist who had been editing *Gulf Coast* magazine for over twenty years, although how he managed to do it in such a cramped, hot room was a mystery. He seemed surprised by Lea's arrival, even though she had called ahead, and jumped up to shake her hand.

'I'm afraid we're rather old-fashioned,' he warned, moving a stack of papers so that she could sit down. 'We've been here a long time because we keep our advertisers happy. We run news items that supplement an aspirational lifestyle.'

The lifestyle was hardly visible from Pignot's headquarters. Around the walls were pinned yellowing *Gulf Coast* covers featuring speedboats, crystal-set dining tables, elaborate watches and women in furs. Below in the street, Lea could see a man selling mobile phone covers from plastic buckets.

'I can work to a brief,' Lea said, handing over a folder containing her resume and some articles she had written for *Eva*. She sipped sweet mint tea and waited for Pignot to read, but he slipped the articles back into their folder, having barely skimmed them.

'I'm afraid that's all a bit progressive for us,' he said apologetically. 'We're looking for upbeat features about hotels, car rallies, summer fashions, that sort of thing. Our readers are mostly holidaymakers. We don't cover crime, politics, social issues. It's all rather bland, but who wants to be troubled with the world's problems on vacation?'

'I could write you some pieces on a trial basis,' she persisted. 'You'd only need to buy them if you liked them.'

'I suppose that might work.' Pignot did not sound too convinced.

Lea decided to reduce his pain. 'Well, you have my number,' she said, rising. 'I'm sure you're a busy man.'

'No,' he said, tapping the edges of his desk in mild bemusement, 'not really.'

Her second appointment took her to a white building that occupied the whole of one side of Creek Square. It took her a while to find the office because the company signage was in Arabic.

A Muscovite, Maxim Karpova, headed *Dream World* magazine, the first issue of which was already printed even though the resort had yet to open. In the icy reception area, blow-ups of the front cover featured an attractively modest girl in a black, gold-trimmed *abaya* standing beside a computer generated horizon pool, flanked by gaudy baroque armchairs. Clearly, *Gulf Coast* magazine's days were numbered, because here was the future; a Western ideal that had dispensed with vanity advertising in order to sell a single cohesive fantasy.

Lea rubbed at her suntanned face. No matter how much moisturizer she used, she couldn't prevent its tightness, and the air-conditioning gave her the sensation of always being about to catch a cold. Waiting to be seen by the assistant editor, she realised how far she had drifted from her student days, when she had only written for the liberal press. Her youthful idealism now felt like naivety.

She was seen by a young Arabic woman called Nathifa who regarded her coolly through tinted oval glasses before offering carefully measured responses to her questions. Nathifa was confident, almost arrogant, knowing that soon she would be fielding requests from the world's press eager to discover more about the resort's roster of celebrity visitors.

'It is in our interests to employ staff with connections with the resort,' said Nathifa, in a clipped manner that suggested she had attended business studies at an English university. 'I would be keen to know how you feel about the aspirational core values espoused by the DWG brand.'

'Are you asking me if I would be uncritical?' Lea asked.

'The resort will set a new world standard for the luxurious bespoke lifestyle,' Nathifa told her without a hint of irony. 'We are unlikely to commission anything'— she searched for an appropriate word—'abrasive.'

'I appreciate that. It would help me to understand whether the magazine is simply to be a quarterly advertorial for the resort's featured attractions or whether it aims at something more.'

'Mrs Brook, we think our magazine can provide the highest level of quality without making people uncomfortable.'

'Then you don't need a writer,' Lea replied, 'you need a publicist.' Rising, she politely thanked Nathifa and left.

On the way home she passed the laughing girl on the Dubai Pearl poster, promising the bespoke lifestyle. *I can't be you*, she thought, *because you don't exist.*

Chapter Twelve
The Locks

LEA BOUGHT AN ice cream bar and sat on the beach wall unwrapping it, feeling the cold radiating against her hands. It made her think of the worker who froze to death on the beach.

She called Andre Pignot at *Gulf Coast* magazine. 'You said you have to keep your local advertisers happy,' she reminded him. 'Suppose you put some fresh pieces into your online version? I know it's little more than a holding page right now but we could make it into something more. Nothing too thought-provoking, just something with a little more meat than the latest restaurant opening. Something that would get readers talking. You could keep the hotel edition unchanged.'

'I suppose we couldn't do any worse than we're doing right now,' said Pignot finally. '*Dream World* magazine is going to destroy our market.'

'I'll write the sample lead for free. Let me try that, at least.'

'All right. But I've no money to pay my freelancers this month.'

'That's fine. If I increase your readership, you can pay me.'

'Then we have a deal,' said Pignot.

'Oh, there was something else. My husband told me about a worker who suffered a freak accident on the beach.'

'The one who froze?'

'That's him. Do you happen to know his name?'

'Well, it's not a secret,' said Pignot, as if attempting to convince himself. 'Mandhatri Sahonta. I heard he was a good company man.'

When she got home, she typed his details into her computer's main search engine. Another name turned up in an archived press article. Sakari. Sahonta's daughter had vanished four months before his death. He'd waited for her in the workers' dormitory one Friday evening and she had never turned up. She had called earlier to say she was stopping by the mall on the way home—then nothing. The Dream World Group would have been holding her passport, so they knew she hadn't left the country. There was no more information to be found, which was hardly surprising given that Sahonta would not have been allowed to break confidence online. But presumably it meant that he had died without ever discovering what had happened to her.

The next day, Lea got organised. She bought a flatpack desk at the Mirdif Mall and converted her spare room into an office. In the evening she visited Harji Busabi, telling him that she was writing an article on the way in which Dream World's eco-friendly technology would set a standard of excellence for other resorts. Harji was happy to talk to her.

Although she was not English by birth, Mrs Busabi had managed to recreate the clutter of a Cotswolds cottage in her villa, fitting a fireplace and hideous ornamental coal scuttles into her lounge. She had swathed the wide windows in heavy Laura Ashley curtains as if determined to keep the sunlight at bay. The room was like the stage-set of a forgotten provincial play, incongruous against the bleached-out view to the street.

Harji was helpful but dull, anxious to provide her with the exact data concerning cubic capacities and kilos of force per square metre. He handed her brochures about swimming pools and shower units while Mrs Busabi poured weak tea and periodically interjected with things her husband had forgotten. Lea slipped home in time to cook Roy's supper.

The next evening she went to the Larvins and asked Ben about the Dream World staff. She preferred their house; Rachel's untidy touch was everywhere, from the crocheted pot holders filled with sickly cactus offshoots that hung in the kitchen to the stacks of newspapers overflowing from the patio furniture. As if to fight her mother-in-law's unruly influence, Colette always dressed as if she was expecting guests. Today she was wearing a blue silk Roberto Cavalli kaftan, and remained in the background through Lea's visit, combing Abbi's hair and finding things to tidy away.

Ben tried to be helpful, but clearly knew very little about how the other staff members felt. 'We don't discuss our feelings around the office,' he explained. 'You get a bunch of guys in the room together, they're going to talk about weight differentials on load-bearing ceilings, not their feelings.'

'Don't you talk about the bombs or the accidents?'

'Sure,' said Ben, looking uncomfortable for the first time. 'We wouldn't be human if we didn't. But we don't get much intel.'

'If you want the inside dope about how everyone really feels, you should talk to Milo,' Rachel said to her on the way out. 'He hired the Persiana's original team and was there for all of the early meetings. He never approved of the new structure though, so don't expect him to say anything complimentary.'

'Don't send Lea off to Milo,' said Ben. 'He's kind of a loose cannon. He exaggerates everything, you know that.'

'He gets a little carried away,' Rachel agreed, 'but I'm sure Lea can figure out when he's telling the truth.' She smiled secretively. Lea felt as if Rachel was pushing her toward something she had not yet discovered for herself.

As Rachel saw her to the door, she placed a hand on her arm. 'Is this really an article for *Gulf Coast* magazine?' Her look was slightly incredulous.

'Of course,' said Lea. 'What else would it be?'

'I'M WARNING YOU now,' said Milo, holding the door open for her. 'I don't do the whole tea-and-cake thing. I don't have a maid. Don't agree with 'em.'

'I let mine stay for Roy's sake,' Lea admitted. 'I'm a coward, I took the easy route. And I don't miss the ironing. Your own coffee is fine with me.'

'Then come in and be poisoned.' He stepped back with a smile.

Milo's lounge reminded her of her grandfather's house in Kent. There was a great dark dresser overstuffed with mismatched crockery in the kitchen, and cartons of junk lined the hall. Milo made mugs of pungent coffee, then led the way along the hall to a small lounge. The room was lined with framed certificates, and there were several photos of a small, severe woman in a deep green forest. 'I moved to a single-level property after my leg started seizing up,' he explained, dropping into an armchair. 'So you're planning to write propaganda for the enemy. I'm not sure I'm the right person you should be talking to. I'm treated as a pariah by the management these days. The board has changed a hell of a lot since it was set up.'

'How?'

Milo shifted a stack of *Financial Times* back-issues and sat down. 'We threw a lot of stuff out of the window. We'd planned for a zero-carbon footprint and the use of sustainable resources, but the other directors deemed it unfeasible, and nobody protested the altered plans. When you're talking about a country that builds ski-runs in shopping malls, local manufacturing tariffs don't really top the agenda.'

'Is that why you left? You were disillusioned?'

Milo released a death-rattle chuckle. 'Hell no, I left because I was dog-tired. This is a young man's game. There are all kinds of social issues.'

'Like what?'

'Bedbugs. As one crew returns from the night shift they take the place of those rising for the day, which causes infestations of bedbugs unless their bedding is properly aired, and Rashad can't get them to do it.'

'Who's Rashad?'

'He's their supervisor. There are all kinds of religious and ethnic divisions. Different nationals have different habits. The Somalis chew *khat* to keep themselves awake on late shifts, and the Indians are known to take a locally manufactured amphetamine when they're driving trucks out to the site. The work is boring and repetitive, and in hot weather it's easy to lose your concentration, so they lose a lot of trucks.'

'Rachel says you have the inside dope on everyone,' Lea prompted. 'Does that include Tom Chalmers?'

'He was more than just a neighbour, he was someone I trusted.' He studied her face. 'Well, I know you a little better now, so I suppose it can't hurt. I was sitting here one night and heard this ridiculous noise outside, so I went to see what was wrong. I found him lying on the kerb and recognised the signs of severe electric shock, so I covered him with a blanket. I can't imagine what he thought he was doing, taking an old-fashioned steel-bladed trimmer out there. He managed to blow half the street lights. The cables for the street are only just below the surface of the grass verges, because there's bedrock underneath. One of them was sliced in half. I called Dr Vance, but he was too late. The next day I had an argument with Tahir Mansour—who was then his assistant—over what we would say about his death. Mansour wanted to call it a heart attack.'

'He actually said that?'

'He said it could cost the resort millions in bad press, so I went along with the story. The company is still paying for my house.' Milo reached across and tapped Lea on the knee. 'None of this is relevant to your little fluff-piece. Don't you want to know if I have any good recipes for your readers?'

'Screw you, Milo, you know what I'd rather write about.'

Milo laughed. 'I knew there was a reason why I liked you. You're not afraid to tell a frail old man to fuck off.' He thought for a moment. 'I was bothered by the whole thing. I couldn't put my finger on it for a while. Then I realised what it was. Tom had recently undergone surgery on the tendons in his right hand. I couldn't see how he was capable of holding the trimmer.'

'So what do you think happened?'

'I wondered if someone else could have been there and set the whole thing up. Of course, nobody ever sees anything. And the

CCTV didn't cover the spot—convenient, that. But everyone liked Tom.'

'Do you think this might have had something to do with his daughter?'

'They were worried about little Joia. She was very flirty and theatrical around men. You can't afford to behave like that here.' Milo gave a sharp laugh. 'Now you're curious! When she vanished we speculated endlessly in cocktail bars.'

'You mean she just—'

'Wait, I have something to show you.' Rising with difficulty, Milo made his way to a pine dresser and pulled a folded page from a drawer. 'You're the writer. What do you think of this?'

She took the page and examined it. 'Where did you get this?'

'It was intended for Jim Davenport, but I was accidentally copied in—somebody used the wrong mailing template. A list of workers' deaths. Mandhatri Sahonta died after a pipe burst on the beach. Deng Antonio got his arm torn off trying to clean out a separator. Obviously you're supposed to shut the thing down first, but it shouldn't have been operating if he was standing in the vicinity. According to this, the motion sensors weren't working, but clearly nobody's supposed to know that now. The third one was Garcia Rodriguez.' He tapped the sheet. 'He fell from the top of the Persiana. Not exactly an uncommon occurrence. They get filed under *misadventure*. These guys have a lot of experience with heights but the wind's pretty fierce up there. It could easily have lifted him. I did some digging, just out of curiosity. His workmates say he slipped on something. When the inspectors went up there they found the floor clean and dry. I bet you someone in his crew spilled something on the floor, and cleared it up so they wouldn't get in trouble.'

She held up the email. 'Are you saying there's something especially unusual about these?'

'I'm just asking for your opinion.'

'Given the size of the workforce, I guess three deaths aren't that strange.'

'Not at all, no.'

'Then I don't understand—'

'What if I told you there was something connecting all three of them?'

'Try me.'

'Sahonta lost his daughter. She just disappeared, never left the country.'

'How do they know?'

'The company holds all the manual workers' documentation. They can't move anywhere without it. Antonio's daughter vanished some weeks before his death, similar situation. And guess what? Rodriguez lost his daughter as well. They found her dead in the creek a month before he died. Nobody knows what happened to her because the police took the body and the report wasn't made public. Right after the funeral he had to go back to work. They clean up accidents overnight.'

'But don't they investigate?'

'Investigations throw the schedule out. It's better for everyone that things keep moving on.' He let the thought sink in.

'Were the girls sexually mature?'

'They were 21, 14 and 12.'

'Did they know each other?'

'Not to my knowledge.'

Lea felt an emotional shift, loss, pain, something momentarily revealed.

'I made a few calls but got nowhere. Could you look into it?'

'Milo, what can I do?' she replied. 'If they won't tell you, they're certainly not going to open up to me.'

'Maybe not, but you have an advantage.'

'What's that?'

'You're the new wife on the block, and you're married to an executive who's tipped for promotion. They'll all want to talk to you. If not the men, then the women. Just keep your ears open for me.'

'Milo, I'm in enough trouble as it is. I'm not an investigative journalist. I'm trying to be good.'

'You mean you're trying to be what your husband wants you to be.'

'Yes, I suppose so, for the sake of our family.'

'Forget it. It was just an idea.' He took the page from her and carefully refolded it. 'It was wrong of me to ask. You're right, you should sit back and relax while he makes a shedload of money, and then get the hell out. This place isn't for you or Cara.'

Lea felt the need to explain. 'It's just that we went through some tough times. I need this to be a success for all of us.'

'Hey listen, don't worry. You mustn't get a reputation.' As Milo returned the email to its drawer she couldn't help feeling she had failed him. She liked Milo and admired his honesty, but had seen something in his eyes when he handed her the email that she could not understand or interpret.

'How's your daughter getting on?'

'She's fine, I think. I don't see as much of her as I expected.'

'Well, keep an eye on her. This place may look like Disneyland, but under the surface it's still an ancient civilisation.'

'What do you mean?'

'Just keep Cara close,' Milo replied, and for a second Lea felt the air turn cold. 'You're in the land of conspicuous consumption, and people get consumed too.'

'You think the girls are connected.'

'I have no proof of that. I've worked in a dozen countries on hundreds of projects, and sometimes you see patterns, that's all. It may be just coincidence. There was a teenaged girl on the other side of the compound called Sarah. She was made pregnant by a local man. We were all shocked when she killed herself.'

'What did she do?'

'She jumped from the bridge near the Autodrome and landed in six lanes of traffic. There wasn't an investigation or an autopsy because there wasn't much left of her.'

'That's awful—did nobody know about her state of mind?'

'That's the point. We know and we don't know. We *choose* not to know. I'm not being dramatic but remember, there are snakes in paradise.'

As she rose to go, waiting for him to see her out, she had a chance to look more closely at something that had caught her eye, a shiny brass box screwed into the inner lintel of the lounge door. It looked like some kind of security device. She was about to ask about it when the doorbell rang.

Milo looked through the window and cursed. 'Jesus, you see what you did now? Mrs Busabi's brought cakes over. She's trying to give me diabetes. Get out while you can.'

Lea promised to reciprocate his kindness another day. 'We'll see about that,' he said, opening the door, 'I'm not sure I'm ready to follow the witches into their perfect world of coffee mornings. They probably sit around casting spells on people they don't like. Come in Mrs Busabi, we were just talking about you.'

Lea waved goodbye and headed home, but when she glanced back she was surprised to see Milo still standing in the doorway, watching her leave. She found herself wondering what had persuaded someone living in a gated community to fit brand-new locks on the inside of his lounge doors.

Chapter Thirteen
The Beach House

THAT EVENING, ROY surprised them by turning up for dinner, and even Cara managed to set aside her laptop and eat some grilled chicken salad. 'Well, this is like old times,' said Lea, unable to resist a comment.

'What's all that junk in the spare room?' asked Roy.

'That is your wife's new office,' Lea replied proudly. 'She has a job, sort of.'

'You're writing again?'

'Well, I'm pitching pieces to *Gulf Coast* magazine, if you can call it writing.'

'Will that leave you enough time for stuff around the house? With the mall being a drive away?'

'We have a maid who has hardly anything to do,' said Lea, taking his briefcase off the table. 'I think I can manage to buy a few groceries. We both worked when Cara was a baby and we coped perfectly well.'

'But I know how you get—you pour all your time and effort into this stuff. I just don't want you getting upset if it doesn't work out.'

'You never minded before.'

Roy sipped iced water, considering. 'I'm just not sure it's a good idea for you to be working here, that's all.'

'What are you talking about? It's not like I'm threatening your status. Perhaps you'd like me to start cookery classes.'

'If you two are going to have a fight, I'm going to take my meal to my room,' Cara warned.

Lea looked down at her plate. 'I was over at Milo's house today. He has locks on the insides of his lounge doors.'

'Maybe he's scared of burglars,' said Roy.

'There's never been a single burglary in the compound. I checked with the guards.'

'You checked with the *guards*?'

'I was just talking to them while they were looking under the car. They're not great conversationalists.'

'Well, I heard ol' Milo has been getting a little weird lately. He probably misses his old job. The guy has nothing to do now except sit around and complain. He hates what we're trying to achieve.'

'Really?' Lea set down her fork. 'That's not the impression I got at all. He seems incredibly proud of Dream World. He kept telling me how well they looked after their people when he was in charge.'

'That's not what I've been hearing.' Roy helped himself to salad. 'He's been badmouthing the directors. They're going to take him out of the compound as soon as his contract expires.'

'Can they do that?'

'Sure. They own his house.'

'That's a shame. He's a nice old stick.'

'He's a disruptive influence.' Roy shook his head. 'It's probably better if you stayed away from him. You don't want to be tainted by association.'

Lea could hardly believe her ears. She chewed slowly, thinking it over, then turned to her daughter. 'Cara, do you think Milo's crazy?'

'All old people are crazy,' said Cara unhelpfully.

'What will he do?'

'Go home, I guess. Hey Cara, I was thinking. With me working such long hours, maybe you'd like to come over some evenings and visit the site. There's an empty beach house just past the East tower, at the end of the beach promenade. It belongs to the resort but they haven't worked out what to do with it yet. It's got power and it has a cellar, so you can put your equipment down there. It'd be perfect for your computer club.'

'I don't know,' said Cara, 'How fast is the broadband?'

'It's the same as the resort, really fast.'

'We have Wi-Fi here, Cara,' said Lea. 'You know that.'

'But she'd have room for her friends,' said Roy. 'They're working on a website.'

'You didn't tell me that.'

'Yes, I did,' said Cara petulantly. 'You just didn't listen.'

'Well, go on.' She held out her hand. 'Expound.'

'You wouldn't be interested.'

'Don't be silly, of course I would.'

'It's kind of about this place. It's going to be called *Bubble Life*. You know, like the boy in the bubble? It was this old movie about a kid who couldn't go outside without catching germs.'

'Is that how you see Dream Ranches?' She caught herself. 'I still have trouble calling it that. It sounds like an American TV show.'

'Of course that's how I see it. We're cut off from the real world. The internet is censored, for Christ's sake.'

'You can use Facebook and Twitter. If stuff is being censored, it's because you shouldn't be looking at it,' said Roy.

'Great new world order, Dad, I hope you're really proud to be a part of it.'

'So what's it going to feature, this site?' asked Lea hastily.

'All kinds of online community stuff you can add to and comment on. But for people of my age.'

'Don't worry, I won't embarrass you by leaving comments,' said Lea. She thought about her conversation with Milo. 'I don't know about spending evenings out at the resort. How would you get about?'

'She'll be nearby, and I can give her a lift back when I'm ready to leave,' said Roy.

'A beach house.' Cara glazed a little, clearly enticed by the idea.

'There you are,' said Lea with a sigh, 'If it doesn't offend your delicate sensibilities to be in such a horribly commercial place, I guess you can go with your father.'

That settled the matter. The rest of the meal passed in the smallest of talk and the most awkward of silences.At ten, Lea went into the garden to smoke, and saw Rachel through the branches of hedge that separated them from the Larvins' house. 'I'm sorry,' she called, 'is my smoke going over there?'

'Hey, I came out for a cigarette too,' said Rachel. 'Besides, you're in the great outdoors. People make such a fuss these days. I can't breathe in there. My daughter-in-law keeps the windows shut and the air-con permanently set at eighteen degrees. She's in one of her rearranging moods tonight. She gets very tense some days and there's no talking to her.'

'I'm starting to write again,' Lea said, keen to tell someone.

'Really? Good for you. What are you writing about?'

'I'm not really sure yet.'

'I took a pottery course last year.'

'How did that go?'

'My first pot looked like a camel took a shit. My problem is I don't take direction well. I do my yoga most mornings, and I'm learning how to make sushi. I got caught using salmon I'd dropped on the floor. You should come with me. We could get thrown out together.'

Lea laughed. 'I'm not sure I'm cut out for group activities.'

'I know what you mean. But we can't hang out with the captains of industry. We're not allowed in *that* club. Besides, the private conversations of company men would totally horrify you. So we get stuck with the ladies who lunch. Mrs Busabi tried to enrol us all in belly-dancing classes. I warned her it was a little late in the day to start shaking my junk in public, but I went a couple of times just to gross out my grandchildren.'

'How are they doing?'

'They were so cute when they were small, but now Abbi's turning into her mother and Norah has become some kind of alien creature. Nothing she says or does makes any sense to me whatsoever.'

'That used to worry me about Cara.'

A coil of smoke drifted around the branches. 'God, no, that's how it's supposed to be. I was beginning to worry that they'd never do anything to upset me. I was in my thirties when punk broke out, and I was so shocked—but you know, nothing has really surprised me since? I feel sorry for kids. How can they rebel if they only know conformity? Colette thinks it's a good thing, of course. She loves it here.' Rachel's cigarette flared orange in the hazy evening air. 'She couldn't even bear Morocco, everybody carrying mattresses and window-frames around on bicycles, all baksheesh and hashish, chaos and dirt.' Another cloud of blue smoke wafted through the leaves. 'You know the funny thing? There's a lot to like about the Arabic culture. The propriety, the formality, the sense of grace. Dream World isn't Arabic, of course—it's not anything.'

'Rachel, do you think Milo is crazy?'

'No, of course not, why?'

'He has locks on the insides of his doors. And he thinks—' She waved the thought aside. 'No, skip it.' *Saying it aloud might really make him sound crazy*, she thought.

'Listen, I'd better get back inside before my daughter-in-law decides to start cleaning out the refrigerator again. She has these fits where she throws away everything that's a minute past its sell-by date.' Rachel blasted a final jet of smoke into the hedge. 'Has Mrs Busabi warned you about the need to refrigerate your perishables?'

'Yes, I had that lecture.'

'Hey, we should meet out here regularly. We can be the Anglo-American alliance, and bitch about everyone behind their backs.'

'It's a deal,' Lea agreed. 'Same place tomorrow night.'

'I'll be here. Keep the flame.'

Lea tried to fan away the last of her smoke but it hung in the still air like a guilty secret. She slipped back inside, wondering why she felt the need for an ally.

Chapter Fourteen
The Car

CARA MOVED HER laptop to the beach house and began travelling home with Roy, so that Lea found there were times when she saw no-one except Rachel through the hedge.

Turning out her bedroom light, she lay thinking about the strange division that had appeared in the family. Cara had never sided with her father before. They were all retreating into their own lives. It wasn't what she had hoped for at all.

She must have dozed, because the next time she looked at the alarm clock the glowing green letters read 12:47am, and blue lights were sliding across the ceiling. Roy was asleep, so she tiptoed to the window and looked out.

A police car and an ambulance had stopped in the middle of the empty road. Two young Indian medics were carrying a stretcher covered in a yellow blanket. The absence of sound was odd. In London, such an event would have been accompanied by sirens and the crackle of two-way radios. Presently, the police car silently followed the ambulance and the street was still once more. Frowning, Lea went back to bed.

Mrs Busabi rang the doorbell just as Roy was leaving for work. Bizarrely, she was covered in flour again. 'I remembered that I promised to bring you some cupcakes,' she said, but Lea could remember no such promise.

'Thank you, that's kind,' she said, accepting a box of lurid, deformed sponges. 'Would you like to come in?'

'I won't stop, if you don't mind.' She hovered on the doorstep, bursting with contained information. 'I suppose you heard about last night.'

'No,' Lea admitted. 'But I saw an ambulance.'

'Poor Milo,' said Mrs Busabi, tutting. 'We've never had something like this happen before.'

'What do you mean? What happened?'

'Why, he was knocked down by a car! They think he was putting out his garbage and walked into the road. You know they turn the streetlights off at night as part of the ecological thing? Well, it was after twelve, I know that.'

Lea had seen the overhead lamps switch to low intensity solar-powered kerb lights at midnight. 'Yes,' she said impatiently, 'I didn't see a car outside.'

'That's just it, they didn't stop.'

'You mean it was a hit and run?'

'Can you imagine? Knocking over an old man and just driving off like that? However did they get into the compound?'

'How do you know it wasn't someone who was already inside?' asked Lea.

'Well, it couldn't have been, could it? I mean, it stands to reason. It must have been someone from outside. Nobody here would leave a defenceless old man lying in the road.'

Maybe they were drunk, she thought. 'How is he? Where have they taken him?'

'I think he went to one of the small private hospitals like the Jebel Ali. No, wait, it was the Omar. I heard he was unconscious.'

'We should go and see him.'

Mrs Busabi shook her head violently. 'Oh no, I wouldn't want to interfere,' she said, backing off the porch. She was happy to divulge information but felt contaminated by involvement. 'I'm sure he'll have family visiting.'

'But that's just it, he doesn't have any family here,' said Lea.

'I only stopped by to give you those, I have to be going,' said Mrs Busabi, seizing the opportunity to flee.

Lea dumped the cakes, grabbed her jacket and her car keys.

* * *

THE OMAR TURNED out to be a low, almost invisible building of antiseptic-white concrete, set back from the glass cathedrals of the commerce district. Its elegant, spacious halls were designed to calm and reassure. Nursing was a profession frowned upon by hard-line Muslim families because it required long hours and overnight stays, which contradicted a woman's devotion to home and husband. Lea found a large number of uniformed Indian women passing in distant corridors, and seemingly few patients. The majority of locals did not need to take jobs in the public sector. They remained only partially visible in public life, following a tradition that had marked them as patient, supine, prone to inanition. The Indian workforce was an expedience that posed little threat to them.

She searched for someone to help her. The wide arctic corridors were sparsely populated and disconcertingly silent except for the squeaking of rubber-soled shoes. It was the opposite of an NHS unit; there were no mismatched posters affixed to the walls with globs of Blu-Tack, just dual-language signs hanging discreetly from the ceilings. She felt as if she had wandered into an Edward Hopper painting.

The duty nurse sat motionless behind a long white reception counter, her hands folded together, almost as if she had been waiting for her. The sense of placidity was supernatural. Lea explained who she was looking for, and how Milo had come to be admitted.

The nurse checked her screen with deliberate, careful movements, then looked back up at Lea. 'Are you a relative?'

'No, a neighbour.'

'I cannot give out any further information.'

'I just need to know if he's okay.'

The nurse discreetly tapped at her phone and spoke very softly into the receiver. She looked back up, her face unreadable. 'Someone will be with you in a minute.'

Lea sat and waited. Five minutes later, an absurdly young Asian doctor made his way over and introduced himself.

'I understand you're a friend of Mr Melnik,' he said.

'That's right. I'm his neighbour. How is he?'

'You're aware that he was hit by a car?'

'I didn't see what happened, but I saw the ambulance driving away last night.'

'I'm afraid Mr Melnik suffered internal injuries and died this morning at'—he checked his mobile—'7:09am. I'm sorry.'

'He *died*?'

'His injuries were severe. He underwent a series of cerebrovascular incidents and was not strong enough to take them. He could not be revived.'

'Do you know if the police arrested the driver of the vehicle?'

'I'm afraid I have no information on that. You would have to check with the police. They'll inform the family directly when the need arises.'

'He had no family living here. Surely you could you give me a contact number?'

'Well, somebody will need to take care of the body.' The doctor took a slip of paper from the counter and wrote on it. 'If you can think of any relations who should be notified, they can discuss the matter with me. Insurance, and so forth.'

Lea stepped back into the heat of the hospital car park in a daze. She had spent no more than a few hours with the old man, but felt a connection with him that had been prematurely severed. His death made no sense to her. Why would he have chosen to put out his garbage after midnight? Why hadn't the vehicle stopped? Where had it gone? These were questions that would not have concerned her in London, but here, where life unfolded at a calibrated pace, they took on greater significance.

Like Tom Chalmers, she thought.

Milo had been afraid of something. He had fitted locks on the inside of his doors. He had kept an email intended for someone else and had asked her to be his spy. He had suspected something and had a big mouth, and that made him a risk. On the drive home she fought down the temptation to start looking for a conspiracy.

Back at the house, seated before her laptop, she tried to write but nothing materialised. Finally she called the number of the police officer the doctor had jotted down for her. After ten rings a voicemail message in Arabic cut in. She severed the call without leaving her name.

Fidgety and unnerved, she decided to take a drive around the neighbourhood. On the opposite side of the road, a street cleaner was dipping the end of a broom into a bucket of bleach and scuffing at the stones. Lea watched as he meticulously scrubbed away at the kerb, eradicating any trace of disorder. There was no police cordon, no incident board, nothing to suggest that anything out of the ordinary had happened here.

Frowning against the sun, she walked out to the carport and crossed the road to Milo's front lawn, trying to imagine the sequence of events.

She checked the bin at the end of his drive and found a black plastic sack inside. The collectors had come the previous afternoon at five, so presumably this was the bag Milo had brought out.

He had appeared soon after midnight, had walked down the path, placed the bag in the bin and—what?

Something must have caught his attention, otherwise why would he have walked further toward the kerb? If a driver had failed to see him, his vehicle must have come from the left, because if he had rounded the corner from the other direction he'd have been travelling on the far side of the road. Unless Milo had decided to step from the kerb into the unlit street, an approaching vehicle would have had to mount the pavement in order to hit him. Surely the police had taken note of that?

Okay, a different scenario. He put out the garbage and walked to the kerb. Why? Because there was a car where it should not have been. Perhaps he thought its driver was watching him.

This is crazy, she decided, *you're doing this because you're looking too hard at things you would normally take for granted.*

Hell, an old man was mugged and killed just five doors down from you in London and you barely bothered to take any notice. But she could take nothing for granted in this place, where Christian women emulated good Muslim wives and stayed hidden at home while their husbands lived separate lives.

Shaking sinister thoughts from her head, she got into the Renault and drove off around the compound. But not before she took the binbag out and placed it in the boot of her car.

Chapter Fifteen
The Barracks

THE CCTV CAMERAS were designed to be seen.

Lea looked at the tops of the wrought-iron lamp-posts and checked the surrounding buildings. On each of them, red LEDs winked from a series of wall-mounted plastic domes. She wondered where the surveillance system had its headquarters.

The police presence on the compound was extremely discreet. There was no way of telling if anyone would bother to find out what had happened to Milo. Would they check the CCTV hard drives? The solar-powered kerb lights that came on after midnight wouldn't reveal much about the vehicle. Perhaps the system was infra-red, and would display green ghost-figures drifting past the fallen old man.

Presumably the investigating officers had at least managed to question the compound guards, to find out if a car had left the grounds? If no-one had passed through the entry gates it meant that the vehicle was still inside, or that it had left via the unguarded underpass that linked to the workers' barracks. It might have been driven by one of the men who lived in the dormitory blocks on the other side of the wall.

You'd better not get any further involved in this, she thought. *But you could just take a quick look.*

She turned the Renault right, toward the underpass. It drew her like a moment in a film she knew she couldn't watch. She felt herself being slowly dragged toward the wrong choices, doing the exact opposite of what was expected.

At this time of the morning, the shadowed depression of the road that passed beneath Highway A6 was deserted. Decelerating, she coasted the car into the unlit tunnel and emerged in an alien world. The route took her between the vast concrete dormitories, aligned at right angles to the road. Dozens of workers sat on their haunches smoking or eating with their fingers from aluminium trays. They regarded her with little hostility and less curiosity. They were inert and exhausted.

Piles of rubbish and crates of rotting vegetables littered the open areas. A few fur-bald dogs snuffled through the trash. A single tap and an iron trough stood at the end of each block for washing.

Being here could only lead to trouble, but she was already inside the unauthorized zone, so why not take a look in one of the buildings? She pulled the Renault over and entered the nearest open doorway unhindered.

There was no lighting inside, just a stairway that stank of sweat and urine. Each floor had entrances leading to open dormitories. The walls were banked with mattresses, half of which were occupied by shapeless grey bundles. The men had pulled blankets over their heads to keep the light out of their eyes; there were no shades on the windows. In the corners of the room were hundreds of fluted aluminium containers, flyblown noodle boxes that had been discarded by exhausted workers.

She was careful not to enter the rooms. It was enough just to glimpse the sleeping shift-workers, lined in rows like wartime sleepers in the underground. Most appeared to be beyond the usual retirement age, or perhaps a combination of punishing sunlight, poor diet and manual labour had prematurely aged them. She counted 120 beds on one floor. A group of men crouching beneath an unfinished window glared sullenly at her as she passed, and she was overcome with shame. She should not have invaded their privacy. *This isn't right*, she thought, *I have no right to be here, I shouldn't see them like this.*

As she walked back out to the light, a broad-chested figure cut off her exit.

'What the hell do you think you're doing?' he asked. She recognised the Afrikaans accent immediately, and heard anger in his voice. *Don't let him scare you, don't apologise. You're new, nobody gave you rules to follow.*

She pushed past him, out into the light. 'I'm sorry, Mr Hardy—the road is open from the compound, and I didn't see any signs forbidding me from entering the place.'

'The road isn't supposed to be like that. We're waiting for permission to seal it off, and if we don't get it I'll do it myself, as soon as a highway maintenance crew becomes available. This is company land, ya? You have no business here.'

'I was curious, that's all. I don't wish to sound ungrateful for your interest in my welfare, but I'm quite capable of taking care of myself.'

Hardy's jaw muscles worked as he tried to keep his temper. 'Do I need to spell it out for you, Mrs Brook? Many of these men have been away from their wives for three years.'

'They look too tired to assault anyone. Besides, I thought you imported prostitutes to take care of their needs. Adultery isn't an imprisonable offence for your workers, is it, because their wives aren't here.'

'You've got quite a mouth on you, Mrs Brook. If I was your husband, I'd take you in hand.' He looked as if he could hit a woman without feeling remorse.

'Well, luckily you're not. Let's just regard this as a friendly conversation between a pair of economic migrants, shall we? We're both in the same boat, Mr Hardy, we should be able to get along.' She turned to go, hoping she sounded more confident than she felt.

'Mrs Brook.'

She turned back to face him, glad that her sunglasses prevented him from seeing her eyes. 'Yes?'

'I don't want to see you anywhere near here again. For your own safety. Or I will take action against you. Do you understand?'

'Perfectly, Mr Hardy. Good day.'

As she slid into the driver's seat, she realised her back was wet with sweat. Her hands were shaking slightly. *If I'm going to survive in this place for two years,* she thought, *I have to learn to keep my mouth shut.*

Chapter Sixteen
The Loss

'HEY, I JUST heard you in the driveway,' said Rachel, leaning over the connecting fence between the villas. The crimson silk handkerchief she had tied around her head lent her a raffish, hippyish appearance. 'Are you going to the mall today?'

'I was planning to,' Lea called back. 'I love the headscarf.'

'Why, thank you. I was going for a kind of Meryl Streep in *Mamma Mia!* mode, but Colette pulled a face and told me I look like a South Bronx gang member. How did my son ever marry such a prude? So many looks get harder to pull off as you age. I saw Mrs Busabi wearing a headscarf instead of her wig the other day and she looked like a chemotherapy patient. God, listen to me, I'm making jokes and a nice old man just died. I heard you were at the hospital.'

'How did you know? I didn't tell anyone where I was going.'

'You underestimate the efficiency of the jungle grapevine, my dear. A nurse told a friend of Betty's, and she called me. If there's anything you want to keep secret around here, it's best to do it off-site.'

'Do you need a lift?'

'Colette has taken the wagon into town. Norah has a dental appointment. I'd really appreciate it.'

'Sure, no problem.'

'Let me grab my jacket. The air conditioning in the mall kills my back.'

'It's funny,' said Lea once they were on the road, 'I hardly ever drove in London. Now I seem to see the whole world from behind glass, either on TV or through a car windscreen.'

'In that respect it's not much different to Ohio,' said Rachel. 'For us, I mean. We lived in the suburbs, never saw a living soul from Monday to Friday except at the mall, and even that wasn't very busy. And the winters were awful. But I feel kind of trapped here. There's really nowhere to go, with the sea on one side and the desert on the other. It's like being inside some kind of weird videogame, where there are only a certain number of routes you can take. There's none of the rebel spontaneity you have in London.'

'Organised chaos, you mean.'

'But that's what I love about your city, the freedom of expression. Even an element of lunacy seems to be encouraged. Everything is so carefully engineered here. DWG knows that the eyes of the world are on them. It's a grand experiment.'

'What do you mean?' Lea searched for her turning.

'Darling, everyone's waiting to see if they'll screw up.'

'The Arabs?'

'No, the consortium, the board of directors and the big money from Guangzhou. We're in the middle of an economic warzone. If Dream World fails, there'll be a mighty big case of I told you so. And I hope he does fail. It's one big power-fucking male conspiracy.'

Lea turned to look at her. 'You have some fire in your belly, Rachel.'

'Honey, I lived through Nixon and Kissinger. I remember abuse of power.'

'Well, I can't afford to start asking questions.'

'Why not?'

'Because if I did, I wouldn't stop until I'd wrecked everything.' Shocked by her own honesty, she fell silent. They pulled into the car park and made a dash from the air-conditioned Renault to the icy mall. 'Come on,' she said, 'let's go and make a mess of some carefully folded cardigans.'

They made their way along an avenue of gleaming empty shops where the sales staff were as listless as children trapped in classrooms, their chiselled cheekbones shining beneath tungsten spotlights like the faces of mannequins. The frozen tableaux they formed at their work stations made Lea feel like a character in a science fiction film.

'My daughter-in-law comes here so often that the store detectives probably keep an eye on her,' Rachel confided. 'Me, I can't stay interested in clothes for more than a few minutes at a time. Let's get something cold to drink.' As they passed a homewares shop she let her hand glide over a smokily elegant vase designed to hold a single aurum lily. 'There's too much stuff to look at. I'm getting nauseous.'

They seated themselves in a slightly scruffy canteen with an outside smoking deck that had been provided for the sales staff. In the background, fountains piddled feebly.

'Poor Milo,' said Lea. 'I keep thinking about him. It seems so weird, the whole hit-and-run thing.'

'Trust him to take his leave so dramatically. He really was one of the good ones. Although he could be a real pain in the ass. His death is pretty convenient.'

'How come?'

'He'd been upsetting people for quite a while. He was campaigning to get the old underpass closed.' She unwound her scarf and set it aside. 'A few months ago some of the workers started coming through into the compound and hanging out around the back of the community centre, getting high.'

'Was he against them?' A waitress appeared and they ordered.

'No, not at all,' said Rachel once they were alone again. 'He didn't want to see them get arrested. He lodged complaint after complaint, but nothing happened. Finally he decided to take matters into his own hands.'

'What did he do?'

'He confronted a gang of workers down by the highway and tried to explain what was likely to happen if they didn't stay on their own side. He nearly got himself beaten up. Your basic failure to communicate.'

'You don't think they had anything to do with his death?'

Rachel shook her head. 'They'd have to be pretty dumb to run him over outside his own house.'

'Maybe he had a fight with them.'

'Wouldn't somebody have heard it?'

'I keep thinking he came outside for another reason, and just happened to grab the garbage sack to give himself some cover.'

'What kind of reason?'

'Suppose there was a car outside and he thought the driver was watching his house, so he went out to check.'

'You mean watching him because he'd become a liability.'

Lea accepted her peach smoothie from the waitress. 'That was kind of what happened to Tom Chalmers, wasn't it?'

'I always wondered about that. Nobody was there when he died except Milo.'

'Milo told me he didn't see anyone else but I got the feeling he did.'

'Nobody sees anything.' Rachel tapped out a cigarette. 'They all sleep with the windows shut and the air-con up. I was woken by the ambulance light.'

'Why was Milo retired?'

'He pissed off the DWG directors once too often. He wasn't happy when the board changed all the green specs. He felt very strongly about that kind of thing. I mean, so did I when I was a student, but you kind of calm down when you have kids, don't you?'

'I went in Milo's house a couple of days ago,' said Lea. 'Did you know he had locks fitted inside his lounge doors?'

'I never noticed that. Why would he need them in the lounge?'

'Maybe he thought someone could get past the front door.'

'I don't know who else would have had a key,' said Rachel. 'He didn't have a maid.'

'Any close friends?'

'Not really. A couple of chain-smoking old codgers who came over to drink his whisky and play poker occasionally. No family to speak of.'

'Maybe Roy's right, and he really was going a little crazy.'

'Why is it that whenever anyone voices an opinion around here they're automatically labelled crazy?' said Rachel with sudden vehemence. She looked out in the direction of the resort, where a shimmering heat haze hung over the silver monorail towers. 'They can control the light, the temperature, the entire environment, but they can't control people. Look at my family. My son is completely stressed out. Have you seen the awful burn he got on his arm? That's what happens when you're not concentrating. My daughter pretends everything's fine. Nobody says what they mean.'

'Milo did.'

'Yeah, he was a terrible influence. One time I was so mad at Colette that I sat in his garden, drank a bottle of Slivovich and threw up in his fishpond. He encouraged me to be disreputable. I liked that about him.' She studied Lea's face. 'You know what's great? I tell you stuff I never tell anyone else. I really feel like I've finally made a pal.'

'Me too,' said Lea.

They finished their smoothies and headed back to the atrium, where they stood before a vast black electronic touch-screen tracing a galaxy of retail outlets in spidery red neon, like a video game for which nobody had the rules.

Rachel looked at it and sighed. 'Maybe we should stick to something we're supposed to be good at.' She took Lea's arm. 'Come on, let's make a proper effort to shop this time. Pretend you're interested in scarves.'

Chapter Seventeen
The Confession

WHEN LEA GOT home, she emptied the contents of Milo's binbag onto the table. He seemed to live on packet meals and alcohol. She counted three whisky bottles. Right at the bottom, unfortunately soaked in tea and orange juice, she found some pages torn in quarters. He'd printed out photographs onto ordinary A4 stationary, so the quality was poor.

She tried piecing them together, but the shots were so similar that they were hard to restore or place in any order. They showed a darkened room, large, concrete, without windows. There was some kind of central structure, also concrete and new-looking, with a square panel in its centre. Milo was an architectural engineer, she reminded herself. This was just the sort of thing such men kept. But ten pages of the same room taken from every angle, then printed out and torn up? It was impossible to tell what he might have been thinking. She kept one reassembled page, taped it together and folded it into her desk drawer, then put the rest back in the binbag.

There were some smaller photographs right at the bottom, printed out in the same way, just shots of a bland-looking lounge. The room looked like it belonged in any high-end property agent's portfolio, an executive suite finished in colours her mother would have lumped together as beige, so generic that its lack of personality almost qualified as an architectural feature.

She also found the email he had shown her. Why had he decided to throw it away? Could it actually be dangerous to own?

No, she decided, *you're being stupid. An old man keeps late hours, hits the whisky and throws out some garbage before he goes to bed. A carload of drunks wings him. You're looking for things that aren't there.*

On Thursday morning, after Roy and Cara had left the house, Lea finished her article and emailed it Andre Pignot at *Gulf Coast* magazine. As if to remind her what people were used to reading, the local paper dropped through the letter box. It was the only one they received in the compound and always featured the same stories. A singer or a minor member of royalty opened a new bank, mall or highway. A Hollywood film star attended a sporting event or a fashion festival. Water shortages in the financial district had been resolved. A new signature restaurant was the hottest place to be seen in town.

The sea droned with speedboats. The coastal highway was peristaltic with luxury saloons. The day drifted.

Casting about for something to do that Lastri had not already taken care of, she decided to properly introduce herself to Betty Graham, the Englishwoman Rachel had pointed out at the Larvins' party.

When she called, the whine of a vacuum cleaner drowned out the doorbell, so she went around to the back of the house and knocked on the glass. Betty saw her and gave a small scream. She opened the window and patted her chest. 'God, you gave me a fright! Sorry, I was in my own little world. Come in.' She was actually wearing a frilled apron, a sixties' sitcom housewife made real.

'I just wanted to say hi,' said Lea. 'I'm sorry, we didn't really get to talk at the party.'

'Please don't be, it was my fault, I was too busy keeping an eye on my son. I caught Dean tipping rum into his punch glass. I must look a fright. I don't usually do my own vacuuming. I missed the bin and accidentally emptied the Hoover bag all over the kitchen floor, but I have to do this myself because the maid we have at the moment is hopeless. Let me get you something.'

'No, it's all right, really,' Lea protested.

'No, no, I insist.' She raced to the kitchen and spoke with the maid. Lea guessed she was about to get the coffee-and-frosted-cupcake treatment. Betty returned with her apron and Alice-band removed and her auburn hair loosened to a pageboy fringe, but it looked crooked. Everything about her was slightly off-balance. 'I never expect to see anyone so I don't put makeup on. I don't know what you must think of me. I mean, a lot of people came around after Harry left us to make sure that we were okay. Everyone was so nice that it all became a bit wearing, to tell the truth.'

Lea assumed Harry was the husband. There was something reassuringly scatty about Betty, the way she took a run at her sentences, hurdling them without thinking or taking a breath, and the way she looked about herself in puzzlement, as if always having to remember where she was. 'Tell me about yourself, though. You settled in okay?'

'I suppose so. I don't see much of my husband, and my daughter hangs out with her new friends, but I guess that's understandable.'

'Oh, the three musketeers,' said Betty. 'They go everywhere together.'

'Sorry, who?'

'My son Dean, your Cara and Colette's daughter, Norah. They're all working on the same computer thing, something to do with bubbles? Dean tried to explain it to me but it went over my head. He wants to go into IT when he graduates—if he graduates.'

'Cara hasn't the faintest idea what she wants to do. Maybe she'll be able to concentrate on choosing a career while she's out here.'

'I know what you mean,' said Betty. 'Dean's driving me crazy. I caught him cutting school a few weeks ago. He's been hanging out with a group of workers from the barracks, and I can't help thinking they're a bad influence. Since he found out that Harry was moving to three-month shifts he's become much harder to handle. They weren't especially close, but at least Harry kept him in check. He doesn't listen to a word I say. It's like I've become a faint annoyance in the background of his life, like a mosquito. I'm sure if he could find a way to blame me for what happened, he would.'

Lea felt as if she had walked into a movie and missed the first twenty minutes. 'What do you mean?'

'Harry and I weren't getting on—we always seemed to be arguing—so he decided to take an engineering post in Abu Dhabi. Call me a cynic but when men say they need space, I think they're talking about other women. We had problems in England, and when he came out here I hardly saw him for two years.'

'That must have been difficult for you'

Betty looked suddenly shamefaced. 'Well, it's common knowledge on the compound, so I might as well tell you. I just don't want you to think badly of me.' She pressed the heel of her palm to her forehead, as if checking herself again. 'I met someone else, someone younger who paid me a bit of attention. It was all so stupid, really. There was nothing to it. Dean heard something from a friend at school—hopelessly blown out of proportion, of course—and he threatened to call the police. Affairs are a punishable offence. I could have been deported.'

'He called the *cops* on you?'

'He was very upset. Oh, I don't think he would have gone through with it. It was just a bit of grandstanding.'

'So what happened?'

'Harry took the transfer to Abu Dhabi, and Dean made me promise not to see this man again.'

'Your own son blackmailed you?'

'You know how boys are at that age. But I stopped seeing Ramiro out of respect to Dean.'

'Wait, Ramiro, our tennis coach?' Lea couldn't imagine the tanned athlete with the woman on the sofa, sitting there like a partially unravelled ball of string.

'I know, what can I tell you, a total mismatch, right? But it was a lifeline for my self-esteem.'

'Did you—?'

'God, no. It was just a ridiculous flirtation. I probably imagined half of it. And Dean was right. I was the one who behaved inappropriately. They say the biggest problems here are alcoholism, adultery and over-medication. We don't even notice how bored we are. Does that sound spoiled? I mean, Harry and I are still married. He's working so hard. He supports us. It's just that we're not really together.' She wiped watery blue eyes and blew her nose. 'I'm sorry. You probably think it's weird talking to a virtual stranger about things like this, but there aren't many people you can have a conversation with around here, not honestly.'

'That's okay,' said Lea. All her life, people had confided in her. She had what her mother had once described as a *listening face*.

'I can't leave until Harry finishes his tour of duty and our apartment in London becomes available next year. It's all very civilised and respectful between us but I just don't think I love him anymore. He always chooses his work over me. I'm the mother of his child, but I'm entirely replaceable, like one of his building beams that's developed a fault.' She reached out and clutched Lea's hand. 'I'm always the villain, and Harry's always the hero, even when he's not there for us. Dean will never forgive me. He can barely even bring himself to talk to me. It's all such a terrible mess.'

'I'm so sorry, Betty. If there's anything—'

'I should never have told you all this, I'm sure you have your own problems. Most of the women here do, they just sweep them under the carpet.'

'But not the men.'

'They work together, they see more of each other than we see of them. God, I get so lonely sometimes. I go to the golf club and order a shrimp salad for one and I just know the others are looking at me, thinking I can't cope.'

'Then we should form our own club,' said Lea, trying to comfort her. 'The kids hang out at the beach, so we could take trips.'

'We'd have to be careful where we go,' said Betty, brightening a little. 'Tahir Mansour doesn't approve of western women going out by themselves.'

'Too bad. If he wants Dream World to be a blueprint of future resorts, he has to accept a certain amount of European behaviour. He can't have it both ways.'

'The law will support him.'

'I'm not suggesting we break the law, just that we stand up for ourselves a little.'

'You really think it would help?'

'Yes, I do.'

As Lea left the house and stepped back into the withering heat, she felt less certain. How could the city be expected to abandon the articles of faith that had remained in place for thousands of years? The families here were passing through, and nothing they said or felt could be expected to make the slightest difference. The wives of Dream Ranches had to learn to live with themselves.

Chapter Eighteen
The Empire Of Light

THE HOTELS WERE almost finished. The hoardings came down around the Helios Wing, the Persiana's annexe of spectacular beach-level suites, to reveal a ziggurat of black glass that followed the tideline, halting sea zephyrs and repelling the sun's force in calculated defiance of nature.

Inside, an immense cascade of blue water arced around the great atrium, falling silently over a series of articulated walkways. The troublesome marble had been replaced, but every day brought new problems.

Roy stood on the white concrete platform of the monorail station that curved down to the hotel foyer. Since the cutbacks, three of the original planned stations had been discontinued. He tried to see where Harji Busabi was pointing.

'It's over there,' Harji insisted. 'The wrong colour.'

Roy raised his shades and squinted into the blazing sun. It reflected from every surface, deliberately mocking his hangover. 'The light's on the sea,' he said. 'I can't see a thing. We need to get up higher.'

They took the express elevator to the top of the Persiana, where the penthouse suites had their own helipad and even gravity felt man-made. The cooling system in the glass external lift was not functioning, and Roy felt the refracted sauna-heat breaking sweat patterns on his shoulders. They emerged into the iced air of the circular floor and went to the window.

'I noticed it when I was checking the pressure in the Atlantica pools,' said Harij. As water projects manager, he was responsible for the regulation of flow in the swimming pools surrounding the Atlantica hotel. 'The gauges were way up into their red zones. I thought at first it was a software malfunction, which would be okay because we're adding patches all the time, but we ran diagnostics and came up with nothing.'

Roy leaned on the low parapet and looked out at the coastline through a vast curved sheet of grey smoked glass. He could see it clearly now; a broad plume of brown water pumping out into the azure bay. 'We've got a problem.' He said softly. 'Look where it's coming from. Let's get down there.'

They took a Jeep from the DWG carpool and headed for the Atlantica marina, driving to the far end of the jetty. Roy alighted and lowered himself down over the side to where one of the tenders waited. Harji followed, but looked doubtful about getting in the boat. 'It's okay,' said Roy, 'I have a licence.'

He took the Fletcher Arrowshaft out a few hundred metres and eased back the throttle. 'Look.' He pointed over the side. A dozen or so fish, red snappers, bobbed belly-up in the water, their chromatic scales glittering like mirror fragments. 'Oh Christ.' Roy put his hand over his nose. 'Can you smell that?'

Harji sniffed the air and recoiled. 'It's shit and oil.' He unclipped his black nylon backpack and removed a clear plastic tube, lowering it into the water to take a sample. As he did so, a bulbous grey squid broke the surface and tenderly wrapped a tentacle around his gloved wrist. Harij leapt back with a yell as the squid released him, returning to the water, too weak to maintain a grip.

'It's okay, Harji, it's dying. Like everything else is going to be around here unless we cut those valves off.' He pulled something else from the filthy water, a torn red cotton pair of shorts. 'It doesn't help if this kind of stuff gets sucked into the inlet pipes. What will it be like when the hotels are full?'

He turned the tender around and headed back to the jetty. 'I'm betting the raised water pressure has cracked one of the sewage outfall pipes. It'll soon start discharging raw effluent onto the nearest beach. Good job the hotel's not open yet. Can you imagine this happening with two thousand occupied bathrooms? That's an awful lot of shit.'

'It's nothing to what we're going to get from Davenport if we don't contain this,' Harji warned.

'Don't worry,' said Roy, 'I'll deal with it.'

Harji was pitifully grateful. 'I'm glad you're here. I wouldn't have known what to do. I keep hearing good things about you. They say you're already on track for promotion.'

'Well, it hasn't been officially announced yet,' said Roy. 'I can't even discuss it with my wife. It will probably mean me staying on, and I don't think she's going to be too pleased.'

They headed back to the treatment plant, shut down the system and closed the staff bathrooms, then set about tracing the fracture.

CARA EMERGED FROM the Abercrombie & Fitch changing room and gave a twirl. 'What do you think?' she asked. She was wearing a tiny red skirt and top that exposed her flat brown stomach. She was flirting with Dean, but he couldn't tell how seriously.

'You look great,' he said.

'My mother would have a shit-fit if she saw me like this.' She darted back into the cubicle and put her jeans back on. While she waited for her purchases to be wrapped, she took his arm and led him to the men's section. 'You need to get some new clothes. Something less boring.'

Dean's arms were thick from his morning workouts at the school gym, and her hand rested on his bicep appreciatively. 'I need swimming trunks,' he told her.

'How about these?' She held a pair of bright green shorts over him, her forefingers and thumbs pressing lightly against his hips. It was as if she had passed an electrical charge through her fingertips.

'Okay, fine.'

'That's it? You're just going to buy the first pair you see?'

'They don't let you try on swimwear. I could get some new baggies.'

'No, no, no. How about these?' She pressed another pair over his groin, smoothing her hands towards his hips, enjoying his discomfort.

The counter clerk was carefully watching them on her monitor. Cara knew she could face jail for a display of public intimacy. She brushed back her newly blonde hair and moved away to the racks, pulling out T-shirts and pairs of shorts.

'What, you're choosing my clothes for me now?' Dean asked.

'I'm good at picking out the right stuff, that's all. It doesn't mean we're like, going out or anything.'

When she was with Norah and Dean she felt as if she could change the world. Dean looked at her stupidly. 'So we're not—I mean, we wouldn't—'

'What? Oh, I went out with lots of boys in London,' Cara said airily. 'Who wants to be tied down? Where's the fun in that? You should see my folks, totally fucked up.' She knew she made him uncomfortable, and she knew he hadn't had a girlfriend. She used her innocent smile on him like a knife.

'Maybe I'm not looking for a girlfriend,' he countered, setting aside the shorts.

'Of course, that's why you spend all your time with the boys. What do you get up to with them?' Her smile held mischief. 'Don't you let girls join your group? I bet you all talk about us.'

'No, we talk about all sorts of things. Politics, technology, the law.'

'Yeah, all talk, no action.' Their sparring always involved a certain amount of spite. 'Maybe you should put aside your boy-toys for a while.'

Before he could think of an answer Cara had collected her bags and headed out into the mall's main walkway, dancing ahead.

*　　*　　*

LEA STOOD ON the patio listening to Maria Callas and sneaking a guilty cigarette. She noted the sepia corner of the lawn where one of the sprinklers had stopped working. Finally she covered her shoulders with a jacket and stepped outside, hoping that a walk would calm her down. Nobody walked in Dream Ranches.

The early evening light was tinted misty blue, the street as silent and severe as a gallery painting. As she passed Milo's darkened house, she carefully avoided walking over the spot that had been scrubbed clean. It had dried now, and looked no different from the rest of the kerbstones. The useless CCTV cameras stared back at her mockingly.

Every evening, a soporific air settled across the estate. The houses camouflaged themselves in stonewash colours, a featureless terrain that smothered dissent, passion or any violent emotion. Its occupants remained hidden in shadowed silences, watching satellite TV or lounging beside pools in drugged entropy.

She passed a house with its porch lights on—the timer must have been set slightly ahead of the rest—and was struck by the property's resemblance to Magritte's painting *The Empire Of Light*. When she reached the end of the road, she took a left turn and found herself in the compound's most expensive section.

Few lights showed from the road. She could smell barbecue coal, lighter fluid. The high-walled villas had central courtyards. There were no cars on the street; every Mercedes, Lexus and Audi had been tucked away in its garage, to gleam in the dark like jewels in a safe. She finished another cigarette and took pleasure in grinding it out on the pavement, a small unsightly blemish, like a fleck on a photograph. Then she went home to start the dinner.

At 9:00pm, Roy called home and told Lea not to wait up for him.

She sat at the table with lamb couscous laid out for three, and ate alone. Cara had belatedly texted her to say that she would be out with Dean until ten, an hour later than she was allowed. Bored, Lea flicked through the TV channels, the spectacularly bad soap operas filled with kohl-eyed women shouting at their husbands and sisters in orange and purple lounges, the simpering girls falling into lovers' arms against badly digitized sunsets. Two TV presenters were discussing the 'Modestkini' swimsuit, a head-to-toe outfit made of acid-lime rubber, this year's hot colour. The BBC World Service channel showed police disappearing into a tent on sodden, muted moorland as a crimson caption ran past: 'Yorkshire police find body of Shannon, aged six.'

She checked her watch; 11:25pm. It was still warm. Suddenly she missed London, the dripping plane trees and cool fecund parks where plants grew unstoppably, not because they had automatic watering systems. She missed the messy streets, chance meetings, rowdy laughter. The mob rule of the city had been replaced with moderated behaviour and calculated glances. If there was any lunatic impulse here it had been carefully hidden away, along with every other sign of life.

Feeling rebellious, she let herself out of the house and started to walk with new ferocity.

Chapter Nineteen
The Fracture

THE STREETS WERE bathed in melancholy aqua light from the overhead lamps, the colour of loneliness. They drained the warmth from the red roofs and green verges so that the world appeared to be under shallow water. No breath of air stirred the branches of the eucalyptus trees.

Lea checked her watch. Just after midnight. She was about to head back when she heard a sound in one of the front gardens, a plastic scrape like a dustbin flap being dropped back in place. She slowed and looked over. As she passed through the blackness between the kerb lamps she could vaguely discern a pair of slender figures in whispered argument. They stopped and loped off, doubled low. Curious, she walked nearer.

She was still trying to decipher what she had seen when the package in the bin exploded. The detonation was muffled by plastic bags, but caught her by surprise. Its vibration set off an alarm inside a garage, and moments later several confused residents emerged on the street to look at the smoking, melted mess of garbage in the driveway.

She found herself sitting on the kerb, unable to recall how she had got there. It felt as if the air had fractured. One of the householders came over and put his arm around her, and her surprise at this intimate gesture was mitigated when she realised she was bleeding. She was taken to a peach-coloured bathroom in the villa, and saw there was a small cut on her forehead caused by a tiny shard of glass, but it had bled enough to make her appearance disturbing.

The wound was already scabbing over as a woman fussed around her with a hot flannel. Everyone seemed overly excited. Her ears were singing. The couple who lived in the house introduced themselves as Bill and Nancy Cooper from Seattle.

'Is there someone we should call?' said Nancy, peering anxiously into her face.

'Did you see them?' asked her husband, storming back and forth.

'No—yes—not really,' said Lea. 'Just their backs. It was dark.'

'What were they like?'

'There were two of them, short, dressed in jeans and grey jackets I think.'

'What my husband means is, were they—you know—'

'Black,' completed Bill. 'Were they from the workers' barracks?'

'I'm not sure,' she said, resenting the question. 'It was hard to see.'

In the disordered minutes that followed, Roy somehow appeared, accompanied by James Davenport. 'Lea, would you mind giving a statement to the police?' he asked.

She nodded numbly. 'Can I do it here?'

'I'm afraid we have to go down to the station,' said Davenport. 'I'll drive you. You'll be home in an hour.'

'No, really, Roy can drive me, or I can drive myself.'

'I don't think that would be a good idea, Lea. You could be in shock,' said Davenport.

'Please, everyone's overreacting, it's just a scratch. It took me by surprise, that's all.' *I lived through the London 7/7 bombings*, she wanted to say, *stop treating me like a child*. But she let herself be led to Davenport's Audi, climbing into the back of the car with Roy.

She could tell Davenport was anxious to question her himself, but Roy deflected his enquiries. 'Perhaps we should wait until she sees a police officer,' he said. 'It's better to keep her answers fresh.'

Good move, she thought, *I don't trust you, James. You're the one who accidentally sent Milo the email.* They talked about her as if she wasn't there, as nurses did beside hospital patients.

The state institutions all shared the same architectural ethic.

School, government building, hospital, police headquarters, all were low white rectangles with airy, empty spaces, built with an odd disdain for human scale. There was something about them that encouraged calm and a sense of respect. Very few members of staff were on duty, but Davenport found someone from the national security office. A tall, goateed man in a crisp white *thobe* introduced himself as Mr Qasim, the Deputy Commissioner, and led her to an interview room.

'Can't my husband be with me?' she asked, looking back over her shoulder at Roy.

'It is better if we take notes from you without intervention from anyone else,' said Mr Qasim. 'People want to be helpful, but sometimes they make our job more difficult without meaning to.' He held open the door to a bright featureless office and seated himself opposite her.

'Please do not feel uncomfortable concerning the question of racial identity,' he instructed, opening a folder and unsheathing a silver fountain pen. 'It is simply a matter of accurately recording what you saw.' There was a computer on the table, but he ignored it.

She did her best to describe the pair, apologising for her disappointing powers of observation. Mr Qasim sat patiently, allowing her to gather her thoughts. His soft, insistent tone teased out details from Lea's memory. He seemed like a good man. Finally, after listening to her account and confirming her contact details, he sat back and regarded her coolly for a moment.

'What do you think actually happened?' he asked, placing his slender hands flat on the table.

'What do I really think? That it was probably a prank.'

'A *prank*.' He turned the word over, slightly puzzled.

'Maybe a couple of the workers got drunk and came into the compound looking to play a joke.'

'These are sensitive times, Mrs Brook. It is not the kind of joke people find funny.'

'Mr Qasim, if this had happened in London, we would probably have dismissed it as high spirits.'

'But we are not in London. This is the Middle East. There are a great many political and religious sensitivities to take into account.'

'I appreciate that, but whatever it was they detonated barely had the strength to blow a plastic bin apart. I hear much louder fireworks at the beach every weekend.'

'You know there were bombs found at the Dream World resort? Did your husband tell you that somebody smashed a sewer pipe today, causing poisonous effluent to leak into the sea?'

'No, he told me he had to work late, but didn't explain why.'

'Because of this we will undergo a heightening of status to the area's security, an inconvenience to everyone. How we handle such situations is as crucial as anything we build. In Britain every move you make is filmed by closed circuit television cameras every minute of the day. We do not wish to take that path, because we must be able to trust our citizens. We cannot afford to start curtailing the freedom you enjoy here.'

'But that's nonsense—there are CCTV cameras all over the place.'

'The compound cameras only record during the day. They don't operate after midnight. The ecological lighting—'

'It's too low to see anything, I imagine.'

'The presence of the cameras is intended to warn, not to control.'

Lea wanted to argue that it was a waste of time having them if they couldn't be properly used, but kept her counsel.

Mr Qasim checked his notes. 'Is there anything else you can remember about the men who planted the bomb?'

She thought for a moment. Something drifted just beyond the edge of her consciousness. 'Something.' She said, trying to remember. 'They both had hats of some kind. White, with no brims—'

'A *kufi*.'

'Maybe, I'm really not certain.'

'Muslims.'

'Surely Christians wear them too.'

Mr Qasim closed his book, clearly disappointed. 'Mrs Brook, I would like you to think carefully tomorrow about what you saw. It could be very important. You must call me if you think of anything else.'

She emerged to find Roy and Davenport waiting for her. She began to wish she had lied to Mr Qasim, and remained silent on the drive home, unwilling to share her thoughts with Dream World's PR chief.

As soon as they were back in their own car, she could sense a bad atmosphere building between them. 'I don't know why you wouldn't speak to James on the way back,' said Roy, nettled. 'He was good enough to wait for you.'

'Anything I say to him will go straight back to his bosses, you know that,' said Lea.

'No, I don't, Lea. He has a difficult job to do. He's here to help you. Anyway, what the hell were you doing wandering about the neighbourhood at that time? I came home to find the place empty. Where did you think you were going?'

'You hadn't come home, Cara was still out with her friends and I needed to stretch my legs. We're not in a police state. I'm still free to come and go, or perhaps you'd like to lock me away inside the house like Mr Mansour does with his wife.'

Roy gave a sigh of impatience. 'Jesus, Lea, try to see it from my side just once. We had a terrorist act at the resort today. Somebody smashed a section of temporary pipe and tampered with the pressurisation software. The police are involved now.'

'I'm sorry,' said Lea. 'It's been a bad day for me too. I know it'll seem like a small thing to you, but I'm trying to find some work that actually pays instead of writing free content for a website nobody reads.'

'You don't have to look for work anymore,' he said gently, touching her arm. 'We've got good money coming in and we're saving a ton each month. I've been meaning to tell you. I'm in line for a directorship.'

'How is that possible? You've only been here a short time.'

'Jeez, I thought you'd be pleased for me.'

'I am but—'

Roy shrugged. 'A couple of group heads decided not to renew their contracts, so I got fast-tracked. I'm just waiting for the confirmation letter.'

'I'm really happy for you, honestly.'

'Well, you should be. There's no going back now. I'm senior management material. Cool, huh?'

'Of course—'

'But what?'

'I need to do something too. It'll put me in a better mood and stop me from moping about the house while you're out building an empire.'

'You make it sound like such a bad thing. It's giving us better lives, Lea.' Roy's anger would not allow him to stop. 'So it's a leisure complex—big crime. It creates employment and pours money back to places where the standard of living is lower, so that people can buy houses and start families. Think about that for a change.'

She forced a smile. 'I'm sorry. I know you think I'm being selfish. I hope the police don't come down hard on your workers. There's no proof that any harm was meant. I hated having words put in my mouth.'

'Why? You were just telling them what you saw.'

'But if I hadn't been there, no-one would have been hurt.'

'Oh, Lea, you're always the liberal. You know the police have a detention protocol that could have kept you in for questioning tonight? They were good enough to let you out. You have to start taking this kind of stuff more seriously.' He shook his head in wonder. 'Boy, I'd love to live in your world for a while.'

'You did, Roy. When we first met, remember?'

'Don't start that again. You know what? You always say you want one thing and then back off when you get it.' He concentrated on the road in silence.

When they reached home, Roy looked in on Cara and sat with her for a while, then went to bed. He held Lea in his arms for a brief moment and kissed her on the forehead, but a distance had opened between them that would not easily be closed.

THEY SAT AROUND the breakfast table in silence as Lastri made buttermilk pancakes. The maid had claimed the kitchen as her own domain, and refused to let anyone help her. Cara was absorbed with her iPad. Lea waited for Lastri to finish so that she could talk to Roy. She still didn't feel comfortable having the young woman waiting on them.

'What are you doing today?' she asked.

Roy had been studying his Blackberry with angry intensity for the last twenty minutes. 'Intermittent electronic faults. The inspectors found non-approved materials above some ceiling panels, and now the whole lot will have to come out. What are you doing?'

'I honestly don't know,' Lea admitted. 'Preparing meals. Looking for magazine contacts.'

He put down the Blackberry and rubbed his eyes. He looked exhausted. 'It means a lot to you, doesn't it?'

'Of course. I don't like feeling useless. Nobody does.'

'Something will turn up. It'll take time.'

'I've never had much patience. I'm sorry.'

'Don't be. I have to run.' He raised his voice slightly. 'Don't do me any pancakes, Lastri.' Roy's electronic gadgetry was lined neatly along the kitchen counter, fully charged and waiting to be placed in his shoulder-bag. She watched as he carefully packed each item, already at work in his head. He kissed her absently and headed to the carport.

That evening, he called to say that he would be late again. Lea decided there was no point in planning family recipes. Instead, she cooked separate dishes and sealed them in plastic freezer tubs. She took no pleasure in eating alone. It was becoming obvious why the wives arranged coffee mornings and lunches at the golf club.

Rachel called to say that Milo had left instructions concerning his ashes, which were to go to a nephew in Hamburg. There was to be no formal send-off. Lea raised her lemonade glass to him.

Roy arrived home close to midnight. His eyes were dark and tired. 'Harji Busabi's team found the cause of the problem,' he said, rummaging in the refrigerator for a sandwich. 'The remains of a pipe bomb attached to the main sewage outlet out by the marina. It was made from a soft drink can, just like your one, with another can finely grated up into aluminium filings for the filling, so that it acted like thermite. They chucked in some magnesium powder, a firework fuse and a cheap plastic wristwatch, that's all. The can is an Indian soft drink popular with the workmen. They have vending machines at the barracks. It's specially imported for them, a brand you can't buy anywhere else.'

'The couple who got bin-bombed,' said Lea, 'you know them?'

'Bill Cooper from Seattle, works in HR. It was his wife who helped you. She remembered you from the welcoming party.'

'There were too many people to take in that day. How do you know it was the same kind of bomb?'

'I shared notes with your Mr Qasim.'

'He didn't call me, and I was the one it happened to.' Lea was unable to keep the tone of irritation from her voice.

'He has my number. Besides, why would he think you needed to know?' He rose from the fridge. 'I don't like cold beef. Isn't there anything else?'

'Look in the bowl at the back. If it wasn't a prank, why do you think they targeted the Coopers?'

'One of Bill's jobs is to release any workman who fails to show at the resort site on time.'

'What happens to the people he fires?'

'They're escorted back to their barracks and sent home on the first cheap flight that becomes available, so it's unlikely to be anyone he'd just let go.'

'Maybe the workers are upset about somebody getting fired. When I saw them in the underpass, they seemed pretty angry.'

Roy looked up from the fridge. 'Why are you so interested?'

'What happens in your job is going to affect all of us,' she replied, trying to sound casual. 'I need to know what's going on.'

He narrowed his eyes at her in suspicion. 'I wonder.'

'What do you mean by that?'

'I don't want you writing about any of this. You have to promise me, Lea.'

'Look in the big bowl, there are hard-boiled eggs,' she said.

Chapter Twenty
The Wives

THE FOLLOWING DAY, she began to make notes for a new article.

Identifying her theme—the problems of moving to the Middle East, seen from the perspective of western women—she drew up a fresh interview-list of the neighbourhood's wives. Some topics would have to be avoided. She could not afford to embarrass Roy and the other husbands, or damage their relationship with DWG.

By now all her neighbours would have heard about the bomb on the compound, and about Milo's lonely death, but she had no real idea what they thought of such things. Did they know about the girls who went missing? If they did, did they care?

Tucking her laptop under her arm, she went to call on Mrs Busabi.

'I hadn't been expecting callers,' her neighbour warned, leading Lea into the cool recesses of the villa. 'It's the maid's morning off.'

Even so, there was an overpowering scent of polish in the still air. With a sinking heart, Lea realised that interviewing her neighbours would require the heroic consumption of pastry. 'When we were in Delhi we had so many staff,' said Mrs Busabi. 'I miss India terribly. But we had to leave when Harji's work took him to England.' Tea was already laid out. 'I always take a little something mid-afternoon, when I get back from the school. We haven't many little ones there at the moment. It's too hot for them now. I simply won't permit you to leave until you've tried some of my famous seed cake.'

Lea was handed a slice and asked questions between dry mouthfuls. Mrs Busabi leaned forward, listening intently. Every now and then a look of puzzlement crossed her face and she found it difficult to form a response, as if she couldn't imagine why anyone would want to try and write in the first place. Lea noticed that there were no bookcases anywhere on the ground floor, just an old copy of *Hello!* on the kitchen table.

'I thought it would make an interesting subject,' she said, although she was already beginning to wonder if she would be wasting her time.

'I suppose there's no harm in it,' Mrs Busabi finally decided. For a moment, Lea thought she was going to call her husband to check. 'After India it's all so private here. Delhi could be very frustrating, especially when three men would turn up to lift a flowerpot or change a plug, but people worked out their problems together. Here you just get smiles and silence. It does make me wonder how people let off steam. When Indian families have a row, everyone in the street gets to hear about it. You never know what goes on behind all these closed doors.'

Lea hoped her subject might feel more comfortable after a few minutes, but Mrs Busabi continued to sit with her knees pressed together and her hands knotted in her lap, as if attending an interview for a position that was far beyond her capabilities. Her replies were impersonal and imprecise. No, she had not found the move difficult, she had lived in hot climates before. Making friends was never hard because women loved to talked about children, and she was a nurturer. There was never much friction with her husband, because when you'd been married for a long time there was nothing left to argue about.

'What about neighbours? How did you get on with Milo, for example?'

'I thought he lacked social grace,' Mrs Busabi sniffed. 'He'd say the most dreadful things after a few drinks. He was openly rude about DWG, and they were paying his bills! And this interference with the migrant workers, well, it was just asking for trouble.'

'You think they deliberately ran him over?'

'Don't you think it's likely that he made enemies? Maybe they just wanted to scare him and it went too far.'

Lea closed the lid of her laptop. 'One other thing,' she said. 'When I first met you, you said you were good friends with Mrs Chalmers for a time. What did you mean?'

'Did I say that?' asked Mrs Busabi. 'I really don't remember. I certainly didn't mean to imply anything bad—'

'No, of course not. This isn't for the article. It's just that we're living in Tom Chalmers' house and I was interested.'

'I wouldn't say we had a falling out, exactly. I don't think Tom was ever happy about being posted here. He didn't enjoy working for the *Chinese*.' She mouthed the last word as if they were listening. 'They're very *driven*. He found the job terribly stressful. And then that awful thing with little Joia, their daughter. She was twelve, I think, or nearly thirteen. They had her very late.'

'Milo started to tell me about her. What happened?'

'My dear, she vanished. She set off for the beach one morning and never turned up there. It was as if she'd been lifted off the face of the earth.'

'I didn't hear about this,' Lea said, surprised.

'Well, there's nothing much to say. The police looked, but decided she'd run away. I ask you, a girl of that age! Of course, I know things like that happen all the time in London, but here— well, it's usually so *safe*.'

Lea knew Mrs Busabi was right. She had seen BBC news items about two missing children just this week.

'Tom never accepted that she'd run away. The police found a single shoe at the resort, but Tom and his wife couldn't decide whether it belonged to their daughter. Then he had that ridiculous accident. I mean, what did he think he was doing outside after dark trying to cut out plant roots? We got together a petition.'

'I don't understand.'

'There had been reports of someone hanging around the houses. It didn't seem right to have the migrant workers living so close to the compound.'

'You think they might have had something to do with Tom's death?'

'I suppose we thought that at the very least they might have seen something. We tried to get the underpass sealed off, but the construction people won't block it up until the resort is finished, because they'll lose their slip road. It's a short cut to the far side of the Persiana, you see. They can make their round-trips more easily. But what's the point of having guards and ID cards and security checks if these people can come and go as they please?'

'Are you sure they're the only people who hang around the compound?'

Mrs Busabi grew defensive. 'Didn't you tell the police you saw them planting a *bomb*?'

'No, I said I saw two people by the bin, that's all. It was dark.'

'But they *were* foreigners.'

'I only saw them for a second. I can't be a hundred per cent sure.'

Mrs Busabi's sensitivity made her uncomfortable. How did she know what Lea had told the police? 'I think I have all the answers I need for the moment,' she said diplomatically, rising to leave. 'By the way, the Larvins said you have some wonderful recipes. You must let me have them some time.'

'I'll put some in your postbox,' said Mrs Busabi, happy to be back on solid ground. 'Perhaps you'd like to come to our cooking circle one afternoon. We're icing party sponges at the moment.'

'Yes, I'd like that,' Lea lied, standing. 'It was so kind of you to spare me some time.'

Afterwards she was ashamed of her cowardly retreat. Perhaps it was better to let the Mrs Busabis of the world enjoy the comfortable lives they had created.

*   *   *

Her other social call of the afternoon was to the Larvins. Only Rachel was home. She was wearing an orange tie-dyed sarong and looked more hippyish than ever. 'Hey, I was beginning to think you weren't talking to me,' she said, throwing open the door. 'I keep sneaking out back for a cigarette and never manage to catch you. I feel like a spy trying to find my contact. Come in. Don't worry—I'm not going to force any sugar on you.'

'Thanks,' said Lea, genuinely grateful. 'Mrs Busabi just made me eat some of her "famous seed cake".'

Rachel laughed. 'Did you ever eat anything that tasted more like chewing a sandbag? I'm making my famous vodka stingers and you're having one. What's up?'

'Oh, I'm starting to think this is a stupid idea.'

'Let me be the judge of that. According to Colette, criticism is my greatest skill. She's pissed at me again because I had an argument with Norah. That girl can do no wrong in her eyes. So, shoot.'

'It's just that, well, I'm not getting anywhere with the journalism, so I thought I could make notes for a more serious piece. Or several pieces. Maybe I could turn them into a book.'

'The psychopathology of the resort widow,' said Rachel, 'it should be a best seller. But not at Dream Ranches, home of the unexamined life. You should get enough material here to last you a lifetime.'

'It's weird. You say that, but outwardly there's really not much to complain about. Everyone seems pretty happy. I feel like I'm the interloper.'

'That depends.' Rachel shot her a knowing look. 'I always think you see what you're searching for. You could paint an attractive portrait of the middle classes in retreat, or lift up a paving slab and study the dark things crawling around underneath.'

'Are there a lot of worms?'

'Are you kidding? Where do you want me to start? Look, this is a formerly Islamic city built on Muhammad's land. The *muezzin* call is heard five times a day drawing believers to prayer, but you have to listen pretty goddamn hard to hear it out here.'

'I've noticed you can only hear the mosque speakers when the wind is right,' Lea said.

'Most people just have it on their phones,' said Rachel. 'It's not about being mindful of Western sensibilities. They chose to build the resort out here because it keeps the infidels away from the mosques, not the other way around.'

'Come on, Rachel, this place is being sold on its cosmopolitanism.'

'And you buy that? I'm going to smoke in the house, don't faint. I expect you to join me.' Rachel lit up a Virginia Slim and offered the packet. 'Don't worry, I keep air freshener in my room. I'll douse the place and then open all the windows before the kids get back.' She sprayed smoke in the air. 'God, that feels good. Listen, there's not a faith in the world that doesn't operate on a double standard. If you believe in something, you have to find a way around the parts that make your life hard. Did you know all UAE nationals are entitled to a number of residence visas? They use them to hire imported servants, gardeners and drivers. But they often have permits left over, so they sell the remainder to brokers, because they can't be seen to be selling their own permits. And who do the middlemen sell them to? Take a guess.'

'I don't know, but I have a feeling I'm not going to like this.'

'They sell them to single young women who want to come and find full-time employment in the city. There are something like a quarter of a million imported hookers living along this coast in the summer months.'

'Come on, Rachel, where are you getting this from?'

'Dear old Milo knew all about it, because a friend of his had to process the permits. And right now is the busiest time.'

'Why?'

'Because it's July. We're hitting the upper forties. Haven't you noticed how empty the cafés have gotten? That's because if you're a wealthy businessman, you send your wife and family away to escape the heat.'

'Where do they go?'

'To the Riviera, the Amalfi coast, the Greek islands, America. As soon as the coast is clear the men go absolutely apeshit. Middle-aged guys turn into hormonal teenagers. They head for the bars on the King's Highway on the other side of the airport, and hire Nepalese and Chinese whores by the dozen. There are certain hotels that arrange orgies, or they'll deliver women to your room.'

'I'm not sure this is the kind of thing I'm intending to write about,' said Lea uncertainly.

'Think of it as background material.' She slammed the fridge door and sluiced fresh vodka over ice. 'You need white crème de menthe for this. I'd be making them at 10:00am if I didn't watch myself.'

'Don't the police do anything about it?'

'No, because they all get a cut. Theoretically paid sex is illegal, but the cops only clamp down when somebody goes too far. Once in a while a bar or a hotel will overstep the mark. There was a famous whorehouse at the edge of the desert that got shut down because it offered a shopping list of services: oral, anal, threesomes and so on in different rooms. The cops made a big show of closing it, but they let the owners off with a warning.'

'What happened to the girls who worked there?'

'I guess they moved somewhere else. Isn't that what usually happens?'

'You're talking about human trafficking.'

'Oh, don't look so shocked. Where do you think your fancy London hotels get their staff from? But you're lucky in England. Your corruption scandals are kind of pathetic. A member of Parliament charges the building of a duck-house to his expenses? Hell, Toronto had a crack-smoking mayor. Isn't it funny how the most God-fearing people always have the most corrupt government officials?'

Lea could see the embers of old fires burning in Rachel. 'What did you do back in Ohio?' she asked.

'When I was much younger and more idealistic I was a state attorney, but then our department got caught up in a scandal,' she explained. 'You see these things happening, but it doesn't mean you can do anything about them. It's like you.'

'What do you mean, like me?'

'Oh, come on Lea, you're not fooling me. You don't want to write about how housewives pass the time while their men are at work, you want to get your hands dirty. You're doing it without even realising. Don't tell me you haven't wondered why nobody's been caught for driving over poor Milo?'

'I assume the investigation is still ongoing.'

'Do you think they even bothered looking for the car that hit him?'

'Why wouldn't they?'

'Because if they did, they'd get reporters following up the incident. Have you seen anything in the news about your bomb or the sabotaged sewage pipe?'

'No.' Rachel was right. There had been nothing in the papers at all.

'Of course not. Once the press senses blood they start hanging around and going through your trash until they find something, and right now that's the one thing Dream World can't afford to have. Their safety record is in the toilet, their labourers have a collective bug up their ass and their budgets are being stretched to snapping point. If this place underperforms, imagine what it will do to Sino-Arabic relations.' Rachel raised her glass.

'You always seem to see the bigger picture. How come—'

'—I didn't continue my career?' Rachel passed over one of the cocktails. 'Because I'm the grandmother. I was broke, honey. I got myself in debt. So that was the deal. Colette invited me here to look after the kids. Abbi's easy. She's the girliest little girl you could ever meet. Norah's difficult. I don't think she agrees with anything I stand for, but then I felt exactly the same when I was her age.' She took a long drag at her Virginia Slim and jetted smoke over the kitchen table. 'I should have been born a boy,' she decided. 'I'd have got a better deal.'

'You don't really think that?'

'Hey, my son has been a great source of comfort to me. I couldn't have gotten work here anyway. It's a young town. Besides, I'd never be accepted as a *Mowatina*, a local. I don't believe that Allah's going to bail me out every time I screw up. It was Milo who fed my cynicism, of course. He had this wild theory about the older gods, a religion that's even more ancient, one born in the rocks and underground rivers. You have to appease the land or lose everything, and everyone who comes here has to do it or fail. He gave me a book on the subject—if I can find it under all my shit I'll lend it to you.'

'Thanks,' said Lea, 'I like history books.'

'No no, not history.' Rachel wagged a finger at her. 'A living, practical mythology. He became an Olympic-sized bore about it when he was drunk.' She squinted out at the light. 'I think the sun accentuates the weirdness in all of us.'

LEA MADE ONE more stop at the end of the afternoon, to Betty Graham's villa. She rang the doorbell and stepped back into the silvery late heat, listening to two voices having an argument. Eventually Betty opened the door.

'I'm sorry,' she began, 'I'm having one of my weekly fights with Dean. It's best to leave him be when he's like this. Can I come over to you for a moment?'

Before Lea could reply, Betty stepped outside and closed the door. 'He's slamming around in there, and when he gets like that there's nothing I can say or do. He's impossible. His grades are slipping. He won't do his homework. He's cut school twice this month to go to the mall. His father was able to control him, I just don't have the same talent. Do you have trouble with Cara? No, of course you don't, her father is there for her.'

They sat in Lea's walled garden as the sun faded below the hedges surrounding the swimming pool. A smell of grass cuttings hung in the air. 'Dean's a good boy at heart,' said Betty, sinking back in her chair. 'I really don't know what to do. He's his father's son. They were inseparable. I thought being here would be good for him, but now I'm not so sure. There's so much temptation.'

'There is?' Lea must have sounded unduly surprised, because Betty gave her a strange look. 'The girls,' she explained. 'They stir the boys up, and they know exactly what they're doing. They mature at an earlier age, you see.'

'Which girls?'

'The *service*.' She dropped her voice, as if someone might overhear, but the only sound in the garden was the hiss of the watering system coming on. 'I had to fire the maid just after Christmas because—well, you know. I caught them together. Fooling around.'

'You mean, actually—?'

'Well, no, but flirting certainly. Eye contact, brushing against each other.'

Lea caught herself stifling a laugh. Was that all? Youthful high spirits? Here in a hot country where Dean was constantly surrounded by pretty girls at the beach, it was hardly surprising that he was showing an interest in sex. 'It doesn't sound like anything to worry about,' she said.

'But there's an unwholesomeness here,' Betty persisted. 'Girls go missing.'

'What do you mean?'

She looked shamefaced, as if the subject itself was taboo. 'There have been—I don't know, indecencies, things covered up. The girls get pregnant. Or they report trouble with men. Then suddenly they change their minds. They stop talking, they move away—and sometimes they disappear. Everyone has an opinion about them but nobody has the facts. They come here and simply disappear.'

Lea returned home to start supper, failing to realise that she had taken hardly any notes.

Later she lay on the garden sofa with a book about the Middle Eastern landscape and its customs.

A unifying religion born in the rocks and underground rivers...

In all of the latitudes at the middle of the world, people supposed that light and darkness were poles attracting powerful magic. The sultans had once believed that the shadows in their courtyards harboured deathlike wraiths that waited to claim their souls. And there were dark corners here.

Something she could sense but not properly define was shifting within those slivers of blackness. It was chill and poisonous, and was rising out of the shadows toward the light.

Chapter Twenty-One
The Boy

THE SCORCHING SUMMER swamped their waking hours in a sunburst of dead white heat.

Out in the sparkling sea, the squadron of red trucks appeared as a shimmering mirage, driving endlessly across the surface of the water. They were dumping rocks, building the marina causeways that extended on either side of Dream World like stone arms ready to embrace the world. The low drone of their engines could be heard behind Cara's radio, a ceaseless soundtrack of activity.

With the arrival of the resort and its surrounding beach hotels, a linear city was rising along the coastline. Here, the usual human hierarchies would be absent, replaced by a single community of sun-worshippers unmoored from time and responsibility, a pagan zone that existed beyond political or religious concerns, the new evangelists.

The sons and daughters of the compound had spread themselves on towels across the only cool patch of beach they could find, beneath some wild acacia bushes at the edge of a hotel backlot.

'We're heading over to the Mall of the Emirates later,' said Lauren. Her coral lip implants looked larger than ever. An iridescent orange wrap floated over her yellow bikini, so that she looked like an extension of the sun. 'Are you coming with us?'

'Yeah, I guess so.' Cara and the others were lying in the shade of an acacia bush drinking beer from cola cans. A sulky-looking Indian-American girl called Madhuri had joined them.

Madhuri had arrived with a legendary reputation; back at her old school in Orange County she had talked her way out of an arrest after her brother had planted marijuana on her for stealing his favourite T-shirt. She still wore the Patriots top as a badge of honour. Her latest idea was to persuade some of the kids to 'liberate' Percodan, Adderall, Valium, Dexedrine, Ritalin and other prescription drugs from their parents. She then searched the internet and matched up the ingredients with various uppers and downers, crushed the right combination of pills with a mortar and pestle and fed them back to her friends.

Cara breathed deep. The air was golden. Even swimming in the sea wasn't enough to cool anyone down, not when you had to walk back over burning sand and could feel the afternoon sun stinging your back. There was hardly anyone else at the beach now.

'How long do you think you could stay out in this heat without dying?' asked Norah.

'It would depend on whether you had fresh water,' said Dean.

'Well, how long without water?'

'In a temperature of about 43°, two days tops,' said Lauren.

'Maybe, but you can lose like, ten per cent of your body weight through dehydration and suffer no long-term effects,' said Cara.

'I think cover would be the big problem. You'd get burned first. You're supposed to cover up, because your clothing stops your sweat from evaporating.' Norah sounded as if she was recalling a science project.

'Nobody was ever meant to live in this place,' said Lauren, stretching lazily.

Cara looked over at them, from Lauren to Dean's tanned body, his thick thighs, his shiny red trunks. His skin seemed to glow with light and energy. In London, the girls in her class prided themselves on looking pale and tough. They wore leggings, shirts, boys' coats, clumpy boots. It was an effort to imagine them undressed. Lauren was wearing immense glittery sunglasses, and always looked like a teenager's idea of a celebrity.

'Can I help you, Cara?' asked Dean.

'What?'

'You're staring at me.' He set down his beer and studied her. 'I want to go to this heavy metal bar in London that's full of rock chicks. It's famous. Do you know it?'

'There are loads of bars. Whereabouts?'

He thought for a moment. 'Camden Town, I think.'

'You mean the place Amy Winehouse used to go. Yeah, I know that.'

'She was a total skank who deserved to die,' said Lauren, shaking her bottle and finding it empty. 'It's getting too hot. Let's go to the mall.'

'Why don't we go to the other one past the gold market?' said Norah. 'There's a place that sells crazy old bootleg DVDs.'

'I've got to get my mom's car back before she gets home,' Lauren replied. 'We have to go now.'

'I think I might stay here for a while,' said Dean, glancing at Cara.

'Whatever. You'll have to get the bus.'

'That's OK. Cara can stay with me. Drop off the car and we'll join you at the mall later.'

'Fine by me.' Cara nodded, feeling the others staring at her.

They watched in silence as Lauren, Norah and the others packed up and left, flip-flopping across the burning sand to the parking lot.

'Why didn't you want to go with them?' Cara asked as Dean pulled himself up into the deeper shade of the bushes.

'They'll spend like an hour in A&F,' he replied.

'Did you go out with Norah?'

'You're joking, right? You need to be careful around her. She and Madhuri are fucking crazy. One day they'll make a mistake and take us all down with them. Besides, she doesn't like guys.'

'You mean—'

'She's not like, gay or anything. She just—doesn't see us, like we're beneath her.'

'Is that why you don't come to the mall?'

'Why would I want to spend my afternoon watching you going into shoe stores?'

'I don't complain about you guys high-fiving each other over your *Gran Turismo* scores.'

'I don't play games,' said Dean.

'Well, that's good. Neither do I.' She rose and stepped back between the polished green leaves of the acacia bushes, keeping her eyes on his.

'Well, what do you want to do?' asked Dean, mesmerised.

'Come over here and I'll show you.'

Cara dropped her sunglasses onto the sand. She slipped the end of her wrap around his neck and pulled him into the bushes toward her. The shadows of the leaves hid her eyes as she retreated, until he could only see her glistening pink mouth. The heat of their bodies was fiercer than the sun.

Chapter Twenty-Two
The Need

RAMADAN HAD BEGUN, and many of the local shops were now shuttered. Bars and cafés kept shorter hours, and were only frequented by tourists. The British Foreign Office had issued warning guidelines about morally correct behaviour.

The trucks crawled through the tarmac delta that led to the resort like dying beasts. It was too hot to pass between buildings into valleys of molten glass, too hot to breathe without scalding the throat and nostrils. At the shoreline, the dump-trucks emptied boulders into the sea until the land rose above the water-level. Every week the shore grew a little, human ingenuity providing what nature could not. The city slowed to an imperceptible crawl, its population becoming invisible, but in the icy offices of the business district, worlds turned.

Lea put a teabag into her ginger cat mug and stared at her notes. The air-conditioning unit was not yet set as high as it could go, an indicator that there was even worse heat to come. The words on her screen seemed indecipherable this afternoon, and reworking them brought no improvement.

Finally, she rose and went to the window.

Outside, the brown patch where the sprinkler was failing had grown larger. The grass was returning to the natural colour of the land. Everything would die here if left unattended. Thoughts desiccated in the heartless heat.

There was no point in waiting around for inspiration to strike. On the spur of the moment, she decided to drive out to the resort and see Roy. A little spontaneity might at least persuade him to take a beverage break.

She arrived at the Dream World sentry gates and waited while the guards examined her photo-pass. As one of them went to phone ahead, she realised that the heightened security around the resort forestalled any notion of a surprise visit. CCTV cameras glared down at her.

'There's no answer,' said the guard, checking his watch. 'What time is your appointment?'

'I don't have an appointment,' she explained. 'I'm his wife. I was in the area and thought I'd look in to see him.'

The guards seemed to think this odd and talked among themselves. One came forward. 'I can get someone to take you as far as the Persiana,' he offered. 'We think Mr Brook may be in the main hall.'

Lea waited while the other guard called ahead. They made the process unnecessarily laborious, glad to have something break the monotony of their day. They were in their late teens, but both carried some kind of squat black weapon in their belts.

A bright yellow electric buggy appeared, driven by James Davenport, who hopped out and shook her hand. He was wearing a blue woollen cardigan over his starched white shirt. The high temperatures had no effect on the energetic young Scotsman. 'Lea, this is a surprise,' he said. 'You can leave your car here.'

She switched the Renault for the electric buggy, and they headed off. Beyond the gates was a white concrete path flanked by vast plots of dead brown earth. 'You should have called first. You might have had a wasted journey.'

'I thought Roy was just working on the Persiana?' she asked.

'They've got him troubleshooting between there and the Atlantica,' Davenport explained. 'Let's see if we can find him.'

The grand portico of the Persiana appeared to be a cross between a church and a casino. In addition, the elaborately carved entrance of white marble was laid with red protective carpets, like the mosques that covered their floors for non-Muslims.

The centrepiece of the atrium was an opalescent chandelier over ten metres high, constructed in the shape of an ornate red and gold tulip, through which the light of a thousand stained-glass windows refracted in chromatic refrain, like a place of worship for Las Vegas showgirls.

'It's extraordinary,' said Lea, marvelling at the expense more than the design. 'I feel tiny.'

'The chandelier was made in Venice.'

'Will anyone be able to come here and visit?'

'The foyer, you mean? Yes, but it will cost them around eighty US dollars to do so. To keep out gawkers. Ah, there he is.' He pointed to a distant figure working beside a dry octagonal fountain of aquamarine quartz panels.

'Lea, what are you doing here?' Roy looked up as she approached, but did not come over to greet her. He didn't seem too pleased to see her at all.

'I was nearby,' she said lamely.

'But there's nothing near here.'

She wasn't about to argue. 'Do you have time for a coffee?'

She caught him glance at Davenport in apology. 'Oh honey, if you'd phoned ahead I could have cleared a space. I'm just about to go into a meeting.'

'No problem, it was just on the off-chance.' She turned to Davenport. 'I'm sorry to have wasted your time, James.'

'Let me drive you back to your car,' Davenport offered.

She waved his offer aside. 'Really, it's no distance, and it's shaded. I can walk. I'm learning to cope with the heat. I seem to drive everywhere these days, I could really use the exercise.' She set off before Davenport could stop her. When she glanced back, she saw him calling someone on his mobile.

As she studied the three great hotels in their unfinished states, the cables of marble-polishing equipment snaking out of windows and doorways like the controls of some long-dead automaton, it seemed that the resort had already been abandoned and that she was wandering a future disaster area, as ruined as the remains of Baghdad or Xanadu.

She knew the resort layout by heart; Roy left maps lying all over the house, yet the sight of the buildings always caught her by surprise.

Nature had been brought to heel. The benign Gulf waters looked like sheet steel, bordered on one side by the promenade and on the other by passing container ships. Dream World was almost ready to open, but she could see dead flowerbeds, dried-out fountains, cracking cement walkways. It was possible to imagine that one day it might exist only as a distant memory as the rocky coastline reasserted itself.

There was a building out of place. She backed up and frowned into the light. Right at the far edge of the resort stood an unadorned hexagon, low and unassuming, like a chapel for religious workers. Everything else was so obviously for a commercial purpose that it stuck out. What was the point of it? She was sure she had seen it before somewhere, but could not remember where.

Then it came to her. In photographs. Milo's torn-up pictures, taken inside and out.

Davenport would be watching her. There was no time to investigate further, and it was probably nothing special. But as she left she couldn't help glancing back. It was a decidedly odd structure.

Her Renault was no longer in the shade. The sun had moved, and as she opened the car door the interior proved so unbearably hot that she suddenly felt ill. As she waited for the dizziness to pass, a gang of workmen in blue headscarves and heavy brown overalls trudged past like transferring prisoners. They seemed oblivious to the luxurious hostility of their surroundings, as if they existed in a parallel dimension.

She wished she hadn't decided to come here. Roy was obviously annoyed with her. Perhaps she had caught him doing something he shouldn't. There was something wrong, and she couldn't understand—the heat made it so hard to think. Her head swam as she tried to concentrate.

Roy was wearing different clothes. That was it. He had left the house in tan cargo pants and a blue shirt, and now he was wearing a white shirt and navy trousers. It made no sense. He used the gym on the compound, he didn't carry extra clothes with him to work. Why would he have changed?

As she left the resort and the car's air-conditioning unit restored the interior temperature, she began to focus once more. She came off the highway and passed the line where the sprinklers ended. The blossoming dragon-green land returned to ochre moon-rock.

As the turnoff for the compound approached there was an odd noise from the Renault's engine, and she realised she had forgotten to fill the gas tank. The gauge sometimes gave false readings in the heat. The vehicle coasted the next curve and slowed, its engine knocking. The road had just enough camber to allow her to coast it onto the hard shoulder.

There was a gas station a few hundred metres off the highway, just inside the compound, but to reach it she saw that she would have to go through the underpass that connected the workers' barracks to the compound. The only alternative was to walk for ages in the pounding heat.

You can do this, she told herself, *it's no big deal. If there's anyone down there, they're liable to be as nervous of you as you are of them. They threw earth at the car, they didn't intend to hurt you.*

But beyond the sunlight, at the edge of the bridge's precipitous shadow, her heart started beating a little faster.

A rectangle of fire at the far end told her that the passageway was no more than a hundred metres, but her eyes had not adjusted to the gloom, and she could not tell if anyone was standing against the walls.

She removed her dark glasses and kept up her pace. As she walked, she heard a shuffle and cough in the shadows. The tip of a cigarette glowed. Another, then a third. There was a muttered phrase in Hindustani. A harder cough. *They can't see me against the light*, she thought, *they can't tell who I am*. Then she was out of the other side, heading toward the garage.

As she filled her gas canister she looked for someone who might give her a lift back, but the cars all had their windows tightly sealed, the drivers remaining in shadow as the pump attendants ran around their vehicles. She no longer saw into people's eyes; the high summer sun meant that everyone remained impassively shielded behind mirrored aviator lenses or rhinestone-encrusted designer eyewear.

After filling the can she looked for a way back that would avoid the underpass, but the grassy slopes that led up to the highway were too steep to climb, and typically, there were no verges to walk along. She could have been in Brazil or California, an insignificant figure casting a long black shadow across the featureless road in late afternoon sunlight. Steeling herself, she headed back to the mouth of the tunnel.

She tried to think about the men in the underpass, to humanise them, to understand why they needed to gather in communal solitude. She wondered whether they had dreams of something better, only to find that an accident of geography had reduced them to this hidden world. They were building a paradise they would never be allowed inside, for people of unimaginable wealth. They were here for one purpose only, to send money back to loved ones they might not see for years, to receive training in skills they might never use again. They were tolerated, controlled, ignored. And if they failed, more would silently appear to take their place.

She thought they might try to rape her.

Checking her rising nervousness, she remembered EM Forster's *A Passage To India* and decided she would never behave like Adela in the Marabar Caves. Giving your fear a human face, she decided, was the best way to defuse it. She walked on into the dark with a surer step. The men were intent on something. An atmosphere of order and concentration seemed to fill the tunnel.

Nobody was watching her, even though she could tell there were many others hidden in the dark recesses.

They were waiting. The cigarette stubs glowed orange in an unwavering row, forming a patient line against the tunnel wall. From the far end she could hear a muffled sound, somewhere between a sob and a sigh.

There was something pale and rectangular on the floor, lying among the discarded boxes and litter of the tunnel's deepest point. She realised now that it was a mattress. As her eyes adjusted further, she saw a frail Chinese girl, her thin brown arms splayed at her sides. It was hard to tell, but in the penumbral gloom she looked extremely young, little more than a child. Her head was turned to one side, almost as if she was asleep. She wore a dirty white T-shirt, and was naked from the waist down.

One of the workers was lowering himself into the crevice between her legs. He began shoving himself at her, bucking and ramming with such determination that he pushed her away in the process. Another men knelt down behind her, holding her shoulders still until his friend had finished.

Lea tried to turn her attention away, but she could hear the fold and brush of loosened clothing, smell the vivid spice of sweat and sex. The girl did not look perturbed, merely dulled with acceptance. There was nothing especially repellent about the process. Its mechanics had been blunted with necessity and repetition.

Lea looked straight ahead and kept moving toward the sunlit slope at the far end of the underpass, praying that she could slip past unnoticed. She wondered if they had got together to pay for her, or if the girl was being kept there against her will.

Despite herself, she looked back.

The man who had been holding her shoulders released her now, and the girl raised herself on one elbow, staring blankly at the wall as the next one came forward and unbuttoned his overalls. Some dirham notes fell beside her. She quickly gathered them up and dropped back onto the mattress, and the man behind her resumed his duties once more, preparing to grip her shoulders. The others crowded around, mercifully blocking Lea's view.

And then she was at the tunnel exit. The sun on her neck felt like a torch of absolution. Having been repeatedly warned away from the area, she knew she dared not interfere with what went on there. It would be easy to believe that sin could only breed in darkness.

Glancing back down the slope, she saw two figures caught in the edge of the light. One was a Chinese workman, bony and ill-looking, dressed in company dungarees. The other was Betty's son Dean. They both had their heads lowered, and were intent on something that occupied their attention. She glimpsed an exchange, some small object passing from one set of hands to the other.

This unnerved her more than the sight of the thin, impassive girl. Whatever transpired here had crossed over into the compound. She walked faster and did not look back until she reached the stalled car.

Back inside the vehicle, thoughts swirled in her head.

Mandhatri Sahonta, freezing to death on the beach.

Deng Antonio with his arm torn off.

Garcia Rodriguez, falling from the tower.

Tom Chalmers suffering a heart attack.

All of them mourning lost girls.

And Milo, believing there were old gods living in the ancient rocks.

They were pieces of an absurd idea and nothing made any sense, but once that the thought was planted it would not go away. Lea suddenly knew that she could not keep ignoring it anymore.

When she reached home, she immediately went upstairs and dug out the family's DWG induction pack. Sifting through the documents from Roy's information folder, she found a slip of paper bearing a login code for the DWG website address, and accessed it. The Excel spreadsheet of accident statistics dated back to the ground-breaking ceremony on the site, four years earlier.

A log had been kept of all mishaps that had occurred at the resort since the inception date. Calculating a norm by multiplying the total of workers involved, she saw that the number of deaths and injuries was only slightly higher than the national average. Dream World had issued regular press releases championing their safety record.

How many accidents had befallen other fathers who had lost their daughters? Just the ones on Milo's list, it transpired. One might as well count the number of accident victims with ginger beards.

Googling related topics, she found an online interview with a construction safety trainer who admitted that over nine hundred workers had fallen to their deaths in 2008 throughout the UAE. He said that more than half the accidents happened in spite of them wearing safety harnesses. The workers were expendable. They came from villages where they had only been used to raising goats and growing rice. Many more died from kidney failure because they did not drink enough water while they were on the skyscrapers. The workers' toilets were often situated on the ground floor, and those on the upper stories could not afford to lose time going down to the latrines.

There was no discernable pattern. Bar graphs and cloud charts scrolled before her eyes until they were meaningless. Logging out of the site, she slipped Roy's access details back in his document pack, none the wiser for what she had read.

There was one last thing to do. Instead of running the names through search engines, she looked them up on local social networks, using translation tools. This time a trace appeared in the ether, a faintly luminous thread that led through the miasma of misinformation.

Sahonta, Sakari

Antonio, Maria

Chalmers, Joia

No mention of Rodriguez's daughter because she had been found dead in the creek. The other three were mentioned on the website of a local parents' group, OurMissingChildren.org, which covered Dubai and Abu Dabi.

There were forty-six other missing girls listed on the Dubai page.

She was sweating in the air-conditioned bedroom. When she clicked on the drop-down menu, it failed to open. It took her a while to realise that the site had been closed down. Only the holding page remained, and there were no contact details listed on it.

Chapter Twenty-Three
The Theft

LEA SAT ON the patio and smelled smoke. She went to the end of the garden.

'Rachel, I know you're there.'

'God, is it that obvious? I'm halfway inside a fucking hyacinth bush. I thought Colette wouldn't be able to see me from in here. I'm always so careful to pick up my butts.' Rachel's false eyelashes fluttered up at her between the fence staves and the leaves. She jetted smoke into the still air and batted it away, stepping closer. 'Are you okay? You look like you've seen a ghost.'

'No, I'm really not okay—I ran out of petrol near the underpass. The men were taking turns with a girl.'

Rachel took a long drag at her Virginia Slim and exhaled. 'Oh honey, I thought you knew. That was why everyone wants to close the road. It's why they made such a fuss when you said they threw rocks at you.'

'Do you know about the missing girls?'

'Oh.' The figure beyond the fence was still.

'So you do?'

'I've heard all kinds of things.'

'Guess how many have disappeared since the construction started on Dream World? Forty-six. That includes Tom Chalmers' daughter.'

'Lea, they're mostly migrants, and there are millions of those here. So many people come and go. Disappearances don't make the news.'

'What about the girl who was found in the creek?'

'She was the only one I read about. But nobody notices, nobody cares.'

'Some people care. They set up a website but it's been shut down. It could be why the mishaps occur.'

'I'm not following you.'

'The parents who make a fuss, the ones who won't go away. Some of the fathers who filed official complaints died in work-related accidents.'

'Jesus, really? How did you find that out?'

'The information's publically available if you know where to look.'

'You're not going to mention this to anyone other than me, are you? You could really screw things up for us all.'

'No. I love my husband too much to do that.'

'You're not the first person to go looking for big bad wolves. Even if you were right and found out that someone here had a taste for little girls, what could you do?'

'I guess that's what Tom Chalmers wondered.'

The cigarette smoke drifted, slowly dissipating. 'Did you stop to think it might be the workers?'

'No, I've seen where they take their women. That's how they cope with their sexual issues. Rachel, you have two granddaughters. I have a daughter. What if something was to happen to them? How would we ever find out the truth?'

'I know one way.' She looked up and saw Colette leaning from the bedroom window. 'Shit, I've been busted. Are you around tomorrow?'

'Sure, I'm not doing anything.'

'I'll be back late afternoon. Let's grab a bite together. Promise?' The leaves rustled and she was gone.

Lea walked back into the lounge and saw that her phone's voicemail light was blinking. Mr Qasim from the police station had left his number, asking her to call immediately. As she waited for the call to go through, she wondered if he had discovered any leads in his search for Milo's killers.

'Mrs Brook? Thank you for getting back to me. I'm afraid this is rather a delicate matter, and I wanted to contact you directly.'

She waited for him to continue.

'We have five young people from the Dream Ranches estate here with us. One of them is your daughter.'

'Why are they there?' Lea asked. 'Have they done something wrong?'

'They were caught on camera at a clothing store in the Mall Of The Emirates. Abercrombie & Fitch, I believe. They had been trying on clothes and left the shop without paying.'

'You're saying Cara stole something? Is she under arrest?'

'It was a silver neck-chain. It triggered the store's alarm. Your daughter told the security guard that it was a mistake, that she had put it on earlier and had forgotten she was still wearing it, and her friends backed her up. The store has a policy of reporting every suspicion of theft to the authorities, so we brought them all in to make statements.'

'I can't believe they meant to steal. Cara has an allowance, she can afford to buy what she likes, within reason. You're not going to charge her, are you?'

'Probably not. This time we're going to let them off with a warning, but the store has insisted on barring them from the premises, and the mall may no longer grant them entry.'

'Thank you for telling me. I'll drive over and collect her.'

'No, you needn't come here. They just have to sign releases and they'll be free to go. However, we suspect one of the boys has been drinking and he's underage, so we'll be keeping him here for his father to collect.'

'Who is it?'

'A Korean boy, Kim Lo. He goes to your daughter's school. We're sending Cara home now. When things like this occur, we try to take an enlightened view and allow the parents discuss the problem directly with their children.'

I won't fly off the handle at her, she told herself. *I have to treat this in exactly the same manner as if it had occurred in London with her school friends.* But at the same time she was furious over the betrayal of her trust.

Her final approach, she later realised, satisfied no-one. 'Your father will be very disappointed in you,' she warned, watching Cara as she focussed her concentration on unpacking her bag on the kitchen table.

'It wasn't deliberate,' Cara mumbled. 'I forgot I still had mine on. I wouldn't lie to you about something like that. It was dumb.'

'And what about Norah? She was with you. Had she forgotten too?'

'We were all trying stuff on.' The rest of Cara's answer was lost below sound level.

'What was that?'

'I said she isn't responsible for me. I can look after myself. I made a mistake, that's all.'

'What about the boy they kept behind for drinking? Who was he?'

'Kim's just some kid who was hanging out with us. He's in the year below. I hardly know him.'

There was something different about her that Lea couldn't put her finger on. Despite her shamefacedness, Cara seemed more sure of herself, more adult somehow.

'Cara, I'm not going to go on about it after tonight, I just want this to be clear between us. You're younger than most of the kids in your class. The girls have more experience than you. They've been here longer, they're not like the ones you hung out with in London. I'm not sure that Norah and Dean are a good influence.'

'Dean wasn't there.'

'That's not the point. They know just how much they can get away with, but you have to be more careful. Answer me truthfully. You didn't steal the chain, did you?

'No, of course not!' Cara was indignant.

'You can't just think about yourself. If you'd been arrested and charged, imagine what it would have done to your father. You could have put his career at risk.'

'And what about me?' Cara turned to her, flushing red. 'What about my future? You pulled me out of my old school, then after a couple of years you're going to shift me around again. For what? So that Dad can help build a fucking amusement park for the super-rich! Did you ever think what I had to tell my friends when I left, how humiliating that was?'

'Go to your room,' Lea warned. 'Roy can deal with you when he gets home. I will not be sworn at in my own home.'

'This isn't even your house, it goes back to the corporation on the day you leave and a month later some other stooge family will be in here.' Cara stamped off to her quarters.

What made her so angry was feeling that at some level Cara was right.

Roy was late home, having dealt with the fallout from a narrowly averted strike after new shifts were announced to workers. Lea listened patiently, commenting where she could. She wanted to tell Roy about Cara's arrest, but was wary of opening up subjects that would not be shut away so easily.

Roy refused dinner, explaining that he'd ordered a takeout earlier, and fell asleep fully dressed on the couch, where it felt kinder to leave him dozing before ancient *CSI* reruns rather than rouse him for bed.

Lea sat in the upstairs window overlooking the deserted street, and read for a while, but she had drunk the best part of a bottle of Vivanco, and could no longer concentrate.

She awoke in her chair with the Persian book in her lap, trying to recall the retreating tendrils of a dream. It scurried away, vanishing beneath the warm streets, behind the artificial hedges. Within it was something dank and malignant, an impassive rock-grey monster. And now that she had found a connection between the accidents, Lea knew it was the enemy she'd have to face.

Chapter Twenty-Four
The Desert

EARLY THE NEXT day, Rachel Larvin rose ahead of her sleeping family, dressed in cream shorts, a long-sleeved khaki shirt and hiking boots, and packed her bag.

She took bottles of water, salt tablets, a cold lunch, a swimsuit and a spare shirt, then set off in her son Ben's luxury BMW 4X4. Once a month she headed out into the hinterlands, just past the Desert Hideaway Hotel, where hawk trainers staged displays for tourists. She usually stopped for a cocktail and a swim in their deserted pool, then drove for a further hour to the edge of the desert.

It was always too hot to leave the vehicle there, but she had discovered an empty spot where there was nothing to see but an undulating horizon of coral sand and the painted aquamarine backdrop of the sky. The sight of it always brought peace, giving her the freedom to contemplate her life. She found the process more therapeutic than going to one of the overpriced coastal spas. She disapproved of having to put a price on what she felt should be the most natural of pleasures.

As a child of wealthy liberals on New York's Upper East Side, Rachel had always enjoyed the run of the city, and the uniformity of life here subdued her. Ben tried to keep her happy, but as much as she loved her family she sometimes needed to be free of them. And today she needed to think carefully.

She reached the desert hotel at 10:30am and slipped into the still cool empty pool. The clear blue panel of water shattered and refracted as she swam laps, calming itself as she ascended the ladder, anxious to return to stillness. Heading back to the 4X4 in her wet swimsuit, Rachel waited for her anxieties to fade. She would be dry within minutes just by opening the windows and turning off the air-conditioning.

It took her a while to find the slip-road that led to the desert's blankest quarter, and although part of it was now striated with highways she imagined she might see a prehistoric creature, a Diplodocus perhaps, lumbering over the distant escarpment, searching for the last remaining oasis.

Within a few minutes she hit a section of the route almost obliterated by shifting sand. As soon as she saw the glittering mica sliding across the blacktop she knew she was within reach of her destination, and felt a warm caul of calm descending over her.

For the last few weeks Ben and Colette had been at each other's throats. The heat outside didn't help. This year it was proving to be so punishing that a record number of employees' families had left for cooler climes. Rachel was tired of thinking about the resort and its problems. Lately it had become the only topic of conversation in the household. Colette was affronted by offers of help, so Rachel had learned to keep her counsel. But she feared that Ben might have good reason to be on edge all the time.

She mopped her forehead with a tissue and closed the car window, turning the air-con higher. As she drove on, the amber rock-strewn landscape, as barren as the surface of a distant moon, softened and was subsumed by sand until the contours of the horizon flexed in balletic arabesques.

She found the spot she was seeking. Only locals would have been able to tell it apart from any other quadrant of the desert, but Rachel had memorised the configuration of the land. Tourists rarely came here, because the new highways took more direct routes. Pulling the 4X4 over to the side of the road, she gently eased it onto the packed-gravel pathway leading between dunes until she could no longer see the highway in her rear-view mirror. There was no danger of becoming stuck in the sand, and there was still enough room to reverse and return to the main road when she wanted.

Switching off the engine, she pushed the air-con down to half-level. She needed to think. She had promised herself that by the time she left the desert today, she would have decided what to do. She would talk to Lea at around five and listen to her advice. Then it would be time to make a choice; either ignore her fears or go to the police and risk their derision. The worst part was trying to understand how it could all have gone so wrong. She was frightened; who wouldn't be? But she was more frightened for the victims.

Looking up through the windscreen, she felt safe beneath the fierce cobalt band of oxygen which protected the earth from limitless darkness. Like ice crystals melting, her thoughts cleared and solutions began to present themselves. She made a mental list of people she could approach, those whom she felt would be sympathetic to her plight. Then she made a second list, consisting of potential enemies who should be avoided at all costs. Gradually, the nagging tension she had felt deep inside her over the last few days began to fade. She closed her eyes, and soon fell into a light sleep.

A clanging noise awoke her with a start. It had sounded like a rock hitting the roof. She was sweating despite the fact that the air-con was still running. Sitting up, she turned it off and listened.

Nothing.

She looked out of the windows. The sun was now at its zenith, somewhere directly above the roof of the car, and there were no shadows. A light wind had picked up and was sifting sand from the phosphorescent peaks of the dunes.

She was sure she had not imagined the noise.

There was a second bang, this time from the rear passenger-side tyre. She could only think, absurdly, that a hawk might have attacked the 4X4 – did they do that?

Her clothes were piled on the back seat, but her swimsuit was dry now, so she decided to get properly dressed. She couldn't very easily do it in the vehicle, but suppose she got outside and was attacked by a bird?

This is ridiculous, she thought, *it's just the heat expanding the metal roof rack. You're jumpy at everything these days, and you know well enough why.*

She slipped out of the driver's door and stepped onto the hardpack of the road, which stayed cooler than the sand. Immediately the sun stabbed down at her, stinging her bare shoulders. She had a bottle of Factor 50 cream in the boot, and urgently needed to put some on. She had been waiting until she had dried off to apply it.

First, though, she took a quick look at the roof of the car, to see if anything really had landed on it. The 4X4 was so tall that she had to stand on tiptoe. There was nothing. She felt a gush of hot wind at her back, and almost lost her balance. There was another thump of rock. She turned in time to see a plume of sand falling about five metres away. What was doing that?

When she went round to the driver's door, she found it shut.

She pulled on the handle, but nothing happened. *You have got to be fucking kidding me*, she told herself, trying it again. The car was not self-locking—at least, she didn't think so. Maybe it had jammed. She felt sure the boot would be open, at least. Moving to the rear of the vehicle, she depressed the catch but nothing happened. None of the doors opened.

The sun was already starting to scald her bare shoulders. She peered in through the driver's window and saw that the keys were missing from the ignition. It made no sense at all. Did she take them out? It was true that she sometimes forgot what she did, but she had no pockets in her swimsuit, so why would she have done? *Think clearly and carefully*, she told herself, trying not to panic. *Your keys are gone and the car has somehow locked itself. Where's your cell phone?*

With a sinking heart, she looked inside and saw it lying on the passenger seat. There was no sign of the keys anywhere. The vehicle was sealed. There was nothing else for it but to break one of the windows. Ben would be mad at her, but this was an emergency.

She set off to find a rock. Most of the loose ones were made of impacted sand and were not up to the task. She needed one that would prove stronger than the window. Hunting around on the hardscrabble she managed to pull free a sizeable chunk. Gripping it with both hands, she slammed it at the centre of the passenger-side window. The rock cracked and fell apart, crumbling into dry brown pieces.

She searched further afield, and came back with four more. Two broke, and two had no effect on toughened glass. Her pulse was rising fast. She could feel her face and shoulders reddening.

Rachel cursed herself for getting into such a stupid situation. This was how people died. She knew that in a few minutes she would start blistering badly. To be shut outside your own car in just a swimsuit, how dumb was that?

Dropping to her knees, she looked under the vehicle. The road had a high camber that almost touched the 4X4's bulky undercarriage. Perhaps there was a slim space on the far side of the vehicle near the back tyre. She might be able to shelter at least part of her body from the unforgiving sun, but that was all.

She was not given to panic, but her present state of mind was not conducive to staying calm for long. Pacing around the car in burning bare feet, she was still trying to think of a plan when she heard the sound of an engine starting up. She hopped to the rear of the car and saw a vehicle rolling forward from behind the nearest dune. When she recognised the licence plate she offered up a silent thankful prayer.

Chapter Twenty-Five
The Tragedies

'WHAT DO YOU know about vortex shedding?'

Roy rubbed his eyes and checked the time on his bedside alarm clock; 6:10am. 'Gee, Ben, I'm not awake yet, let me get some coffee first—' He switched the phone to his other hand and looked back at his sleeping wife.

'Listen, you know the Compass Towers are designed to sway four metres at their tops in high winds? Well, the swaying causes a wave cycle that emits a regular pulse—'

'I know that part.' He sat up and slipped out of bed, trying not to wake Lea.

'But if the wind matches the tower's natural bend cycle you get shedding, which is why the sides of the seaward buildings are stepped, to break the synchronisation. And it works, but not on the ground. The wind came up last night, the cycles matched and ripped all the tiling away from the fountains. It's a real mess.'

'You're already there?'

'Been here since five.'

'Let me take a shower and I'll meet you on site.'

'Nothing you can do here. You could get legal to dig out our contract with the construction team.'

Roy closed his phone and headed for the shower. He glanced back at Lea's sleeping form and wanted to touch her, but he needed to work. *Best not to wake her,* he thought.

Arising from an uneasy sleep, Lea found the other half of the bed rumpled but empty. She was vaguely aware that Roy had come upstairs late, but there was no sign of him now. She slipped on her dressing gown and opened the door to her office. 'Ah,' she said, ' you *are* here.'

'Sorry, I thought it was best to let you sleep. I'll just be a few minutes.' He returned his attention to the computer printer.

'Do you want breakfast?'

'No, I raided the fridge before I came to bed, I'll get something later.'

Lastri arrived and insisted on cooking breakfast for Cara, even though she only ate Cheerios in the mornings. Lea looked in on her daughter but found her bad-tempered and unresponsive. She had made the mistake of asking her about a rumoured boyfriend just before she went to bed, and had been accused of denying her a private life. Realising that she had violated some unwritten law and would now be punished with a complex series of sulky silences, she walked around the lake to clear her head of bad dreams.

The sun was rising behind the hedges, dispelling lavender mist from the lush parkland. Slats of gold striated the sculpted hedges. No-one was allowed to walk on the lawns that sloped to the water's edge; baroque railings fenced off the grass. A phalanx of gardeners was busy trimming any sign of untidiness from the acacias, hyacinths and black willows. No desert plants were allowed to flourish in the painted landscape; wildflowers were regarded as parasites.

She passed the back gardens of the villas where the maids were setting breakfast tables. A flock of plovers rose and settled repeatedly at the far end, like a videogame resetting itself. A few matronly ladies were walking tiny inbred dogs. By mid-morning an army of strangers would be minding pets and toddlers in the shaded areas of the park. The nurses and maids of Dream Ranches were respectful and distant, careful to avoid the comfortable intimacy of mothers and owners. The scene felt oddly Victorian, as if she had been stationed in some doomed and distant fort owned by the East India Company.

Lea removed her sunglasses and studied the sky, a deep topaz that made the earth's oxygen layer appear dangerously thin.

When she reached the communal swimming pool, she found the gate closed with a red and white plastic chain. She leaned over the railings and saw that the pool was half empty. Something flopped and rolled in the shallow end, a large shiny brown insect she had never seen before. Unable to escape, it seemed likely to die. Disconcerted, she headed home.

'Roy?' she called to the other room, 'why are they draining the pool?'

He appeared at her side, tightening the knot of a grey silk tie. 'What do you think?'

She touched the tie, straightening it. 'Kind of sexy. Do you remember when Cara was little and we hired that horrible French villa?'

Ray chuckled. 'God, we managed to pick the only unpicturesque village in the whole of Provence. No towels and a wasps' nest on the patio. Why?'

'Cara was asleep and we sat watching the shooting stars. And you said nothing bad could ever happen to us, so long as we stayed together. Remember?'

'Sure. What is this?'

'I don't know, I miss you.' She reached up and gave him a kiss on the cheek. 'Why are you all dressed up?'

'I have to sit in on a presentation tonight. I'll be late.'

'There's breakfast ready on the patio. Try and eat some, you'll make Lastri's day.'

Roy checked his tie in the mirror. 'What did you ask me?'

'The pool—it's half empty.'

'I don't know, honey. You know who to ask, go over and see if they're around. I need to use your computer for a few minutes.'

There was no sign of the maintenance man, so she collected the spare key to the pump room, a small breezeblock building accessed from the rear of the garden.

She'd been shown how to do this. Checking that the long red handles of the pool valves were pointing in the right direction, she made sure that the tank was filling, At first she thought there wasn't enough water coming back into the header tank, which would mean a leak in the recirculation system, but then she decided to check the concrete pool itself. In the corner of the deep end was a faintly visible crack, a deep blue line that ran for a little over a metre.

She returned to find Roy draining his coffee. 'Looks like a fissure has opened along a join,' she explained. 'I'll give maintenance a call.'

'I'm sure somebody over there is already figuring out what the problem is,' said Roy. 'I have to go. Lastri brought in the paper.'

She looked down at her copy of *Gulf News*. 'Reading that will take up thirty seconds of my day.' A movement caught her eye. Colette was coming up the drive. She looked as if she had been crying. Lea went to the front door and opened it.

'What's the matter?'

'It's Rachel.' She pulled out a wet tissue and rubbed at her eyes, making them redder.

'You'd better come in.'

'She's always been so damned headstrong, she refuses to admit she's getting any older, acting like she's still a teenager, for God's sake.'

'Why, what's happened?'

'She went out to the desert yesterday morning—she's done it before, we can't stop her—and somehow managed to lock herself out of the car. She was found by a passing motorist. She'd been in the sun for six hours without any protection. We've been at the hospital all night.'

'My God, is she all right?'

'The doctors tried to bring her temperature down but her arteries weren't flexible enough—they'd narrowed, and they just couldn't do it. She died a little after six this morning.'

'Oh no, Colette, I'm so sorry,' said Lea, placing an arm around her. 'Can I do anything?'

'No, really—there's nothing anyone could have done.'

'I don't understand. How could something like that have happened?'

Colette shook her head violently. 'We don't know. She must have panicked. She was in her swimsuit—she always dries off in the car after she's used the pool at the Desert Hideaway. She thinks we don't know she goes out there, but Ben knows the manager and he always tells us when she's been. She must have got out of the car, thought she was shut out and collapsed of heatstroke. I don't understand it, because that car is impossible to lock yourself out of. The police said it looked as if she'd been trying to break one of the windows with a rock. But why would she try to do that when the door was open? The keys were still in the ignition. The police have taken it away for analysis. Poor Rachel, she hated the sun but loved to sit and look at the desert. We should never have brought her out here.'

'Where's Ben now?'

'He had to go to work for a few hours. He couldn't get out of it. We can't do anything until they release the body.'

'Do you want me to sit with you?'

'No, Lea, it's okay—I may call you later though. I'm looking after Abbi. I just thought you should know. You got on with her so well, and I had to talk to someone.'

'If there's anything either of us can do, will you promise to come over?' said Lea. 'Can Lastri at least fix you some breakfast?'

'No, I'm not hungry. I have to get back. I guess there'll be calls to make.'

As she watched Colette trudge back down the path, exhausted, it felt as if she had somehow lost more than a friend. Rachel had possessed the kind of rambunctious spirit that turned the world.

Lea sat at her desk trying to work on her notes, but it was hopeless. Dark conspiracies winged into her head. What if there was more to Rachel's death than a stupid mistake? She'd been to the desert many times before, she knew her way around. How could she have locked herself out of the car if the keys were inside? Perhaps the air-conditioning had broken down and she had suffered heat-stroke. She seemed surprisingly youthful, but

Colette said she got confused sometimes. What other explanation could there be?

She found it impossible to concentrate; other people's tragedies crowded in. Three deaths in the same street. Okay, over 90% of the workforce transient; some people were bound to fall. Perhaps their safety was an illusion. Despite two decades of westernisation it was still a harsh dry land, best suited to hardy Bedouin, camels and desert thistles. The verdant veneer that lay across the baking rocks could be removed at any moment with the twist of a water-valve, the entire country reverting to its primeval state within the space of a single summer, the old gods returning to reclaim their kingdom.

The day crawled past, bogged down in a sinister molten heat. The setting sun brought amber skies, hot breezes and flurries of sand, and the street became a sepia photograph. She watched an old DVD, Luc Besson's *Le Grand Bleu*. The underwater sequences failed to relax her as they usually did.

She felt as if something more was expected of her, but really, what could she do? Talking to the authorities led nowhere and flagged her as a troublemaker.

Toward the end of the film, she heard the front door open. Roy looked terrible. He threw his briefcase onto the couch and followed it down. 'Want me to fix you a drink?' she asked.

'Maybe a whisky.'

While she broke up ice, she told him about Rachel.

'Well,' he said finally, 'she was a headstrong woman. Ben and Colette had been worried about her behaviour for some time.'

'God, Roy, her lack of conformity didn't exactly mark her out for death. It just sounds so unlikely.'

'You have to be vigilant here. We have cases of heat-stroke every day at the resort.'

'You don't sound surprised.'

'Sorry, I've got a lot on my mind right now. From Monday we'll be working until eleven every night, until we can be sure that the resort will launch on time.' He accepted the amber glass and took a slug.

'When are you planning on seeing your daughter?'

'After work I guess, when she's finished at the beach house. She can come over to the Persiana.'

'Then that just leaves me.' Lea found it hard to keep the irritation from her voice.

'Let's not have this fight again, Lea. It's not going to be forever and the potential rewards are enormous.'

'You're right.' She went to touch him, but he looked dead on his feet.

'S'okay. I'm really sorry about Rachel. It's going to be tough on the Larvins. I guess they could get someone in to look after Abbi.'

Now, as she lay in the master bedroom watching him sleep, she felt bad about giving him a hard time. Dream World was his big chance to make good. Perhaps it was her test, too.

Even with the air-conditioning unit turned up high, she twisted and turned in bed until she was forced to throw off the sheets. She could not bring herself to touch Roy—lately his skin had become hot and tanned and hard, not at all like the flesh of the man she had married.

It was easy to entertain fearful thoughts now. As Cara slept next door, it felt as if, for the first time, the beast of chaos could cross into the sanctity of her home.

Chapter Twenty-Six
The Book

11:00AM, FRIDAY MORNING. Hot enough to fry breakfast on a sheet of tin.

Lea sat in the chill air, determined to write. So far, she had managed a few sections composed of her first faltering interviews with the compound's wives. She wondered how Cara managed to generate content for her website, and looked for it online. *Bubble Life* turned out to be filled with mystifying band reviews and teenspeak manifestos as indecipherable as hieroglyphs, annoyingly condensed versions of sugar-rush conversation that she quickly gave up on.

She found herself drawn back to the holding page of OurMissingChildren.org. The names of the children led nowhere. She imagined a fearless journalist making connections, bullying out answers, exposing wrongs, but the reality was completely different. Here she was nobody, and could do nothing.

On the other side of the garden hedge, two Indian workmen were standing in the emptied pool, examining the cracked stonework. Kicking back in the chair, she went downstairs and stood at the window.

Mid-morning, and the street was deserted. In mechanically chilled rooms, housewives baked and cleaned and tucked themselves from sight. How could they survive with so little human contact? Did they drink alone, invent online identities, create phantom liaisons, spend their days blissed out on pills? When the time came, would they flee to better pastures without taking anything from their past lives, like the Arabs did when they abandoned their date groves for oil?

The computer screen showed a hopeless jumble of sentences. She was about to scrap the pages and start over when the doorbell rang. Lea looked at her watch. The traditional calling hour. She prayed it wasn't Mrs Busabi.

Colette stood on the doorstep, her eyes as pink and swollen as a rabbit's. 'Can I come in?' she asked.

Lea led her into the kitchen and sent Lastri off to change the bed linen. Colette seated herself at the breakfast bar and meekly accepted a mug of tea. 'Ben went straight to the resort without any sleep,' she said. 'That's the way he deals with problems. When his father died he stayed at the office for weeks. I feel really strange about all of this.'

'That's understandable, given the circumstances,' said Lea. 'I have some sleeping pills if you need them.'

'Thanks, I have plenty. Dr Vance is very keen on supplying medication around here. I have to make sense of things. I'm just so angry.'

'Angry? Why?'

'That she could have done something so stupid.'

'What do you mean?'

'Rachel could be difficult, she was always the first person to admit that. Heaven knows we had our ups and downs.' She took a gulp of coffee, gathering her thoughts. 'She was so stubborn. This business of sneaking off into the dessert, a woman alone, at her age. To have made such a basic mistake, it's just so typical of her. She knew the risks and she deliberately—'

'I don't think she did it deliberately, Colette. I mean, I didn't know her for long but it seems to me she was street-smart, a real survivor.'

'I told you, the doors were unlocked when they found her. She got out of the car, something she should never have done. I think I know why. She wanted to smoke. Did you know she smoked? She thought I didn't know but I used to find her cigarette ends in the garbage.'

'Where there any footprints near the car?'

'No, the wind wiped away any tracks.'

'What did the police say? Have they had a chance to examine the vehicle yet?'

'They pulled it apart yesterday and said there was nothing mechanically wrong. They found some grit between the door and the floor, and think it could have got into the lock and temporarily jammed it. They've already said that the coroner will return a verdict of accidental death. Rachel was in a swimsuit, she'd even left her sandals inside. She knew how sensitive her skin was. She usually took a strong sunblock with her, but there was nothing in her bag.'

'She had to have left the car for some reason.'

'The way I see it is she got out, shut the door, it jammed and so she walked around to the other side and threw rocks at the glass. The trapped grit loosened and the door lock popped back open, but by that time she was either too confused or too panicked to notice, and collapsed from heat-stroke.'

Lea shifted uncomfortably as she remembered the rocks that had been thrown at her by the workers in the underpass. 'You're right, maybe the air-con stopped working for a few minutes and the heat made her light-headed,' she suggested. 'I was coming home with the shopping the other day and honestly thought I was going to pass out.'

'Not the air-con.' Colette was resolute. 'It never went wrong.'

'Maybe something else happened, did you consider that? Maybe she saw something that encouraged her to leave the vehicle. You don't think she was meeting someone, do you? Could someone else have been there?'

'No, of course not. The police don't think so, either. There were no tyre-marks, but the wind clears everything. Entire dunes have a habit of shifting and disappearing out there. Sometimes whole sections of that route simply vanish. Hardly anyone uses it, precisely for that reason.'

Things get covered up, thought Lea. *It's as if the desert is intent on sealing away the truth.*

'She was a ridiculous, impossible woman,' said Colette vehemently. 'She never wanted me to marry her precious son. I wasn't 'creative' enough for him. If she'd just stayed in town where I could have kept an eye on her—'

'I don't think it's good for you to keep thinking about what might have happened,' said Lea. 'Perhaps it would be better to concentrate on the practicalities for now.'

Colette worried at her knuckle, her head turned aside. 'You didn't know her like I did. This was just so damned typical of her.'

'What's going to happen about the funeral?'

'We have to organise it as soon as the coroner has delivered his decision. That will probably be later today. They do things quickly here. We'll cremate because it'll be too expensive to ship the remains to the US.'

'If there's anything I can do to help, will you let me know?' Lea asked. 'I'm sure Ben has enough to worry about right now.'

'Thanks,' said Colette. 'Ever since he got his promotion I hardly ever see him.'

'Oh, I didn't know he got promoted.'

'Didn't Roy tell you? I'm sorry, I'm just not dealing with this at all well. I'm glad you became friends with Rachel. Tom Chalmers was a sweet old stick, but she didn't have much to say to him.'

'They never found out what happened to his daughter?'

'I don't think so. Why?'

This was her moment to say that she thought there was a connection, but seeing the pain in Colette's face she could not bring herself to make the claim. What would be the point of furthering her grief?

'Oh, before I forget.' Colette removed a hardback from her pocket and slid it across the counter. 'Here's your book back.'

Lea looked at the green and cream cover, which featured a lion wearing spectacles. A very old edition of *The Wonderful Wizard of Oz* by Frank L Baum, with illustrations by WW Denslow, 1900. Surely not a first edition? She carefully opened the flyleaf and checked the receipt inside: *Kinokuniya bookstore—Dubai Mall.* She had been to the store but would never have been able to afford anything like this. The date on the receipt indicated that it had been purchased three months earlier.

'I don't think this is mine,' Lea said warily.

'Rachel asked me to return it to you,' said Colette. 'She was anxious that you should have it back.'

'Are you sure she wasn't just confused?'

'She didn't seem to be. I don't know why she didn't bring it over herself.'

Because she was going to the desert first thing, thought Lea, but said nothing. She placed the book among the cookery volumes on her counter shelf. 'If you want me to look after Abbi and Norah while you make Rachel's arrangements it's no problem.'

'I think we're covered,' said Colette absently. 'I can drop Abbi off at the daycare centre, and Norah—well, I don't know where she is. On a study date, probably.' She rose to leave. 'You know, Rachel had a good life. I think Ben wants her funeral to be some kind of celebration, but none of her old friends will be here. Perhaps you'd come?'

'Of course,' said Lea. 'I'm sorry I only knew her a short time. I think we would have become good friends.'

She watched as Colette headed back down the path once more, carefully avoiding the new-mown grass, as if she was afraid of leaving footprints that might mar the striped pattern. *That's the word,* she thought, watching her neighbour leave, *afraid.*

She went to her computer and checked on the book.

Baum's very first edition had been for friends. The main imprint ran to 10,000 copies. Prices for an original varied between $100,000 and less than $4,000, depending on quality. It turned out that the book largely owed its success to a musical version that opened two years after its publication. There were thirteen sequels. She flicked through the faded pages, and for the first time it crossed her mind that perhaps Rachel had been unbalanced after all. But then she remembered her very first sighting of the city's towers, and the thought that they reminded her of the Emerald City of Oz. There were no bookmarks or letters slipped inside, so she placed the volume on top of all the others yet to be properly arranged.

Cara returned from school, passed through the kitchen without speaking and carried a stack of toast off to her computer. Occasionally a car crept along the street in near silence. The sky remained so uniformly blue and cloudless that the house appeared to be in some kind of film set representing limbo.

We are adrift and becalmed, she thought, *floating far away from the everyday world, vanishing one by one. We have to leave here before it's too late, or do something about it. Either way, it will be the end of everything.*

Chapter Twenty-Seven
The Promotion

LEA CALLED THE Deputy Police Commissioner to see if there had been any progress on the search for Milo's attackers.

Mr Qasim sounded harassed and in no mood to talk. 'We found an old Toyota abandoned in the workers' barracks,' he explained briskly. 'The owner said it was stolen from him. Unfortunately, he had lent the car to many of his fellow workers—they all paid a share to use it. Therefore we have no useful forensic information. Is there anything else I can help you with?'

'I guess you know about Rachel Larvin. She'd been to the desert plenty of times before, but somehow she got locked out of her car died. What do the police think?'

Mr Qasim sounded surprised to hear that she had already been informed of the death. 'I'm afraid I am not at liberty to give out that information,' he said carefully. 'How did you hear about this?'

'I'm her next-door neighbour, Mr Qasim,' she said. 'We had started to become good friends.'

'The police have no reason to presume that it was anything other than an unfortunate accident.' Qasim was obviously anxious to halt any spread of disinformation. 'Please,' he said, 'if any of your friends ask, tell them not to worry. The police will issue a statement soon.'

'One other thing. What about the pipe bombs? Any further news on those?'

'There is no danger. We believe them to be the work of a single angry individual, and will shortly be making an arrest.'

'Single? I saw two people.'

He ignored the point. 'You understand that we are anxious to resolve this matter as quickly and quietly as possible.'

Lea had no more time to dwell on the subject. Roy had called to warn her that one of his supervisors, Alexei Petrovich, was coming to dinner, so she would be forced to marshal her meagre cooking skills and prepare something that would please him. She found a recipe of her mother's, chicken with lemons, and reluctantly went to the mall.

CARA SAT ON her favourite rock and looked out at the sea. Her conversion was now complete. Her skin had tanned a deep, rich caramel, her hair lightening and growing coarse. She looked more like a Californian wild-child than a Chiswick schoolgirl. She had abandoned her track suit top and black jeans, and now wore a faded blue Superdry tee, checked shorts and flip-flops. Her manner of speech was altering. Surrounded by the polyglot conversation of migrant children, she had shaved away the clip of her Britishness and had begun to soften and elongate her speech, so that she sounded American. She called Dean and waited for him to pick up.

'Hey.'

'Hey.'

'I'm down at the beach. Wanna meet up tonight?'

'I can't. My father has grounded me until I finish all my fucking homework. Did you finish already?'

Cara was used to having far more homework than she was given here, and got through it easily. 'Yeah. I can help you if you like. My folks have got some Russian guy over for dinner. I don't want to be there. We could meet up later.'

'Not tonight.'

'Why, what are you doing?'

'Just stuff. I'll call you tomorrow, okay?'

'Sure.' She rang off, wondering if he was starting to lose interest in her. She should have kept more of a distance from him, showed less enthusiasm.

'Hey, Cara.' She turned to find Martin Tamworth heading her way, armed with his skateboard. Although he was older and almost absurdly muscular, Tamworth was in the year below the rest of them. He wasn't too smart, and had been held back to retake his tests. The others avoided him because he had some kind of inner ear problem and shouted when he spoke.

'Hey, you hear about Norah's grandmother?' he asked. 'She fucking fried out in the desert.'

'I heard,' said Cara, still checking her phone. 'She was my neighbour.'

'She was like, a hundred years old or something, and got sunstroke. Right in the middle of the desert. Crazy old bitch.'

'Hey, she was okay.'

'I fried my pet rabbit back home, left it in the greenhouse during a heatwave. I wanted to cook it for dinner but my old man said that was gross.'

'He was right, it is gross.'

Tamworth kicked the rock disconsolately. 'I thought I'd see you guys at the mall last night but you didn't show. You guys are never around anymore. You're not avoiding me, are you?' The amiable Californian worked in a GAP store in the evenings, and enjoyed it so much that everyone assumed he would probably end up working there full-time.

'We're not avoiding you, Martin, we just don't want to spend our evenings hearing about what you saw in the changing rooms, okay?'

'I get that. Listen, I got to get to the store or they'll dock my pay. Later, babe.'

'Later.'

Cara slid down from the rock, dusted her shorts and walked off across the empty road to the ice cream parlour, a glitzy art deco confection of rippled chrome and pastel neon. She could see Lauren, Norah and some of the others seated near the window.

They locked fingers in greeting, and Cara slid into a red plastic bench-seat beside them.

'We're taking a break from schoolwork,' said Norah, looking slyly at Lauren. 'Wanna come with us?'

'No, it's okay,' said Cara slowly. 'I've got things to do tonight.'

'Aw, come on, I already apologised, didn't I?' The pair had argued the day before.

'Why, what are you going to do?' asked Cara.

'It's gonna be fun.'

'Tell me what first.'

'Nah, anyway you'll probably be seeing Dean anyway.' Her voice was loaded with insinuation.

Cara bristled. 'What do you mean?'

Norah exchanged a look with the others. 'Come on, everyone knows you guys are doing it.'

'Where did you hear that? Not from me.'

'So it's not true then?'

'If you've been listening to Martin, you should know he talks shit.'

'So you're still a *virgin*.'

'Fuck you, Norah.'

'I'm just messin' with you. We're cool. Anyway, we need to be cool together, don't we?'

'Yeah, I guess we do,' Cara said, and let the subject drop.

ALEXEI PETROVICH WAS not a man given to spontaneity. He studied his companions, remained alert to his surroundings, listened patiently before offering a lugubrious non-committal reply and got slowly, inexorably drunk.

The evening was a disaster. Cara had gone missing, the chicken had dried out, Roy was late and Petrovich was early. The Dream World supervisor was in his late forties, grey-templed, grey-suited and handsome in an out-of-shape, exhausted way. He looked like the manager of a failing provincial football team, but his immobile eyes betrayed a cold alertness. It was the first time the dining room table had been formally laid out since the family moved in. Seated at its head, the Russian drank iced oak vodka at a measured, constant rate. Roy had reminded his wife to buy the brand he liked.

Petrovich was the most senior building supervisor at the resort, and had no conversation except work. Lea struggled to find something to talk about while she prepared the chicken, and found herself matching her guest's drinking pace with glasses of white wine. She had not eaten lunch, and by the time Roy turned up, was on her way to being drunk.

Petrovich lacked social grace but he liked facts, and recited statistics about the resort whenever the conversation failed. Finally Roy walked through the door, and Lea virtually dropped at his feet in gratitude.

'Alexei was telling me all about the sterilisation units,' she said, glaring at him in a signal that meant, *For God's sake take over.*

Roy looked from his boss to his wife in obvious discomfort. He helped himself to vodka and toasted Petrovich, after which things became a little easier. But by the time Lea served dessert, the Russian was explaining company financial policies, and Lea found herself opening a fresh bottle.

At first she drank out of nervousness, but Petrovich's determination to outline the resort's technical achievements in relentless linearity annoyed her.

'When we open, it will be the biggest party in the world,' said Petrovich. 'We are booking the cultural superstars of the West. The New York Philharmonic. Beyoncé. Richard Gere.'

'I'm not sure Beyoncé and Richard Gere are superstars anymore,' said Lea, just to be argumentative.

Petrovich ignored her. 'Our team created the opening ceremony for your Olympics. They are staging a display of fireworks that will be televised in many countries.' He pushed aside his chicken and concentrated on refilling his glass.

'Aren't you worried about terrorists at the resort?' asked Lea.

'There are no terrorists. Why would there be?' Petrovich's face clouded.

'The bombs. I thought they raised the security levels all through Dream World.'

'You must not concern yourself with this. We have already located the culprits and have full admissions of guilt.'

'Is that right, Roy?' Lea asked her husband.

'I know the security guards made some arrests,' said Roy.

'And someone admitted planting a bomb?'

'Certainly,' said Petrovich. 'Mr Hardy located the troublemaker for us.'

'Of course, Mr Hardy,' said Lea. Roy shot her a warning look.

'I think you'll find that our security services are more efficient than you give them credit for, Mrs Brook.'

'So Dream World's public park will be open to everyone?'

'That is correct, with fountains and picnic lawns for families.'

'How will the public get into the park? The resort is gated, yes?'

'Obviously there is security.'

'Then how will they get past the guards?'

'They will need to show an identity card issued by the resort for which anyone may apply,' said Petrovich.

'So you can't just show up,' Lea insisted, waving Roy's agonised warning glances aside. 'It's not a public park.'

'We are not a public service industry, Mrs Brook. We are a private company seeking to maximise profits for our shareholders, and we decide who can use our facilities. But within that group, all will be free to come and go as they please. It is the capitalist system adopted by both East and West, but mostly denigrated by those who enjoy the comforts of it.'

'So you've created a secure enclave. With its own private police and privately made laws. It's a separate state where you can do whatever you like.'

'We have designed civility and good citizenship into the project, just as art and science were designed into the Parthenon.'

'But hardly for the same reasons.'

'Lea, I think you're being extremely unreasonable,' said Roy.

'If someone has an accident in your park who is liable?' Lea persisted.

Petrovich looked flustered. 'I'm sorry, I don't—'

'There are so many accidents at Dream World. Employees go missing. Their daughters go missing.'

'This is not my area of expertise.' Petrovich looked to Roy for help.

'I was just trying to make a point,' Lea replied. 'I'm sorry, Mr Petrovich, I didn't mean to embarrass you.'

'YOU HAD TO keep going, didn't you?' said Roy later.

They were in the kitchen, clearing up after Petrovich's chauffeur had called to take him home. 'Your old self appears out of nowhere with no thought about how difficult you might make life for me.'

'He was completely pissed,' said Lea, refusing to feel ashamed. 'I don't suppose he'll remember anything in the morning.'

'Well if he does, I'll know who to blame. I know you, Lea, you're upset about what happened to Rachel. You're bored here and you're looking for something to upset the applecart. Find a hobby. Join the damned cookery classes. Just don't interfere with my job. And leave the clearing up to the maid, for fuck's sake.' He took the tray from her hands and set it down on the counter with a bang.

'I thought we were in this together. I was just asking a few simple questions.'

'If you were really in this with me, you wouldn't ask questions. I had my promotion confirmed. I'm a full director now. I'm expected to behave with decorum. And so are you.'

Roy headed upstairs and closed the bedroom door behind him, something he never normally did. He seemed very different now from the man who had charmed her into bed on a second date.

She sat at the top of the stairs for a while, then went out in the garden for a secret smoke, but there was no Rachel on the other side of the fence, and it was no longer the same.

Chapter Twenty-Eight
The Important Stuff

SHE KNEW THE hotel was called the Desert Hideaway, and found it easily. From there, the trail grew more difficult to follow. Sand had closed the road Rachel had presumably taken, so she was forced to make a detour and enter the area from a connecting route on the far side. Even then, she wondered how she would ever be sure that she had found the right spot.

But there, straight ahead of her, beneath a double hump of ochre sand and bracken, a series of red and white striped plastic poles marked out the spot where Rachel's 4X4 had been found.

She checked the temperature gauge and found that it was 42 degrees outside. She didn't know what she expected to find here. It had been foolish to think of duplicating Rachel's final journey, slipping out at dawn without telling her family, but she wanted to see for herself and put some errant feeling at rest.

Even though she was wearing desert boots and a long-sleeved shirt, she was reluctant to leave the safety of the vehicle. Heat was radiating up from the ground like the fan-assisted air from a convection oven. She pulled a raffia shopping bag from the back seat and slipped it over the corner of the car door so that it couldn't shut, then walked over to the arrangement of poles.

There was nothing to be found, of course. The sand had slipped across the road and the landscape had no doubt changed. The wind had written its signature onto these spines of rock, which history was relentlessly eroding and sifting away. If Rachel had left any mark of her existence in this barren region, it had been buried with the fossils of long-dead creatures beneath micrite and silt. Some bird tracks and a shed snake skin provided the only obvious proof of recent life.

She tossed the single red rose she had brought with her into the centre of the poles, and offered up a silent prayer. *Talk to me, Rachel, tell me what happened. I need to know.*

A bird cried in the sky, a terrible tearing shriek. Her cheeks were moist for a brief moment before the desert dried them.

As she arrived back at Dream Ranches she realised that Betty must have been watching out for her, because she came over moments after Lea left the Renault and entered the house.

'I need to speak to you for a moment,' she said, stepping onto the pristine front lawn with her arms defensively folded, clearly wishing not to be heard by anyone else.

Lea came down and joined her. 'What's the matter?'

A few minutes later, Lea returned indoors and went up to Cara's room. It was Saturday and there was no school, but she knew Cara was in because her computer was chattering to itself. She entered without knocking. Cara was lying on her bed, working on her laptop.

'You're supposed to give me a warning before you come in,' she complained. 'We had a deal.'

'The deal's off.'

Cara sullenly closed her laptop and sat back, awaiting a lecture.

'Do we need to have a conversation about contraception?' Lea asked.

'What? No.' Cara looked grossed out.

'You're spending a lot of time with Dean.'

'*So?*' Never had two letters of the alphabet sounded more defensive.

'His mother says—'

'His *mother* doesn't know anything.'

'She found condoms in his room.'

'You really have no idea what's going on, do you?' Cara replied hotly. 'That's the incredible part. Nothing breaks through to you. What we do doesn't matter, Dean and I hang out together and let off steam, it's not important. You never notice the important stuff.'

'What important stuff?'

'Dream World stuff.'

'Oh, you know all about that?'

'Ask your pal Hardy over at the resort how many workers he beat up yesterday. Ask that Russian thug you had over for dinner about his "special" security force and the deal he has going with the secret police. Ask yourself why they won't block up the underpass. You have no idea what really goes on around here.'

'You seem to know so much, why don't you tell me about the underpass?'

'They keep it open to give the workers somewhere to take their whores. It's where they buy the drugs that keep them awake and working.'

'How do you know? Is it because Dean told you?'

'I know a lot more than you think.'

'That has nothing to with the way you and your pals behave. I want you to think about what you do and be careful. You're not even sixteen yet.'

'You can't choose my friends for me,' said Cara, reopening her laptop to signify that their conversation was at an end. 'I'm old enough to decide for myself who I want to hang out with.'

'Not until you cease to be my responsibility, and that doesn't happen until you're eighteen. You get a very easy ride here, and you know it.'

'I know right from wrong. But I have to experience things for myself, and then decide.'

'You have to promise me you'll be sensible and take control of your life. I really mean it. Do you have any idea how much you mean to me?'

But an email pinged in and Cara returned her attention to her laptop, pecking at the keyboard, indicating that the topic was closed.

* * *

CARA STAYED IN Lea's thoughts throughout the day. She knew that Colette was just as worried about Norah's behaviour. The kids spent a lot of their spare time on the internet together, creating material for *Bubble Life*, but what else were they getting up to? She wondered how her daughter had formed such strong ideas about Petrovich. *You were exactly the same when you were that age,* she remembered. *You did some pretty crazy stuff and didn't grow out of it until you met a boy at college.*

Still restless, she drove to a deserted section of beach at the edge of the city and walked between the last of the shorefront cafés, down onto the scalding yellow sand. One sickly date palm had collapsed on itself, providing a small area of shaded relief from the light.

In the distance, through a shimmering heat haze, she could see the silvered towers of the Atlantica and the Persiana, an as-yet uninhabited Xanadu available to the highest bidder. The "twice five miles of fertile ground with walls and towers girdled round" were an earthly vision of paradise unimaginable to Coleridge, and just as unaffordable. *This is the world we are making,* Lea thought, *stripped back to its barest essence. The pleasures of the few, built on the burdens of the many.*

Sweating, she headed for the new boulevard that had been constructed along the seafront. The grey concrete paving stones of its promenade petered out, as if marking the point where time ceased to matter. She found an empty coffee bar, a neutral zone where she could sit and think.

You're trying to forget, she told herself. *You don't want to think about what happened to Milo and Rachel. If you cease to care, they'll cease to exist. You have to do something before it's too late.*

But even if she discovered concrete proof of wrongdoing, she knew it would be ignored by the men. They had all the power here. Women were to be humoured and ignored. And as for sisterhood, that was just a forgotten term that belonged in one of Rachel's yellowed student books.

Chapter Twenty-Nine
The Fire

A MEMORIAL SERVICE for Rachel Larvin was held two days later. The company gave families from the compound time off to attend the event. The blinding sunlight seemed profanely ill-suited to such an occasion. It threw black shadows around the mourners and set the little white concrete church in sharp relief, so that it resembled an insubstantial paper cut-out.

Colette and her daughters had elected to wear light colours in celebration of Rachel's life, and it was obvious that some of the families did not approve of their choice.

'I don't think it's in very good taste,' said Betty Graham, emerging from the service. 'Not in this place. It's bad enough that everyone's wearing sunglasses, as if they're all going to lunch. You should be able to see the mourners' eyes. It seems disrespectful. Colette said Rachel had once told them she should be buried in rainbow colours, but they've already cremated the body. That's wrong, isn't it?'

Lea and Roy offered their sympathy and help. Ben kept searching around, as if expecting to see his mother come to his rescue in the difficult social situation, something he had doubtless done many times in the past. Norah kicked at the ground with her hands in her pockets, demonstrably bored.

'Ben wants to send Abbi to stay with my sister in Connecticut,' Colette told them. 'There are some things we have to sort out here, and he says it will be best for her.'

'Well, if there's anything we can do—' Roy began.

'No, they—that is, the company—they organized everything.

They've been absolutely wonderful. I couldn't fault them.' Colette's unqualified support of DWG felt uncomfortable in the light of her husband's obvious distress. Lea watched as Colette fumbled for her daughter's hand and slowly led her away, walking tentatively across the car park like a child venturing into the dark.

There was no wake for Rachel. Awkward in company at the best of times, her son and daughter-in-law clearly had no desire to spend time with the other compound residents. Three days later, without a further word to anyone, Ben and Colette sent Abbi back to the USA.

LEA AND ROY were invited to dinner with the Larvins at Peruglia, an expensive Italian seafood restaurant with overwrought gold and crimson seventies décor some twenty kilometres further along the coast, where occasional Gulf breezes gave some respite from the overheated nights.

They were surprised by the invitation, but figured Colette was making an effort to be friendly now that time was weighing more heavily on her hands. Her youngest daughter and mother-in-law had gone, Norah was rarely home and her husband worked far into the night.

The restaurant was filled with Westerners. Two tables over, Hiromi Morioka and her husband Dan were eating lobster spaghetti. Hiromi had designed the elegant sushi kitchens in the Persiana, and was one of the few female executives brought in by DWG. She gave a friendly wave when she saw Lea. On the other side of them sat the electronics manager Richard McEvoy and his wife.

Ben and Colette arrived late and were out of sorts. Despite the stifling heat of the night, Colette was overdressed in dowdy winter colours, and had thickly applied makeup as if seeking to hide behind it. Struggling to maintain an interest in the evening's small talk, she sat quietly drinking, letting the others hold up the conversation. Ben looked tired and preoccupied.Considering the long hours he'd been working lately, Roy was in a surprisingly good mood, and Lea was anxious to honour the truce between them.

'Did you hear what happened last night?' he asked. 'Elena Ribisi and Ramiro Gonzales were arrested for adultery.'

'You're kidding. How? Where?'

'The police stopped them while they were out walking together in a park in Al Muraqqabat. They took them to headquarters for questioning. They both tried to deny it.'

'So what happened?'

'The police confronted them with two signed witness statements. They've been released on bail pending a court hearing.'

'But who acted as witnesses?'

'Bruno, her husband, and the pool man, who's fed up with the situation because he's sleeping with Ramiro's wife and wants him out of the way.'

'So the stories are true,' said Lea. 'Who'd have known Dream Ranches was such a hotbed of vice? I never see anything from my window.'

'You should get out more,' said Roy. 'Actually, maybe that's not such a good idea. You should definitely stay away from the pool man.'

'He'll be staying away until the pool is fixed,' Lea reminded him. 'I suppose I could go to the golf club if I fancy a dip. And they still can't seem to fix our sprinkler system.' She set down her fork. 'God, listen to me. You're sorting out multi-billion dollar stuff and all I do is complain about luxuries.'

'It's okay,' said Roy. 'You've been really patient with me lately. I want you to know I appreciate it. Alexei really liked you. He told me he thought you were "feisty". Then he suggested I should keep you more under control.'

'He said that?'

'In so many words.'

'He's the one whose wife charged a white wolf fur coat to his credit account without telling him?'

'The very same.'

'Then he's hardly in a position to offer advice.'

'That's what I thought.'

'Did Roy tell you the bad news?' Ben asked suddenly. 'We're having problems on delivery dates. We'll be going through weekends from now on.'

Ben already looks like he's about to have a heart attack, thought Lea.

'Even Tahir Mansour's wife has been giving him grief,' said Colette. 'She says they don't do anything together, and it's making them unhappy. I keep thinking we should have been around more for Rachel. I don't accept the coroner's verdict. The whole thing stinks. The business with the car door just doesn't make sense.'

'Few accidents really make sense,' said Roy. 'People have them because they don't pay enough attention to what they're doing. They stop concentrating for a moment and end up falling off buildings. How's Norah?'

'Teenagers are pretty resilient,' she said, picking at her food. Looking up, she saw Mrs Busabi heading their way with a folder under her arm and a look of determination in her eye. 'Oh God, not tonight. Does she have to be everywhere we go? She keeps coming around with petitions.'

'Hello there you strangers, I don't want to interrupt your meal, I just thought you might be interested to know how we're progressing,' said Mrs Busabi, patting her paperwork. 'I've presented our requests to the British Consulate and to the prefecture of police. We're all at risk until they stop the immigrants having access to the compound. I've seen them down by the nursery at night, hanging around and smoking. I've picked up their cigarette butts.'

'The air's cooler in the compound,' said Lea reasonably. 'There are more trees.'

'The underpass can't be sealed off at the moment,' said Roy. 'Even when the main work is finished, the construction teams will still require access to the road.'

'But that could be two or three years away. Who knows what could happen in the meantime? We could all be murdered in our beds. The other day one of them spat at me, just because I told him to pick up his litter. Harji and I don't feel safe in our own houses. We always felt safe in Delhi.' She looked down at the crab linguini cooling on their plates, and checked herself. 'I'm sorry, I'm keeping you from your meal.'

Lea watched her waddle back to the table where her husband was draining his second bottle of red wine. 'Poor thing, I almost feel sorry for her. It's all she ever talks about. She's hardly seen Harji in weeks. I know.' She smiled and raised her glass. 'Let's toast. To the end of Dream World.'

That night they made love for the first time in weeks. Cara was on a sleepover at the beach house with Norah and they had the house to themselves. Lying in cool air without clothing was a rare luxury. 'We could move from Chiswick if you like,' she said. 'Wait for Cara to get fixed up at university and get a place at the coast. How about France? Normandy, perhaps?' The street was a vacuum of silence. Only the clock could be heard ticking on the bedside table. It was twenty to two. 'It's so quiet out there. You'd think we were the last people left alive in the world.'

She fell asleep with her head on his shoulder.

Her dreams were odd and unsettling. Some time later she muzzily awoke and raised herself on one arm. She felt the sheet. The other side of the bed was empty. 'Roy?'

Silence.

'Roy, where are you?'

Roy was outlined in the doorway, pulling on his shorts. 'I got up to get myself a glass of water.'

'What time is it?'

'Early. Lea, you'd better come and see this.'

She slipped a T-shirt over her head, freed her hair and joined him on the landing. 'What's the matter?'

A crimson glow pulsed in the windows opposite. 'I think something's on fire,' he said.

PART TWO

Just because you're paranoid doesn't mean they aren't after you.

– Joseph Heller

Chapter Thirty
The Dark

THREE GLEAMING RED trucks still stood around the house, hoses snaking to hydrants. Lea watched as the firemen cleared debris away from the site. They had been at work for the last two hours, making sure that no cinders drifted to other parts of the compound. Several other neighbours had come out of their houses, but although it was only 6:45am it was already hot, so most stayed indoors and watched from their windows.

There was nothing left of the Busabis' house. Lea could see the blackened contours of the rooms and some loose timbers, but no more than that. The air was acrid with the tang of smouldering varnish.

Tahir Mansour alighted from his Mercedes and spoke with the fire officers. After a few minutes, he headed back to his car. Lea stopped him on the way. 'Mr Mansour, do you know what happened to the Busabis? Are they all right?'

Mansour turned and stared at her, as if trying to recall her face. 'Mr Busabi is being treated for smoke inhalation. He will probably be kept in the hospital for a day or two, just for observation. They were very lucky.'

'Have they said what happened?'

'Mr Busabi is a smoker,' said Mansour with disapproval in his voice. 'A terrible misfortune.'

'We saw them in Peruglia last night.'

'I heard he had been drinking earlier in the evening. It appears he may have failed to put out his cigarette properly when he came home. This is why we discourage smoking in the compound or at the resort. Please excuse me.' Having performed his official duty as perfunctorily as possible, he returned to his waiting car. He seemed to find the tragedy distasteful, another sign of foreign sloppiness.

Lea felt it was her duty to visit Mrs Busabi. After Roy headed to work, she drove over to the Dubai Hospital and found her seated alone in a perfectly white visitors' waiting room, sipping from a Starbucks cup. The icy air smelled antiseptic. There was no sound of life anywhere.

'Oh, Lea, you shouldn't have come, really,' Mrs Busabi said, holding out her hand. For once she was wearing no makeup. She suddenly looked old and unprotected. 'Harji's in having tests and can't have visitors until this afternoon.'

'I came by to make sure you were all right,' Lea replied. 'If you want to stay at the hospital, I can pick some stuff up for you.'

'Really, I'm fine. I'm going to stay with my sister tonight. We lost everything, Lea. There's not a stick left. Mr Mansour virtually accused us—'

'Mr Mansour says Harji left a cigarette burning.'

'That's an outright lie. Why would he say such a thing? Harji gave up smoking six months ago. He'd been having trouble catching his breath, and I begged him to stop before it was too late, so he did.'

'Perhaps Mr Mansour didn't know that.'

'It's true Harji was downstairs by himself, but I believe him when he says he wasn't smoking. He called upstairs to say that he could smell something burning. The next moment, the hall was alight. If the back door hadn't been open we'd have been trapped in the house. We'd have burned alive.' She wiped her eyes, trying not to cry. 'I asked the police to test for traces of petrol but they say they don't need to, that it was obviously an accident. How can they possibly know such a thing? They're not planning to investigate it at all. They're just sweeping it under the carpet like they do everything else.'

'Why would they do that?'

'Isn't it obvious? It's because we're so close to the resort's opening date now. They don't want any trouble. I know who did this. They wanted us out because we complained about them. *They* destroyed our home.'

'Who are you talking about?'

'You know very well who.' Mrs Busabi's eyes hardened with hatred. 'The Somalians, the Nigerians, the Indonesians, the mixed-race whatever-you-want-to-call-them, they want what we've got and when they see they can't have it, they try to take it from us. We're the minority here.'

'But you were in the minority in India too.'

'That was different. We once *owned* India. There was still respect for all we had done, despite all the damage that self-serving little lawyer Gandhi did, with his fasting and his fancy dress. Well, we took out plenty of insurance when we moved here. We'll replace everything.'

'I'm glad you're not going to let something like this upset you, Mrs Busabi.'

'Oh, we're not going to be intimidated. We're made of sterner stuff. Harji and I had a contract job in South Africa, where they think nothing of butchering a cow and leaving it on your front doorstep when they're upset with you. That's the trouble with these outposts, you always walk into someone else's territorial disputes.'

'Where will you live now?'

'The company has already promised to sort out the compensation and rehouse us on the north side of Dream Ranches. There's another nursery over there where I can work.'

'What will you do until then?'

'They offered to put us up in a hotel until then, but I told them I've made other arrangements.'

It was Lea's last sight of Mrs Busabi for a while, seated on the white plastic couch in the waiting room, angrily shredding a paper napkin around her Starbucks cup.

The next morning, Harji Busabi was released and they left for his sister's house on the far side of the city. When they returned to Dream Ranches two weeks later they stayed away from their old neighbours, only stopping to nod briefly at golf club dinners, as if everyone else was somehow to blame for what had happened.

YOU REALLY HAVE *no idea what's going on, do you?*

Cara's words had stayed with her. Now Lea was starting to wonder if she was right. She thought about the Busabis and wondered if their house had been deliberately torched because they had become a nuisance. The idea seemed ludicrous until she applied it to all the accidents and disappearances. Then a paranoid pattern started to emerge.

The next morning, she presented herself outside Leo Hardy's office at 8:45am and waited for him to arrive. When he walked into his office, she told him she was writing another article for *Gulf Coast*'s website, and needed five minutes of his time to conduct an interview.

Hardy let out a harsh mirthless laugh. 'Is that still going? It's not a magazine, Mrs Brook, it's a bunch of perfume ads for rich old women.'

'Andre Pignot has launched a new online edition.' It was something of an exaggeration, but Hardy's attitude irked her.

'Has he now?' Hardy seemed amused. 'Pignot is a bankrupt womaniser and a drunk. He can't have thought that idea up by himself.'

'I thought that as the most respected security officer working for DWG, you could give me your take on a situation,' she said. 'Especially now that you've had a promotion.'

'Flattery isn't going to work on me, Mrs Brook,' he said, but she could see that it at least stood a chance. 'Grab a seat, but you'll have to be quick, ya? I've a hell of a day ahead.'

'We have... an unusual situation at the compound,' she said. 'Mrs Busabi is convinced the migrant workers were responsible for burning down her house. She'd been collecting signatures for the petition to close the underpass.'

'I think you know how absurd that sounds.' Hardy tipped back in his chair, openly staring at her legs. 'If you're going around talking to people, you should cover yourself up a little more. You'll get no respect otherwise.'

Lea bit back her reply. She knew that he had declared war on her. The interfering bored housewife—he had seen plenty of those.

'I wondered if the other residents who signed her petition might be at risk. Do you have an opinion on that?'

'Hell, I have an opinion. My men are good workers. They keep to themselves. If they behave badly, they know they'll be punished. They can't afford to lose their jobs. They're the breadwinners, and their families are entirely dependent on them. There are literally lives at stake here. That's why none of this is taken lightly. Do you understand?'

'I appreciate that. Alexei Petrovich told me that arrests were made in connection with the bombs.'

'They were, but I'm not prepared to discuss that with you. You were a witness to one of the attacks. You were prepared to blame my workers. You said you saw Muslims, didn't you?'

'I thought they might be foreign workers, based on their headgear—nothing more.'

'Well, there you have it.' He rocked his chair. 'The wife's opinion. Was there anything else?'

'So, that's the end of it? Everything is back to normal now?'

'I have a suggestion for you, Mrs Brook. Instead of making a nuisance of yourself, why don't you and the other wives do something useful?' Hardy checked his Rolex. 'Organise a party at your compound for the opening weekend. I'm sure the men would all enjoy a chance to relax after so much hard work. Now I have to attend a meeting. If you have any further questions, contact our press officer.' Hardy opened the door for her and virtually pushed her out.

In a state of barely controlled fury, Lea returned home to finish the article. When she calmed down, she marinated steaks for a barbecue. Norah and Cara were planning to do their homework at the beach house, so Colette and Ben Larvin came over to eat with them.

Seated on the patio, facing away from the spreading patch of dead grass, her neighbours looked more tired and miserable than ever. Ben's shirt collar was a size too big for him. He was losing an alarming amount of weight, and periodically forgot what he was saying, drifting off into his own thoughts. Every now and again he frowned suddenly, as if failing to understand something. Colette tried to sound light-hearted, but lapsed into silence after a while. Lea noticed that both of them were drinking more heavily than usual.

There was still a faint aroma of charred wood in the air. The fire chief had warned that it would take several weeks for the smell to go away. Realising that the mosquito candles around the barbecue had gone out, Lea rose to put the outside lights on.

'No, leave it like this,' said Ben suddenly. 'The dark is good.'

'So, Lea, Roy tells me you're writing for a magazine,' said Colette with forced good humour.

'It's just an online piece about the resort. It won't have as much detail as I'd hoped.'

'Why's that?'

'I've only got space for 2,000 words. I'd like to write about some of the things that have been happening here, like the hit-and-run incident and the Busabis' fire.'

'Yeah, well—I have a solid theory about that,' said Ben, anger suddenly colouring his voice, 'but I wouldn't want you to write about it.' He sat back, his face unreadable in the darkness.

'Why not?'

'Because you can't trust anyone around here. Did you know the estate's Wi-Fi network is being hacked into by our police bureau?'

'Ben, don't start,' Colette pleaded.

'You don't know that for sure,' said Roy hastily.

Ben jabbed a finger at him. 'Ask Dick McEvoy—he should know. He oversees the resort's electronic traffic, and that includes mail coming in and out of the compound.'

'Ben, please.' Colette laid a restraining hand on her husband's arm. It seemed to Lea that she hated any public exposure of emotion.

'So, what's your theory?' Lea asked.

'Ask yourself how many more "accidents" have to happen before somebody starts to make a noise? It's the whole fucking thing. We're all complicit.'

Lea had never heard Ben swear in front of his wife before. 'What do you mean?' she asked.

'Ben's exaggerating as usual,' said Colette, panicking that anything her husband said might be reported back. 'Didn't you say the safety record has been unusually good for a site of this size? You can't count things that have happened in the compound. Everything's fine. Really. And what happened to Rachel—well, she was always doing crazy things. Once she went out in Ohio when the highway safety people were advising everyone to stay home, and she got stranded in a snowdrift overnight. She could have died. She told me she'd gone out for cigarettes—in a snowstorm!'

Ben held up a hand to silence his wife. 'There's something I have to say—'

'No, Ben—'

'After the autopsy, we received Rachel's clothing and personal belongings back from the coroner. The one thing that was missing—the only piece of jewellery she never removed apart from her wedding ring—was the silver neck-chain my grandfather had made for her twenty-first birthday. She was crazy about Indian gods, so her father crafted a piece, a Ganesh. She never took it off.'

'You think someone stole it?' asked Lea.

'I damn well know they did And I know who.'

'These things happen,' Colette said quickly. 'It could have been someone in the medical unit.'

'She wasn't the only one who lost something,' said Ben. 'That guy Rodriguez, the one who fell from the tower. His daughter was found dead in the creek without her ring. She wore her mother's ring for so long that she couldn't get it off. Someone cut off her finger.'

'We've been over and over this, Ben,' said Colette. 'Please, let's forget about it and try to enjoy ourselves.'

But nobody did.

The dark is good, Ben had said. It would have been more accurate to state that in all this searing light, the dark had become a necessity.

THE BLACK AND yellow-striped cement mixer churned. Six men alighted from the yellow construction truck and began unloading wooden battens. They were preparing to seal up the underpass.

Lea pulled the blue Renault over and watched for a while as the barriers slowly rose. Grabbing her laptop, she stepped out of the car and headed for a grass slope, preparing to make notes. She was about to sit down when she noticed a group of sullen-looking young Indian men standing on the embankment staring at her.

'Hey missus, fuck you!' called one of the youngest, a boy in a blue headscarf and vest. 'You have no business here! Go back to your fucking house!'

The others stirred in agreement. A couple began shouting in Hindi. Another ran closer. 'You got no business here! This is our territory! Go home, fucking rich woman!'

One of them stooped to pick up a rock.

It had been a mistake to come here. Lea took a step back and stumbled. Stupidly, she put out her right hand to break the fall, the one holding her laptop. As she landed on her knees, the computer cracked against the concrete kerb. A rock bounced on the grass beside her, then another. She groped around for the laptop as a lump of concrete passed her head.

A hand reached down to grab her arm. 'I think you should get back inside your car.' The man led the way and opened the door for her, running around to the passenger side as more rocks fell around them.

He picked up the laptop, which had come apart. The screen had split from corner to corner. 'I'm sorry, I couldn't save it,' he said, handing it back.

'It was my fault,' said Lea, 'I should never have come here.' She started to turn the car around.

'Are you okay?' he asked. The Indians were still shouting insults and hurling rocks.

'I'm fine.' She crunched the gears and reversed. 'I didn't mean to upset them. Can I give you a lift somewhere?'

'Could you drop me off at the main gate? I came out in the truck with them. I can't go back through the underpass, not when they're like this.'

'Thank you for your help,' said Lea as they set off, 'I'm Lea Brook, Roy's wife.' She held out her hand.

'I know. Rashad Karmeel.' When she looked back, he was still looking at her. He was a powerfully built man with thick tied-back hair, strikingly handsome. *A strong face*, she thought.

'Why did they decide to go ahead with the closure after all? Was it because of the petition?'

Rashad shook his head. 'No, I heard there was one but I don't suppose anyone even looked at it. They're building a new road further along. The barracks is going to be torn down. Our work will soon be at an end.'

'You live there with the other workers?'

'Of course. They're my responsibility. I'm sorry they reacted so violently to your presence. There will be repercussions over this incident, I can assure you.'

'Please no, I don't want to make the situation worse.'

'They just want to be left to do their jobs,' said Rashad. 'The men gather there because they have nowhere else to go.'

'They never go into town? To the beach?'

'They cannot afford to go into town. And they are not allowed on the beaches.'

'I didn't know that. I'm afraid I must appear very ignorant to you.'

'No. You live in your world and I live in mine. They don't touch each other.'

'Well, I'm sorry for it. It isn't the way things should be. People should not be divided by the colour of their skin.'

'They are divided by money first, Mrs Brook.'

The Renault was approaching the main entrance to the compound. 'You can drop me here,' said Rashad. He turned and solemnly shook her hand once more. 'I hope you will all feel much safer now, and I am sorry for your trouble.'

As he unfurled his powerful body from the car and strode away, she wondered how he could possibly have any sympathy for the white residents of Dream Ranches.

Chapter Thirty-One
The Whores

SHE MISSED HER laptop. The general-use desk computer they had brought out from London was overloaded and slow, but would have to do until the newly upgraded models came out next month. Lastri insisted on vacuuming the entire house every day, and nothing Lea said could dissuade her from her routine. The whine of the vacuum cleaner passing doggedly back and forth along the landing broke her concentration, so she pushed herself back from the screen and went next door to visit Colette.

The Larvin household had become a sterile environment since Rachel's presence had been removed from it. Colette obsessively cleaned the kitchen and lounge, tidying away all signs of life until the interior resembled a set in a furniture catalogue. The smell of bleach and polish was everywhere.

Colette looked unsettled by Lea's sudden arrival, as if she regarded her as an unwelcome force for chaos. She was wearing even more makeup than before, a beige mask that almost succeeded in concealing her facial expressions. 'You've missed coffee,' she warned sharply. 'Everything got put away.'

'I've had enough coffee to last a lifetime,' said Lea. 'How are you doing?'

'I'm fine. I keep telling everyone that. Ben's the one they should be worrying about. He's virtually stopped speaking—to me, at least.'

'Why?'

'Why do you think, Lea? He's somehow got it in his head that I should have stopped Rachel from going out to the desert by herself. You saw what she was like, she wouldn't be told anything. I couldn't have stopped her if I'd tried.'

'I'm sure he's not trying to blame you. I can see what kind of pressure he and Roy are under.'

Colette moped at the kitchen counter, looking for something more to do. 'The company's aware of the problem. I know they think they helped with the Friday thing, but I guess that's cancelled now.'

'What Friday thing?'

'You know, the time off.' When Lea gave her a blank look, she added, 'Early leave?'

'What early leave?'

This stopped Colette in her tracks. 'You mean you don't know?'

'Colette, I have no idea what you're talking about.'

'The senior architects and engineers are allowed to finish early on Friday evenings because they put in so much time over the weekends.'

'Roy never mentioned that to me. He never gets back before eleven on a Friday. What do they do?'

'I think they go off drinking somewhere,' said Colette vaguely. 'They're not supposed to, of course, but I'm sure that's what they do. Ben never tells me much about what goes on at the site anymore. He thinks I won't understand.'

'Well, where do they go?'

'I don't know, somewhere offsite. Down to the King's Highway, you know where all those bars are past the airport? I've never been out there myself. I don't think they're the kind of places women go.'

'You're telling me they go to brothels on Friday evenings?'

Colette looked stricken. 'I really don't know, I don't suppose they're actual *brothels*. They need to let off steam. I'm sure it's all harmless.'

'That depends. Which ones do they go to?'

'I know there's one called "The Pink Panther" or something like that. Ben's always had a habit of picking up matchbooks even though he doesn't smoke. I found one in his pocket.'

*　　*　　*

LEA WAITED UNTIL 6:00pm, then set off. Under normal circumstances, there would have been no question of trusting Roy, but lately they were being pushed further and further apart. She wanted to see where her husband went on Friday evenings.

She reached the strip just as the dipping sun had rippled and expanded, turning the horizon to a bilious shade of nylon pink. She had driven along the street once or twice before, but in daylight the dusty plastic bar-fronts were shuttered.

A neon arcade suddenly came to life, twinkling with phosphorescent geometries. Signs in Arabic and mangled English sought attention from passing cars. The Desert Bloom. The Whirlwind. Sexy Sexy. Arabian Nites. Fluorescent tubing crackled with errant electricity. Doorways were illuminated with faded photographs of Chinese girls in the kind of old-fashioned nightclub gowns she associated with drag queens. There were no direct calls to action, but the images were unmistakably clear; girls were available here.

The sidewalk was deserted; vehicles circled and slipped furtively into rear parking lots. Lea took a left turn and followed the route to the car park of a bar called Glamour Cocktails. At the back doors of the clubs, the inferences were more explicit. One sign said *Girls At Your Table – Private Rooms*. Another read *Oriental Or American – She Always Say Yes*.

Lea applied the handbrake and waited, watching. Two Korean girls in low-cut shiny red bikini tops, thongs and high heels came out to the back step to smoke. A young Indian man parked his truck and headed over to talk to them, but an older Korean woman appeared and ordered him around to the front of the club, determined to receive her commission.

Lea wondered what these places were like after midnight. She remembered what Rachel had said about Nepalese and Chinese girls working the strip. *I have to take a look inside*, she decided, getting out of the car.

She chose the emptiest-looking bar, whose neon Pink Pussy logo featured a cartoon cat with disturbingly human breasts lounging in a martini glass. Inside was a single rectangular room, painted purple, hung with incongruous Christmas lights, smelling of disinfectant and incense. An old Elton John song was playing on the bar's tinny sound system. Along the left-hand side was an American-style drinks counter with unoccupied swivel stools. In the centre of the room stood a square stage with a steel pole at each corner and a selection of mirror-balls hanging at different heights from the ceiling. An LED board displayed more cats with breasts, advanced technology conjuring the most juvenile fantasies.

She felt as if she had wandered onto a porno set before they had begun shooting. A line of gold-painted kitchen chairs were occupied by a few bored girls in red nylon gowns. Each one had a number on her wrist like a beauty contestant. Clearly the rush-hour had yet to start.

She was about to investigate further when a fat little Chinese woman started wheeling across the room in her direction.

'You husband not here, missus,' she shouted, flapping her hands as if batting away an annoying insect. 'Nothing for you here. You go home now!'

Mortified, Lea lost her nerve. Was the purpose of her visit that obvious? How many other wives had followed their husbands to the strip? Flustered, she turned and left, pacing past the gaudy venues lit purple and pink, the colour of bruised flesh.

Peering through the doors, she saw crimson interiors, straw lamps, metallic stages. In some, girls in one-piece swimsuits were penned into corners like mannequin displays awaiting removal from long-derelict department stores.

The last bar, Pussy Ranch, was themed like a spit-and-sawdust Wild West saloon. Above its counter fake ham-hocks hung in string bags, each with a garter attached so that they looked like severed thighs. It was early; the night's main activities had not yet begun, but men were already arriving to get the best tables.

She felt suddenly sick, and had to get away. Nothing Roy could say would dissuade her that these clubs were anything but brothels. She felt betrayed and disgusted, but there would be no way of resolving the issue without an argument that would paint her as the enemy.

Roy arrived home at ten as usual, but Lea could not bring herself to respond. He went to the refrigerator and rummaged for the ingredients of a sandwich before noticing the silence.

'Come on then, out with it,' he said finally, 'what's wrong now?'

It was important that she kept her temper. She tried to sound casual. 'I was talking to Colette and she mentioned you're allowed to finish early on Fridays. How long has this been going on?'

If Roy was surprised, he did not show it. 'Not long. It's a PR exercise. We don't really take advantage of it.'

'You mean you just stay at work?'

'We do for a while. Then we go for a few drinks.'

'To the bars on King's Highway.'

'We've only been there a couple of times.'

'They're whorehouses, Roy.'

'Some are. Some are strip-joints and some are just bars. The city's three-quarters male, honey. We put in long hours. There has to be some level of tolerance. You know how guys can get.'

'Is that how you get?'

'Jesus, Lea! We go there for a drink, that's all.'

'Which bars?'

'I don't know—a country and western-type place, a couple of others, one with a Mexican theme, I can't remember.'

'You could go to any number of hotel bars but you go out there.'

'The men don't want to pay the prices at hotel bars. They're not tourists, they're saving their earnings.'

'Aren't you meant to set some kind of moral example?'

'Morality only covers our work conduct, it doesn't control what goes on inside our heads.'

'If you're going there for any reason other than to have a drink with the boys, you really need to tell me right now.'

'Or you'll do what, Lea?' Roy's patience had run dry. 'What are you going to do? History is not going to repeat itself. I have a tough job. We all have to cut loose sometimes. You just have to trust me.'

'I want to believe you. I was prepared to fight for you before, but right now I don't know if I'd do it again. I love you, Roy, and I love Cara. But things feel different between the three of us now.'

'You're making too big a deal of this.'

She wanted a drink, a cigarette, anything but the conversation they were having. 'You know, when I was a girl I used to think that love was this fragile thing, but it's not. It's tough and strong, and it can survive almost anything. I just need a word from you to tell me we're okay.'

'Well, I thought we were. I don't tell you every little thing because I know how you get. Cara keeps her distance from you because you smother her. In the back of your head there's always the knowledge that you can't have another kid. Maybe you should explain that to her one day.'

'You know I want the time to be right—'

Roy suddenly rounded on her. 'You know why I don't tell you where I go? Because the bars are pretty seedy. We know what goes on here, a blind man could see they're hookers, we look and the conversation gets rough but that's all, nothing else. We're not stupid. We know what's important. Our wives. Our homes. Our families. Okay? Is that good enough for you?'

He popped a beer and headed out of the kitchen, into the pale moonlit garden. He was still standing there, looking up into the inky star-filled sky, when she went to bed.

Chapter Thirty-Two
The Stories

LEA AWOKE IN a sweat and looked at the bedside clock. 1:45am. She shook her head and tried to banish a tangle of dream-images: sunset neon, thin-armed girls in cheap satin gowns, Rachel wandering lost in the unforgiving glare of the desert. The blackened shell of the smouldering Busabi house. Somebody smiling in the dark. Somebody lying.

Roy was buried in pillows, snoring lightly, one brown arm trailing on the floor. There was no point in trying to get back to sleep. She got up and went to her desk to think. Andre Pignot had posted her new article on the *Gulf Coast* website, softening her prose. She logged onto Skype, just to see if anyone else was awake.

To her surprise, Betty Graham was online. She suddenly appeared in a ridiculously English pink quilted dressing gown, looking confused, as if she had only just discovered how to operate the application. There was an empty wine bottle and glass next to her.

'You're up late,' said Lea.

'I think the clock in the lounge is wrong,' said Betty. 'I'm always forgetting to wind it. I should get an electric one. What are you doing up? Hang on, you're upside down. Don't worry if I lose you, it just means I've pressed something.'

'I'm having trouble sleeping,' Lea admitted.

'I called you this afternoon but you were out. Did you hear, they sentenced Elena and Ramiro?'

'Your Ramiro?'

'Oh, please, don't call him that.' Betty shook the idea from her fingertips, anxious to forget the flirtation. 'A 2,000 dirham fine and one month in jail. But the worst part is, they're going to be deported upon release.'

'Sounds like they're sending us a message.'

'What do you mean?'

'Well, the police—about infidelity.'

'Oh. Gosh. I hadn't thought of that. Quite a few of the other women around here would miss Ramiro, I can tell you. I wasn't the only one who fell for his line. Are you okay? You don't look too good. Or perhaps it's my screen. I really need to clean it.'

'No, you're right, I feel unsettled.'

'I know that feeling, like a cat when it knows something bad is about to happen. I can't make sense of anything right now.'

'What's all that?' Lea pointed to the brightly coloured translucent objects lined along the table at the base of the screen.

'Oh—I'm making fruit jellies. I'm not a great cook but even I can make a jelly. These ones on the right have got gin in. I needed something to do while I was waiting for Dean. He still hasn't come home yet. He's meant to call me but he's not answering his mobile.'

'Have you two had another fight?'

'We don't fight exactly, we just sort of—disagree on everything. He's missing his father. He stays out late on school nights and never thinks to call. Harry knew how to control him.'

'Sounds like he's testing the boundaries, pushing back a bit. When's your husband due home?'

'In just under three months. Harry's allowed to take a weekend off once a month to come back and visit, but he's not using the time. He knows that when he returns we'll have to have a proper talk, and I honestly don't know what the outcome will be, whether we'll give it another go for Dean's sake or if we'll actually separate.'

'God, do you really think you might break up?'

'To be honest, it feels like we already have. I hardly ever see him. Dean knows what's going on. Kids always do. But I can't sort anything out until he gets here. I just feel as if I'm in limbo.' Betty looked around the room. 'Don't you hate this time of night? It's even quieter out there than usual. It sounds silly but I miss hearing sirens.'

'Yeah, me too. I'm keeping a diary, so sometimes when I wake up in the night I make a couple of entries, just until I'm tired. There's something here I didn't note down and was meaning to ask you. You said there was a Muslim family living on one side of you.'

'That's right, and Tom Chalmers and his poor wife were on the other.' Betty thought for a moment. 'It couldn't have been long before you arrived that Tom had his accident. He took his daughter's disappearance very badly—well, who wouldn't?'

'What was she like?'

'Oh, a pretty little thing. Very mature for her age, and far too smart.'

'Did the police ever say what they thought happened to her?'

'Well of course there were theories. There was talk of a sex attacker. They deported several construction workers. It was Milo who found Tom.'

'So I heard.'

'He was convinced Tom had been murdered. At least, that's what he used to say when he was drunk. Something about a voltage limiter. He said Tom couldn't have electrocuted himself, and there was blood on the pavement. He said he saw someone running off, but of course nobody believed him.'

'Why would he have been murdered?'

'Because he knew what really happened to his daughter. But you know what?' Betty leaned forward, sharing a confidence. 'There are always stories in places like this. They count for nothing.'

'Why do you think that?'

'Because nobody ever gets to know the truth, not the *real* truth. We sit around and speculate but we're on the outside. We're not important enough to be given answers. You just have to accept what happens and move on. Milo and Tom were both deeply unhappy men. Harry's the opposite, he thrives on the life out here. He never liked London, commuting by tube, the dirt, the noise, the overcrowding.'

Lea wondered if Betty's husband was one of the men who visited the brothels when his wife was not around.

'Lea, do you think everything's all right?'

'What do you mean?'

'It's just—everyone's so jumpy. Poor Rachel. And the Busabis' house. You look out in that street and it seems like everything is just the same as it always was. No matter how many bad things happen, none of them show. I try not to worry, but you can't help wondering—' She saw Betty look up, hearing something offscreen. 'Listen, Lea, I think Dean just came in. I have to go and read him the riot act. You'd better try and get some sleep.'

'Okay. Goodnight.'

Lea logged out and went to make herself a fruit smoothie. She stood before the picture window in the lounge, looking out into the dark, dead street. *The men love it and the women hate it,* she thought. *Of course we hate it. The men prosper and we vanish.*

All she could see was a reflection of herself in the window, framed in the bright empty square of the room behind. Her shadow stretched across the street, a negative space where a woman had once been.

THE WIVES' ACTION committee had finally decided on a name: the Dream World Grand Opening Gala Weekend Dinner. A meeting was hosted, somewhat reluctantly, by Betty Graham, whose maid provided the Patisserie Valerie cupcakes and a selection of fancy teas. Lea sat listening to the various arguments for and against a marquee, balloon and banners, an English menu versus an American menu, and found it hard to concentrate. Certain members were noticeable by their absence; no Mrs Busabi, no

Colette, a couple of other women had dropped out and several fresh faces had taken their place, interchangeable wives in pastel tops, one of whom seemed to have inherited Mrs Busabi's fixation on improperly rinsed salads.

Looking at the assembly, Lea knew that Rachel wouldn't have been caught dead here. The irony of meeting to discuss fancy dress outfits and table decorations after years spent fighting for women's rights and equal pay would not have been wasted on her.

'—don't you think, Mrs Brook?' said the lady opposite, and suddenly Lea realised that everyone was looking at her, waiting for an answer.

'I'm sorry,' said Lea, 'I didn't—'

'Mrs Garfield just suggested we could hold the dinner in the nursery hall, as it is air-conditioned and would save the cost of a marquee.'

'Wouldn't we have to clear it with someone?' asked Lea, trying to show an interest.

'Mrs Busabi handed over the responsibility for the hall's bookings to Mrs Garfield before she left, so I don't foresee any problems. Plus it has a kitchen, so the catering can be handled on-site.'

'And it's preferable to provide a hot food menu,' said the salad-rinse lady. 'We wouldn't want to find ourselves in a Spanish cucumber situation.'

Minutes were taken. Tea was drunk, cakes daintily devoured. The meeting broke into looser groups so that the wives could discuss other topics of the day; gardeners, book clubs, a swimming group, the creation of a weekly newsletter outlining progress.

'Perhaps you'd like to write that, Mrs Brook? You used to be some sort of writer, didn't you?' The woman asking the question was one of the new ones. Dressed by Jaeger, preserved by surgeons and pickled in a kind of venom peculiar to the English Home Counties, she leaned forward with a mean smile on her thin lips, waiting for an answer. This was Mrs Garfield, a career colonial married to a flight lieutenant whose exploits were followed by a ground-crew of reverential military housewives from the other side of the compound.

'I'll be happy to help out,' she heard herself saying.

'We'd do it ourselves, of course, only we'll be too busy with the physical arrangements.'

'Surprisingly, writing is a physical process too,' Lea said.

'I'm sure Mrs Garfield didn't mean to denigrate your abilities,' said the lady opposite, 'it's just that we're running short of time.'

'All you have to do is write down who's doing what in simple, clear terms,' said Mrs Garfield, as if talking to a particularly dense child. 'Do you think you could manage that for us?'

'I've done research on your husband's civilian bombing raids in Afghanistan,' said Lea, 'I think I could manage to remind you who's in charge of cupcakes.'

Savouring the massed floral recoil in the room, she rose and left.

GULF COAST'S WEBSITE had increased its visitor figures. A glance at the homepage revealed dozens of positive comments posted after the appearance of Lea's online article. When she rang Andre Pignot, he cautiously committed himself to a new piece. She had already thought of a subject: *The Human Cost Of Building Dream Worlds*.

'I think we'd need to talk about that title,' said Andre uncertainly.

'I can be there in half an hour,' Lea replied.

Visiting Andre in the Al Qusais area, she headed for the pungent, shabby café below his office on Creek Road. Most of the coffee houses were shut for the duration of Ramadan.

They seated themselves among the crisp linen *thobes* and sparkling *abayas* of the few non-observing Arabs who visited the blue-collar zone. After the bland European cakes and teas at Betty's house, the pungent aroma of Arabic coffee and honey-coated pastries was intoxicating. Lea ordered *basbousa* with almonds, and another with pistachios.

'I like your work,' said Andre, seating himself beside her. 'I didn't expect such a good response.'

'There aren't many forums where these kinds of discussions can take place,' she reminded him. 'There are various ways we can build reader loyalty.'

'That's what you want to do? Even though I can't pay you?'

'If I stop writing, I'm scared I might go rusty and forget how. You'll be doing me a favour. It would be interesting to know what people think about the psychology of living here. Nobody mentions that. It's fine for the locals—whenever someone drives off the road due to lack of sleep it's *Inshallah*, but nobody talks about how non-Muslims cope.'

'The will of God governs the land,' said Andre. 'We are merely guests here.'

'Then that's my angle. Stress is a subject everyone's interested in.'

'Fine, so long as we agree not to say that this is simply the fault of DWG. That would be misleading. There are international companies all along the Gulf coastline. A lot of people made their fortunes in the good times, then the ex-pats got trapped in negative equity. They started leaving their houses behind and abandoning their brand-new BMWs at the airport. I don't want you trying to point the finger of blame at anyone. We could get into serious trouble.'

'It's not about apportioning blame. We might be able to do some good.'

Andre thoughtfully sipped his coffee. 'All right,' he said finally, 'but remember, I'm running a lifestyle magazine, not the *Washington Post*.'

'I'll find a positive spin, I promise. Maybe list some meditation centres, spas, desert resorts, places where you can go to chill out.'

'That's a good idea. I heard you went to interview Leo Hardy.'

'Who told you?'

'He called me and suggested that I should reconsider my decision to employ you. He thinks you're some kind of Bolshevik troublemaker.'

'I'm afraid Mr Hardy and I got off to a bad start.'

'You might want to remember that Leo Hardy has the power to end your husband's contract,' said Andre. 'He was Alexei Petrovich's EPS for ten years.'

'EPS? What's that?'

'Executive Protection Specialist. It's a fancy title for a bodyguard. He's a former head of the South African Police. He's also the godfather of Petrovich's son.'

'I didn't know that.'

'So he's upset that he was never made a director.' Pignot drew a line on a napkin with his finger. 'It's because of the scandal.'

'What scandal?'

'The girl they found in the creek,' said Pignot, not looking up. 'She was unloaded from his jeep.'

'You're sure about that?'

'It's what people said.'

Lea was appalled. 'But wasn't anything done?'

'Hardy said the jeep had been taken the night before. The police met with the directors and after that nothing more was heard.'

'My husband was just made a director.'

'Don't think it entitles him to discuss anything with you. He'll report only to his fellow directors on the board. It's dangerous to speak out about such things. And you're a woman.'

'What does that mean?'

'That your opinion is invalid.'

She sat back. 'So everyone turned a blind eye.'

'You just arrived here and suddenly you want justice? Such things have gone on for hundreds of years. Go on and write your piece—just remember who we answer to.'

Lea took her leave. Cara was out with Norah and Lauren, and Roy called to warn her he would be working late. Relieved at not having to prepare an evening meal, she stood at the window and studied the lonely rectangle of light cast across the tarmac. Hardly any of the other houses were lit after 11:00pm.

I was never going to be a crusading journalist, she thought. *Are there even such people anymore? I met Milo and Rachel a handful of times. Really, what did they mean to me? We're all visitors here. Soon the resort will be open and we'll be back at home.*

She opened another bottle of Vivanco and drank it, the better to be angry with herself.

Distant lights striated the sky. The coastal development was busiest after dark. Trucks rolled back and forth along the promenade in relay, pouring gravel and rock into the giant jack-shaped seabreaks. The stars were obscured by the immense spotlights of the resort, just as the old gods were obliterated by the desires of their earthbound counterparts.

Lea wavered at the window, empty bottle in hand, breath condensing on the glass. *You've failed,* she told herself. *Failed as a mother. Failed as a wife. Failed yourself.*

Chapter Thirty-Three
The Dedication

For the DWG employees, time sped up until it was a blur of heated meetings and deadlines, snatched meals, naps, rising before dawn and returning long after midnight. Roy hardly ever spoke to his wife anymore. His eyes were focussed elsewhere, his mind far away. He heard parts of her sentences and tried to guess conversations, but Lea saw that it was a waste of time and resolved to stay out of his way until the resort was open.

The last of the building rubble was cleared from the site. The remaining planters were filled. The fountains were switched on. The plastic sheets came off the marble flooring. An army of cleaners moved in to dust and polish every brass rail, every gold-plated tap. One million bright blue LEDs were stretched in a plastic trellis over the atrium of the Persiana.

The guest list was confirmed. There were pop singers and football heroes, film stars and politicians, entourages and press agents. Flowers were flown in from Amsterdam, caviar from Russian, fireworks from China. Security reached a new level around the resort, with colour-coded passes and computer-readable ID badges. There were flaws in the system. The barcode readers that were meant to be installed at the gates of Dream Ranches failed to materialise, and extra security guards had to be hired to patrol the resort.

The Dream Ranches Opening Gala Weekend Dinner menu was planned without Lea's involvement. The compound's impenetrable pristine houses and immaculate lawns defeated her. The event would take place in the nursery under the guidance of the fearsome Mrs Garfield, who took pleasure in ordering the other wives around like field-troops.

Lea hunted for things to do. A small mountain of boxes and books had accumulated in the spare room since they had arrived, so she enlisted Lastri's help and together they bundled everything for the trash. As she sorted paperbacks into stacks, planning to take them to the children's centre, she came across the tattered volume Colette had given her.

She was certain she hadn't purchased it; she didn't collect rare books, and had only ever watched the film version. Turning it over, she tried to recall if she had ever seen it before. Either Rachel had confused her with someone else, which seemed unlikely, or she'd been sending her some kind of a message.

There were pictures of the crying old lion and a creepy, bald tin-man. The winged monkeys looked too jolly and Oz was just a castle. There were no soaring emerald towers to remind her of this city.

A terrible thought crossed her mind. Could Rachel have simply lost her wits and committed suicide?

The phone rang, making her jump.

Cara was stranded at the mall. 'The stupid ATM ate my card,' she said. 'Can you come and pick me up?'

'Oh honey, can't you take the bus?'

'I have *no cash*. That's why I was trying the ATM.'

'Okay, give me twenty minutes.' Lea leaned over the bannisters. 'Lastri, could you keep bagging everything while I pick up Cara?'

It had been a long time since her daughter had asked a favour of her, and she decided that the trip back from the mall would give them time to talk. But Cara proved as uncommunicative as usual, and instead of having a proper heart-to-heart they spoke of clothes and homework. Even the subject of the beach house seemed not to interest her. When they arrived back at the house, Cara headed straight for her bedroom.

'I've got an English essay to finish,' she called down. 'I have to imagine that a famous historical figure has written a book for future generations. Could I use Lady Gaga?'

A book by Lady Gaga, thought Lea with a sigh. *The book.* She ran upstairs to the spare room and searched, but it was gone.

'Lastri,' she called, 'did you take the books that were on the floor?'

'Yes, Miss.'

'Where are they?'

'I take them out to the garbage with the boxes. You want me throw them out, yes?'

She ran downstairs and out into the street. Looking around, she saw that the bins had been emptied. The truck had moved several houses up the road and was about to turn the corner. She ran after it. 'Wait,' she called, 'wait!' It was picking up speed.

'Please! Stop!'

The driver saw her coming and slowed down.

'I need to get something.' She pointed into the crusher.

'It is too late,' said the garbage man riding the rear of the truck, a white worker who sounded Polish. 'I am not allowed to open the back.'

'Please, it's very important.'

She remembered the folded bill she always kept in the pocket of her jeans for tips, and passed it to him. He looked at it, pocketed it and called out to the driver. The truck jerked to a stop. The driver pulled a red steel lever that opened the crushers at the rear of the truck.

The sweet, hot reek of garbage punched out into the still air. She climbed onto the fender and looked inside. There, behind several burst and leaking garbage bags she could see the box of books that she had intended to be taken to the children's centre.

'Wait, I'll get it,' said the garbage man, climbing inside. 'You're not allowed to go in there.' As he pulled the box toward him, it split. Half of it had already been crushed into a pulp.

'There,' she said, pointing, 'that's the one I need.' She could see the book's faded green cover, but it was soaked in something that looked like vinegar or oil. Half the pages were sodden. Clutching it to her chest, she ran back inside the house. The garbage man looked on in puzzlement.

Lea tried to unstick the reeking pages but they were too wet to pull apart. She saw now that Rachel had written something to her in violet fountain pen on the blank page after the title, but the ink had formed a Rorschach blot that rendered her words indecipherable. She needed to dry it out first, so she placed it in the back of the airing cupboard. After an hour the warmth had turned the page brown and brittle. Taking the volume to her study, she held the page beneath the desk light.

Lea

Look behind the curtain

Love

Rachel

There were no other markings on the pages. She settled herself on the end of the bed and began to read. In places, the narrative was very different to the film version. The wizard appeared to each of the main characters as something different: a horrible monster, a beautiful woman, a ball of flame. And the wicked witch tried to kill them by sending hungry wolves, and crows to peck out their eyes, and a storm of black bees to sting them to death. And there were no ruby slippers. Dorothy wore silver shoes, like Rachel's trainers.

She made a hot drink before continuing to the next chapter, but caught the arm of the sofa as she returned, sending the ginger cat mug to the floor. It shattered, spattering tea like a bloodstain over the tiles. Roy had bought her the mug in Spittalfields market soon after they met. Breaking it felt like a bad omen.

As Lea mopped up the mess, she thought about the inscription Rachel had written. Perhaps she felt she couldn't leave behind anything explicit in case someone else read it. But what did it mean?

The thought was pushed from her mind as doorbells began ringing.

Chapter Thirty-Four
The Accident

NEWS OF BEN Larvin's accident spread around the compound within minutes of its occurrence. It was impossible to contain. Long before the husbands had returned home, the wives had visited each other to compare notes.

Mrs Garfield's cookery class was interrupted by Mrs Busabi, making her first reappearance on this side of the compound since her house had burned down. She took a vicarious pleasure in informing everyone of the drama. It was not that she had anything against Ben Larvin, but to die like that, well, it had to be a case of negligence, and although the story was truly awful it tinged the bright dead days with the stain of scandal, and made her life a touch more exciting.

The first wave of gossip merely outlined the dreadful fate of the hypertense American. The second package of information, endlessly embellished and altered to fit the opinions of the spreader, described the circumstances of the tragedy, a collapse of some kind, legs trapped, screams, appalling injuries.

Naturally Mrs Busabi, who called at Lea's house next, ostensibly to collect money for the compound residents' sponsored run, had a theory involving immigrants. Thank God her timely petition had resulted in the underpass being blocked up. It was a disgrace that things had got this far, and who might be next? The company did nothing to ensure the safety and well-being of their executive employees and their families. They should all buy guns and keep them under their beds.

Lea listened with impatience, then did her best to remove Mrs Busabi from her kitchen. She needed to think. For the first time, seemingly random events began to take on a terrible geometry. The book preyed on her mind.

Colette's phone went straight to voicemail and her car was missing from the garage, so she was presumably at the hospital. Lea was tempted to head there, but was hardly likely to be welcomed. She decided to wait until Roy could accompany her.

'You hear about Norah's old man?'

'No, what's happened?'

'He only got fucking crushed flat, that's all,' said Martin Tamworth, unable to stop himself from grinning. Cara had been heading back from the beach house when he had come lolloping toward her. 'Hey, where is everyone?' he asked, looking around. The others had taken to avoiding him lately. 'A concrete pipe steamrollered him. There was a whole stack of them and the top one rolled down over him and turned his legs to mush. Imagine, man! How fucking gross is that?'

'Don't believe everything you hear,' said Cara.

'It's true, everyone's talking about it. Nobody knows why it fell. There might have been another pipe bomb. They're really easy to make. You and Norah are good at science. I bet even you could figure it out. I seen all that stuff you do.'

'What stuff?'

'Designs and shit. It can't be harder than building a website, right? Imagine being flattened! What are they gonna do at his funeral service, roll him into a cardboard tube? Where's Norah?'

'She's at the hospital, where do you think? said Cara in annoyance, pacing away across the sand.

'Right, of course. Hey, when you see her, can you ask for my Warhammer shirt back?'

Cara ignored him and kept on walking.

*   *   *

THE FOLLOWING MORNING, a little after 9am, a small group gathered in the antiseptic white waiting room at the Creek Hospital. It was becoming an uncomfortably familiar place. Hiromi Morioka found Roy and Lea waiting for news. 'I was in the area when Leo Hardy called me,' said Hiromi. 'Where's Colette? Is she all right?'

'I couldn't get hold of her. There's no reception here. We can't use phones because of the scanners,' said Lea. 'I just saw her out in the corridor talking to her son. Have you heard anything?'

'Ben's still unconscious.'

Lea blinked in surprise.

'They didn't expect him to survive the trauma, but apparently he's stabilising. I don't understand.' Hiromi sat down, defeated. 'How could this have happened? When the medics arrived they thought he was dead. His legs are shattered. They filled him full of antibiotics and gave him a transfusion, but it doesn't sound as if it was enough.'

'What do you mean, not enough?' asked Lea.

'Blood poisoning. They've completely removed his right leg from the hip, but even that may not halt the spread of infection.'

'—infection—'

'There was some untreated sewage in the ditch where he fell.'

'But if he's alive there might be something I can do for the family.'

'I think Colette is in shock,' said Hiromi. 'She doesn't want to see anyone.'

'Ben knew his way around the place,' said Roy. 'He knew the risks. It's a good job Leo was on site when it happened. You're not supposed to try and fix things yourself without someone else there.'

'You didn't tell me you'd spoken to Leo Hardy,' said Lea. 'What was he doing there so late?'

'Christ, I don't know, Lea.' Roy tried to think. 'He's always around. He's upset that he couldn't do more for Ben.'

'Do you think this was negligence?'

'It was an *accident*,' Roy replied, 'but someone from their team should have checked that everything was okay. Ben shouldn't have been down there by himself.'

'That poor family,' said Lea. 'Doesn't it seem odd to you that this pipe-thing should suddenly go wrong just when he was near it?'

'Sometimes if you need to check on something and there's no access ladder you hang onto the nearest pipe. Maybe it came away. They're stabilised with steel ties but the ties can sometimes expand in the heat. Nobody knows the truth yet, okay?'

As Colette came back into the waiting area it was clear she had overheard the last part of the conversation. 'You know the truth as well as I do,' she told Roy. 'If my husband lives, it'll be without his legs. He's thirty-nine, for God's sake. This isn't about someone forgetting to put a tick on a timesheet. There was no-one on duty. Nobody ever accuses Leo or his cronies in the police.'

'Leo is as shocked as the rest of us,' said Roy. 'I'll make sure Ben gets the best care available. And he'll be granted the maximum compensation allowed.'

'I didn't know you and Leo were such close buddies,' said Colette. 'When you next speak to your homie, you can tell him I'm hiring the best damned lawyer I can find—a real East Coast shark—and I'll find out exactly who is responsible for Ben's injuries. I'll find out what's going on around here if I have to shut down the entire fucking resort to do it. Excuse me, I have another meeting with the physician scheduled in a few minutes.'

Turning away from the waiting group, she marched off toward the ward doors.

'Roy, I'm going outside for a cigarette,' said Lea.

'When did you start smoking again?'

'I never stopped, I just don't do it in front of you. I figure we shouldn't keep any secrets from one another. You should try it. Smoking, I mean.'

She stepped through the tinted glass doors and stood in the last of the evening light, lighting up and angrily savouring the smoke in her mouth. The endless shifting of blame changed nothing. She knew what was expected of her; to show no concern and mind her own business.

An engorged red sun sank below the horizon in a haze of smoky pink pollution. Feeling slightly sick, she ground out the cigarette and returned to the waiting room. Something had been bothering her for hours.

Roy was talking with Hardy and an elegant Arabic man she had not seen before. She waited for a break in the conversation and touched Roy's arm.

'Where were you?' she asked.

Roy looked confused. 'What do you mean?'

'When Ben had his accident. You called to say you were working late, but I tried your mobile and got no signal.'

'I was working over at the main office. I went for a quick drink with a couple of the lads.'

'Which ones? Are they here?'

'No, Lea, you don't know everyone I work with. What's the matter with you?'

She sighed wearily. 'It's as if everything's become poisoned here. In case it's escaped your attention, we're being decimated, family by family. Anyone with a disagreeable opinion is being removed. For all you know, I could be next.'

'You spend too much time at that computer. All that imagination's not good for you.'

'I'm writing about this place,' she told him. 'I'm putting down what I see.'

'Maybe you should take up a different kind of hobby and renew your sleeping pill prescription.' He turned away to catch something Hardy had said.

'Thanks for the advice,' she said aloud, digging out her keys and heading for the door.

Chapter Thirty-Five
Dream World

EVEN WITH THE help of some of the area's best doctors, the infection in the tissue of Ben Larvin's remaining leg proved too virulent to bring under control. By the time it subsided, he had also lost his left below the knee. His therapy sessions were expected to last many months, but his state of mind was of greater concern. He had sustained serious head injuries, and would have to undergo months of cognitive testing. His wife remained at home with the blinds drawn, and stopped speaking to any of her neighbours.

Lea searched the web for any details about the accident. All she found was Colette's own angry account on her blog.

Elsewhere, as August came to a close, the surface of life returned to normality. The swimming pool was repaired and refilled. A wooden construction fence went up around the remains of the Busabi house. New smart-ID cards were printed, but proved hopelessly faulty. Extra guards were placed at the entrances to the compound and the resort, and a strange late-summer lassitude descended upon the area.

The heat outside was beyond endurance. Lea was tired of spending her time scurrying between ice-blasted public buildings as if sheltering from meteor showers. The wives reduced their visits to one another's houses, as if they could no longer be bothered to keep up the pretence of friendliness. Mrs Garfield took to holding court at the golf club on Friday lunchtimes with the other military wives. Only the children maintained their loyalties to one another, living separate lives.

Their worlds were disconnected now, and Lea wondered what it would take to repair the damage. As the final countdown to Dream World's September opening began, Roy spent most of his waking hours at the resort. During the weekends he seemed distracted and barely capable of speech. If Lea interrupted him, he would look at her as if trying to place her name.

Their plans to visit other states or take trips into the desert evaporated. Even a trip to the movies seemed impossible to organise. She knew it wasn't just her family who was affected; life for everyone in the compound was deeply and irrevocably altered. Standing at the window, she sometimes thought she could sense its pattern brushing at her fingertips, only to feel it dissolve.

Ramadan came to an end. The celebration of *Iftar* took place on the last evening of the month-long fast. After dark, meals would be laid out all across the city. Muslims were heading home to be with their families. There were just three weeks left before the resort's grand opening. In the cool shadows of their courtyards the Arab women prepared their feasts. At the Dream World resort, workmen erected the steel bleachers for their honoured guests. A stadium stage had been constructed in front of the Persiana, but without its decorative lights turned on it looked more like an arena designed for public executions.

One afternoon the doorbell rang, making Lea start. Madeline Davenport stood on the step with a snuffling highland terrier on a plaid lead. She stared down at the dog as if waiting for it to improve its behaviour.

'I hope I'm not disturbing you,' she began. 'I was just passing. I wonder—can I come in for a minute? Outside it's too—' She looked around uncertainly.

'Of course, please come in.' Lea stepped back.

'I haven't spoken to many of the neighbours since Mr Larvin's accident. I imagine Colette has her hands full and I wouldn't want to interfere.'

'Let's go in the kitchen. I think Lastri has a coffee pot brewing.' She led the way.

Madeline set down her dog and lowered her wide-beamed bulk onto a bench. She looked as if she was about to speak, but suddenly stopped herself.

Lea tried to help. 'Roy and I have been to the hospital a few times. There hasn't been much change in Ben's condition. He's on so much medication that he doesn't know you're in the room with him. He's dosed up for pain control and depression.'

'The poor man, one feels so helpless,' said Madeline. She sipped her coffee, watching the dog. Lea was puzzled as to why she had stopped by. She waited for her to explain the purpose of her visit.

'I'm staying for the opening, then going home for a good long holiday at the end of the month,' she said finally. 'I know Colette was planning a break too, but she won't be able to take it now. I was wondering if we wives couldn't do something to help that poor family.'

'What did you have in mind?' Lea asked.

'Well, they'll have to get the house refitted with wheelchair ramps and special handles in the bathroom, things like that. If DWG isn't taking care of it quickly enough we can hire someone to carry out the work. You know, to save Colette from having to worry about it. I heard the company has been very generous with compensation, but money's not the answer really, is it?

'I'm glad that DWG recognised they were in some way culpable.'

'Did you hear about the results of the enquiry?'

'I didn't know there had been one.'

'James told me, so I don't suppose it's a secret. There was an electrical fire and it burned through the cables holding the pipe in place. He explained the whole thing to me in great detail but how it happened hardly matters, does it? It can't change anything. I just wondered—' Lea waited for her to continue, but Madeline was struggling with her words. 'You see, there's been a lot of talk. About the accidents, I mean. It's just that—there's a rumour that Leo Hardy was with Ben that night—and I thought you might have heard about it.' Madeline Davenport had always championed the company. Lea wondered if something had happened to mitigate her opinion.

'I believe he was, yes.'

'Because Mr Hardy was with my husband as well, just a short while before the accident happened.' Madeline twisted her hands together in her lap. 'James saw the pair of them talking just before Ben Larvin went down to the pipeworks. He says Leo Hardy summoned Ben to the resort and sent him in.'

'You think Hardy knows more about what happened than he's letting on, is that it?'

'Lord, I wouldn't want to get anyone into trouble, I just keep going over the sequence of events in my head. But if you do know anything, perhaps we should tell someone.'

'Roy never mentioned it.'

'I've just been trying to understand. People think the workmen are deliberately sabotaging the project, but that doesn't make sense to me. I mean, it's their livelihood, isn't it? Why would they want to destroy their own jobs? They have so many dependents. It's Mr Hardy I don't trust. What if he had a reason for wanting to get rid of poor Ben Larvin? Don't tell me, I know I'm being stupid. We've all become so—*suspicious*. And now here I am, virtually accusing a man of murder. It was never like this before. I must get back.' She rose to leave. Lea stood watching her, unsure as to whether she had just been accused.

Madeline paused on the doorstep and turned. 'It never seems to upset the men, does it? They just get on with their work. I've hardly seen James since he got promoted.'

'He was promoted as well?'

'I think it incentivises them, being taken into the board's confidence. It makes them feel powerful,' said Madeleine. 'They can do whatever they like. I sent Colette a note asking if she needed anything. That's all any of us can do, isn't it? After all, we're only the wives.'

The wives, she thought. *You're all living in a dream world.*

*   *   *

THE CURTAINS WERE drawn, making the house look like it had been closed up for the summer. Lea rang the bell and stepped back. She was about to give up when the door opened a few inches. Colette blinked out into the fierce light. She looked as if she had just been aroused from a troubled sleep.

'I'm sorry, Colette, I wondered if I could have a word with you? It's important.'

The door opened a fraction further. Slipping inside, Lea found the Larvin household dark and icy. The maid kept everything so tidy that it seemed as if no-one lived there.

'I'm sorry, I don't know what—' Colette stopped and corrected herself. 'I was going to say I don't know what you must think of me, but to be honest I don't care what anyone thinks. This is how things are now.'

'How are Abbi and Norah doing?'

'You know Norah. She spends most of her time with her own friends, why would she want to be here? And Abbi's on the other side of the world.' She looked around, pushing her hair back in place. 'What was it you wanted?'

'I know it sounds odd, but if I wondered if I could have a look at Rachel's room. I think it would be easier to explain afterwards.'

The request clearly took Colette aback. 'I tidied up her room after she died. It was a tip,' she said, mystified. Her arms folded in suspicion. 'Why do you want to see it?'

Can I trust her? thought Lea. 'It's nothing, just a silly thing really, but I need to put my mind at rest.'

'I don't know what you hope to find there, but go ahead, knock yourself out.' Colette threw her a mean stare. 'Oh, and my husband, thanks for asking, is never going to fully recover from his accident.'

'I went to the hospital to see him just two days ago, Colette. I just missed you. And Roy has been to see him regularly.'

'I know, everyone's been very *kind*.' She made it sound like a bad thing. 'Then you know he's not responding very well. There have been other complications. His immune system—' Her face suddenly crumpled. 'Fuck. Fuck, I'm sorry. I don't know what's happening, Lea. I really don't.'

'It's okay, Colette, nobody expects you to be superwoman...'

'I can't get any kind of a handle on it. The doctors say he'll eventually walk with the aid of prosthetics, that he'll be able to lead some semblance of a normal life if he wants to, but they can't say what he'll be like inside. And right now he doesn't want to live. Who will he be? Not the man I knew and fell in love with. I know it sounds terrible, but I'm not strong enough for this. I think about it and feel sick.'

'Perhaps you'll feel different given time.'

'No, I know I won't. Rachel's death affected him so badly, and now this has torn him apart. How could everything have changed so fast? He so wanted to see the resort open. He was so proud to have been taken into the confidence of the board of directors. They told me to attend the opening, to make a show, but I can't be there without him.' She started crying again.

Lea could not bear to see her so distraught. 'The book you returned to me from Rachel,' she said. 'It wasn't mine. I think you should have it back. I don't know why she wanted me to have it.'

Colette drew herself up, trying to listen. 'Rachel was kind of weird toward the end. She drank too much and believed all kinds of stuff.'

'Like what?'

'Spirits, legends, conspiracy theories, I don't know. She was difficult with the kids, filling their heads with crazy ideas. She wasn't good with technology and had trouble loading apps on her phone, so she asked Ben to get her a paper map of the Dream World site.'

'Why would she do that?'

'I honestly have no idea. Look, Lea, I know you're searching for something too, but it isn't here.'

'I'm just trying to make sense—'

Colette had not heard her. 'In the early days Rachel and I used to go down to the site with Ben and he would point out where everything was going to be, and I just couldn't imagine these great silver buildings rising up into the sky. But he could. He only had to look at the floor plans and he could see the finished resort.'

'Maybe she was just trying to connect things too. I promise I'll let you know if I do find anything.'

'Her room is up there, first left. I don't go in it.'

The blinds were drawn upstairs as well. Lea made her way along the shadowed passage and tried the door. Rachel's room was sparse and neat. There was a hint of lavender and patchouli oil in the dead air. Her fountain pen lay on a table beneath the window, but there was no accompanying stationery of any kind. A bookcase was filled with volumes of philosophy, biography, various social sciences. There were a few trashy paperbacks— virtually the only physical reading material that could be purchased without a trip to the immense Kinokuniya bookstore. The wastepaper basket under the table had been emptied. In the drawer beneath the table she found a fold-out map of the coastline, and took it.

How long had Rachel sensed that something was wrong? Lea opened her desk diary and flipped through the pages, hoping to find something of interest, but only the most mundane notes appeared.

Buy conditioner

Post sweater

Birthday present—DW North

Dream World North. The four towers that were set to house the resort's signature restaurants, arranged at the four points of the compass. She vaguely recalled a conversation about the North tower. Roy had mentioned it some time back, but in what context? Why would Rachel be taking a birthday present there? If there was an answer here, it didn't easily show itself. She returned downstairs.

Colette looked as if she'd been crying. Rachel was tempted to put an arm around her, but as she stepped forward she saw Colette flinch. 'Did Rachel buy a birthday present for someone the week before she died?' she asked.

Colette dried her eyes with the back of her sleeve. 'I don't know. She was very independent. She did all her own shopping, never came to the mall with us. She never quite turned her back on her hippy years. She drove out to California in a VW van in the sixties and met her first husband there. Smoked too much pot and burned her bra. She thought she was liberated. I thought she was ridiculous.'

'Well, thanks anyway,' said Lea, turning to go. A thought struck her. 'How much longer are they going to keep Ben in?'

'I don't know yet. Mostly he sleeps. If he doesn't start his rehabilitation therapy soon the doctors are worried that his long-term prospects will be affected.'

'When is his birthday?'

'Not for another two months. Why do you want to know if Rachel was buying gifts?'

Lea shook her head. 'Sorry, it's just something she mentioned, a crazy idea. It's really nothing.'

'She sent a hideous sweater to her brother John in Ohio, and it was Norah's birthday the week she before died,' Colette volunteered. 'Rachel doted on her, always spent way too much money.'

'What did she get her?'

'A new laptop. Norah maxed out the memory on her old one. Rachel took it to the beach house to surprise her.'

'Why there?'

'Your husband had his carpenters come in and set everything up. You must know more about it than me.'

'No—I don't.'

'Norah shouted at me because I unplugged the cables in her bedroom to clean behind the desk. So I suggested she went to hang out with your daughter at the beach house in the evenings, while Roy and Ben were finishing up.'

'I knew Roy said that Cara could take friends there. The sweater for her brother—she posted it?

'No. She hated waiting in line at the post office and she was near the resort. I think she took it to Ben to post. You know, using the internal system.'

'Thanks, Colette. I'll catch you later.'

She stepped outside into the heat-bath, and darted back to the lighter chill of her own house. In the hallway she stopped and caught sight of herself in the mirror.

Colette thought her mother-in-law was crazy. But she hadn't been crazy. She'd been frightened. She'd gone to the North Tower to give Ben the package containing the sweater. Then she had returned home and written an inscription to Lea in the book of fantastical nonsense. What had happened in between those two events?

Her skin prickled in the air-conditioned chill of the kitchen. Rachel couldn't risk coming to talk to her. She feared she was going mad, or feared something else. Something within the resort's maze of tailored lawns, flowerbeds and fountains. Something hidden in plain sight that she alone had spotted.

The evening light was fading. Lea picked up Rachel's book, searched for her car keys and headed to the garage.

Chapter Thirty-Six
The Heart

AT THE EXIT gate of the compound she was stopped while her departure details were laboriously logged by listless teenaged guards. Lea waited impatiently as the boy hunched over his notebook, writing longhand, the tip of his tongue between his teeth, finally stamping it and releasing her. Wiring hung from the guardhouse counter, awaiting to be attached to a barcode-reader.

The sun had started to set as she drove toward the resort, passing in the opposite direction of traffic leaving the business district of the city. Streams of light swagged the hoods and roofs of the vehicles that pulsed along the highway, a golden river that passed through the financial canyons like the flow of passing money. The drivers were mostly men in dark suits or *kanduras,* their eyes hidden behind reflective aviator glasses. They were living the dream.

Mist had smudged the horizon, removing the distinction between sea and sky. Slowly, the glass and steel towers of the DWG complex stretched themselves across her windscreen. She spun the wheel and turned away from the shining highway, onto the site, drawing up to the intimidating new steel security barriers set in a concrete platform on the road.

An immense bank of steel bleachers ran beside the road for the entire length of the resort perimeter. Workmen were still bolting together hospitality marquees, bars and boxes for the invited VIPs.

She showed her laminated ID card at the red and white security booths. After a lengthy period of examination, the guards punched buttons that lowered the wedge-shaped ramp and raised the barriers.

'From midnight tonight the entire resort is off-limits to everyone,' one of them told her.

The resort was almost deserted. Perhaps inside the chilled control rooms and service corridors staff scurried back and forth, but the overall atmosphere was of orderly calm.

The four observation towers marked the boundary lines of the resort like *campaniles*. Much of the area had been cordoned off in order to prevent the invited guests from wandering into other parts of the resort. Her path took her through a forest of purple bougainvillea and perfumed white night-flowers.

She knew that Roy had been occupying an area on the seventh floor of the North tower, and that Ben most likely had an office on the same level, so it made sense to try there. The main plaza was deserted; it was still too hot to spend any more time than was absolutely necessary outside. She searched the windows of the surrounding buildings but saw no-one.

Most of the exterior work had now been completed. Inside the buildings, trunking was being routed through floors and ceilings, marble had been polished and the last few chandeliers were wired in. Somewhere an angle-grinder yowled and scratched. When it ceased, the site fell completely silent, but there had to be men somewhere, burrowed deep below the gardens, in the delivery tunnels, in the maintenance rooms.

She parked and walked to the sea-facing tower. Emerald lizards darted across her path like rush-hour pedestrians. The main doors were unguarded but the bank of silver elevators was taped off, so she searched around for another way up. The shining marble halls reminded her of a grand mausoleum, a monument to a forgotten race. In the centre of the hall stood the immense figure, a leaping athlete carved in indigo glass, his musculature as sharply defined as the compressor blades of a jet engine. He rose from a sunburst of inlaid flooring to tower above visitors' heads, like a shrine to a dead dictator.

Passing beneath the statue, she found herself facing a glass observation elevator. The main security CCTV globes would have already noted her features by now and matched them to a list of personnel permitted to visit the site. Her ID card opened the doors.

The gleaming curved pod rose smoothly to the seventh floor, the doors opening to reveal ice-blue walls. The hiss of air-conditioning was discernable through the partially exposed ceiling cavities.

Apparently Roy was attending a meeting in the city's garment district to talk about the tracking for the thirty-metre curtains that would eventually screen the Persiana's atrium. She tried his number but the call went directly to voicemail.

His office was on the shore side of the great open floor. The architects' cubicles were filled with building plans, meticulously constructed working models and half-eaten meals in cardboard boxes. She found his briefcase and papers scattered around his computer. Picking up his favourite work-shirt, she carefully folded it on a chair. It smelled of sweat and Dior aftershave.

In one drawer she found a set of swipe cards in a plastic wallet with his ID on the back, along with a photograph of the three of them, taken when Cara was a baby in the garden in Chiswick, in happier times.

She went to the window and looked down into the settling darkness. The view of the vast brown land was extraordinary. From here you could be forgiven for believing that you were the king, living far above your subjects, surveying all that you owned. As she removed her hands from the glass, her palm-prints evaporated like ghosts.

On the other side was an immense quadrangle bordered with clipped trees, steel walkways, newly planted date palms, arabesques of copper fountain jets. Mosaic murals were arranged in low geometries. The final plants had gone in, the auto-watering system installed.

I'm missing something, she thought. *I have to see it through*

Rachel's eyes. She hadn't come here looking for anything—it had jumped out and caught her attention.

She took out the map and unfolded the single sheet. It felt like years since she had opened an old-fashioned paper map, and orienting herself on it proved difficult. Rachel had ringed a building in blue biro. She turned slowly around, examining the resort's perfectly symmetrical ground plan, but could see nothing that matched it.

Her iPhone rang, startling her. She checked the name on the screen: Leo Hardy.

She froze. It seemed to her that Hardy appeared whenever anything bad was about to happen. She caught the call just before it went to voicemail.

'Mr Hardy.'

'Mrs Brook, I need to find your husband quickly, but he's not answering his phone. Do you know where he is?'

'He's at a meeting in the old town, something to do with the screens for the atrium, and he has other appointments after that. I didn't really expect to hear from him today, with the opening coming up.' She looked out at the aquamarine sky, wondering how Hardy had got hold of her number. He had never rung it before. 'Why? Is there a problem?'

'I have to talk to him.' A pause. 'Where are you?'

'I'm—' She thought for a moment. Something made her lie, even though she knew the lie could be found out. 'I'm at the Mirdif Mall.'

'I think you need to get back to the compound.'

'I still have quite a bit of shopping to do.'

'Are you alone?'

'Yes, why?'

'I'm not sure it's safe for you to stay out by yourself.'

'That's ridiculous, I come here by myself all the time.'

'I'll send someone for you.'

'No, it's fine. What's wrong?'

'I need to discuss this with your husband—'

'I'll go home as soon as I've finished.'

'All right, but get Roy to call me as soon as you hear from him, ya?'

She rang off and went back to the window, looking down at the concrete patterns below, wondering who to call for help.

Behind the buildings, the dying day held the glowing contrails of arriving flights, sewn across the sky like golden threads. The first stars of the evening were starting to appear. The constellations seemed as ordered as the grounds below. A pair of workmen in green resort overalls walked across a connecting bridge, vanishing into a side entrance of the Persiana.

Rachel had come to deliver the sweater to Ben and had looked out on this scene, the very heart of Dream World. Then she'd gone home and left the house early on Wednesday morning. Colette said she went to the desert whenever she needed to clear her mind. Rachel couldn't decide who to talk to. Why not? Because she had no idea who to trust anymore. Lea felt her stomach shift as phantoms stepped from the shadows. *What did you see, Rachel?* she wondered. *What did you realise when you looked out on all this?*

On an octagonal concrete building behind the flowerbeds, an exuberant mosaic pattern had been engraved in emerald green tiles. A row of sprinklers fussed into life, popping and fizzing as they doused the hibiscus bushes and acacias, splashing the main concourse between the landscaped gardens. The walls of the building darkened like poisonous night blooms.

She checked Rachel's map again. She had ringed the octagonal building. Next to the circle she had written something that looked like: *2,400 yards*. No, not yards, *years*.

Sealed behind glass in the air-conditioned tower, Lea rubbed her shivering shoulders. She headed downstairs. In the reception area of the hall that bordered the North tower, a guard sat behind a hectare of grained glass and stared blankly at his phone, like an electrical device waiting to be powered up. He barely took in what she had started to say.

'My husband, Roy Brook, he might return here tonight. It's important that you get him to call me straight away. I can't get hold of him.'

'It's very busy,' he told her. 'Everyone is in meetings. For tomorrow. You can leave a message.' He slid a pad toward her and indicated that she should write the message. She scrawled a hasty note, passed it back across the desk and headed outside, running across to the green-tiled building.

Colette had told her that she and Rachel regularly came here and watched Ben pore over the plans for the resort. What was so special about this place?

The building was little more than a concrete stump, probably an air vent of some kind. An unassuming iron door marked its entrance. As she got closer, she saw that its swipe-card box had been disconnected and the lock had been drilled out. In the last-minute rush to change all of the pass-protected doors, it had not yet been re-sealed. It opened easily, but with a metallic whine.

Without thinking twice, she stepped inside the vault.

Chapter Thirty-Seven
The Conspiracy Of Men

THE DARKNESS WAS so palpable that she hardly dared move for fear of falling. She turned on her cell phone and used it as a torch. The interior was disappointing, a bare space with some stacked gardening implements. A black square on the floor.

The square turned out to be an unlit stairwell. There were wall-lamps, but she could not find a switch. She held out the cell phone but its feeble light illuminated nothing.

There was nothing sinister here. A flight of clean stone steps, bare walls, no handrail, the smell of bleach. She descended slowly.

A small low-ceilinged vault, blank, empty and dull. Some gritty sand on the floor. A square iron grating set in the floor. A couple of channels leading away from it. Flood drainage. Her torch followed the wall. Another staircase down, half as wide as the last. She listened and heard no-one, nothing. These steps were wooden and creaked. They led beneath the grating.

This room was smaller still. There was nothing to see here either. Standing beneath the iron grille, she knelt and placed her hands flat on the floor. It was soothingly cold and wet. That was to be expected, she supposed—it was below sea level. Around the edges of the room was the sludge of drainage, just run-off. It was all very disappointing.

Under her phone-light, she looked at her fingertips and saw that they were covered in blood.

No, not blood—rust. Wet rust from the grating.

She searched the floor again, using her phone. In one corner, caught down a narrow crevice, something shone dully. A short piece of chain. For no particular reason, she pocketed it.

At the back of the room was a standard metal door with a fire exit bar. Pushing it, she found herself in an ordinary service corridor with an automatic lighting system that detected her presence and flickered on. The floor and ceiling were tiled cheaply and plainly. The pale blue illumination made her feel as if she was moving underwater.

At the end of the long corridor was an extravagantly panelled hardwood door, an absurdity considering its location. Digging into her jeans, she removed the plastic wallet she had taken from Roy's desk and tried the swipe card.

The door swung back in silence, its automatic lighting revealing a blandly decorated foyer partitioned off by a floor-to-ceiling red curtain. She pulled the curtain aside, feeling like Bluebeard's wife, expecting the worst.

Instead she found herself looking at some sparse white leather Italian furniture, two tall steel lamps, a fan of design magazines on a marble table, several plush rugs in teal and stone, a panoramic glass wall of the city and the sea which proved to be fake dioramas discreetly illuminated by LEDs. It could have been the room from the photographs in Milo's bin.

At the back of the main living room was a large bedroom furnished with photographic blow-ups of Bedouin women in traditional head-dresses. The bathroom had empty cabinets and freshly folded towels. There was nothing more to see.

She left the same way she entered, from the octagonal vault, and skirted the deepening shadows that had dropped across the resort grounds like chasms.

The rust beneath her fingernails still looked like blood.

Driving away from the coast, she caught the heavy homegoing traffic and sat creeping forward, anxiously waiting for lights to change. Her head was filled with lies and betrayals.

The lights changed and she edged the Renault ahead. *Move*, she wanted to yell at the Porsche in front. The traffic filtered to a single lane, where a pair of mirror-shaded cops bent to see through car windshields before waving them on. It was impossible to tell what they might be looking for. They barely glanced at her, a woman no longer young, before moving to the next vehicle.

Fears looped themselves through her mind. Rachel had figured something out. She had gone to the desert, planning to return that day because she had taken no spare clothes with her. Couldn't she have talked to the authorities? No, she was worried that she wouldn't be believed. *The crazy grandmother who gets drunk with Milo at parties.*

As the road widened again she stepped on the accelerator, opening the window as she overtook, feeling the hot sea air on her sweating face. The book with the faded green cover was still lying on the passenger seat.

The book.

She pulled the Renault over so suddenly that the Mercedes behind her gave a long, angry blast on his horn. As she tipped to a stop, a cloud of dust settled over the car, then drifted across the road to the sands.

She threw the hardback open and flicked through the pages. Dorothy, the Tin Man, the Scarecrow, the Cowardly Lion. The Wonderful Wizard.

Look behind the curtain, Rachel had written. What had she been trying to tell her? Had she seen the story as some kind of parable? Oz, the distant land into which they had all been blown, including the wizard himself, a carnival trickster who set himself up as its all-powerful ruler.

If you wanted to become all-powerful, what would you do?

The Renault rocked violently as a truck roared past.

She looked down at the illustration once more.

The Emerald City. The people of Oz. The visitors.

Reaching for her phone, she typed an address into it. An instant later the shimmering DWG website unfolded. She flicked beyond the home page to a display of the company's corporate structure, represented in a scrolling, spidery graph.

At its head was the cabal of directors, existing only as a company logo, a neat little gravatar, a hotlink revealing no more than a basic paragraph about the founders, Oxford and Harvard educations, corporate fellowships and societies, the kind of undetailed information James Davenport was paid to invent on a daily basis. There were no other names or images. None at all.

As she glanced back at the book and studied the drawing again, it became clear that she had made a mistake.

The Wonderful Wizard of Oz did not blow in from a far-off place and reinvent himself. He was created to control Oz.

There was no such man as the Wonderful Wizard. There were only the company's directors. The conspiracy of men, an exclusive group with unlimited power. They could enter the room via the vault whenever it pleased them. They could do whatever they wanted, and take whoever they liked there.

Abuse, destroy, conceal. The way of all those who controlled worlds.

Chapter Thirty-Eight
The Secret History

LEA PULLED INTO the car park of the Dubai National Geographical Institute and turned off her engine. Like the rest of the city's municipal buildings it was monumental yet somehow understated, as if the architects sought to misdirect people away from it.

A woman at the front desk issued her with a visitor's pass and allowed her into the public archive, a pristine area which looked as if it had not been visited by anyone since it opened. Illuminated glass displays explained the history of the city and its region, but there was no-one to read their story.

Finding maps on the coastal region was easy enough, but the electronic files only referenced the present. To follow the timeline back she had to go into the print archives, a series of tall blue steel cabinets on tracks that traversed the lower ground floor, sharing the space with a library.

The strange thing was, it wasn't at all hard to find. It featured on every map and diagram, in every sketch and fanciful painting, a circular stone dwelling that had once stood at the edge of the ocean, with a cart-track leading from it to the only tall rock in the area. An aerial photograph taken two years before the work on Dream World began showed the blurred outline of a circle submerged beneath a veil of sand. It was captioned: *Ancient meeting-place of the Ka'al*. She found a young attendant and asked him.

'It is probably a tribal reference,' he told her solemnly. 'Please follow me.' He led the way to a glass temperature-controlled room and unlocked the door. 'You must wear gloves for these books.' He brought her a pair of white cotton gloves tied with a blue cardboard band, then set out a large album covered in grey linen. It was published in 1892 but she supposed that in a city like this, which had only existed for a handful of years, it must have seemed like an ancient artefact. She read.

The first human settlement in Dubai was in approximately 3000 BC, when the area was inhabited by nomadic cattle herders. In the 1st century AD the Ka'al (lit: 'Men of the Sand') became the first known tribe to stay in the coastal area. Their elders met in a small circular building (Site A attached to Site B), the High Rock, where sacrifices were made to the sun. In the 3rd century AD, the area came under the control of the Sassinid Empire which lasted until the 7th century, when the Umayyad Caliphate took control and introduced Islam to the area.

Ka'al Tribe: Secretive tribal settlement whose members were periodically wiped out due to public disapproval of their sacrificial practices. The Ka'al believed that prosperity could be assured by virgin slaughter. Ka'al elders held positions of high tribal status. The cult returned in considerable numbers in 430, 1200, 1560 and at other times later still before being finally eradicated. The last known adherents of Ka'al rituals died in 1908. Members of the Ka'al could be recognized by a ceremonial burn-mark made on the left arm. Their status may be derived from a more mythological meaning of 'Ka'al', suggesting 'doom' or 'doomsayer', one who grows strong by dooming others of lesser, more innocent status.

In his book Corruption of The Gods *Dr Omar Shamon explains how the Ka'al sought to infiltrate the ranks of local property owners in order to buy land and establish permanent bases, therefore providing sites for commerce.*

Modern-day re-interpretation of the Ka'al: Rumours continued to persist throughout the 20th century that the

> *Ka'al would return in a new, more commercial guise, and
> that the souls of the young would once again generate
> wealth for the old.*

How could people not have noticed what was hidden in plain sight? The Ka'al had returned. Perhaps they had never been away. They took the girls to their ancient sacrificial site. They dumped their bodies afterwards. They got rid of anyone who suspected.

She scrolled down the DWG page on her phone. The directors' list had been expanded to include its latest pair of inductees: Ben Larvin and Roy Brook.

If we could see inside men's minds, the truth would appal us.

Were the directors of the Dream World Group knowingly following in the footsteps of the Ka'al, or had the tribe simply reappeared like spring water bubbling up through the rocks, impossible to eradicate because it was part of the landscape, part of its history, part of its existence? A secret enclave within a private company, the lines of responsibility and guilt blurred like charcoal on parchment, until it was impossible to tell whose hands were stained.

As she pulled out and inched the vehicle forward through the sea of hot engines, she understood everything. What horrified her most was its sheer inevitability. The worst fears were always true, even though they were clothed in kindness and rendered acceptable. Power was like water or stars or the arid soil, something that was simply there.

A truck horn blared at her, snapping her attention back to the outside traffic; she had missed her turn at the lights. The few people on the streets were walking faster than normal, as if they had all been energized by the thought of the world's gaze once more turning to this desert land.

The journey home took forever. She pulled in to the compound entrance and a new young guard shambled out to check under her car with his mirror, moving as slowly if he was underwater. Suddenly everything was normal again, and her fears seemed as absurd as the plot of a multiplex movie.

Just ahead, across the white demarcation line on the tarmac, were the rows of perfect villas with neat green turf and white garages, every bush and flower in place, down to the last leaf, bud and petal. Somewhere a dog yapped. Sprinklers hissed. Droplets shivered on acacia leaves.

As she waited for the guards to finish, she recognised one of the men standing behind the booth, Rashad Karmeel, the construction workers' supervisor. She rolled down her window.

'Mr Karmeel,' she called, 'could I have a word with you?'

Rashad broke off his conversation and came over. He looked overheated and uneasy. Dark patches showed beneath the armpits of his white workshirt. 'Hello, Mrs Brook, is everything all right?'

'Have you seen my daughter or any of her classmates?'

'Not today. Quite a few of the kids are helping to decorate the nursery for your dinner party tomorrow, aren't they?'

She had forgotten that Mrs Garfield had persuaded them to volunteer their services. 'Thanks, I'll check there,' she said. 'How long are you staying on?'

'I'll be here for a few weeks yet. My men are looking forward to seeing their wives and families again.'

'I hope they're being properly paid.'

'Our contracts were extended by a month, without any extra pay. There are some people who do not like to see black men making money, Mrs Brook.'

She closed the window and drove off. The streets were silent and empty. She parked the car at the kerb and went into the house. Lastri had returned to her own home at five, and the rooms were in darkness. Roy was presumably stuck in his meeting with his mobile turned off. She had to talk to someone, but had no idea whom to trust.

She remembered the young woman who acted as an off-site assistant to the senior architects. She existed as a voice, a conduit without an identity of her own, which made her easy to talk to. What was her name?

'Irina, it's Lea Brook. Do you know when my husband is likely to get out of his meeting?'

'There are sessions running right through the evening, Mrs Brook. I have not heard from him in a while.'

'Roy told me one particular appointment was arranged late downtown. Something to do with curtains or blinds.' She was amazed by the calmness of her voice. She held out her left hand and found it was shaking.

'I can't see anything,' Irina replied. 'He might not have had time to add it to the central diary.'

'Have you spoken to him at all this afternoon?'

'Not since this morning. He has not called in. Do you want me to pass on a message?'

'No, it's okay.' She rang off and called the nursery, but the line was busy. Had Cara and her friends forgotten that they'd offered their services and dashed over there, running late? She found it hard to imagine Cara rushing anywhere.

There was still no response from Roy. Outside, a Mercedes passed her front door slowly, and she ran to look. The driver leaned over in his seat to check out the house. His face was in shadow, indistinct and unfamiliar. Before she could find her glasses, he had driven off.

Evil was unfolding in the silvered dusk. The phantoms were flesh and blood after all. They had moved from a world of sand and silence to one of steel and silicon. The days of enforced lethargy were crawling to a close, to be replaced by a virulent, relentless malevolence.

Chapter Thirty-Nine
The Disappeared

As if daring herself to doubt its existence, she checked again on the Dream World plans that Roy kept in their shared desk. Long before the resort had been started, the map showed the old sites to be cleared. At their centre was a faint octagonal dotted line. The vault had always been there, once filled with elders deciding what was best for their people. She imagined the cabal becoming corrupted over time, old men taking children from the caravan trains that passed through the area. Terrible things, obscene things happening in the cool stone shadows.

There was nothing she could do about it. What could anyone do? Milo, Rachel, Ben and all the others had failed to expose the truth.

It seemed pointless staying inside the dead-aired house waiting for something to happen. Picking up her phone, Lea stared at the list of speed-dial names, all polite acquaintances with impassive faces, no real friends anymore.

Then she remembered that Andre Pignot was once an archaeologist.

'Lea, it is nice to hear from you. How are things?' Pignot's tortuous French accent was suddenly familiar and reassuring.

'Andre, do you know anything about the site DWG chose for the resort?'

His reply was guarded. 'What do you mean?'

'There was a building belonging to a tribe called the Ka'al, an ancient monument. They never dug it out. They never destroyed it.'

'Lea, now might not be the best time.'

She caught herself, wondering how much was safe to say. 'I thought you might know something more, that's all.'

His reply was measured and unemotional. 'No, but then I'm not very up on things over there. I could call a couple of people for you.'

She heard another voice in the background, asking a question. 'Is there someone there?'

'I'm with Nathifa and Sergei from *Dream World* magazine. Let me ask them—'

Fresh doubt assailed her. 'I picked a bad time. I'm sorry to have bothered you.' She rang off before he could protest.

She paced the floor, then looked out into the darkened street. It was better to see someone not directly connected with Dream World, a neighbour, one of the wives. Betty's lights were all off except the one in her kitchen. Lea decided that she was probably still at the mall. She went outside and walked over to Colette Larvin's house.

'I was just about to come and see you,' said Colette, opening the door and stepping onto the lawn in front of the house before Lea could say anything. Her neighbour's distracted gaze flicked beyond Lea's shoulder to the roadway, as if she was expecting someone to drive up at any moment.

'What's the matter?' Lea asked.

'Have you seen Norah?'

'No, and I can't get hold of Cara. Her phone is dead. Not just turned off or out of range, I know how that sounds.'

'Norah was supposed to be back over two hours ago. You don't suppose something has happened, do you?'

'Have you tried any of their friends?'

Colette hugged her arms. 'I called Dean, but there was no answer. And there's a Swedish boy he hangs out with, Roslund. Same thing.'

'Rashad says they were due to help out with some of the party preparations, but I can't find anyone. I should go over there but I might miss them.'

Colette managed to look cold in the evening heat. 'I don't know what to do. Sometimes I ask myself if I even know who

Norah is. I only have the faintest idea of what drives her. Wherever we go, whatever we do, the one thing that never changes is her alien nature. I thought she'd help me with Ben but now she's even further away. It's almost as if she expected it to happen.'

'Colette, the book Rachel said she'd borrowed from me, I told you I never lent it to her. There's more to it than that.'

Colette regarded her with puzzlement. 'What do you mean?'

She held up her hands, pleading to be heard. 'Rachel discovered something at the resort. There was a site that she and Milo knew about. She wanted me to understand—'

'Lea, you don't fully make sense at the best of times,' Colette warned. 'We need to find the children. Where are they? The last time they all went off together it was because of the *Iftar*. I don't want them to get into more trouble.'

'Maybe they went to the mall,' she said lamely, changing her mind about taking Colette into her confidence.

'I guess so. Some of the stores have only just restocked after Ramadan, and you know how obsessed the girls get. They lose track of the time. Maybe there's a connection issue with the phones. The servers are probably overloaded, all those folks arriving from around the world.' Colette was already stepping back into the house, vanishing into the shadows as she convinced herself. 'That's probably it. I guess I'll have to wait for her here.'

She gently closed the door, sealing herself away. Lea was about to ring the bell again when she heard the sound of a car pulling up. Betty was negotiating the kerb in her Audi. Lea ran over.

'Where's Dean?' she asked as Betty climbed out of the car. 'Have you seen him?'

Betty's eyes widened with fright when she saw the look on Lea's face. 'Why, do you know where he is? We were supposed to meet at the marina and he never showed up.'

'I can't find Cara, and Colette hasn't seen Norah,' said Lea levelly. 'I haven't been able to raise any of their friends either.'

'Then where are they?' Betty looked as if she was about to cry.

'We've been closing our eyes to it all,' she said aloud, not meaning to, 'right from the start.'

Betty glared at her. 'You know something, Lea? Everything was fine until you came here. There were never any problems. We all just got on with our lives. Then as soon as you arrived there was trouble.'

'What are you talking about?'

'It all seemed to start around the time you arrived here.'

'All what seemed to start?'

'Everything—Milo got hit by a car, didn't he?'

'Yes, but there had been bombs before we got here, and Tom had already died,' said Lea. 'You can't seriously think that we're to blame—'

'That girl of yours, setting up her computer club and getting everyone to hang out with her, digging up heaven knows what. If kids access illegal sites they can be arrested, do you realise that?'

'Betty, they're good kids, they wouldn't—'

'Everyone was happily minding their own business, and then all the trouble started, and there you were, going around poking your nose into everyone's affairs, never mind our feelings, always siding with the shiftless workmen. If you want to know why there's trouble try asking the migrants, not the decent families living here.'

'You're being unreasonable.'

Betty took a timid step forward, as if trying to check on a dormant firework. 'Am I? When did Milo get hit by a car? Just after you arrived. He was always mouthing off about the management to anyone who'd listen, and suddenly you were all ears. He found someone who would take him seriously. I saw him at the party, drunk, and you hanging onto every word, buying it all. If you were so important in London, why didn't you stay there?'

Lea decided there was no point in trying to reason with her. 'I'm sorry, Betty,' she said, 'I must find my child.'

As she walked away, Betty continued to shout after her. 'It was all right until you came here!'

That's how the Ka'al resurfaced and survived for so many centuries, she thought. *The blame is always shifted. Nobody sees what the Sand Men do outside the closed circle. Oh, people suspect but they ignore what should be more obvious than anything else. Conspiracies are like oysters; it takes some grit at the centre for everything else to form around them.*

Her hands were shaking as she opened her phone's address book. A rare wind was rising, mustering in the trees, lifting sand into the street. Marking down the house numbers, Lea walked to the next road to call on other families.

She halted before the house of a couple she remembered from the golf club and rang the doorbell. Silence. Stepping onto the tightly clipped grass, she peered in through their darkened lounge window. A boxer dog slammed itself against the glass, spittle flying. It bounced about barking as she backed away.

She headed for Lauren's house, walking as fast as she could, eventually running down the middle of the deserted roadway.

Lauren's mother answered the door on the second ring. She touched her lacquered copper hair and pulled at her low-cut blouse as if going on a date.

She was as mystified as Lea. She had not been able to reach her daughter for several hours. Lauren had left school at the normal time and was supposed to be coming straight home, but still hadn't arrived. None of her friends had turned up. 'Didn't they say they were going to the nursery? The number seems out of action, but then it often is,' said her mother, puzzled but not unduly worried. 'Lauren is kind of a wild card but she at least sends a text if she's going to be held up. You have to trust your kids to show some common sense, don't you?'

'I think this is something more serious,' Lea began, but just then a white Toyota Prius pulled up and Lauren climbed out, waving goodbye to a girlfriend.

'Where have you been?' asked her mother, eyeing her short pink skirt with alarm.

Lauren shrugged, pouted, resented being questioned. 'I had coffee with some friends down at Sheikh Zayed Road, so what?'

'Didn't you hear your phone?'

Lauren dug it out and checked the screen. 'Battery's out. What's up?'

'Have you seen my daughter?' asked Lea.

Before Lauren could reply Lea's mobile suddenly rang, making her start. 'Roy, where are you?'

'I'm still in town, waiting for final approval on the plans. There's like, a dozen missed calls from you. What's wrong?'

'Have you heard from Cara?'

'No, isn't she with you?'

'She didn't come home. And some of the other kids are missing. Several of them have just disappeared.'

'Did you try the beach house?' The shack had no dedicated phone line. 'They're bound to be there. I can't get away but I could send someone over in a little while.'

'No, I can drive over there.'

'Listen, things are really crazy here.' Roy was having to shout above the sound of a drill. 'It's a really tough night for us. Everything has to be just right. I can't stay on the phone, they're holding everything up for me. I'll be finished soon, I'll come home, okay? I'm sure Cara's just lost track of the time. The traffic looks real bad from my window. Why don't you go home and wait for me? She might be back at the house by now, anyway.'

No, she thought, *she's not, she's gone, along with the others. They've been taken by the Ka'al and no-one will believe me, just as nobody ever believed Milo or Rachel. We could have done something about it but we didn't, and now it's too late.*

She looked across at the roofs of the compound houses and suddenly longed to see the land reclaim its natural geography. To watch the clocks speed up, the water pipes split, the pools drain, the grass desiccate. Cracks would appear in the walls, tiles loosen, paint peel, sand silt up against the dulled and splitting front doors until the pressure caved them in, drowning them in the sparkling silicate of the returning desert.

The compound would join the other lost and ruined towns that dotted the landscape of the Middle East, abandoned by families made newly rich from oil. Instead of acacias there would be thorn bushes, instead of overbred pedigree dogs, gazelles. Instead of concrete and air-conditioning, nothing, nothing at all but yellow sand and blue sky.

But the Ka'al would still resurface because it belonged to the oldest of old worlds. It was here first, along with the sand and the stars.

She headed home to get the car.

Chapter Forty
The Enemy

IT FELT AS if there had always been something going on behind her back, beyond the mirrors and glass, obscured by the sun, always just out of reach. As she walked, she tried to recall the exact order of events that had brought her to this point.

It had started with Milo being hit by a car. Why had the police never managed to trace the vehicle? They would have contacted Leo Hardy, they would have made him check every truck and saloon in the workers' compound. Why had they never found it? Because Hardy reported to the Ka'al.

And Rachel's lonely death in the scalding desert heat. What had happened in the hour of her death? How could she have accidentally locked herself outside, knowing that she was at risk in the heat?

The Busabis' house, burned down because Harji smoked, but Mrs Busabi swore he had given up. Ben Larvin almost crushed to death beneath the concrete pipe, another absurd accident that should never have happened. There should have been enquires launched, questions answered. Instead there had been quiet confusion and silence. The Ka'al left no trace. They were the Sand Men; they scattered themselves to the winds, only to reappear when they were hungry once more.

She recalled reading about the energy blackouts in America, how executives had turned off power to those in most desperate need. They had no shame, no conscience, no guilt, because this was how companies had always been run and would always survive.

Milo hadn't been the first tragedy. Tom had died and a worker had frozen to death on the beach. *Everything was all right until you came here,* Betty Graham had told her. But it couldn't have been. It must have started earlier.

As she was letting herself in she heard the sound of an approaching vehicle, and turned to find Leo Hardy's green Land Rover in the street. He spotted her and pulled up before the house.

'You always seem to be in my way, Mrs Brook,' he said, taking an unnecessarily heroic leap out of the vehicle.

'I was going to say the same thing, Mr Hardy.'

'I'm checking the security arrangements,' he warned. 'You have to get back in the house and stay there until this thing has passed.' He narrowed his eyes at the street. There was an absurd, outdated masculinity about him.

'What thing?'

'It's a security alert. A big day tomorrow, ya?'

'I need to find my daughter. Some of the children are missing.'

'They haven't been in touch?'

'Their phones go to voicemail.'

Hardy prowled around his car as if checking for enemies. 'I just came from the North Side nursery. A few of the older kids are helping to paint the room for the parents' celebration dinner. Who exactly is missing?'

'My daughter, Norah, Dean, Roslund, some others, I can't remember all their names. We haven't seen or heard from any of them since before dark. They were supposed to be coming home but never got here.'

He shrugged, barely listening. 'They probably stayed late at school or went to the beach.'

'I rang the school. Cara always turns her phone back on as she leaves.'

'Okay, let me make a call.' He speed-dialled a number on his iPhone and cupped a hand over the microphone. 'I'm checking with the nursery staff.' Lea waited while he spoke, studying his pressed scoutmaster shorts and high beige socks.

'You're absolutely sure of that?' Hardy put his hand over the phone. 'They haven't seen your daughter, but some of the others are there.'

Her head throbbed with the effort of remaining calm. 'That's what I said, they've—'

'Wait, let me finish.' He listened—or pretended to listen—for a moment. 'The supervising teacher only just came on duty. She thinks your daughter and her friends went to get burgers.'

'Then why aren't they answering their phones? The directors—' She caught herself.

'What?'

'It doesn't matter—'

He rang off. 'You might as well tell me.'

'My husband's promotion—'

'Roy's a lucky man. The board trusts him with everything.'

'I still can't believe he rose so quickly.'

'It was always on the cards, Mrs Brook. They like well-educated men.'

'Was it on the cards even when he was back in London? Was he told he'd get a promotion then? Did you ever meet the board of directors?'

'I deal with their people. We all deal with their people. Nobody has to meet them.'

She studied his bare forearms and saw no evidence of burns. 'Have you ever heard of the Sand Men—the Ka'al?'

'I don't know what you're talking about.' Hardy shifted impatiently. 'I have to go. I'm trying to get everyone back to the compound. I've lost most of my best men this week. The new compound guards are a bunch of illiterate bastards who can't fill in a simple form. I don't know where everyone is.'

'People think the workmen caused your security breach but they didn't, did they?'

'Maybe someone is planning to leave us with a grand gesture.' Hardy stopped and looked at her in the ghostly blue light of the street lamps. 'There have been warning signs.'

She rubbed at her temples, trying to forestall a headache. 'The warnings came long ago, Mr Hardy, and they started on the inside, right in the heart of Dream World, but everyone ignored them. When people find out that you did nothing to stop it, guess who'll get the blame?'

'That sounds like a threat.' He opened his mobile and made a call, speaking in Afrikaans. She stood waiting for him to finish, chilled in the warm night air. 'My men are going to be on duty all night anyway, so I've instructed them to look out for your kids. I need you to go inside your house and stay there until your husband and daughter arrive, ya? Go and write something, assuming your laptop is repaired, do something that will calm you down.'

'How did you know about my laptop? I didn't tell you.'

'You women have no secrets from us. I don't want you wandering around the neighbourhood, do you understand? From midnight nothing bigger than a mosquito is going to get through our security. Everything must be kept orderly, and you can help by not frightening the hell out of people.'

'Are you with them,' she asked, 'or with us?'

'It depends on who you call them? Liberals—you all make the same mistake.'

'What do you mean?'

'You come to a strange land and think you're surrounded by devils. You never identify the real enemy. It's you people.' He jabbed angrily at her chest. 'It's always you.'

Waving her away from the vehicle, he jumped back in and roared off, accelerating with a squeal of tyres as he barked commands into his phone.

Chapter Forty-One
The Abduction

BEN LARVIN HAD been moved to the rehabilitation clinic, but was still in a hospital bed. The ends of his lower limbs were now capped in what appeared to be perforated blue shower caps. He still had the nub of a saline drip protruding from his plastered left wrist. The nurse warned her that the patient was still undergoing the after-effects of pain relief and might not respond to her, but Ben raised his hand in a weak greeting as Lea entered the room.

She seated herself beside him. She hardly knew where to start. 'Ben, I know what you've been going through. I don't mean since the accident—before that.'

He turned his head slowly and studied her.

'When you first found out about the Ka'al.'

No response.

'After they made you a director, you realised what was happening. That's why you sent pretty little Abbi away. You feared they might take her.'

'Abbi is safe.' His voice was slurred and low, like a recording that had been slowed down.

'Yes, she's safe. I know the truth now. How did you find out?'

He licked his lips. Lea poured some water into a plastic jug and put the straw in his mouth.

'Sewage outlet,' he said finally. 'Went there after Roy and Harji, to look at damage. Found shorts.'

'Whose shorts?'

'Tom Chalmer's daughter. Was wearing them when she went missing.'

The air-conditioned room felt colder still. 'Did you tell anyone?'

'No. But I listened.' He tried to raise his head but fell back against the pillows. 'So tired.'

'Ben, why didn't they just deport Mandhatri Sahonta when he made a fuss about losing his daughter? Why did they stage the accident?'

'Avoid investigation.'

Of course, she thought. *Once they'd found out how easy it was to get rid of anyone who pointed the finger of blame, they used the same method again and again.*

'Ben, is there anyone I can talk to, anyone who knows?'

His eyes had closed. Moments later he was asleep.

'Ben? Who else knows the truth? Who can I trust?'

He spoke without opening his eyes. 'Betty Graham.'

'Betty *Graham*?'

'She was there.'

He started to snore.

HER NEIGHBOUR WAS coming out of the corner shop in the compound and actually started when she spotted Lea. For once, Betty Graham had removed her apron. She was struggling to carry a large carton filled with jars. Knowing Betty, it didn't seem likely that she would still be upset.

'Let me give you a hand with that,' said Lea, taking one end of the carton and looking inside it. 'What are these for?'

'Oh, Mrs Garfield has enlisted me in jam-making,' she explained. 'She's got us all under the cosh. A real martinet.'

They reached Betty's front door and carried the box to the chaotic kitchen. 'I'm glad I saw you,' said Lea. 'There's something I wanted to ask you about.'

A look of discomfort immediately came into Betty's eyes. 'I don't suppose I'll be able to answer, I never know what's going on.'

'This is rather serious, so I was hoping you'd be able to confirm something... you see, I talked to Ben at the hospital.'

'Oh God.' She turned away, busying herself with unpacking the empty jam-jars.

'Remember when I Skyped you in the night? I asked about Tom Chalmers' daughter and you changed the subject. Ben tells me you were there. When it happened.'

For a moment Lea thought she wasn't going to answer. *Clink* went the jam-jars on top of each other. Betty raised her head and looked out of the window. 'It was cloudy and close,' she said. 'Not a good day for the beach. We were down by the lake, where it was cooler. I can't remember why I'd agreed to take Joia down there. Funny, you'd think it would be the part I'd remember most clearly. We sat on the grass and she read for a while, but she was smart and I think she'd grown too old for the book—it was *The Wizard Of Oz*.' There was an odd distance in her voice. 'It got even muggier and she grew bored, so I said we should go to the pool. She had her swimsuit with her, and went off to the changing rooms. I was putting away our things when I looked up and saw two men in those grey hooded sweaters, and I thought they must be workers. It was so hot, only the workers wear clothes like that. While I was watching, they changed direction and headed toward the changing rooms, and something made me get to my feet and go after them.

'When I reached the cubicles the men had gone, and so had Joia. Her T-shirt and swimsuit were still on the bench, which meant she was just wearing her red shorts. She was at the age when she was becoming self-conscious of her body, so I knew she'd not let anyone see her half-dressed. Mrs Chalmers—well, I think she blamed me even though she knew it wasn't my fault. She didn't speak to any of us much after that.'

'And the police did nothing.'

Betty came back a little. 'Oh, they looked. They *said* they looked. They made enquiries and two workers were deported. It all happened so fast.'

'What did you do with Joia's book?' Lea asked.

'Mrs Chalmers didn't want it back so I gave it to Rachel. She said it was proof.'

'What do you mean, proof?'

'Joia had taken it with her to the changing room. Some of the pages were torn, as if they'd tried to pull it away from her. Rachel said there would be fingerprints.'

'But you didn't hand it in to the authorities?'

'No,' she said in a small voice. 'I was frightened.'

'Did you tell Rachel what you saw that day?'

'I did, but I shouldn't have done.'

'Why not?'

Betty looked forlorn. 'Because they'll come for me one day, just as they did for the others.'

'Who is going to come for you?'

Her neighbour's cheeks were wet. She wiped them with the back of her hand. 'The men who were always here,' she said. 'The Sand Men.'

'But a modern company like DWG.' The idea defied rationality. 'How is such a thing possible?'

'Modern?' Betty spoke as if dealing with a particularly stupid child. 'Men don't change. They'll live with any cruelty and still believe in their innocence, if it gives them power.'

Chapter Forty-Two
The End Of The Dream

THE DRIVE TO the beach house was hell. It seemed as if the whole of the city had been tipped out onto the roads. Lea had trouble parking near the low breezeblock villa, which was more accessible via the coastal dunes than from the road. To reach the entrance, she passed through a thicket of parasitic thorn-bushes and clumps of maroon and yellow desert hyacinths.

She knocked on the front door but there was no answer. A dim light pulsed inside, but the place looked empty. Stepping back, she studied the house. The sea air had cracked and warped the window surrounds, and one side panel had clearly proven impossible to shut. After thumping it with the heel of her hand a few times, she managed to slide it high enough to climb inside.

Several cheap plastic chairs had been set around the edges of the single large room. Electrical cables trailed across the sandy floorboards. The place reminded her of Cara's bedroom. Jumbo Coke cups, pizza boxes and empty junk-food delivery cartons overflowed a wastepaper basket. She was like her father; they both had the ability to lock into screens and lose all sense of time.

On the central trestle table lay an assortment of laptops, one of which was set to the website's homepage. The soft light emanated from the brightly coloured *Bubble Life* logo which revolved, burst and reformed. The room was free of paperwork—Cara assembled all her information online—but signs of the kids were everywhere. Norah's favourite baseball shirt hung on the back of a chair. Dean's sneakers were under a desk. An expensive cardigan, some drying swimwear, a skateboard, some rollerblades. It looked as if the group had left in a rush. Cara's wristwatch, given to her by her father, lay on the counter. There were other signs of youth; small change, a candy-coloured wrist bracelet, a plastic hair-slide, still-damp swimming trunks, flip-flops. It was as if someone had set off a fire alarm and the building had been evacuated.

She looked under the table and found an iPhone. Cara's name was inscribed on the back. She never went anywhere without it. Pieces of the broken screen were scattered across the floorboards. Everyone knew that the kids hung out together at the beach house. They would never have left so suddenly under their own volition. Apart from anything else, they didn't possess the organisational skills.

A threadbare rug lay near the far wall, its corner rucked.

It has a cellar, Roy had said, *you can put your equipment down there.*

Hardly any buildings in Dubai had cellars. The city was built on solid rock, but the beach house stood on sand and soil. Kicking back the rug she found a single wooden flap fitted with a recessed brass ring. Underneath was a flight of sandy plank steps.

The room was not much bigger than a telephone booth. On one side a grey metal door had a thin strip of light showing beneath it. There was neither lock nor handle, so she shoved. It grated against the floor, but moved easily.

Inside was a room half the size of the one above. On a trestle table, four monitors glowed. The laptops connected to them all showed the same thing. The crimson and blue *Bubble Life* logo grew and burst, to repeatedly reveal:

6-6-6 THE DREAM IS OVER 9-9-9

Cara was seated with a laptop on her knees and another on the desk, writing code. A joint burned in an ashtray. Behind her, tacked to the wall, was a poster of Ed Snowdon. She was wearing headphones. Lea placed a hand on her shoulder, making her jump.

'What are you doing here?' Cara asked, yanking off the cans and turning to face her. 'You're supposed to be at home.'

She had pushed back her sunbleached hair, and looked older. Behind her the screens pulsed into fresh life. A computer-generated image showed the silver towers of the resort crumbling and collapsing into the sea. Across the destruction ran article headlines in red ribbons of lettering.

LUXURY SLUMS: MULTINATIONAL CAPITALIST VENTURES LIKE DREAM WORLD WILL BE USED BY 0.0001% OF THE WORLD'S POPULATION.

SLAVE LABOUR: DREAM WORLD STEALTH-HIRES BELOW MINIMUM WAGE, ABUSING THE POOR TO AMUSE THE RICH.

RESOURCE PLUNDERERS: EACH DAY DREAM WORLD DRAINS MORE RESOURCES THAN AN ENTIRE AFRICAN NATION USES IN A YEAR.

FUTURE NIGHTMARE: 23 NEW DREAM WORLD RESORTS AND APARTMENT COMPLEXES ARE SCHEDULED TO OPEN IN AFRICA, THE MIDDLE EAST, RUSSIA AND AMERICA IN THE NEXT DECADE.

'This is what you've been doing,' said Lea, staring at the screens, 'playing at being a revolutionary.'

'Not playing. Doing something.' Cara eyed Lea warily as she approached.

'Did you send warnings about the bombs?'

'We tried to but we're not sure they went through.'

'How did you get the call sign?'

Cara closed her eyes in sufferance. 'From Dad, obviously.'

'I should have realised.' Cara shrugged, more intent on the screen than listening to her. 'Look at me, Cara, why would you do this?'

She tore herself away from the scrolling sentences. 'To open people's eyes. You always go on about wanting to do something but you don't. You never do. You couldn't even get your so-called writing career started, you just wring your hands and complain like all the other wives.'

'Where are your friends? How many are involved?'

Cara evaded the question and looked back at the screen. 'We're not children. We can look after ourselves.'

'You're not even sixteen, Cara.'

'I will be next week.'

Lea's mind raced back over the events of the last few months. 'You couldn't have made the pipe bombs. The first one was found before we arrived.'

'Dean made the first one and smuggled it into the resort, but he got the timing wrong.' Her face betrayed no emotion as she spoke. 'Norah and I showed him how to do it properly. We're not hurting anyone, we're aiming at disruption. It's better that you stay home until all this is over.'

'All what?' Lea took a step closer, watching the messages drift down the screens. 'Tell me how this works.'

'You wouldn't understand.'

'Try me.'

Cara tapped the nearest monitor. 'The site is a call to action. It looks normal when people first open it, but they get to the sub-site by following coded clues from other sites. And they only get those once we've checked out their personal details. We've created a private universe. We only talk to people we trust.'

Behind her head, the largest screen showed a computer graphic of buildings being consumed by an electronic apocalypse. The firestorm threw fierce orange light across the room.

'We're showing others what's going on here. How the workers are being treated, how they're deported when they fail to reach targets. How the owners are importing rare hardwoods for hotel bedrooms to please the Chinese. Buying drugged-up dolphins from Japan to stock the aquariums. Taking bribes from contractors, stealing land, poisoning the sea. We're waking people up. It's a mechanism for protest. The next war will take place here, and you won't even notice it. The stuff out there isn't real. It's a dream. You don't see how far you've fallen. You're terrified of just being a housewife but you have no dreams left.'

Lea looked into her daughter's eyes and saw naivety, innocence, hope—all the things that would be taken from her. 'You really don't see what you've done, do you,' she said, watching the screens.

Cara barely heard her. 'We thought we could take the resort offline during the opening by hacking the digital management program. We removed the existing OS and transferred the symbolic role of the integer 999 to the digit sequence 9-9-9. The building's secure but the network isn't. Their IT team is rubbish. We had everything we needed to take it down. Then the security patrol turned up. Dean and Norah got away. I stayed down here. I have everything I need. I can get out after dark.'

'Cara, listen to me. You've been set up. You've played right into their hands. They wanted you to do this.'

For the first time, Cara looked unsure of herself. 'What are you talking about?'

'James Davenport said the system was failsafe. They made you think it could be hacked, and you fell for it.' She leaned in and wiped the sweat from Cara's forehead. 'Oh baby, you weren't to know. You did everything they expected of you. Right from the day your father told you about the beach house.'

'I don't understand what you're saying.'

She sat down in the chair next to Cara. 'You're the distraction, the release valve. Now if any questions are asked they can say it was you.' She tried to explain about how the vault had always been there, an ancient spot where the Ka'al elders gathered, set deep in the rocks. How the company had built the complex around it, adding the private apartment, a meeting place for modern elders. She explained why it was on every single map going back through the centuries, and what they used it for now. She mopped at her forehead, feeling dizzy. 'Do you have anything cold to drink?'

Cara stayed silent, but reached under the table and pulled a plastic bottle of water from a mini-fridge, rolling it across the table-top to her. Lea drank a third and pressed the bottle to her forehead.

'They didn't want the whores from King's Road, the ones everyone else used. What's the point of having power if you still have to do that? They started taking girls. Afterwards they dumped them at sea but one washed up in the creek. It wasn't enough to take the workers' children, and they made a stupid mistake. Her name was Joia. Tom Chalmers' daughter. She was thirteen. Tom suspected the truth. He told Milo they had taken her. Milo told Rachel and Rachel said something, so they followed her out into the desert and staged another accident. They took her pendant as proof. Rachel was found without her neck-chain.'

'This is insane. You're talking about—'

'The rituals were secret and sacred,' said Lea. 'Now they're just expedience. They provide... an outlet. This land has only just turned its back on the old ways.' She wanted to reach over and touch her daughter, but Cara shifted away. 'Your father and the others, they let you build the website and do all this. They encouraged you. You think they didn't know about Dean right from the start? An angry kid with a backpack, planting home-made bombs on a high-security site? Now they can make you disappear. You and anyone else they want. Your father sold you to them, Cara. A new city built on ancient ground, that's what they promised to deliver. They even brought back virgin sacrifice. The sins of men never change.'

Cara rose to her feet, looking back at the shimmering screens. 'You're crazy.'

'They're cleaning up before the resort opens. Getting rid of anyone who knows and keeps making a fuss. That won't be hard; we're all contracted to the company. The police will come back here. You'll be taken to the vault and your disappearance will be explained away.'

'You're wrong. You're sick, everyone says so.'

'You're in danger, Cara. We need to go back to the house and get our passports. We'll have to be fast. They're looking for you.' She grabbed Cara's hand, but the girl pulled away and stood her ground.

'I don't believe you. I don't believe that Dad—'

'Your father made his choice long ago. Before we moved out here.' She spoke with slow deliberation.

'*I don't fucking believe you!*' Cara shoved at her furiously.

Lea grabbed her hands. 'I went there, Cara. I saw it for myself.' She waited for Cara to stop fighting her, then slowly released one hand. Digging into her jeans, she pulled out the chain she had found in the corner of the vault. 'They always take something.'

Cara turned the identity bracelet over in her hand and read the inscription:

Joia Chalmers

'You're lying, you're lying!'

'Am I? Think about it, Cara, use your brain! Think about everything that's happened. You play at being rebels, but if you decide I'm right then you have to do something real instead of all this—posturing.'

'I can't—get away from me.' Cara leapt up, pushing Lea to the ground, tipping her chair over and knocking down the computer screens. Lea felt a searing pain through her right elbow as it connected with the concrete floor. By the time she had climbed to her feet and ascended the stairs, her daughter had gone. The beach house was surrounded by rustling dark bushes.

As she left the building, she saw the dark outlines of men hopping and running across the distant dunes, slowly coming closer.

Chapter Forty-Three
The Escape

FROM THE MOMENT she had arrived, the Sand Men had told her where to go and what to do. They all just wanted her to shut up and go away. There was never any proof of wrongdoing. No evidence, no guilt, no shame. *The private conversations of company men would horrify you*, Rachel had said.

She had nothing on her but the money in her purse, and there didn't seem to be any stores open. She would go back to Dream Ranches and wait for Cara to return.

There had to be evidence against the directors somewhere. Andre Pignot ran the oldest local magazine. He'd been here since before the oil boom, he had to know about the vault.

She knew then that she had to see him. He was the only one she could trust. As the Renault approached the run-down building that housed *Gulf Coast*, she began to get a bad feeling. Nathifa and Sergei from *Dream World* magazine had been at Pignot's offices the last time she called him.

The cab stopped outside the door, and she saw that it had been removed and was being painted. Pushing past the decorator and climbing the stairs, she smelled turpentine and fresh varnish. Andre's office had been emptied out. The rooms were completely bare. Dust sheets were down and the walls were being painted white. A stocky unsmiling woman with strong Russian features stood on the landing. She was writing notes in a sequinned pocketbook that looked as if it should belong to a teenaged girl.

'I was looking for the offices of *Gulf Coast* magazine,' Lea explained. 'They were here.'

'Gone now,' said the woman curtly. She squinted at the wall and made another note. 'Everything has gone to Dream World head offices,' the woman replied. 'Same company now.'

'Do you know where I can find Andre Pignot?'

The woman looked up for the first time and studied her. 'He's gone too,' she said, her voice lower.

'Where did he go?'

The woman studied her properly for the first time. 'Are you a friend of his?'

'Yes, I am.'

'Then I am sorry. He was drunk. He fell down stairs. Those stairs. Whisky.' She pointed to the steep, narrow staircase ahead of her. 'He broke his head. He did not live until ambulance arrive.'

She saw now that the wooden landing was petalled with blackish-crimson bloodstains. She had to get out of the building fast. Turning, she pushed down the stairs, past the decorators and out into the deserted street. She scanned the road to see if anyone had seen her enter the building, and ran to the car.

Nobody could afford to let Dream World fail. Not the Russians or the Europeans or the Arabs. Everyone kept telling her that. There would be firings and cover-ups and acts of damage limitation but nothing would change.

After getting no answer from Roy, she texted *Call me—urgent*. She needed to hear his voice, to see if she could discern betrayal in it.

Just as she was pulling back into the compound he rang back. She gripped the wheel, trying to stop her hands from shaking any harder.

'Did you go to the beach house?' he asked casually. 'Did you find her?'

'I couldn't get there,' she lied. 'Hardy's put the compound in lockdown.'

'We've had more bomb threats. The security at the resort can handle the problem. So you haven't heard from Cara?'

'No, perhaps she's gone to the mall with friends.'

'Okay. I'll be back later than I hoped. I have to go to the resort before I finish for the night. You know how important tonight is for all of us. Why don't you go and prepare a nice meal, it'll give you something to do.'

She refused to let her anger reveal itself. 'Good idea, I'll do that.'

I don't know what to do, she thought, suddenly overwhelmed with panic. The wives could be trusted; they would not have been made privy to the secrets of their men. But they were unlikely to trust her in return; she had been branded the troublemaker, the catalyst.

Heading upstairs, she added Cara's passport to her own and filled a bag with clothes. She had some loose cash kept aside for tipping and her credit cards. Cara would have to come back to the house and when she did, Lea decided they would get away together even if it meant kidnapping her.

All she could do now was wait.

In the bathroom she found a packet of Zimovane sleeping pills in the cupboard, popped out two and washed them down with a glass of hot mint tea. She needed to rest, to gather her strength and be ready for Cara's return.

She remembered something Rachel had said. *The world is divided into those who look for others and those who are looked for.* The men weren't remotely concerned. Only Ben Larvin had suffered a crisis of conscience. How long did he live with the burden before becoming a liability?

Her thoughts fragmented. In the shadowed lounge she lay back on the couch, turned up the air conditioning and drifted into an uneasy, dislocated sleep.

SHE HEARD HER neighbour's front door snick open. A homely figure in pink carpet slippers tentatively stepped out. Betty Graham was in her cornflower-blue apron once more, but now her hands were tied behind her back and she had been blindfolded with an absurd floral dishtowel. She was being gently led out of the house by two men in hooded grey tops and black jeans. Behind her, orange clouds pulsed like jellyfish, rising slowly in the night sky as the compound burned.

Puzzled, Lea slipped out of the car and followed. As they disappeared around the side, she heard Betty say something that sounded like 'But I don't want to leave.' She had scratched her arm somewhere, and was dripping black spots of blood. She didn't seem frightened, just confused. She still trusted the men who were leading her. She knew them, or at least recognised their voices.

They were Hardy's men, and they were still talking softly to her as they carefully lowered her onto her knees in the side-alley. She addressed one politely while the other pulled a Swiss Army knife from the pocket of his jeans. When he opened the impossibly long serrated edge, only Lea's sense of self-preservation kept her from crying out.

It was over very quickly. While one held Betty by her shoulders, the other pushed the blade into her pale throat, leaving it there for a moment while he wiped his hands on his jeans. Grasping the red plastic handle, he pulled it hard across and Betty fell silently forward, banging her head on the concrete with an audible crack. The whole operation had only taken a matter of seconds. Moments later a grey plastic body-bag was being unfurled and she had gone, as if she never existed. A trusting housewife, blindfolded and led to her death in a floral apron and dishtowel.

Tall figures shifted around her, watching and whispering. At first they seemed familiar and friendly, members of her family, her mother and father, her daughter. As they moved closer she began to panic. She tried to explain, but they weren't listening. Nobody was listening. Hands guided her gently downwards, soothing voices were telling her to calm herself and rest…

* * *

LEA AWOKE.

The room was in deep darkness. Her back was wet with sweat. A crushing pain pulsed behind her eyes. She could smell freshly baked bread. Puzzled, she opened her eyes and turned her head to one side.

There were thousands of stars above the rooftops.

'You're awake at last,' said a figure beside her.

Mrs Busabi was knitting something, a vast unravelling maroon shawl of some kind, although how she could see the stitches was a mystery. A single candle flickered in a saucer on the side table. She rolled her armchair closer and smiled. She had put on weight. 'I was beginning to think you'd sleep right through the night.'

'Mrs Busabi, what are you doing in my house?' Lea raised herself on one elbow and looked around.

'Rosemary,' said Mrs Busabi. 'Call me Rosemary.'

Her head was swimming. The sofa was the wrong shape, and the chairs had been moved. A dresser full of floral crockery stood against one wall. A clock ticked.

She was not in her own home.

Shadows stretched and flickered about the room. Outside, there were no street lights. The road was pale blue, illuminated by the starfield above. The sky was pressing down over the compound, brighter than the black buildings.

'Why is it so dark?'

'The lights all went out. There must be a fault. A good job I had candles. I always keep plenty of candles for emergencies.'

'Where am I?' She tried to clear her throat. Her mouth tasted as if it had been filled with sand.

'You'll probably want some tea,' said Mrs Busabi. 'Let me get it for you.'

'Wait, I should be in my own home, why am I here?'

'Dr Vance is here, I'll just get him.' Mrs Busabi set aside her shawl and hastily rose, leaving the room. Lea tried to sit up but felt suddenly light-headed. She had taken sleeping pills on an empty stomach and then...

'Mrs Brook, you're with us again.' A pleasant-faced man, American or Canadian, with thinning blond hair side-parted, and ridiculously bleached teeth. She'd seen him playing in a jazz band. Dr Vance was avuncular and old-fashioned, a character from a Norman Rockwell painting. He seated himself on the arm of the sofa and smiled. 'It's lucky you've got good neighbours, Mrs Brook.'

'I don't understand,' she said thickly, 'what am I doing here? I don't remember leaving my house.'

'You were in the street, very distraught about not being able to find your daughter. Mrs Busabi was driving past and brought you here. Don't you remember?'

'But she doesn't live here. She moved to the other side of the compound after... something bad happened—'

'Yes, and that's where you are. On the North side. It's only a short drive from your house. I was due to visit her and found you here. You felt quite feverish. I gave you a sedative.'

'But I'd already taken sleeping pills.'

'Don't worry, it wasn't very strong, it won't do you any harm. You just needed to shut down that busy mind of yours for a while. Are you feeling better now?'

She tried to rise. 'I have to find my daughter.'

'She'll be here soon. You had a text message.' He held up her iPhone so that she could read the screen.

Staying late with the others. We're working at the beach house. We'll get something to eat out. Love, Cara.

'That isn't from her,' said Lea firmly.

'Then who else could it be from?'

'From them.'

'Who are they?'

'It doesn't matter, you wouldn't understand.' She tried again. 'That text is not from my daughter.'

'You know what I think?' said Dr Vance patiently. 'You've been upsetting yourself unnecessarily. I've seen it happen a lot with the ladies here. When you've got so little to worry about, you make yourself fret over the tiniest things.'

'Can you stop fucking patronising me? I don't have a fever, I'm not imagining things. I know when there's a problem. I'm not a child.'

Dr Vance winced at the use of coarse language. 'Of course, but you must admit you're overwrought, and it's really over nothing. The children are quite safe.'

'The children are safe? Do you have the faintest idea about what's going on here?' She looked around herself, trying to understand. She vaguely remembered standing on the lawn, a conversation which had turned into an argument. What had she said? How much had she given away?

'Let's try this another way,' said Dr Vance. 'Do you know what we mean by the term *paraphrenia*?'

'I don't know—'

'It's a less recognised state to that of paranoia. A mental disorder, characterized by an organised system of delusions that may or may not include highly lucid hallucinations, without any deterioration of intellect or personality. Of course, everyone's a little paranoid. I often think people are taking my pens. Do you see what I'm saying? Paranoia is thinking everyone's out to get you. Paraphrenia is creating a belief system that explains *why* everyone is out to get you. A classic example is conspiracy theory. People who believe in complex conspiracies are simply trying to reorganise their fantasies into a rational pattern. And I think that's what you're trying to do.'

'But if I'm determined to organise my fantasies, that's just what I'd be expecting you to say.'

Dr Vance chuckled. 'Very good, Mrs Brook. You catch on very quickly.'

You have no idea how quickly, she thought. She gave what she hoped would be mistaken for a genuine smile of relief. 'I'm sorry. Perhaps you're right. I've been stressed for a while and I'm not sleeping well. I think I just needed to rest. In fact, I feel much better now. But I think I should go home, just in case my husband is worried.'

'I don't think you're up to it just yet. Why don't you stay and rest a little longer?' Dr Vance's smile was safe and vacuous. 'Get yourself back to full strength. We don't want you falling over in the dark. The street lights are out. We think there's a problem with the substation.'

She turned to the window and saw that the power was off across the entire compound. Above the rooftops was the distant glow of the city's business sector, which clearly still had electricity.

'I still feel very sleepy,' she said, measuring her words carefully. 'You're right. Maybe I should have another nap, if it's not putting anyone out.'

'That's better. I'm sure Mrs Busabi won't mind.' Dr Vance placed his hands on his knees and rose. 'Perhaps you'd like me to get her to make you a nice hot drink. Then she can come back and sit with you for a while, just until you doze off.' He took his leave with some reluctance, watching her. 'If you think you're going to be all right now, I should really be heading home to my family.'

As soon as he left the room Lea climbed out from the cushions and searched around for her shoes. She found them neatly tucked under the sofa. Holding them in her hand, she walked to the door and listened. Voices came from the kitchen. She pulled the door open a fraction.

'—keep her here for a while, if that's no inconvenience—'

'—fine, I have no plans for this evening—'

'—because she really can't go home yet. You know how distraught some of the ladies get—'

Lea opened the door wide enough to slip out, walking on tiptoe into the hall. She could see the doctor and Mrs Busabi in the kitchen with their backs to her. Gently depressing the latch of the front door, she tried to open it but it was stuck. She pulled harder, but it would not move.

There was a bolt on the inside of the door, like the one she had seen in Milo's house. Why did they have them in a secure compound? Rachel had known why. The enemy was inside.

She slid the bolt back as quietly as she could but it squeaked painfully. She froze, holding her breath. No sound came from the kitchen.

She tried again, gently easing the bolt out. Opening the door as quietly as she could, she ran down the steps and tiptoed barefoot across the lawn, out into the street. She was remembering more now; she had yelled at Mrs Busabi. The poor woman must have thought she was having some kind of a nervous breakdown. No wonder the doctor had given her a sedative.

As she wandered out into the road, her shoes still in her hand, she felt the world tipping on its axis. She hadn't smoked grass since college because it had thrown her sense of balance, and the sensation returned violently now, tilting the road at a drunken angle. Glancing back, she saw that Mrs Busabi's front door was still pulled close. They hadn't yet noticed her absence. She could not stop to put on her shoes; that would mean sitting down, and she doubted she would be able to rise again.

Concentrate, she told herself, *keep putting one foot in front of the other and don't look up until you're home.*

The identical streets passed on either side, differentiated only by the species of plants and makes of cars. Moonlight had flattened the landscape, robbing it of light and life. The spacey sensation distanced her. It was like walking on a planet with a different atmosphere.

She turned into her street, no more familiar than any of the others, and watched as her house approached. A red flatbed truck swung around the corner and slammed to a halt in front of her. It was too dark to see who was driving, but her instinct was to get away. She remembered what Ben Larvin had told her. No-one could be trusted.

Chapter Forty-Four
The Ganesh

'MRS BROOK.' As if to prove her wrong, the voice was recognisably one that belonged to a friend. Rashad Karmeel came around the truck and took her arm. 'I'm sorry, I didn't see you. The streetlights aren't working. Did you find your daughter?'

'No, not yet.'

'Are you all right?'

'I don't know. The electricity—'

'The phone mast at the compound entrance is down, some of the networks are out and the street lights are off. I think it's a pretty big fault. Hardly surprising, with so much energy being used by the resort tonight.'

They've vandalised the mast and the substation, she thought. 'Everyone's been telling me there's nothing to worry about,' she said. 'I have to find Cara.'

'Have you got a signal? Maybe you're on a different provider.'

Lea checked her phone. 'No, nothing.'

'It could be coincidence,' said Rashad. 'I can call the emergency services again.'

'The lights are out for a reason.'

'What do you mean?' He looked at her. 'What sort of reason?'

'Are you a director, Rashad?' she asked.

'No, of course not. Why?'

I was going to wait for her, she thought, *but that's what they want. They want us to stay home. They stage accidents to preserve their secrets. How would they keep me quiet? What would they do? It would have to be something believable. A gas explosion, perhaps. No-one would ever investigate it properly.* At some point she realised that she had been speaking out loud. 'You know the worst part? I have no proof that it's even happening. How could I convince anyone? But I've seen for myself, I know what they do in the vault. It's right there in plain sight. You can see for yourself too.'

Rashad did not look at her as if she was mad, or pity her. 'I have to go back to Dream World. I can check it out for you, if you like.'

'You believe me?'

He shrugged. 'I'm not sure I understand, but I have no reason not to believe you.'

'Then could I come with you? Roy said he has to finish up there tonight, and Leo Hardy was heading back there. I don't trust Hardy, but I trust the police even less. Do you think you can get back in?' Her head was starting to clear. Paradoxically, Dream World felt like the one place that might provide a safe harbour. Cara would call if she chose to believe her.

'I have a Premium Pass. It should work until the security seal is activated at midnight. Only directors will be allowed in after that.'

'I can show you what I saw.' She came around to the passenger side of the vehicle. The Renault could stay at her house. It would make them think she was still in the compound.

Rashad put the truck in gear. 'If your husband and daughter aren't there you'll have to get a taxi back. Most of them have been commandeered for VIP use tonight.'

'I'll figure it out. Just give me a lift.' She tipped her head and listened. 'It's so silent. The calm before the storm.'

They set off across Dream Ranches, the only vehicle moving through the dark deserted suburban streets. Shortly they reached the blacked-out perimeter wall and traced it around to the entrance gates, passing only one other car along the way.

'Maybe you should drive slower,' she said. 'There could be anything out there.'

When Rashad pulled up, they found the barriers down and the sentry booth empty. The highway beyond the compound was brightly lit and busy, a world away. Lea looked back at the darkened houses. The compound had turned into a jail, and the people inside it didn't even know they were inmates.

'The guards are supposed to be here twenty-four hours a day,' said Rashad, climbing out. 'The next shift doesn't end for another two hours.' He walked over to the deserted booth and tried the door. It was locked. Inside, the computer terminals were powered off.

Lea joined him. She pushed against the barrier but felt no give. 'Could we move these back manually?'

'No. They're electronically controlled and made of galvanised steel. I watched them being installed.'

'The other gate at the rear of the compound, near the old underpass, there's only usually only one guard on it,' Lea pointed out. 'We could try that.'

'Look.' Rashad pointed up at the black phone mast that stood above the acacia bushes beside the entrance. The top antenna had collapsed on itself. It looked as if it had been hacked off at the point where it joined the base.

'You think they cut the mains power as well?' Lea asked.

'Maybe. Come on.'

As they drove back across the compound they passed a grey steel electricity substation at the side of the road. Its doors had been wrenched open and stood wide. The wiring had been pulled out in fistfuls and thrown on the grass. There were no emergency service vehicles to be found.

'Where are the police? They're usually patrolling. Why aren't they around?'

'Maybe they're tied up with the opening,' Rashad said.

They had pulled up against the rear exit, but that, too, was closed, the barrier firmly locked in place, the sentry box empty.

'Is there any other way out?'

'When we sealed up the entrance to the underpass, we reopened a small slip-road to remove materials to the other side of the freeway. We closed it after we finished, but I don't think it was properly sealed. I could probably get it open again.'

'Let's go.'

Rashad drove his truck off the road and across the hard scrubland beyond the houses, keeping his headlights on low beam. After five minutes of bouncing over pack-earth they came to the grassy freeway embankment, where a narrow section of the slope had been patched with sheets of corrugated iron.

'I have some tools in the back of the truck,' he told her. 'Can you give me a hand?'

Rashad turned off the truck lights. They found a hammer and a crowbar in a rucksack on the flatbed, and began prising off the panels, working by the light of the stars. The panels were easily removed, but Lea could see a lot of debris inside.

'Is it wide enough to get the truck through?' she asked, standing back.

'Just about. We'll have to clear some rubble.'

They dragged the last of the panels aside and entered the tunnel. Rashad's headlights sent rats scampering. Slowly working their way through, they shoved aside bricks, barrels and planks, until they had reached the far end. Rashad gave the panels a few hard kicks, then nudged them with the truck's fender. They came down in a spray of dust.

The truck rejoined the highway, and its cabin was flooded with light. The night guards were manning the Dream World gates, and argued with Rashad about his pass. Apparently, he now required an additional admittance code because the resort's security status had changed in the past hour. It seemed that everyone had been caught by surprise. The guards argued with each other, then with Rashad. Finally, one of them waved the truck through.

'How did you do that?' she asked.

'I get his brothers cheap cigarettes,' Rashad replied with a grin. 'Camel Lights.'

'I need to show you proof of what I'm talking about,' said Lea. 'It's down there on the left. Pull over just past the next junction.'

She checked her original eyeline from the North tower and indicated the octagonal concrete building. She had expected to pass Hardy and his men. The security officer's Land Rover was sitting in the car park.

Jumping down from the truck, she headed for the vault. As she walked toward it, she saw that the door now sported a newly fitted electronic swipe-card box. She tried to move it, but it had been firmly bolted into the steel. 'It was open before.'

'Problems have a way of disappearing quickly around here.' Rashad walked along the wall, trailing his fingers over the emerald tilework.

'I went inside. There's a stairway leading to an apartment.'

'It's an air vent, Mrs Brook.' He turned away from her. Solar lights sent a cold wash over the pathways between the hotels. The rest of the site was in darkness.

Lea looked around. 'There's nobody left here now, but that's Hardy's jeep over there so he must be around somewhere. Wait.'

Rashad seemed to make up his mind and walked swiftly back to the truck.

'What's that around your neck, Rashad?' She caught up with him and flicked open his collar, exposing a silver chain hung with a small pendant of Ganesh. Rashad said nothing, but stared back at her.

'Where did you get it?' she asked. 'It belongs to somebody I know.'

'Have you been to the creek market, Mrs Brook? There are millions of these things.'

'Not like that one. I should know, Rachel's father made it for her. He was a silversmith.' Before he could react she reached forward and flipped the heavy pendant. 'His initials are on the back.'

'Okay, let me tell you what happened,' said Rashad, suddenly uncomfortable. 'Someone left it in my locker. When people go home at short notice they leave stuff behind. The men often leave items they've found.'

'When was this?'

'Two days ago.' He unclipped the chain and handed it back. 'Take it, please, I didn't want it in the first place.'

Rashad didn't seem like the kind of man who would lie, but if someone had placed the chain in his locker it meant they were deliberately stirring up trouble. Worse than that, they could be trying to implicate him in Rachel's death.

There was an odd look on his face now, something between guilt and a loss of nerve. 'I wish you hadn't done this,' he said quietly.

'What are you talking about?'

'Okay, look. Here's what we're going to do. I want you to sit inside the vehicle for a few minutes and wait for me. It's going to be safer this way.'

'Safer? I don't understand. Safer than what?'

'Please. You must not argue.' He stood close to her and held up a hand. 'I'll only be a few minutes, I promise.'

Lea watched as Rashad padded off across the car park and slipped into the ground floor of the Persiana, leaving her alone. She looked across at the building. Everything was still and dead. While she waited, she tried to recall the exact order of events that had brought her here. She looked for anything that might prove she was wrong.

She wished she had a cigarette. She glanced back across the car park and saw the glass doors to the Persiana atrium slowly swinging open.

Rashad was walking purposefully toward her with Leo Hardy.

Hardy's face was impassive. The South African moved forward, grabbing her forearm and hauling her out of the vehicle. 'I need you to come with me now, Mrs Brook,' he told her.

'Keep your hands off me,' Lea warned. 'Rashad, why did you bring him here?' Rashad looked away from her, embarrassed.

Hardy seized her wrist and began to gently pull. 'Let me get you to—'

'Leo, leave her alone,' said Rashad.

'The more people who find out, the greater the risk,' said Hardy with a shrug of his wide shoulders, but he finally released her arm.

Rashad led Lea to one side. 'We've had intelligence that there's going to be some kind of attack on the resort,' he confided. 'They used a recognised call sign that's only known to the directors.'

'It's not a real threat,' she said. 'They deliberately gave the call sign to the children.' *You can say anything,* she thought, *it won't make any difference.*

'Hey, we've got to go,' called Hardy.

'There's nothing you can do right now, Mrs Brook. You'll be better off at home,' said Rashad.

'The power's been cut, remember?' she told him, stalling. 'It's not safe for me there.'

'Then maybe you should stay in one of the hotels on the promenade until tomorrow morning. You can easily walk there from here.'

'Rashad, come on, man,' called Hardy again.

'Where are you going?' she asked.

'To deal with the problem. I'll catch up with you later. Don't worry.' He gave an apologetic shrug and ran to the truck.

The car park was overlooked by closed circuit cameras. They couldn't do anything underneath the lights. They were just following orders.

She watched Rashad drive out of the parking lot, then set off in the direction of the main road.

Chapter Forty-Five
The Hunt

As Lea headed toward the taxi rank, she decided not to go to a hotel. She had no spare clothes, nothing but the money in her purse, and there didn't seem to be any stores open. Rashad had warned her about the difficulty of getting cabs tonight, but an empty cab sporting a local company logo was parked at the kerb beside a takeout shop. Its driver was leaning on the bonnet eating pungent *gulab jamun* from a plastic cup. She tapped his arm and climbed inside.

As the hotels and cafés ran out, the concrete parquet of the road pixelated into loose uneven rectangles. The taxi drove on until the promenade became desolate and half-buried. She paid off the cab and ran with her sandals in her hand, over the still-warm dunes.

Once she reached the sidewalk she looked back, but could no longer see the shoreline. Over at Dream World, police vans and security vehicles were crowded near the guard's post. All of them had their lights off. There was no sound, and she could see no personnel moving about. *Nothing to see here*, the silent lights said, *just men going about their business.*

At this end of the promenade the only cabs to be found were illegal. Climbing into the nearest one, its dashboard festooned with gold garlands, she sat back and listened to the driver's English news channel. Most of the items were about the feasts and parties that were being planned across the capital to celebrate the opening.

'Sharon Stone is there,' said the young Indian driver. 'She is old woman. Why no sexy Bollywood girls? Where you wan' go?'

She left the taxi near the road that ran parallel to the compound's outer perimeter, paid the driver and ran across to the cleared access tunnel.

Once she reached the interior, she saw that most of the street lamps were still off. It took her another twenty minutes to walk home. She was glad she had worn trainers. As she crossed the deserted, darkened pavements she tried to formulate a plan. She wouldn't be able to do anything if she was arrested.

The safest thing would be to drive out the same way in the Renault and try to book two flights online as soon as she could get a signal. She didn't know how she would ever track Cara down in time, but she had to try.

She ran up the drive, dug out her keys and let herself into the house. The alarm system was down. The rooms smelled of disinfectant and polish, nothing human, as if it was being returned to a pristine state by Lastri, ready for the next occupants.

Poking around in the dark proved challenging, but she finally found a decent torch under the sink. She decided now to take only the bare minimum. She would buy everything she needed at the other end.

She had wanted to shake Cara and shout, *How could you have been so stupid, couldn't you see what would happen?* But how could she have, when she had been just as blind? The important thing now was to find her and make it out alive. Survival was the key.

She was zipping up her flight bag when something caught her eye at the window.

A police car was creeping forward silently from the next street, its roof-light sliding crimson panes across the lawns. Grabbing the keys to the Renault, she headed downstairs. She ran to the car via the kitchen door and threw her bag onto the passenger seat just as the police car turned into the street.

The car's interior was filled with red light. She prayed that the patrol driver hadn't seen her, but a moment later the whoop of a siren cut through the night air. She put her foot down, swinging the Renault hard into the next street. It was best to head away from the compound's main entrance. They would be waiting for her there. Rashad had shown her another way out. Nobody would know it was open.

She pulled the Renault up onto a front lawn, tearing over the grass, stopping under the low boughs of an acacia tree. Turning off the engine, she kept her head down until the police car had passed the turnoff. Across the gardens, she saw the glow of another red light. They would have her license plate; they would not expect her to continue on foot.

Grabbing her bag she slid from the car, running down the side of the nearest darkened house. The gardens backed onto the meandering path that led around the lake. The fountains were turned off and silent.

She realised she did not know the way to the embankment tunnel from here. She and Rashad had found it from the main road. It had to be at a point where lights shone from the other side of the highway, but if she ran in the wrong direction she might never locate it.

Two torches switched back and forth between the houses. Vaulting the low steel fence and falling to the ground, she lay in the soft dry earth, partially hidden by the low leaves of the bushes. One of the torches came closer, wavered in the overhead branches.

She waited a few minutes to be sure it had passed by, then set off around the lake.

She had reached the far side when the glistening helicopter came over, its tail swinging round, its searchlight casting a perfect oval of light on the smooth glass of the water. Hardy must have arranged to have the search stepped up. She could feel the chunking vibration of the overhead blades in her bones. The top branches of the plants and bushes were fluttering like candle flames.

She would have to cross the lake's bridge. The only other way was to go all the way around, and the path would take her along the exposed edge of the road. The chopper's searchlight swept the undergrowth. She broke cover, leaving the circle of brush that surrounded the water, and ran for the bridge.

She had reached the mid-point when the searchlight caught her. Some kind of order was being barked from above but it was in Arabic, and she could barely hear above the throb of the chopper blades.

The police would be armed, and trained to kill.

Chapter Forty-Six
The Road

LEA WAS ONLY a few metres from the far side of the lake bridge. If she ran into the bushes the powerful searchlight would spot her through the cover. She would be seen as easily as if she was moving through open territory. But there was no way back.

At the edge of the lake was a covered walkway that offered daytime shelter from the sun. It had a curved steel roof, and allowed the maintenance staff to pass between buildings. She reached it knowing that even though the chopper could probably see her, its marksmen would not be able to shoot through the canopy.

She ran as hard as she could, covering the five hundred metre span to the park edge.

When she looked ahead, she swore. She had run the wrong way. Straight ahead lay the entrance to Dream Ranches. The two young guards had reappeared at their post. They seemed bemused by the helicopter. Craning up and shielding their eyes against the spotlight, they were trying to see what was happening. Lea realised that nobody had yet informed them of the search. It meant that she might be able to brazen it out and walk right through.

She tried to control her breathing and calm herself. She still had her ID card, but it would look odd being on foot. Nobody walked anywhere here.

The guards looked even more surprised to see her step from the undergrowth onto the road in front of them.

'My car broke down,' she called cheerfully, hefting her bag onto her shoulder. 'I couldn't find a torch, and can't see to fix it—the power's out.' Getting no reaction, she pointed to the street lights. Still nothing. The guards looked at one another.

She pulled out her ID card and handed it to the one who had always seemed friendlier towards her. The chopper was banking and coming nearer. Lea waited while her card was slowly passed between them. The searchlight swung over the trees behind the guard booth.

'Come on,' she said under her breath. 'Come on.'

'Where are you going?' asked the guard.

'To the other side of the highway. To get a taxi.' The searchlight was creeping nearer.

'There are no taxis from there. You can't get across the road.' He was right. The city had not been built for pedestrians. There was no walkway.

'I'm hot,' she said. 'Can I wait in your box? Do you have air-con?' She darted inside just as the helicopter beam reached them.

'You can't go in there—security,' said the other guard, but now the pair of them were arguing with each other and looking up into the chopper's light, unable to hear what was being announced from above. The beam crossed back and forth, checking the entrance, and found nothing.

Seconds after it passed overhead, Lea stepped from the box and quickly walked away. The guards were still arguing. She had left her ID card behind, but figured she would no longer need it.

When she glanced back, she saw one of them opening his cell phone. They were going to run a check on her. She needed to get off the road.

It means he's got a signal from another phone mast, she realised. Lea checked her phone and watched as it picked up reception. She kept a taxi service on speed-dial, and tried it now.

The chopper was tilting back. She didn't dare look up at it, but kept moving forward. Cars and trucks roared past her on the eight lane highway. There was no possibility of getting across it, or of flagging anyone down. The taxi service answered.

She remembered that there was an Arabic grocery store somewhere up ahead, a cracked red and green plastic fascia tacked on a breezeblock building, one of the old local shops that had been left behind in the gold rush. What the hell was it called? 'Hi, I need to be collected from the Palm Supermart,' she said.

'I don't know where that is, miss.'

'It's a few hundred yards past the main entrance to Dream Ranches, maybe a bit further. I think there's a slip road.'

The steel and glass chopper swung back and forth over the highway like an immense dragonfly, but could not descend because of the power cables. Frustrated, it passed up and down the lanes, finally heading off.

She needed to call Colette and Betty, to warn them of what might happen if they stayed. Her thumb hovered over the speed-dial. They would ridicule her, blame her. She pocketed the phone instead.

She had no idea how long she walked. All she remembered was the noise of the passing traffic, dust and gravel, petrol fumes, the sound of the overhead blades approaching and receding.

The long curve of the neon-lit supermarket occupied the corner of a road she had never paid much attention to before. Displays of shiny crimson tomatoes and lurid green cucumbers stood in ranks before her.

She entered the store and looked about. Her heart was in her mouth as she walked to the ATM. There was a limit on the amount she could withdrew in a single day. She waited and watched while the machine read her Visa card. She punched in a request for the maximum withdrawal, and felt a pang of relief as the money slid into the tray.

The supermarket was as overlit as any garage forecourt. She felt sure someone was checking for her on a bank of TV screens, but there was only the cashier, watching an old Arabic film on his monitor. She studied the locals drifting through a nearby shopping arcade, seemingly without a care in the world, shopping for fruit and vegetables.

She tried to work out her next step, and was still staring at the shoppers indecisively as a blue and white ABC taxi slid to a stop beside her.

Lea instructed the driver to head for the airport and fell back into the seat, feeling the cool air wash over her. As she watched the traffic slide past, she wondered if there was any point in attempting to get out of the country. It was unlikely that she would clear airport security. Her name would already have been relayed to the police on some trumped-up charge by now. Why else would they have sent a helicopter into the compound?

She supposed it was possible to go up to Sharja and fly out from there, at least take a flight to Greece, Turkey, down to Africa even. There had to be a way. But they would stop her credit cards as soon as they realised that she was missing.

As the taxi approached Dubai International Airport she saw a line of squad cars waiting in the drop-off zone's slip road with their lights off, and her nerve failed. 'Take the nearest exit,' she told the driver. 'I've forgotten something.'

The silent driver was not being paid to question her instructions. He deftly turned away from the main highway as Lea checked her phone.

She found what she needed just outside a small town on the edge of the scrubland that led to the desert; a locally-owned garage that rented battered old cars.

Paying off the driver, she headed into the *AYMAN* garage and picked out a sand-covered Jeep with cracked plastic windows and no air-con, renting it with her Visa card. While the forms were being processed, she headed back to the washroom.

She stood looking at herself in the filthy mirror, wondering what she could do to make herself look more presentable. Throwing some cold water on her face, she tried to flatten her hair in place. She had no comb or makeup bag.

Facing terrorist charges and on the run from the police, that'll be one for the CV, she thought with bitter amusement.

She wondered what was happening back at Dream Ranches. Her imagination ran wild; troublemakers being rounded up in a single swoop, a frenzy of arrests, the burial of secrets before they tidied everything away and continued exactly as before. *We accept such corruptions as normal now. We've all been taught to assume the worst. I never thought it would involve the man I married.*

It was possible, she supposed, that Cara and her friends might decide to act and survive as agitators, forever changing their IPs, hiding behind a thicket of fluctuating code, staying one step ahead. It *was* possible, wasn't it? Or would the infinitely-resourced DWG always outpace them?

She tried not to think about what lay in the future. Speed was of the essence. Having decided to run, she had no choice but to go on. She could reach Sharja in a little over an hour. Cleaning the dirt from her jacket as best as she could she left the bathroom, and forced herself to stop thinking about Cara. Back at the beach house her daughter had seemed calm and confident, suddenly mature, yet she was really little more than a child.

Lea had wanted to sweep Cara up and crush her to her chest. *My husband, my daughter.* The sense of loss had barely begun to bite.

Chapter Forty-Seven
The Return

SHE NEEDED TO avoid the main freeway but was not sure of the route via the back-roads.

Many of the signs were only in Arabic. The lanes were abnormally busy because of the influx of tourists to the state. She kept the rental car just below the speed limit, and allowed herself the luxury of thinking that things were going to be all right, that Cara and the others might find safety, that the helicopter had been searching for someone else, that it was all some kind of absurdist nightmare that might yet dissolve and disappear.

A green and white signpost indicated the old road to Sharjah, so she took it. On this alternative route, the traffic was lighter and slower. Rusting trucks laden with wooden crates of vegetables, ironwork and coils of cable trundled back and forth through the night.

As she reached the approach road to the airport, she saw more police cars waiting on the hard shoulder. She only just managed to turn off in time. The next town was little more than a dusty strip of neon-lit shops and a single road of unfinished houses, their first floors consisting of concrete pillars and ferruled rods. She pulled into the forecourt of an electrical store and disturbed some local men watching a football match on an immense lurid screen. The brilliant pitch turned everyone's faces green. Nobody bothered to look at her.

She bought things she had forgotten in the darkened compound; soap, a T-shirt, cigarettes. The shopkeeper gave her directions to a hotel that was owned by his cousin.

When she arrived outside the Desert Orchid Lodge, Lea saw that it was little more than an ordinary house with a piece of yellow plastic strip-lighting nailed to the front, the electricity supplied by lethal-looking loops of untethered cable.

The owner offered her what appeared to be his only guest room, on the ground floor, behind a café that had been constructed by removing a wall and adding a corrugated plastic roof.

The room had no air-conditioning and no curtains, but at least there was hot water. The night passed in a sweat of horrific dreams. The men in the vault, the bodies in the creek.

The next morning, she was awoken at dawn by the blazing golden slant of the sun. She showered and dressed, then went outside for a cigarette. On the dusty forecourt the temperature was already in the high thirties. She turned on her phone and found four missed calls from Roy. She had turned off her phone's GPS. Hiding herself behind dark glasses, she looked at the vast emptiness of sky, the flat bare landscape, and saw only its disfiguring blankness.

There was nothing else for it. Despite the risk involved, she had to go back to Dubai. She had to find Cara and get her away somehow.

She checked out of her room, settling the bill in cash, and set off. As soon as she hit the freeway, she took a deep breath and called Roy.

'Lea, where the hell are you? I thought you were going to be here. The Renault's gone. What's going on?'

'I'm sorry—I ran out of petrol and had a terrible time getting back to the car, so I checked into a hotel and fell asleep.' Lying was easy now.

'Everything's been kind of crazy here. Cara hasn't turned up yet but I'll find her. She can't be far.'

I'll make sure you never find her, she thought. 'I'm on my way home now. Is the power back on?'

'Yeah, it's been fixed. We think it was sabotaged. I had to come to work for a security meeting. Have you heard anything?'

'No, nothing.' *Say anything to keep him from suspecting. Lie and lie again.*

'I have to attend a last-minute session with the directors. I'll try to come home immediately afterwards. How long will it be before you get back?'

'I don't know. The traffic looks bad. Maybe an hour.'

'Okay, I'll be there soon after you. Don't go anywhere else, okay?'

'Of course not.'

Dubai was going to work. The resort was due to be officially opened an hour after sunset, and cars were streaming into the city. In the sidewalk cafés the women in *abayas* and *hijabs* and gold sandals and smart black suits were eating muffins and ordering hot chocolate. The men in sharp white *dishdashas* and *thobes* and Prada sunglasses were meeting on street corners, hailing taxis, heading into offices, and reading newspapers. There was nothing in the day's news to indicate that there was anything unusual. Nothing about stolen children, bomb threats, communications blackouts, security alerts. Nothing about the raping and killing and disposing of bodies. Nothing about lies and bribes and infinite degrees of complicity and silence, nothing about smiles hiding fears, heads turned, eyes unseeing.

Lea felt dirty and exhausted. She was sure she smelled of sweat and fear. As she pulled off the freeway in the nondescript Jeep, she tried to imagine how she could confront Roy.

She entered via the tunnel once more, slightly surprised that the police had still failed to find it. They wouldn't have been searching for a new way onto the compound. Right now they had more confounding problems.

The streets of Dream Ranches were as deserted as the canyons of the moon. Telecoms engineers were replacing the phone mast. The old pylon had been dragged away and disposed of. Only the splintered branches of a hibiscus bush attested to the removal.

It was strange to turn into the street and find everything normal. She alighted from the Jeep and dug out her keys. The rooms were cool and shadowed. There was no sign of Lastri or Roy.

The house felt marked now that she knew the children had gone and would not be coming back. There would be no more 11:00am coffee calls, no more pointless social visits, no more complacent amiability. There would only be blame and fear and pain.

The imported yellow tulips in the vase on the kitchen table had collapsed. The brackish smell of ullage filled the room. Lea emptied them into the bin and ran the vase under the tap.

She threw away a pile of magazines, washed some cups, then turned on the news. She half-hoped to see footage of a bombing campaign; blackened concrete, collapsed walls, punched-out windows, a broad scattering of glass shards on the emerald grass like a crystalline aurora, police cordons and workmen sweeping up debris. Instead she saw a piece about a jet-ski race held at Jumeira Beach, and a Versace fashion show attended by Sharon Stone.

The natural order of Dream World had already re-exerted itself.

Chapter Forty-Eight
The Nightmare

SHE NEEDED TO stay calm. Plugging in her iPod, she put on Lakme's *The Pearl Fishers* and went out to the porch. The sprinkler system had ceased to function altogether now, and the lawn had turned brown. Digging out her last pack of Davidoffs, she sat on the deck, smoking.

As the aria came to an end and she finished her cigarette, she went inside and changed the track to Maria Callas singing as Elvira in *I Puritani*. Slowly she raised the volume until it reverberated throughout the villa. She allowed the sound to wash over her, until there was nothing else but the purity of the music. Gradually her fury ebbed, but the tension refused to leave her temples.

She became aware that there was someone standing outside the patio windows. Colette was slapping on the glass with the flat of her hand, flushed and angry.

'What are you doing?' she shouted as Lea opened the door. 'You can hear that right across the neighbourhood.'

'I'm sorry, Colette. I didn't mean to disturb you.' She went to the iPod dock and turned the music down. 'Have you spoken to Norah?'

'No—did you find Cara? The police told everyone to stay in their houses while the power was out. There was no answer from your house. They were worried.' Judging by her unsteadiness in her voice, she had been drinking.

'Cara will call me in her own time.' She couldn't let anyone know what she was about to do. 'Are you and Ben okay?'

'No,' said Colette, shaking her head violently. 'He had a fight with one of the nurses. She had to sedate him. He kept saying he should have done something. Do you have any idea what he means?'

'Colette, he's trying to tell you that you're in danger. They will find our children and take them, and they will come for you.'

'But why us? Why is this happening?' Colette reminded her of the women who emerged from the rubble and dust of the World Trade Center: *Why us? Why do they hate us?*

'Because it's our children who've been sabotaging the resort,' she said. 'I have to go.'

'Wait, what did you do to them?'

'I didn't do anything.' Lea tried to keep calmness in her voice. 'But they won't come back.'

'They're minors. They're our responsibility.'

'People go missing here. There's nothing we can do.'

Colette was not listening. 'I hope the police pick them up. They won't detain them, they've done nothing wrong.'

'We did something wrong,' said Lea vaguely. 'We ignored what was right in front of us.'

'Why did you have to keep digging and pestering everyone?' Colette all but shouted. 'Just because you were bored and dissatisfied with your own life, you had to infect your daughter with the same irresponsible attitude. They're only children.'

'They're not anymore,' said Lea. 'They're fair game. But you're right, it's my fault. I neglected Cara, I should have been watching her more carefully, like Milo told me to.'

She stopped, breathless and angry, realising that Colette was crying. She stepped forward and hugged her without thinking, staying tight even as Colette fought to push her away. 'I'm sorry, I'm sorry, it should never have happened. We have to stick together and see it through, for their sake. My husband is involved, and your husband too. But Ben couldn't go through with it and they tried to kill him.'

Colette disentangled herself and stepped back. 'Will you listen to yourself? You make up these stories. Dr Vance warned us about you. He says you're not well. Why would you say such a thing? All I want to do is be with my family. I want my daughter to come home. I want my sweet girl back.'

She turned and ran to the safety of her house.

Lea was watching Colette leave when she realised a car had pulled up, and then Roy was there with Rashad and Hardy, standing before her with his arms held slightly out, looking at her as if he expected her to rush into his embrace. He was wearing new chinos and a white shirt she'd never seen before.

On the front lawn, a small hand-held garden fork had been left in the flowerbed. She picked it up and kept it ready in her right hand.

'Leo and Rashad told me what happened,' said Roy, keeping the others back and taking a step toward her. 'I'm sorry it came to this. I know you're thinking lots of crazy stuff right now, but can you at least let me explain.'

It was as if she was looking at him for the first time. She saw blackness in his eyes, the taint of greed. She saw that he would say anything now for it to be over.

'I just want to know,' she said. 'How did they phrase the deal to you? Did they drop it into the conversation casually, over lunch? How do you tell a man you'll give him everything he ever wanted in return for his daughter? Or did they even fool you at first?'

He took a step towards her. 'It's not like that, Lea—I've spoken to Cara and everything is going to be all right. There's nothing that can't be fixed. The kids didn't realise what they were doing. We need to sort this out with the authorities as quickly as possible.' He could no longer look at her. Lea recognised the change in his features. It was the attitude he adopted when he had made up his mind and would not be turned.

'We need to know who's helping you, Mrs Brook,' said Rashad.

'What are you talking about, Rashad?'

'Your prints are over everything at the beach house, Lea,' said her husband. 'They think you've been in contact with a terrorism organisation.'

She ignored him and turned to Rashad. 'You must be able to see what's going on. Don't you see what they're doing?'

'There were bomb threats,' said Rashad. 'They came from your house.'

'Of course they did—the girls—'

It was too late. She saw how tightly the noose had been drawn around her neck.

'Please, darling, you just need to tell everyone the truth. Did you plant the bomb outside the Coopers' house? Did it go off before you could get away? Did Milo put you up to it?'

'I think we should take your wife to the police now, Roy,' said Hardy, moving toward her. 'She can make a full statement there.'

'You all know the truth,' she said coolly. 'I don't know why we have to go through this charade. I don't need to explain anything.'

'Then let me take you in so that we can clear it all up.' There was a darker tone in his voice now.

'You're not the man I married,' she said evenly. 'But I know what you are.'

'What am I, Lea?' he asked, walking forward, daring her. 'What am I?'

'You are the Ka'al.'

She raised a hand and struck Roy's face hard with the hand-rake, dragging its tines down across his cheek. As the flesh of his right cheek split wide he cried out and tried to cover the stream of blood with his hands, humiliated at being attacked in public. She brought the handle down hard on his nose, feeling the crack of cartilage and would have put out his eyes if Hardy hadn't jumped at her.

She turned to the security chief. 'How much do they pay you to look away, Leo? How long do they keep the girls down there before they decide to get rid of them?'

'I knew you were trouble the first time I met you,' said Hardy with soft menace. He was physically imposing, but was wary of coming within range of her weapon. Roy had fallen back against the vehicle, his white shirt soaked in blood.

Across the road, the curtains flicked in a dozen houses but no-one came out to help her. Hardy feinted to one side, then the other as she brandished the fork, knowing even as she did so that he would easily take her. When he charged forward she was caught by surprise and thrown over on her back.

'Let me take care of her,' said Roy, spitting through red teeth and split lips.

'Keep the fuck away from me,' said Lea, clawing at him as Hardy dragged her to his Land Rover one-handed, holding her wrists. He shoved her into the passenger seat as Rashad climbed into the back, then centrally locked the doors.

Roy kept his hand over one half of his face as he took one last look at her. Then he headed for his BMW.

Lea fell back in her seat, defeated. Hardy started the engine and tapped out a cigar.

'Those things are going to kill you, man,' said Rashad.

'I'm not asking you to smoke them for me.' He cupped his hands over the end and drew hard until it glowed, tossing the match out of the window.

'My daughter,' said Lea quietly. They ignored her. 'She's fifteen years old. Norah is sixteen. Dean is sixteen. Joia Chalmers was just thirteen years old.'

'You could have told me you were behind me, brah,' Rashad told Hardy as they drove off, ignoring Lea.

'I was hanging back, trying to stay out of your rear-view mirror.'

They were talking about the trip she made to the resort with Rashad. Hardy had followed them. Her heart sank.

It's a power-fucking male conspiracy, Rachel had told her. 'You've both been played and you don't even see it,' she said, her interest in them fading.

'I think she's taken a shine to you,' said Hardy over his shoulder. 'I never had you down for a ladykiller, being a Hindu.'

'You were a fucking ignoramus in Kenya,' said Rashad, 'and you're no better now.'

'Really? I'm smart enough to leave you with the shit work, ya?' He laughed.

Rashad checked his Rolex. 'Man, I was supposed to be home ages ago, and now we got to go via the police.'

Hardy compared his watch to Rashad's. 'That's a fake, right? You should buy yourself a real one. That thing looks like shit. I'm taking the other exit, the cops by the main entrance are running around like a bunch of *Iftar* chickens. If they see her in the back, they'll stage an intercept to get all the fucking credit.'

The Land Rover was heading toward the tunnel Lea had cleared with Rashad, the exit that would take them under the main highway. Hardy was driving fast. The door locks were down.

She tried to think of a way out. They would have to take her to the police, where she would be charged with conspiracy to kill under the terrorism act, and she would disappear along with Cara and the others.

She sank further into her seat, realising she had travelled to this young country carrying the seeds of harm within her own family. The worm had always been in the bud. She had imported it from the West, like someone slipping through customs with a banned import.

The Land Rover turned off and descended to the tunnel. Hardy couldn't risk taking her through the main checkpoint, just in case she tried to pull something. He was heading for the Central Dubai Police Headquarters.

She knew what would happen now, had read about it often enough. Her request for legal representation would be denied under the prevention of terrorism ruling that allowed her to be indefinitely held, but a deputy from the British Embassy would doubtless appear with suspicious speed to act as a go-between.

Perhaps Mr Qasim would come along to watch another westerner disgraced. They would carefully explain their reasons for holding her. They would treat her well. Perhaps he would agree to release her in Roy's custody after certain statements had been signed.

If they covered their tracks cleverly enough, Cara and her friends might manage to stay free, but only if she believed what Lea had told her. She was the only adult who admitted the truth, and nobody would listen now. They wouldn't hear her unless she said what they wanted her to say, that she had made bomb threats to the resort in a misguided attack on the phantoms who had supposedly taken the compound's children. That she was not well, that she needed medical help. Roy would probably prefer it if she was held at the station until she could be charged, just to make the grand opening of Dream World easier.

She could see the progression in seamless continuity at last, beginning with the man who froze to death on the beach, moving through Tom and Milo and Rachel and Ben, culminating in the resort's public launch, broadcast live in sixty different countries. Share prices soaring, companies growing, multi-million dollar deals, a round-up of troublemakers that turned the world's attention away from secret detentions, torture, paedophilia, rape and murder, then on to the next resort with no chance of ever stopping the cycle, the most extreme perverts gradually replaced by subtler new members. An entropic cascade of corruption, always learning from the past, becoming ever more insidious and sophisticated.

As Hardy swung the Land Rover toward their final destination of the evening, she knew all that was left was for the players to follow the predetermined script. Corruption was controlled in the same way that modern warfare was conducted, from a distance, behind banks of flickering screens. Jail a tourist, send a signal, sign the big deals behind closed doors.

Hardy flicked on the headlights as they entered the tunnel. 'Shit, you could have cleared this better,' he complained, looking at the broken pallets pushed against tunnel walls.

'Mrs Brook helped me,' said Rashad. 'We were in a hurry.'

Something ran in front of the car. She tried to see between the headrests.

'Fuck, man. What was that?' asked Hardy.

There was a odd puckering sound and something obscured part of the windscreen. She thought at first that someone had thrown eggs at the Land Rover, then realised that there were holes in the spiderwebbed glass. She had never heard real gunfire before, and was surprised that it sounded so oddly undramatic. Hardy swore and ducked, then grunted and flopped toward the centre of the car. A flap on the side of his head had dropped down like a red trapdoor, and a fine mist of blood darkened the window.

She reached forward and tried to work out the central locking system as Rashad grabbed at her.

Punching down at the switch, she slipped her sweat-slick arm from his fist, kicking at the passenger handle as the windscreen took another hit. With the high door acting as a break she dropped low, falling to the ground and moving back behind the vehicle. Rashad was coming at her now, and she could hear others moving.

She ran back toward the tunnel entrance with Rashad in pursuit and shouts rising from the fire-blackened walls. Rashad threw himself at her and they fell into the rubble. A pile of bricks grazed her knees and arms, tearing skin. She tried to rise but he dropped hard on her, holding her down.

Rashad punched her in the side of the head and she dropped back, blunted. When she could see once more she tried to rise, but his weight was heavier on her than before.

He wasn't moving. Her right hand rose to his forehead and came away scarlet. His shaggy black hair was disturbed, and she could see a hole exposing meat that glistened inside the curls. She wriggled from beneath him and tried to rise, but he convulsed, gripping her more tightly.

And then he fell away, a dead weight, and she realised he had lost consciousness. Slowly, she pulled herself out and climbed to her feet.

There was no more gunfire now, no more shouting. There were only the dark shapes of slender young bodies. It was impossible to tell how many there were. She looked back into the dark of the tunnel but her eyes could not adjust to see their faces. They were motionless now, waiting.

They watched her go in silence.

The workers were letting her leave.

Without looking back, she limped away.

She still had the passports on her, and some money. Her credit cards might work for a while yet, until the others discovered Hardy and Rashad. Once the police found out that she was still alive, they would search the compound. She knew how they thought now; she was a woman, she felt comfortable at home, she would return to her house to await arrest and explanation, accepting the role that had been granted to her, like someone who always waited to be told what to do.

To prove them wrong, she headed for the coast.

Chapter Forty-Nine
The Paradise Of Sunlight

THE AIR-CONDITIONING kept the office at a perfect nineteen degrees centigrade all year round. Dr Vance put the window blinds back in place and settled in his chair to study what he had written in neat black biro:

Patient Name: *Lea Catherine Brook*
Referral Comments:
Patient suffers from an advanced form of paraphrenia and is adept at reconfiguring events around her into any number of unifying conspiracy theories. She has no previous history of the condition, which seems to have started when she first moved here and mistook the mezuzahs attached to Milo Melnik's doorways for security bolts. After this she began to construct a series of intricately connected fantasies around various 'key events' in her unifying conspiracy theory. She entered a dream world of her own making and constantly found new evidence to support her life within this bubble of make-believe.

As is common in such cases, her condition is based around a confluence of latent fears: loss of control over her family, diminishment in her role as a wife and mother, inability to integrate within her new surroundings. These fears may have become exacerbated by outside events, in particular the heightened security alerts affecting the resort prior to its opening, a number of unfortunate accidents affecting her friends and neighbours, and the presence of immigrant workers intruding into the compound.

The patient's paraphrenic state developed more sharply after she suffered a minor injury from an incendiary device planted within the DWG compound. Following this event she became increasingly delusional and was convinced that the DWG corporation was involved in various criminal pursuits. None of these fantasies need to be outlined here, but will be examined in subsequent documents.

Following an episode in which the patient became disoriented and confused, she was given a mild sedative and requested to attend a referral session for psychological assessment, to see whether the condition could be modified by a medication regime. She failed to attend the session, and subsequently left the city without providing any contact details. At present, her whereabouts are unknown. Once the patient is located, assessment and treatment can resume.

Copies to: Roy Brook, Leo Hardy

Dr Vance searched around his desk for something he could use to sign the page. He called out to the other room, 'Who keeps taking my pens?'

LEA DUG HER heels into the warm saffron sand and leaned back, feeling the sun on her face, listening.

It was supernaturally quiet. For once, she could hear the sound of the waves breaking all along the shoreline. No trucks rumbled across the Dream World resort. No cranes turned; their arms were frozen like clock hands set at different times. No workers trooped across the heat-rippled concourses. All work had stopped for the grand opening. Soon there would be amplified music, Western pop songs blasting from the immense speakers placed at each corner of the Persiana hotel. Then the sky would be smeared with streaks of coloured fire. Strontium, lithium, titanium and magnesium would poison the atmosphere, detonating like diseased blossoms. The man-made starbursts would be seen from space.

Soon the assembled guests would be sitting down to steaks imported from Scotland, lobsters from Canada, *foie gras* from France, gulls' eggs from England. Nothing came from the desert. How could it?

Back in the compound, the Dream World Grand Opening Gala Dinner would be under starters' orders. Mrs Garfield would be alternately punishing and rewarding her troops, planning the arrival of each course with military precision, marshalling a fresh phalanx of compliant foreign waiters, a Dream World for the lower orders.

At the resort, a cast of obedient performers was awaiting its cue, preparing to smooth away international doubts and jitters with a spectacle of pre-recorded songs. Speeches of empty rhetoric would rise into the night like hot air balloons.

Lea regulated her breathing until she could feel her heart slow. For the next few hours she was under the protection of a clandestine amnesty, less important than an orchestrated eruption of gas-powered fire and chlorinated water, pulsing in time to a robotic medley of hits. After the officially sanctioned oratories, recited like witches' confessions, the hunt would recommence.

She lit her last cigarette and savoured the taste, tossing the packet into the sand. She would give up after this. It was time for some changes.

The seabirds from the wildlife sanctuary were screaming overhead. On impulse, she tried Roy's mobile and found it switched off. She knew he would be doing what he always did best, holding endless, interminable meetings. *Never leave men in a room together*, her mother had once told her, *there's no telling what they might come up with.*

The beach was almost deserted. The tourists always preferred the imported white sands of the hotels around the Jumeira Palm. The fine powdered coral was shipped in from the Far East. Small white birds ran along the water's edge as if they had been deprived of the power of flight and were trying to outrun the tide. A lone camel, disdainful, inelegant and apparently without a driver, was slowly lolloping toward the dry grasses of the dunes.

She checked her watch and looked along the line of the beach.

The children couldn't win, no matter how right they were to believe in their cause. Nobody could live off the grid forever. Geopolitical manoeuvring was about playing the long game. Vested interests always won in the end. And yet there was the illogicality of hope. *Wouldn't be much of a world without that,* she thought.

The final result seemed unimportant now. It felt as if Dream World had only ever been a place of mirages and phantoms. For all of its thrill rides and spas and underwater restaurants, it wasn't that special or even that interesting. There were other resorts coming, bigger and better ones, all along this coast and the coast of the next state—and the coast of the country beyond that.

Raising her sunglasses, she scanned the shore and saw the blurred figure walking toward her. She rose to her feet, dusting the sand from her shorts.

Cara's forehead was sunburnt, her blond hair hacked short and thickly crusted with salt. She was dressed in grey linen trousers and a baggy brown T-shirt, and glowed like a lantern. There was little trace of the child left in her.

'What did you decide?' Lea asked.

'You make it sound like I had a choice,' said Cara, keeping her distance. 'Look at the sun. We're out in it now.'

The wavering molten orb was starting to sink toward the sea, but its heat was undiminished. The sifting radiation transformed them into golden statues. She understood what Cara meant. There was no need to hide from its light any more. It was time to leave the shadows and step from the moon-pale air-conditioned rooms. They had been sheltered for too long, playing at rebellion but hedging their bets, just to be on the safe side. Well, now there was no safe side for either of them. She felt the solar energy tingling her skin, replenishing her. Soon she would become like her daughter, unrecognisable to others, unrecognisable to herself.

'I guess we have to go,' said Cara, taking a last look at Dream

World. A faint pink-tinged mist has settled around its base, as if it was a mirage preparing to evaporate. 'Do you want to say anything?'

Lea looked back at the silver spires, unmoored from gravity, no longer susceptible to the laws of physics. From this distance the resort seemed like a drawing from a book of Arabian fairy tales. Seams of gold glinted from the neat rows of Mercedes saloons in the Persiana's car park, carriages drawn up against a castle of wonders.

'Why did you change your mind?' she asked.

Cara scuffed at her hair, thinking. 'I guess I'm more like you.'

'They didn't come after you?'

'I'm not a virgin. I thought you'd realise.'

She hadn't thought of that. 'I suppose I should have. We need to leave.' Lea shifted her backpack higher on her shoulders.

'So, what's your plan?'

'Who said I had a plan?' She fell into step beside her daughter, heading back from the water's edge, walking away from the computer-calibrated celebrations, toward the weeds and broken pavements where the highway ended, and the edges of the night unfurled to the darkening sea.

Chapter Fifty
The Ghost Town

FROM A DISTANCE, the grocery supermarket looked much as it had always been, but as they approached, Lea saw that it was abandoned. The yellow plastic fascia was split and caked with dust, but some of the outside fruit trays still contained the remains of dried-out pomegranates, prickly pears, figs and apples. The building had been compulsorily purchased by the government when they had planned to build a junction leading away from the East Highway, but with the scrapping of the extension it had been left derelict. A single streetlamp lent it a melancholy air of neglect.

'Wait here,' said Cara. 'I'll go and talk to them.'

Lea knew the others were waiting inside the deserted store, and wondered if they would receive her with hostility. Cara picked her way across a waste ground filled with detritus, an ocean of discarded blue plastic water bottles, rusty cables, washing machines, shelving units, coffee pots, broken crockery, baskets, glassware and old tyres.

She needed a cigarette. Pacing back and forth at the edge of the lot, she watched the distant roads for signs of the police. After fifteen minutes, Cara emerged and beckoned.

Lea entered the dusty supermarket, walking between shelves of sand-crusted cereal boxes, cloudy bottles of balsamic vinegar, packets of couscous and luxury shower gels with peeling price stickers. It was as if the owners had fled a regime change, fearing for their lives, leaving the store just as it always looked in opening hours.

There was no electricity. She walked slowly forward, trying to see into the shadows. Dean appeared before her, flanked by a sullen-faced blond boy she did not recognise. In their khaki camouflage jeans, beige string vests and dirty white T-shirts, they looked more like freedom fighters than English schoolchildren.

'We couldn't find Norah,' said Dean.

'What happened to her?'

'I don't know. We found her bag on the walkway near the beach house,' said the sullen boy.

'That's Arendt,' Cara said. 'We have to move.'

'How are we going to get around?' asked Lea. 'The highways will have checkpoints, and he's blond. He'll stick out like a sore thumb.'

'We're going to take the backroads, but we'll need your help.'

'I don't see how I can do that. The police are looking for me too.'

'We'll feed them new information,' said Arendt, crouching down to grab a handful of dirt. He sounded Danish. 'We can tell them that your body has been spotted in the sea at the resort.' He rubbed the earth in his hair, but it didn't make much difference.

'Do you think they'll fall for it?' Lea asked.

'I don't know,' said Cara as the others gathered up their laptop cases and knapsacks. 'It'll buy some time.'

'We have to hit the road,' Dean said. 'We've got to get out tonight.'

Cara led the way to a sleek black Mercedes that Lea recognised as Dean's father's car. 'You managed to get away with driving this?'

'I look old enough,' said Dean, getting behind the wheel. 'We'll have to take the desert road to the Oman border and cross at a quiet outpost. Then head East to a port, the obvious choice would be Muscat.'

They loaded the Mercedes and headed out.

*   *   *

IT HAD NO name now, and few were left who remembered what it had once been called. The town had filled the valley of date palms at the foot of the great hill, its rock striations sweeping through the pale stone in amber arabesques.

The farmers below had made a good living there for centuries, but when the oil money arrived they had left their homes for bigger profits and grander residences with cool cement rooms. Dates still provided incomes, but the ancient mud villages where they were harvested had been outgrown. The residents had taken little more than they could carry in a single trip, piling furniture and possessions onto handcarts in the rush to abandon their past. Jeeps, trucks and horses had been loaded with crockery, televisions and clothes.

The empty red clay houses still stood, their intricately carved doors and window frames waiting to be stripped and converted into coffee tables by French antique dealers looking for the next ethnic trend. The streets twisted and doubled back on themselves, a maze that afforded protection against marauders, but they were also defeating Cara and the others.

The group walked along the line of palms through dry river beds, into the dusty, deserted alleys, following the wadis, the emerald pools that formed as rivers made their way from the mountains to the sea.

Lea stopped to catch her breath. Although they had plenty of water, their backpacks were heavy with laptops and bundles of technical equipment. They were passing an overgrown graveyard with odd headstones—two for a man, three for a woman. Lea watched as a family of lizards scuttled from a dried-out burial site. 'They say you plant an extra one to make sure your wife does not come back,' said Arendt with a laugh.

'What about going into the desert?' asked Cara. 'The Bedouin have camps where we could stay until things calm down.'

'Bedouin movement is regularly checked by the police,' said Lea. 'They're not as cut off as you think. The old days when they used to keep three or four wives are over. One of them told me there was a time when you could have bought another wife with a good camel. Now you need a plasma TV, a bigger house and a pool to amuse her.'

Cara smiled. Lea looked at her daughter and could no longer recognise her as the Chiswick schoolgirl who spent every weekend in her room. The transformation was complete.

They halted at a further dead end, this one created by a dense thicket of date palms that had broken through the earthen road, nature reclaiming the town as its own.

'It has to be right around here,' said Dean. 'The signal showed it at the far end of the gulley.'

They were looking for a new car that had been left for them by some sympathetic Omani teenagers. Dean's phone signal had cut out before he had time to enlarge the map of the area.

The separation between the two countries was porous here, the region's immense outcrops of rock forcing a staggered borderline around the landscape that sometimes disappeared altogether.

'There,' said Lea, 'under the fig trees.' She pointed ahead to a dust-greyed Subaru van listing to one side of the cambered red roadway. Dean had refused to allow her to lead the group, but she was determined to stay near Cara.

Inside the vehicle they found a box of provisions, a map and several cell phones. The Subaru had a full tank of gas. While Dean drove, Cara and Arendt studied the map.

'It can't be far from here,' said Arendt. 'We may even be over the border already. Some of these ghost towns lie right on the dividing line, and their streets are impassable.'

It was hard to imagine the shadowed, crumbling houses filled with families, the streets bustling with life. Tough, spiky date-shoots pierced through the clay roads, cracking and raising them like overbaked pie-crusts. Branches had forced their way through walls and ceilings. In several places dried-out timbers from the buildings had fallen across the street and had to be hauled out of the way.

The sun had risen an hour earlier and the abandoned houses were still bathed in apricot light. The climate was more temperate here, with muddy streams crossing the ruptured earth.

The group possessed the wired energy of youngsters who had spent the night awake. Dean and Arendt took turns driving. Lea could not be allowed to take the wheel in case someone saw them—no woman would drive males through small villages. Arendt lurched the Subaru out of the shattered ghost town and onto the blacktop that crossed the valley floor.

After seven kilometres they came within sight of a pair of grey boxes, positioned on either side of the road. Directly in front was a car park filled with traders' vehicles.

'Shit—border police patrol,' said Dean. 'Go around it.'

'I can't. We haven't seen a turn-off for miles.'

'It's okay,' said Cara, checking the contents of the box they had been left. She held up a handful of false ID cards. 'Pull into the car park.'

'How did your friends manage this?' asked Lea, examining the cards in amazement. Cara ignored her.

Their vehicle was identical to dozens of others. Dotted between the cars were trucks and vans filled with produce. Cara opened the carton and produced two *burkhas*. Lea's was too short. She checked her appearance in the wing mirror and noted that it hid her identity well enough.

'If they ask anything, you'll have to do the talking,' Cara told Arendt, who was the only one who spoke any Arabic. 'If they speak to you, show them your ID and get out of the car, but keep them away from the rest of us. They're fat old guys, they won't want to move around too much.'

'That's not going to be enough,' said Lea. 'They're experienced. They'll be less interested in ID cards than how you behave, whether you're suspicious in any way. If they look in the back of the van they'll see all the laptops.'

'We can't get rid of them,' said Cara. 'We need them on the other side. They're our lifeline.'

The two middle-aged border policemen had machine guns strapped to the backs of their beige uniforms. They were moving from one vehicle to the next, checking the contents. The boys had donned ragged brown shirts, caps and jeans, and looked like local agricultural workers. Lea watched the traders, trying to think of a diversion.

'I'll be back in a minute,' she told Cara. 'I have an idea.'

'You're not going anywhere,' Dean warned her. 'Stay in the van.'

'You have to trust me on this. I'm not going to try and turn you in. I came this far with you, didn't I?' She studied his eyes, but a man she barely knew stared back at her.

'All right,' he said finally. 'Go.'

Chapter Fifty-One
The Border

ARENDT AND CARA stood beside the mud-caked Subaru as the border guards approached. Lea watched as the guards finished chatting with a man selling eggs and dried beans. There seemed to be a surreptitious trade taking place, the usual covert commerce that existed at borderlines. The farmer parcelled up a packet of shrivelled-looking greens and handed it to one of the guards, who buried his levy within a voluminous pocket and moved on toward the Subaru.

Lea felt sure they would be found out. The guards were bored and in no rush, and that was dangerous. Right now, a hastily erected roadblock would present less of a problem. The one thing the group had in its favour was youth; in their makeshift clothes and caps Dean and Arendt looked like every other farmhand in the region. The *burkha* was making Lea's face sweat. She had applied kohl around her eyes, and hoped that it wasn't running. Her dark colouring helped.

The guard who had taken the farmer's bribe was talking to Arendt. The Danish boy was very good at affecting a level of bored indifference. The other guard had badly puckered skin on the right side of his face, either from a burn or a serious childhood illness. He was walking around the vehicle, idly examining the tyres. Perhaps he wasn't looking for anything in particular, but was just killing time. The faces of the security guards at Dream Ranches had always proven unreadable. These ones were more amiable and dangerous.

'What is he looking for?' Dean whispered.

'There's yellow mud everywhere,' said Lea. 'He knows we've been through the date valley. They have trouble with looters stealing from the ghost towns.'

'But if nobody wants the stuff—'

'I don't know, maybe they want everything left exactly as it is. Don't do anything to piss them off, okay?'

The guard with the burned face stopped by Cara and asked her something. Arendt quickly stepped in and replied for her, indicating her mouth—he was saying she couldn't speak. The guard listened with hooded eyes for a minute, growing visibly bored, his interest waning. Finally he stepped away. Neither of them appeared to notice Lea. In the *burkha* she was middle-aged and sexless, a homemaker and mother, modest and invisible.

A belt radio crackled and the guards listened. Lea moved back against the side of the car, trying not to draw attention to herself. If they crossed successfully here, they would be free to reach Muscat.

The burned guard had moved to the back of the van and was making a gesture, turning a key in a lock. He was asking them to open it.

'Shit,' said Arendt, 'the four laptops are still stacked in the back.'

'Did you shut them all down?' Cara asked.

'I didn't have time. There won't be a connection open.'

'No, but the Dream World screen-savers are on the desktops,' said Dean. 'Fuck, even an idiot could tell what they are.'

Arendt was improvising, saying something about a lost key, but he clearly wasn't being believed. Now the other guard had sensed resistance and had joined his friend, and they were both ignoring him as they tried the rear door handle.

The door sprang up. The laptops were sitting right in front of them, piled in a stack, but on top was a wooden tray filled with dozens of bright yellow baby chicks. The moment they were released into the light they began chirruping and hopping out of the tray, spilling all over the back seat, tumbling down onto the tarmac. Lea ran forward and gave a startling banshee shriek.

The guards were as alarmed by the cry as they were by the sight of the runaway chicks. Cupping their hands they ran back and forth, but it was like trying to hold sand; the chicks slipped through their fingers and shot under the van, while Lea harassed them, yelling and darting about, increasing the confusion. Taking their cue from her, Cara and Dean indicated to the guards that they would only be in the way if they stayed. They bore them no grudge, they would clear up the problem themselves.

With thankful gestures, the guards beat a hasty retreat. Most of the chicks had dispersed beyond hope of retrieval, but some of the farmers came to them with the tiny yellow creatures palpitating in their cupped hands, and they could not turn down the offer. The Subaru sped away with its interior still resounding to the chirping of tiny birds.

The landscape had changed now. It was greener and cooler, and they had entered an area of well-made new roads. Even so, they were surrounded on all sides by signs of ancient civilisation. Human settlement here dated back to the Stone Age. The country existed in distinct Muslim faiths and tribal zones, roughly matching city, desert and woodland. After its civil war ended in the mid-seventies Oman began to enjoy a new prosperity, and the first signs, most noticeable in the form of ubiquitous plastic water bottles, had begun to mar the landscape.

'The Sultan brought in social housing, cheap healthcare and good roads,' said Cara. 'At least, for as long as the oil holds out. Eventually he'll have to give in. This will become another playground for the rich unless someone can stop it from happening.'

Lea looked at them in wonder. To hear this small group of dust-caked teenagers speaking as if they had the power of an international peacekeeping force was oddly touching.

The Subaru coasted down into the town of Nizwa, their last stop before Muscat. As always, there were few women in the streets, mostly men drinking coffee outside their shops or playing checkers. They turned into the main street and found the pavement lined with immaculately dressed Omani boy scouts holding tall red banners.

'What the fuck, man?' Dean looked about. Another troop of scouts was heading toward them. Arendt picked one of the smallest and had a word with him.

'The King of Sweden is visiting the country,' he reported back. 'Apparently he's the head of the World Scouting Federation.'

Arendt laughed, and the tension between them broke. They parked under a fig tree, and bought fresh supplies from a kiosk at the edge of the town's souk.

'That was fast thinking back there,' Dean told Lea. 'Where did you get the tray of chicks?'

'I bought them from one of the farmers,' Lea replied. 'I didn't understand what he was saying so I just stuck a pile of notes in his hand.'

'He probably got most of them back,' Dean said. For a moment it looked as if he might smile.

Even Cara seemed less grudging. She leaned against the side of the van, fanning herself in the shade. 'We need to find an empty café where we can check what happened last night on the laptops,' she said, pointing across the road. At the shadowed entrance to the souk, the proprietor of a small coffee shop sat dozing in the sun. Above his head was a red plastic sign that read *Kahwa – Halwa – Wi-Fi*. 'Over there.'

Heading across the road, they awoke the owner and ordered bitter coffee flavoured with cardamom and dates. Lea ate *lokhemat*, deep-fried dough-balls served with sweet limes, while the boys tapped into their connections and solemnly viewed the news reports.

It felt unreal, the sunlight dappling over the little sepia-painted coffee shop, the smell of roasting *Kahwa* in the kitchen, the fat little café owner dozing on a fraying wicker chair, the scent of sticky sweet *halwa* in rosewater, the *Muezzin* call in the distance and four intense young people furiously typing, muttering to each other, operating as a single organism.

Beside a thorny, ancient myrrh bush stood a kohl-eyed old man, older than anyone she had ever seen before, leaning on his cane, dressed in a traditional tribal cloak, his withered brown arms bare to the shoulders. His left forearm bore the diagonal scar of a terrible burn, long-since healed. The mark of the Ka'al.

And there, just behind him, were two policemen.

'Look,' whispered Lea.

Dean glanced up, annoyed at being interrupted. 'Shit, the fucking scouts. The king of Sweden. He's probably being escorted by someone from the royal family. Heightened security.' They closed their laptops as one and rose, pulling her up, but the police had seen them.

'They've got machine guns on their backs,' said Cara. 'File out slowly.'

Lea placed money on the table for the coffees and led the group out, but as they left the officers began calling to them.

The group broke into a run, heading into the deeply shadowed souk. Sunlight filtered through the wood slats overhead, casting matchstick stripes across the confluence of narrow alleyways. In front of each store sat a boy with nothing to do, too many vendors selling the same things, shoes and bags and lamps, shopkeepers peering out of the gloom to collar passing trade.

The police called out to shopkeepers to stop the infidels, but on Dean's command they broke apart, and Lea found herself running hard to keep up with Cara. Arendt and Dean darted off into one of the many winding alleys filled with carpenters and metalworkers.

Lea glanced back and saw Arendt sprawling across an angled spice display, the great wooden trays of cardamom, marjoram, caraway and sumac tipping and bursting clouds of eye-stinging spice into the air, ochre and crimson, ginger and jade.

A young man popped up in an opened panel among the spices, so that he appeared to be buried to his shoulders. Rubbing his saffron-covered face, he started yelling and grabbing at the boy. Arendt was seized by one of the officers and fought hard, kicking and twisting until strong arms came around his chest and held him still.

Cara hurtled into an alley festooned with wheels of electrical cable, charging through reeking puddles between ducks and flea-riddled cats, around a cart stacked with hundreds of bubble-packed purple plastic dinosaurs. She knew the officers would be calling for more help to seal off the other end of the alley.

'Here,' she shouted, catching up and pulling Cara into the musty interior of a carpet shop. They climbed between the folded towers of rugs woven in burnt oranges and reds that rose from floor to ceiling all around the narrow shop, and ran for the stairs at the rear, pushing past a confused shopkeeper.

Every inch of space was filled with silks, tapestries, scarves, tablecloths, runners, and cloths graded by shade and shape, endlessly refolded and arranged. On the second floor was a small wrought-iron balcony. Here, the sides of the streets were so close that the opposite balcony was not much more than a metre away. Pushing Cara ahead of her, she clambered onto the railing and jumped across, praying that the ironwork would hold.

Somewhere below they could hear the two policemen shouting to one another as they tried to track the dispersing Europeans. Lea was still dressed in her burkha, and Cara could have been mistaken for any black-nailed youth toiling in the dense, dust-filled air of a workshop, except that she had lost her hat and now her sun-bleached hair tumbled about her face. Lea grabbed a brown woollen cap from a pile and jabbed it onto her head.

'Tuck your hair in,' she instructed as they made their way downstairs, through a dingy room where cross-legged boys sat carding twine on wooden frames. They headed into a quieter part of the souk where few might notice their flight.

'What do we do now?' Cara asked when it was safe to stop running. 'Arendt had the keys to the van.'

'We have to keep going,' said Lea.

'We can't get caught.' Cara was bent over with her hands on her thighs, breathing hard. 'There's a lot more to do yet.'

'I don't care about your plans. I just want to keep you safe.'

'You never worried before.'

She grabbed at Cara's face and pulled it around to hers. 'Of course I worried! I always cared. We caught a kind of blindness, you and I. The one thing I can't do is lose you now. There's nothing else, don't you see? If we throw this away, there's nothing else left for us.' They cautiously emerged into sunlight, keeping to the shadowed edges of the buildings. 'At the moment it's only worth thinking about the things we can control. We need to stay out of sight. We have to get a ride to Muscat. I have our passports and some money, we could get a passage to Karachi, head into India, make our way home from there.'

'What home are you talking about?' said Cara. 'What's home anyway? Dad's not coming back. If what you say is true, he left us a long time ago. The time for families is over. This is all the home we need now.' She led the way, checking the road ahead, and for once it was her mother who followed without question.

Ahead, a colourful boy scout parade was spread across the road out of Nizwa. Carmine banners had been hung across the sidewalks, offering some shade from the punishing sunlight. As the King of Sweden's motor cavalcade passed, they turned to watch. Marching in front was a local band, an odd mix of trumpets and *ouds* playing the *maqamat* that gave songs their distinctive Arabic temperament. The procession of vehicles was followed by a small squad of soldiers and military officers, with a mix of security guards and regular police bringing up the rear. All of the men had ceremonial rifles strapped across their backs.

Cara and Lea stood beneath the oleander bushes on the far side of the road, separated from their destination.

'We'll have to wait here until they've passed,' said Lea. 'There are plenty of trucks going to Muscat. We should be able to get a lift in one of them.'

Cara turned to her and smiled. She looked happy again. 'You understand, don't you? That if everything you've told me is true, it all has to go?'

'I don't know how.'

Cara swung down her rucksack and opened it, showing Lea. Inside was a gun. 'Leo Hardy gave it to Norah's dad. He found at in the workers' barracks,' she explained. 'It works okay. The scouts will be going to Dream World.' Still smiling, she took a step forward into the street.

'Come back,' Lea warned, 'don't draw attention to yourself.'

'It's okay, Mum.' Cara raised a placating hand. 'I have to go.'

Lea's stomach tipped. 'We're going together, we agreed—'

'No, *you* agreed. As usual, you decided what you wanted to hear. We can't, we're western females among all these men, they'll stop us sooner or later.' She took another step into the road. 'Do this one thing, okay? Don't follow me. I'll find a way back and I'll stay in touch somehow.'

'You can't do it alone,' Lea implored.

'I won't be alone. There's one phrase I learned in Arabic. انا الصالحين. It means *I am righteous*. There are plenty of people who'll help me.'

Her smile was filled with the light of the day.

Cara touched her face and held the sight of her, then walked away, into the glare of the sun, through the thicket of beige uniforms.

Lea's instinct was to run after her, but for the first time she held herself in check.

The tribal elder was still leaning on his cane, watching with a half-smile on his lined face. He had been joined by several other men of his age. The gathering of the Ka'al had occurred as if by some form of spontaneous magic. The Sand Men watched and smiled and waited, and did nothing.

Lighting the last of her cigarettes, Lea remained beneath the bushes, pushing back into the dusty hot leaves, hardly bearing to watch. Cara carried on walking. She did not look back. Soon she had passed through the crowd and was lost in among the buildings.

My daughter, she thought, *my own daughter.*

The scout troops were being followed by a great mass of mothers and children. In her *burkha,* Lea look no different to any other Omani woman. She allowed herself to be absorbed by the crowd.

She looked back one more time to see if she could find Cara, but the girl was lost in the dust of the people following the parade.

The sun shone and the band played on, and the procession of scouts followed the gleaming black cars along the road with small children running behind them, all filled with an absurd, irrational hope for the future.

About The Author

BORN IN LONDON, Christopher Fowler has written for film, television, radio, graphic novels, and for newpapers including *The Times*, for more than thirty years. He is a regular columnist for *The Independent on Sunday*. Fowler is the multi-award-winning author of more than thirty novels, including the lauded *Bryant & May* mystery novels. He is the winner of the 2015 CWA Dagger In The Library award.

For more information visit www.christopherfowler.co.uk